THE WIDOW

Silver Linings Mysteries Book 1

A Regency Romance

by Mary Kingswood

Published by Sutors Publishing

ISBN: 978-1-912167-27-2 (paperback)

Cover design by: Shayne Rutherford of Darkmoon Graphics

Version 7

Author's note:

this book is written using historic British terminology, so *saloon* instead of *salon*, *chaperon* instead of *chaperone* and so on. I follow Jane Austen's example and refer to a group of sisters as the Miss Wintertons.

About the book: *A traditional Regency romance, drawing room rather than bedroom.*

Nell Caldicott awaits the return of her violent sailor husband with trepidation, but for once her fears are not realised. Her husband's ship, the Brig Minerva, has sunk off the Cornish coast. Nell is free, but her husband has left her with little money and many questions about his past. Gradually, as his secrets are laid bare, she realises she didn't know her husband at all. Can she uncover the truth? And can she ever learn to trust a man with her heart again?

Nathan Harbottle is on a quest to find his missing cousin, but the tragic wife of the Minerva's captain attracts him more than he cares to admit. He wants to help, but he's powerless to intervene. However, their lives are destined to collide in unexpected ways, and his resolve to be nothing more than a friend to the beautiful widow is sorely tested. Can he set aside his own past and convince her to take a chance on love?

This is a complete story with a HEA.

Isn't that what's-his-name? Regular readers of my books will know that occasionally characters from previous books pop up again. There are a few in this book. Sagborough residents Sir William and Lady Harbottle were seen briefly in *The Seamstress*, as was Barbara Drabble, whose lovely daughter Celia became a great success after Fanny dressed her. The Marquess and Marchioness of Carrbridge first appeared in *Connie*, and Daniel Merton, Lord Carrbridge's very clever secretary, was first seen in *Amy* as Sir Osborne Hardy's friend. Lawyer Mr Willerton-Forbes and his flamboyant sidekick Captain Edgerton have been helping my characters solve murders and other puzzles ever since *Lord Augustus.*

About the Silver Linings Mysteries series*:* John Milton coined the phrase 'silver lining' in *Comus: A Mask Presented at Ludlow Castle*, 1634

Was I deceived, or did a sable cloud
Turn forth her silver lining on the night?
I did not err; there does a sable cloud
Turn forth her silver lining on the night,
And casts a gleam over this tufted grove.

Ever since then, the term *'silver lining'* has become synonymous with the unexpected benefits arising from disaster. The sinking of the *Brig Minerva* results in many deaths, but for others, the future is suddenly brighter. But it's not always easy to leave the past behind...

Book 0: The Clerk: the sinking of the *Minerva* offers a young man a new life *(a novella, free to mailing list subscribers)*.

Book 1: The Widow: the wife of the *Minerva's* captain is free from his cruelty, but can she learn to trust again?

Book 2: The Lacemaker: three sisters inherit a country cottage, but the locals are surprisingly interested in them.

Book 3: The Apothecary: a long-forgotten suitor returns, now a rich man, but is he all he seems?

Book 4: The Painter: two children are left to the care of a reclusive man.

Book 5: The Orphan: a wilful heiress is determined to choose a notorious rake as her guardian.

Book 6: The Duke: the heir to the dukedom is reluctant to step into his dead brother's shoes and accept his arranged marriage.

Want to be the first to hear about new releases? Sign up for my mailing list at http://marykingswood.co.uk/.

Table of Contents

The Harbottle Family

Hi-res version available at http://marykingswood.co.uk/.

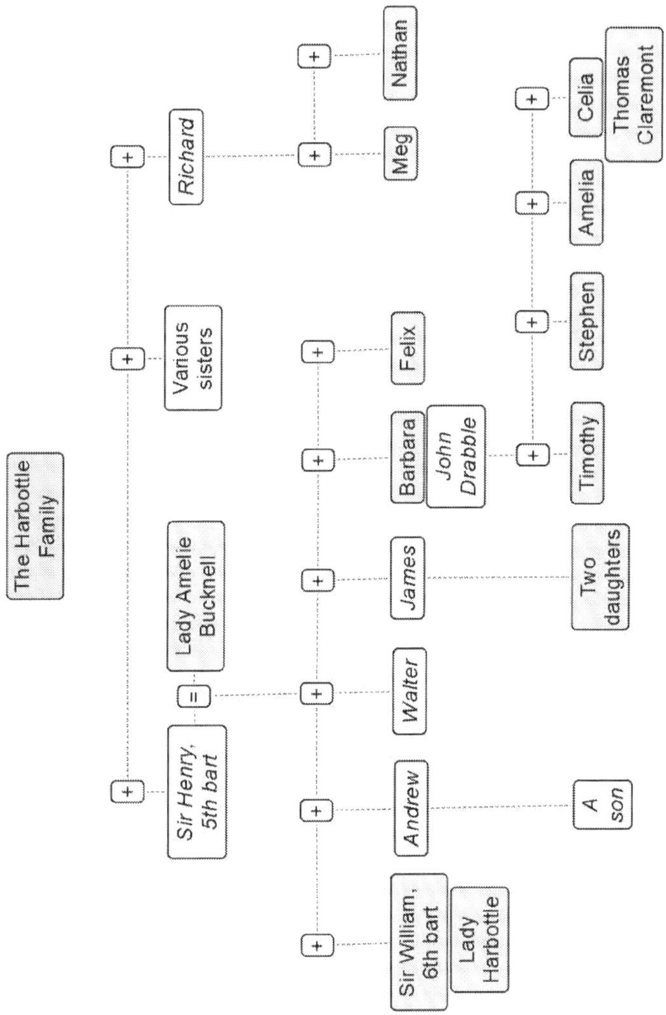

1: A Missing Captain (February)

Nell examined her reflection in the cracked looking glass. The bruises had almost disappeared, and perhaps in another two days she could set aside the high, ruffed chemisette and the large cap with lappets in favour of more refined garments. By the time of the Sherrards' ball she would be completely healed, and need not fear to wear full evening dress. She sighed. Her best velvet gown would do for one more outing, perhaps, but then... yes, this might be the last ball she would ever attend.

But she had made her choice, and would not repine. Her punishment was fitting, after all. She who had been the acclaimed beauty of the parish... of several parishes... of the county, even. Helen of Hampshire, she had been called, and it had been gratifying, even if the epithet did not resonate quite as strongly as Helen of Troy. Suitors had fluttered around her like butterflies in their brightly coloured coats. Would they even recognise her now, so thin and pinched as she had become? If only she could curl her hair properly and afford new slippers and stockings.

No, she must not regret. She had so much to be thankful for, after all. Her son, her home and a husband who loved her... sometimes. She slapped her cheeks to bring some colour to them, adjusted her ruff slightly, then turned away from the unflattering glass, head high, ready to face the day.

The two hours before breakfast were the most pleasurable of the day. With all the other occupants of the house busy elsewhere or still abed, she had her son to herself. Louis had been a sickly, undergrown child from the moment of his birth, and no amount of nourishing food had succeeded in giving him stature or the energy that came so naturally to most children. But when there is a deficit in one quarter, often there is an overabundance elsewhere, and so it was with Louis. He had such a quickness of mind and contemplative nature that he bid fair, at eight years of age, to leave his mama behind him before too long.

After morning prayers, he read aloud from the Bible, and Nell answered his questions on the passages covered as best she could. Then they moved on to Italian, which he had begun to learn after discovering a book of Nell's in that language on the shelf. Finally, Nell read three of Shakespeare's sonnets, which rested her own brain somewhat, for Louis regarded poetry as pointless but would listen quietly while she read it aloud. And finally Louis insisted that they pray again, this time solely for Papa, who was currently plying the Irish Sea as captain of the *Brig Minerva*, and therefore in constant danger, in Louis' mind, from storms and winds and powerful waves and tides and all the destructive majesty of the high seas.

"When will he be home, Mama?" he asked, as he did every day.

"In a few more days, or a week perhaps," she answered as she tidied away the books in the morning room, and laid out the slates for the ciphering lesson later.

A week perhaps, and then Jude would be home, smiling and holding her tight and calling her his dear love, and then her insides would tie themselves into knots until he went away again. But she would not repine. There was no point.

Breakfast was in the grandeur of the dining room, since the breakfast parlour was in the Lloyds' part of the house. All three families dined together, but at breakfast Nell and Louis were joined only by the widowed Maria Delanoy and her daughters, who had moved in after being swept up in the great disaster of five years ago. Since she could afford to pay little rent, Maria had taken upon herself the rôle of cook/housekeeper.

The two mothers discussed domestic matters while they ate, deciding on dinner, determining what needed to be bought that day and wondering whether they needed to order an extra quarter chaldron of coal to see them through to Lady Day.

"We have been rather lax about fires, I fear," Nell said. "Or rather, the Lloyds have been lax. Lydia is forever lighting fires in the bedrooms."

"Her boys have been greatly plagued by the grippe this winter, poor things," Maria said in her soft voice. "One cannot begrudge them the warmth while they recover."

"Those boys have been greatly plagued by mischief, more likely," Nell said robustly. "I do not think there is anything much amiss with them that a box around the ears would not cure. Lydia is too gentle with them."

"Oh, Nell!" Maria said. "She is hardly well herself just now, with another mouth to feed by summer, and she has been very unfortunate with her nursery maids. One must be sympathetic. You do not mean it, I am sure."

Nell paused and gazed at her friend. Maria was a gentle soul who thought well of the world, despite the world not seeming to smile upon her in return. It had not occurred to her that perhaps Lydia would retain her nursery maids more readily if she were to refrain from shouting at them.

"No, I do not mean it," Nell said in milder tones. "Something about Lydia rubs me the wrong way, that is all. I suppose they pay good rent for their half of the house, and coal is included. Well, if we run short of coal, we shall just have to eat our breakfast in the kitchen. That would save one fire a day, which would help."

"Aye, it would, and Jude will be home soon with money in his pocket. Perhaps he will not mind paying for a little extra coal this year, do you think?"

"Perhaps," Nell said colourlessly, but they both knew that she would never dare to ask him for such a thing.

At ten o'clock, Becky, the housemaid, came in to clear away, and Maria scurried away to the kitchen to begin her preparations for dinner. Nell took Louis and the two girls upstairs to the morning room for their lessons. The morning room was handsome, although small, since most of the frontage of the house on this floor was given over to the drawing room. Still, it was easy to keep warm, and it always felt pleasantly cosy on a cold winter's day. February was such a depressing time of year, but next month the weather might permit a day or two without the need for a fire. And the end of March brought Lady Day — the Lloyds' rent money and Jude's salary. Then it would not be long until summer.

After Louis' quickness at his lessons, Lucy and Jane were rather a trial. They were docile enough, sitting side by side in their dainty aprons, with matching ribbons in their hair. Maria had an annuity of only twenty pounds a year, and contributed half for her keep, and sometimes Nell wondered if she spent every penny of the remainder on ribbons for the girls. They were pretty enough, with wide blue eyes, long lashes and the sort of dark, tumbled locks that would drive men wild in a few years, but they would need more than looks to get them through life unscathed.

Nell sighed, and handed out the slates. "Today we will practice money," she said. "Lucy, Jane — you will write down the amounts to be added together on your slates and work out the answer. Louis, you may write the answer directly, but do not say it aloud, if you please. First addition — if I buy three pounds of sugar at eight pence a pound, two pounds of meat at seven pence a pound and a quarter pound of tea at eight shillings a pound, how much will I need to pay for it?"

A quarter pound of tea… oh, if only she could afford tea more often! However frugally she used it, somehow it never lasted long. She closed her eyes for a moment, as the three children tapped away on their slates. Tea… and the best china cups, which were presently packed in sawdust and stowed in the cellar. And her drawing room back again. All the best rooms had been given over to the Lloyds, and although it had been her own idea to take in paying lodgers and it had saved them from having to sell the house, she could not help but resent it just a little.

"Are you quite well, Mama?" Her son's voice was sharp with anxiety. He worried about her, she knew that, but there was not much she could do about it. There was not much she could do about anything.

She opened her eyes to find all three of them staring at her. "Perfectly well, thank you, Louis. Lucy, do you have an answer?"

"Six shillings. I think."

"Jane?"

"Ten pounds."

Louis burst out laughing. "Ten pounds? You could buy half the shop with that much."

"No, I'd get change. Mrs Caldicott asked me how much I'd need, and I couldn't work out the exact amount, so I decided I'd take more than enough. Is it a lot more?" she added, suddenly anxious.

"You would only need five and tuppence," he said. "I tell you what, Jane, if ever you have ten pounds, you may send me to do your shopping for you."

"May I?" she said. "That's very kind of you, Louis."

That set him laughing again.

"He did not mean it as a kindness, Jane," Nell said. "He meant that he would pay five and tuppence for the goods and keep the remaining amount, which is—"

"Nine pounds fourteen and tenpence," he said at once, before starting to laugh again.

"Another one," Nell said wearily. "Perhaps something a little easier. I need six yards of muslin to make a gown, and muslin costs one and six a yard. How much will it cost me altogether?"

Oh, for a new gown! If only—

The knocker sounded below. The girls at once scrambled from their chairs and raced to the window, peering down at the street below.

"It is a gentleman!"

"With a red coat!"

"And a great tall hat!"

"It will be for Mr Lloyd, I expect," Louis said.

Becky's quick steps were heard on the stairs, then the front door opening, followed by the murmur of a man's voice. Then silence. Becky's footsteps returning up the stairs, more slowly this time. There was a quick scratch on the door of the morning room, before she entered.

"Beg pardon, madam, but there's a gen'leman to see you. Askin' for you by name."

By name? Someone she knew? One of her brothers, it must be! "Did he give his name?"

Silently Becky proffered a card. It had been so long since anyone had called with a card that the girl had forgotten to bring it on the silver salver that lay in the hall for the purpose.

'N Harbottle, Davygate, York', she read. No one she knew, then. Her excitement waned a little. But a gentleman visiting was still something, even if it was not anyone from her former life come to rescue her. No, she must stop expecting rescue. Such foolishness. Well, whoever Mr Harbottle was, she would see him, but not alone, and three children were not sufficient protection.

"Is Mrs Delanoy still in the house?"

"Yes, madam. She found some nutmeg left in the pantry, so she don't need no shopping today."

"Ask her to step up to the morning room, if you please — without her apron. Then show Mr Harbottle in." With a bob of a curtsy, Becky hurried off, leaving Nell to be thankful that she had not let her standards slip by a single iota. The servants got their uniform quota each year, so that Becky always had a clean gown to wear, and Nell and Louis looked respectable, if not exactly fashionable.

She and the children abandoned the slates on the worktable, and rearranged themselves according to Nell's hasty instructions. Again, she regretted the loss of her drawing room, purposely designed for just such eventualities. There were so few chairs in the morning room. However, there were enough to make a tolerable circle for conversation, and a window seat where the children could sit, rather squeezed together. "Not a word to be spoken, or you will have to leave," Nell told them sternly, and they nodded solemnly.

Maria hastened in, her cheeks rather flushed, and took the seat on the sofa next to Nell moments before the door opened.

"Mr Harbottle, madam," Becky said, in her very best announcing voice.

Nell rose smoothly to greet him. He was young, handsome and stylish, a man one might meet at a fashionable rout or ball. Well-shaped legs, broad shoulders needing no padding to enhance them, a warm smile and a pair of roguishly twinkling blue eyes... all of this Nell observed appreciatively as he entered the room.

He looked from Nell to Maria, and then settled his gaze firmly on Nell. "Mrs Caldicott? Wife of Captain Jude Caldicott?"

"I am, sir. This is my friend, Mrs Delanoy."

He bowed. "Madam." Another bow, fractionally less deep. "Mrs Delanoy." The two women curtsied in response. Then he spotted the children. "And these must be... no, no, let me guess, if you please. I think... the Miss Delanoys and... hmm, Master Caldicott?"

"That is so," Nell said, with a small smile. Lucy and Jane were clearly Maria's, for they had her dark curls, but Louis was more difficult to place. He had his father's blond hair, but his nose and mouth were all Nell and his eyes were his grandmother's. "Please sit down, Mr Harbottle."

She sat herself, and he then took the chair opposite.

"Thank you so much for agreeing to see me, Mrs Caldicott. Were your husband available, I should not have dreamt of troubling you, but I understand that he is at sea, and not expected home for some days yet."

"That is so. He commands the *Brig Minerva*, which is due to return in a few days, but with the vagaries of the weather and so forth..."

"Oh, quite, quite. Then perhaps I may be permitted to address my enquiries to you, in his absence?" She nodded her assent. "You are most gracious, madam."

He made her a small bow, and there was a brightness in his eye as he looked at her that she recognised. Such looks had once been very familiar to her. She had danced or moved about or talked or simply walked into a room, and men had looked at her with just such admiration. It startled her to realise that she still had that power. How gratifying that, at the age of six and twenty, she could arouse such a response in a passing stranger. She was aware of a little bloom of pleasure inside her, for who could not delight in having an admirer, even one so fleeting as Mr Harbottle?

He went on, "Let me not try your patience with useless chatter, but get straight to the point. I am searching for my cousin, one Felix Harbottle from Yorkshire, who was a naval officer at one time with the rank of captain. There was a breach with the family some twenty years ago when he married against the wishes of his father and mother. We lost touch with him, although he wrote to his mother every year on her birthday — each time from a different port. So we know he is still alive, and still hearing the call of the sea, although no longer with the navy. Now his mother wishes to set aside the past and reconcile with her son, so she has charged me with the task of finding him. For two years, Mrs Caldicott, I have been searching diligently, but so far in vain. The navy has no trace of him, his former friends have had no word of him, and so I have moved from port to port, enquiring."

"From port to port? There are a great many ports in this country, sir."

He laughed, and again Nell noticed those deep blue eyes, and his hair just that colour she so admired — like pale honey. But she had been driven astray by fair hair and amused blue eyes before, she reminded herself sternly.

"It is indeed one of the disadvantages of an island nation that there are a great many ports, and sometimes I feel as if I have ventured into every one of them. However, most are fishing ports only, and I cannot feel that a former naval captain would be commanding a trawler, so I have restricted myself to the major ports only. I began with those from which a letter had arrived, and have now extended my reach to others, and here I am in your fair town, Mrs Caldicott. Southampton is a charming place and has... many attractions..." Here he paused and looked at Nell in a manner which there was no mistaking. "However, in one respect it differs not a whit from every other port in the country, in that no one has ever heard of Captain Felix Harbottle. May I hope for better tidings from you, Mrs Caldicott? Has your husband ever mentioned such a person?"

"I am very sorry, Mr Harbottle, but he has not."

"Am I correct in thinking that Captain Caldicott was also in His Majesty's Navy at one time?"

"He was, but it is a very large navy," she said with a smile. "I do not imagine Captain Caldicott knew more than a small number of its officers. Besides, he rarely speaks of his time in the navy. One or two of the battles, sometimes, with his son, who has an interest in such things, but nothing of the people he knew."

It was a thing she had always thought odd, that he could talk impersonally of this battle or that, almost like an account in the newspaper, yet never mention the men involved. She had supposed it was his way of coping with the horrors of war, and had never pressed him.

"Do you know of any man, any officer on a ship and formerly in the navy, answering to my cousin's description? A man of three and forty, with fair hair and blue eyes?"

Nell considered that. "Captain Walker?" Mr Harbottle shook his head. "Captain Phillipson, then. Oh, but he was never in the navy, I believe."

"I have already talked to both those gentlemen, and neither of them has graced His Majesty's Navy."

"It is a common combination of features, but the navy... so few men leave the navy entirely. And then there is the age. My own husband would fit that description precisely, except for the age. He is not yet forty. Also, he married only nine years ago, not twenty, so his history is very different from that of your cousin. I am so sorry I cannot help."

"There is just one more chance. May I show you my cousin's likeness? It is possible you have encountered him under a different name, perhaps, or passed him by in the street." He produced a small framed miniature from a pocket, and handed it to her. "It was taken when he was but fifteen and only a midshipman, almost thirty years ago, but it is all we have of him."

She gazed at the boy's face, youthful and optimistic, and remembered the time when Jude had been just as hopeful of life, his eyes bright and lips curved into a perpetual smile, before disappointment had soured his disposition.

"I am very sorry," she said. "I do not recognise him. Maria, you go about the town more than I do — do you know anyone like this?"

Maria examined it, but then she shook her head. "He is a fine looking young man, but I don't know him."

"Ah." Mr Harbottle sat back in his chair, disappointment written on his countenance. "That is a pity. But perhaps you would be so good as to tell your husband of my enquiry, Mrs Caldicott? He may write to me if he has any information."

"I shall certainly tell him, sir. May I offer you some refreshment, Mr Harbottle? I am afraid that I have no tea or wine today, but there is ale and cake if—"

"You are too kind, but I will take up no more of your time, madam," he said rising gracefully to his feet. "And you three," he added, looking at the children, "may return to your studies. What is the lesson today?"

They sat mutely, staring at him.

Nell laughed. "Do not imagine them to be ill-mannered, Mr Harbottle. They have been given the strictest instructions not to speak a word while you are here, on pain of— Well, I shall think of some dire penalty, I daresay."

"Then they are exceptionally dutiful, and I commend them," he said at once. "And their mamas, who have instilled such obedience into them. But may I examine your slates and see if I may guess the topic?"

Permission granted, he bounded across the room and picked up one of the slates. " *'Six yards of muffin at one and six the yard'*. Muffin? Oh, *muslin.* That should be easy... let me see... that will be... four and fivepence three farthings... no, wait... twelve guineas... no, no, that cannot be right..."

The children giggled, and Nell smiled, too, and exchanged a glance with Maria, who was trying not to laugh.

"No, I cannot work it out," Mr Harbottle said. "You will have to tell me the answer."

"You are just funning, I can tell," Louis said. "You *do* know the answer. It is nine shillings."

"Is it?" Jane said. "Is that correct, Mr Harbottle?"

"It is indeed," he said, "and a very pretty gown it will make for one of the ladies. Let me see now... green, I think, if it be for Mrs Delanoy, and for Mrs Caldicott... blue, to match her eyes. Or even white, if there be some blue upon it also, and a shawl of gold, with a gold chain about her neck, and sapphires on her fingers. Yes, that is what you should be wearing, Mrs Caldicott."

He smiled at her so charmingly that she could not possibly take offence. Nevertheless, she was very glad that Jude was not there to hear such flirtatious words.

2: A Cup Of Tea

Nathan crammed his hat onto his head anyhow and strode off down the street. He had never found it more difficult to hold his tongue. Such a gloriously beautiful woman — those eyes, so dazzling in the intensity of their gaze — and yet her cap and the high-necked gown could not hide the bruises. They were faded now, but he could not mistake what he saw. Then there was that tiny hesitation every time she mentioned her husband. She was afraid of him, clearly. And there was not a thing Nathan could do about it.

His anger carried him out of East Street and the full length of the High Street before he began to take note of his surroundings again. He had been in Southampton for four days, and so far his enquiries had led him to the wharfs and quaysides, to a few lodging houses within the town and to two or three estates outside it, but he had not allowed himself the time to look around the town. Now he noticed a number of respectable people passing through an arch in the ancient walls. He followed and found himself on a pleasant walk bordering the river, and he was able to cover some distance at his most rapid pace until his rage had abated somewhat.

At length, he flung himself down on a seat, gazing unseeing out at the wide river, and thought about Mrs Caldicott. She was a lady, of that he had no doubt. Her bearing, her well-modulated voice, her manner all proclaimed it. Her husband had been a naval officer, so he must have some aptitude, even if he were not well-born himself. He had won himself a lady of quality, and established her well, for although the house on East Street was not as large as some, it would not be cheap to buy or to rent.

Yet she was poor. She had no tea in the house, even to offer a guest, and that was a desperate degree of poverty for a gently-born lady. Everyone drank tea! Her gown was no longer fashionable, and her slippers were worn. How sad! He had joked about dressing her in blue muslin and a gold shawl, but how he longed to see her in silk, with diamonds at her throat and a little more colour in her cheeks. She was pale and a tad drawn, but then if her husband beat her—

Here he jumped up, as his anger boiled over again. A wife was her husband's property, naturally, but to injure her in that way was despicable, the work of a coward. Had she no family to remonstrate with the fellow? Had she nowhere to go, but must stay with him and tamely submit? And perhaps one day he would hit her so hard that she would fall and not get up again...

His footsteps drew him back to the High Street, where he passed a grocer with a sign in the window — *'Finest Souchong tea from only 4/9 lb, Green Hyson 14/- lb'.* Tea... how she must miss it! Would she be offended, or feel obliged to refuse for propriety's sake? Yet it would soothe his own turbulent emotions to offer her something, some tiny thing, that would improve her life a little.

He entered the shop, a bell jangling above the door, and found himself wreathed in the familiar smells of boyhood, when he had accompanied his mama on her quarterly round of the shops to settle bills. The feathers at the poulterer and the bloodstained sawdust at the butcher had fascinated him, but it was the grocer who most drew him, the wooden floor covered with sacks and boxes with exotic labels from all over the world, and the air heavy with spices. This one was not much different, and he walked about, peering at the currants and rice and blocks of sugar, while he waited for the grocer to attend to him.

When it was his turn, he said, "I should like to buy some tea for a friend. Perhaps you know her — Mrs Caldicott of East Street? Do you know what she would most enjoy?"

"Ah, Mrs Caldicott! Indeed, sir, indeed. She used to buy a quantity of the Black Pekoe — that was her favourite when first she came to Southampton. A lady of refined taste, for few of my customers have the discernment to prefer it. Latterly, she buys a Souchong... sometimes. Or perhaps I should say that Mrs Delanoy buys it. She buys most of the provisions, being in charge of the kitchens since the cook left. We seldom see Mrs Caldicott these days, more's the pity. Yes, Pekoe is what Mrs Caldicott likes best."

Nathan understood him. The expensive taste for Pekoe had given way to something cheaper, and even that was perhaps too dear towards the end of the quarter. She was a careful manager, it seemed. And the cook had been let go, replaced by the friend with the widow's cap who lived with her.

"Very well. Let me have a quarter of the best Pekoe, and do you have any gunpowder tea? That is my favourite, so I will also take a quarter of your best for Mrs Caldicott to try."

Thus provisioned, he continued down the High Street, stopping briefly at a bookseller, before returning, rather pleased with himself, to his hotel.

~~~~~

The next day was busy, for it was Nathan's final day in Southampton and there were letters to be written and arrangements to be made. Everything must be well-ordered for the journey. He could not travel with the slightest hint of confusion. Not for him the impulse of
~~~~~

leaping onto a horse with only a couple of spare shirts in a saddle bag, or rushing to the nearest coaching inn to procure a seat on the next stage that passed by. No, everything must be arranged with meticulous care. His mind was not entirely engaged with these matters, however, for images of clear blue eyes and a lovely face marred by bruises would keep intruding. Late in the morning all was done, and he set off for East Street with his packages.

The same neat maid answered the door, and without hesitation showed him upstairs to what he supposed must be the morning room. It had surprised him not to be received in the drawing room, but now that he was more aware of her circumstances, he guessed that it was the only room with a fire during the day. And perhaps there were few callers to notice.

She was alone with her son, the two of them sitting side by side on a stool before the pianoforte, as the boy slowly picked out the notes of a tune. As Nathan entered, the boy said something and she laughed in response, her whole face suddenly alight with merriment. Nathan's breath caught in his throat — she was so beautiful! She could walk amongst the incomparables of London society and not be out of place.

The smile faded to surprise as she turned to see him enter the room. Pleased surprise, he thought. She was not angry.

The maid bobbed a curtsy. "Mr Harbottle, madam."

"Why, what a pleasure to see you again, Mr Harbottle." She rose gracefully and crossed the room to meet him. So tall and elegant — her posture, her carriage! He could watch her walk about all day. "Do you have more questions for me?"

"No, nothing of the sort. My errand is, I hope, a more agreeable one. As I am to leave Southampton tomorrow, I wished to bring you a small gift in gratitude for your courteous reception of me yesterday. I had no right to expect you even to receive me, yet you were graciousness personified. I thought… I hope you will have no objection, but… some tea for you, and a book for Master Caldicott."

He waited anxiously. It was an impertinence, he knew, and perhaps if there had been no bruises he would not have thought of it. Or if she had been less beautiful, his heart whispered. No, it was more than her beauty. Her dignified manner drew him powerfully. Even in adversity, she was completely a lady.

She smiled, and he released his breath. "How kind of you! And tea… you remembered that we have none. Oh, Pekoe, my favourite… and a gunpowder, too. I thank you a thousand times! We must have a cup at once. Will you stay and take tea with me, Mr Harbottle?"

"I should be delighted," he said, with the greatest sincerity. "Here you are, young man. Open your present."

"Thank you, sir!" the boy said, sitting down at the table to unpick the string and remove the brown paper from his parcel.

Mrs Caldicott rang for the maid and ordered the tea, then looked around for a seat. The circle of chairs had been scattered about, so after a moment's thought she took a seat on the sofa beside the fire. Nathan did not quite like to sit beside her, for that would look too particular, so he pulled forward a chair from the worktable.

"Are you departing tomorrow to investigate another port, Mr Harbottle?" she said, with a sweet smile of enquiry. Such a lovely smile she had!

"I… no, tomorrow I must return home to Yorkshire to report my findings regarding Felix to my aunt. Not that there is much to report."

"Presumably you have advertised in the newspapers?"

"Naturally, but with no response. We have even posted a reward for information, but although a number of people claimed the bounty, none had any information of value."

She wrinkled her forehead prettily, considering the matter. "Mr Harbottle, I am sure it has occurred to you that your cousin does not wish to be found, and has changed his name, the better to remain hidden."

He smiled. "Indeed it has. It is, in point of fact, the only sensible explanation. However, I do not see what can be done about it, if so. If Felix wishes to hide behind another name, why, he could be anywhere, and unless I passed him on the street, I would be quite unable to find him. Even then... I have never met him myself, and he may look nothing at all like the miniature I showed you yesterday. It is frustrating," he said, with a sigh. "If only my cousin had been possessed of a squint or a hunchback or a wooden leg. My task then would have been immeasurably easier."

She laughed, a melodious sound, and as Becky arrived just then with the tea things, the subject was allowed to drop. Louis could not be pulled away from his book, a history of England's great naval battles, so Mrs Caldicott poured for the two of them, and handed him a slice of cake. They sat together in the most companionable way, and Nathan was filled with yearning for such a life — to take tea every day with such a woman, to listen to her musical voice, to watch her cross the room in that elegant way she had... Yet tomorrow he would drive away from this town and would never see her again.

A peremptory knock on the door was immediately followed by its being thrown open to admit a woman he had not seen before. She was small and not especially pretty, particularly so at this moment when her face was creased with rage.

"Nell, have you been at my tea supply? For I won't have it, I— Oh!" Her hand fluttered to her throat, and her voice suddenly became caressingly high. "I didn't know you had a *gentleman* caller."

Her clothes were well-made and fashionable, but heavily burdened with lace and decorative bows and flourishes so that beside Mrs Caldicott's simple elegance she looked like an overdressed doll. The accent placed her solidly in the shopkeeper class.

Mrs Caldicott set down her tea cup carefully. "Mrs Lloyd, I could not possibly have used any of your tea, since you keep the key by you at all times."

"Oh yes, but I saw Becky bringing the tea things, so..." She halted, looking from Mrs Caldicott to Nathan and back again, clearly wanting to be introduced, but not quite confident enough to ask for it.

"Did you?" Mrs Caldicott said, and Nathan could only admire her tone, which was perfectly polite yet tinged with the slightest degree of coolness.

"Nell, dear," the intruder began, in a carefully mannered voice, "I am not sure that you should be receiving a gentleman all alone. It is not quite correct, I feel."

"How kind of you to be concerned," Mrs Caldicott said. "However, I am not alone, as you can see. Louis is here."

"Oh, Louis!" she said in disparaging tones. Again she looked from one to the other. Mrs Caldicott calmly picked up her tea cup again, and took a delicate sip. Thus dismissed, the woman in lace turned without a word and flounced out of the room.

"My lodger," Mrs Caldicott said, with the hint of a smile. Nell... Helen, perhaps, or Eleanor. Nell Caldicott. Mother of Louis. Wife of Jude. Judas the betrayer — how apt.

Nathan politely made no comment on the lodger, but everything fitted. Mrs Caldicott had not received him in the drawing room, most probably, because she no longer had a drawing room. There was some tension between the two women, though, and he could not guess where that might have its roots. Women's lives were complicated, and the lodger looked the sort of woman to stand on her dignity. She would not like giving way to Nell, who was so clearly her superior.

Because he was curious about her, he said, "Where is your family from, Mrs Caldicott?"

She set the teacup down again. "About fifteen miles from here, a place called Bishopswood Cromby. Just a small village not far from Winchester."

At a guess that her father was landed gentry, he said, "Is your father's estate a large one?"

She smiled. "Not especially. There are so many fine estates in Hampshire, but I do not think Papa's was ever accounted one of them. More heathland than good agricultural. My older brother has Daveney Hall now. Sir James Godney. Perhaps you know him?"

Sir James… a baronet, most likely, of Daveney Hall. He would look it up. "I do not, but then I have never moved in that level of society beyond my own county. Do you see your brother a great deal?"

"Not at all. We are… estranged."

So she could not turn to her brother for help against her husband. "That is a pity," he said. "And your husband's family?"

She simply shook her head.

"Then you are all alone," he said.

"No," she said quietly. "I have my son. I have a good friend in Mrs Delanoy, whom you met yesterday. I have… my husband. I am very far from alone, I assure you." She smiled, but he thought it unconvincing, a brave effort that spoke of her dauntless spirit.

Her words filled him with sorrow. Her only friends were her child, a glorified cook and the man who beat her. She would have no friends in her own level of society, for she could not afford to return hospitality, and she could hardly mingle with the shopkeepers and attorneys of the town. How isolated she must be! She was indeed all alone.

But he could not express such thoughts, so he said only, "It is always sad when families are torn apart, and old grievances held for far too long, as in my cousin's case. There was a quarrel when he was thought to have married beneath him, after which he stormed back to London and was never heard from again, apart from his one letter a year to his mother. It is hard to imagine a catastrophe of such magnitude that the breach can never be healed."

"Men can be stubborn sometimes," she said with a slight smile, and he wondered if she was thinking of her husband. "At least your cousin has written to his mother, so she knows he is well. He is kind, even if he chooses to live his life in his own way."

"That is how I view the matter, too," he said, pleased to find their opinions in such good accord. "This is an excellent tea, Mrs Caldicott. I shall have to tell my housekeeper to buy some Pekoe."

It was, he thought, as pleasant an hour as any he had passed. The tea, the cake and the company were all excellent, and although Mrs Caldicott was loath to talk about herself, he gleaned a few nuggets about her husband — that he came from Ireland, that he was not yet forty and that he had owned his own ships at one time, but was now a paid employee, not an owner. That accounted for the family's state of poverty, he supposed.

At length, propriety dictated that he could stay no longer. When he rose to take his leave, Mrs Caldicott said, "Thank you so much for the conversation, Mr Harbottle, as much as the tea and book. I have greatly enjoyed your visit today, and if ever you are in Southampton in the future, I hope you will call again. I wish you success in your search for your cousin."

"You are most kind, and may I likewise thank you for your company." He bowed. "I have rarely been so well entertained." She acknowledged the compliment with a gentle inclination of the head. He hesitated, then, but he could not leave without a word on the matter which most worried him. Impulsively, he raced on. "Mrs Caldicott, do you still have the card I gave you yesterday?"

"Oh, certainly."

In a low voice so the child would not hear, he went on hastily, "Pray keep it by you and... if ever you stand in need of a friend, one who wishes for nothing but your welfare, then you may write to me and I will come to you, wherever you are. Or you may come to me at York, if you prefer. Purely as a *friend*, you understand, one who wishes you well and will do all in his power to ensure it."

She did not pretend to misunderstand him. Her eyes widened, and at one point she opened her mouth to speak, but thought better of it. At the end, she merely nodded, not looking him in the eye.

After a few words with Louis, and a final farewell to the lady herself, he left the house and walked slowly back to his hotel. He had done all that he could. Now it only remained to finish his packing and try very hard not to think of those fading bruises and the husband who would be home before too long.

3: Coming Home

Nell retrieved the card from the mantel, where it had been propped up behind the clock. *'N Harbottle, Davygate, York'* A gentleman, and wealthy enough to spend two years jaunting around England searching for a cousin he had never met. And he would protect her, that was the intent behind his words. He would protect her from Jude, as a friend. That was not the usual meaning of the word, though. A man protected his family — his parents, his sisters, his younger brothers, his wife and his own children. A man also protected his mistress, yet she did not think he meant his offer in that way. *Purely as a friend.* That was what he had said, and he seemed like an honourable man. And if she were desperate... she tucked the card away in her work basket.

Louis could not be torn away from his book, so Nell sat down at the instrument and played for a while. Music soothed her when nothing else could. When she had been so ill, Kitty Sherrard had come every day and played for her, while Nell lay prostrate on the Louis XVI *duchesse brisée*, and it had somehow made everything a little better. Kitty was gone now, replaced by the haughty Theresa, and Lydia Lloyd's silk-clad behind rested on the *duchesse brisée*. The grand piano, so far as she could tell, was never played at all, while

Nell made do with a battered old thing that had been one of Jude's earliest apologies. At least she had a pianoforte to play.

After a while, her mind began to drift while her fingers played on, unregarded. *'N Harbottle, Davygate, York'* Nigel, perhaps. Neville. Norman. A gentleman who looked at her with clear admiration in his eyes. A gentleman who made her feel like a lady again. A gentleman with a housekeeper to order his tea, and a place in society. Unlike Nell. She who had once been—

No, no, no. She would *not* repine. She had made her choices, made her mistakes and now she paid for them. There was so much to be thankful for — her son, her home and a husband who loved her, sometimes. She would *not* repine. It was best not to think too much, so she forced herself to play a harder piece that required her total concentration.

Becky had to cough to gain her attention. "Beg pardon, madam, but a note came from Mr Sherrard." She had remembered the salver this time.

Nell grabbed the paper and unfolded it with shaking hands. *'Mrs Caldicott, Please be informed that the* Minerva *arrived in Dublin on Monday last, and is scheduled to depart for home today, Wednesday. Flack'* From Mr Flack, the secretary. Just a routine note. Her racing pulse settled a little.

"Is it good news, Mama?" Louis said.

"The best," she said brightly. "Papa is on his way home. His ship will be in port early on Saturday."

"Hooray!" Louis shrieked, racing round the room in excitement. "Now we can have proper dinners again."

Oh, the honesty of childhood! To him, his father's return meant only that dinner would be more elaborate, with removes and wine and puddings. Not that Louis ate much, but he loved the ceremony of dinner, the candles and crystal glasses and conversation. Jude was always at his most charming at dinner, witty and slightly flirtatious and urbane. To see him thus, no one would ever suspect his darker side.

Nell rose from the piano stool. "Thank you, Becky. Tell Mrs Delanoy that I will come down directly to discuss arrangements. Remind her that Jude and I will be at the Sherrards' ball on Saturday night."

There was a decided bustle about the household in preparation for the master's return. The maids cleaned and polished with gusto, Maria planned special dishes for dinner, and precious bottles of Madeira and claret were brought up from the cellar. Everyone smiled and said how lovely it would be to have Jude home again, and how fortunate the weather was so settled for the time of year, so as not to delay his return. Yet their eyes did not quite meet Nell's, and there was a brittle edge to all the busyness, the studied activity of those who were pretending that everything was as it should be.

Nell's immediate concern was prosaic — what on earth was she to wear? She looked at her wardrobe with despair.

"A new ribbon for your hair, perhaps?" Maria said timidly.

Nell heaved a great sigh. "I cannot justify the cost. Besides, he has not been away for long this time — only three weeks. He will not expect me to have anything new."

"No, but—" Maria stopped, but she did not need to go on. Nell remembered all too vividly the last time she had displayed no improvement to her appearance when Jude returned from a trip.

"I have one or two ribbons I have not worn much," she said at length. "That might work."

"There are some I bought for the girls," Maria said. "If you will allow it?"

"Maria, you have so little..."

"But you have given me so much," Maria said quietly, resting one hand on Nell's arm. "Please accept a little gift in return." Then, after a brief hesitation, she said firmly, "You know it is better if—"

"Very well," Nell said quickly. "But a loan only, just for a few days." Just until the excitement of Jude's return had died down. Just until they knew his mood. Or until he went away again. Sometimes — most times — he arrived in good humour after a successful trip, and nothing occurred to throw him into a rage. Most times his leave passed uneventfully. But sometimes... it was as well to take every precaution.

The meals were settled, the house smelt of lavender and beeswax, and Nell had new ribbons on an old gown, and more for her hair. Then she waited for the *Brig Minerva* to bring Jude Caldicott home.

~~~~~

Nathan hated London, but it was an inevitable part of travelling from south to north. Every major coach road led to the capital, and so his journey from Southampton to Yorkshire brought him to London first. At least he did not have to put up at an hotel or inn, for he had a good friend to turn to.

Harry Smethurst was a Yorkshire man who represented an East Riding constituency as a Member of Parliament. He was not a conventionally handsome man, nor did he dress in the manner of the London dandies. He looked exactly what he was — the son of the Squire, descendant of a long line of Squires, solid, worthy men, the heart of England. Having objected to the dilatory record of his local Member of Parliament, on a whim he had stood himself and, to everyone's astonishment, not least his own, had been elected by the farmers and burghers of his constituency. Ever since, he had
~~~~~

diligently represented their interests, living in two rooms in a cheap quarter of town when Parliament was sitting, and quietly making a name for himself. After some years of laboriously climbing the ladder of his chosen profession, he had recently been taken up by a noble patron, who had provided him with spacious accommodation.

"This is excessively comfortable, Harry," Nathan said, admiring an elegant vase on the mantel. "Every convenience provided. How many rooms do you have?"

"Drawing room, dining room, study and three bedrooms, as well as the usual domestic offices. You should see the kitchen, Nathan. The cook I have engaged was almost in tears at the sight of it. I have had no hand in any of it, for it is all Lady Carrbridge's doing. She likes to be busy with a project, seemingly, so she saw to all the refurbishments."

"She has excellent taste," Nathan said, adjusting his neckcloth minutely with the aid of a gilt-edged mirror. "Lord, how grand you are getting, Harry, mingling with the likes of Lord and Lady Carrbridge. But you are made, now, my friend. You may consider marriage at last."

Harry flushed, and gave a nervous laugh. "I don't know about that, Nathan. I shall have to see how my finances stretch now that my expenses are so much higher. I am expected to entertain, you know."

"And a wife would be the perfect aid to such an enterprise," Nathan said. "Surely you will—"

"I must wait and see," Harry said quickly. "Did you read all the letters that were awaiting you? Two from your aunt — she is keen for news."

"My cousin is unwell, so she is in rather a flap. If he dies—"

"Ah, yes. And you had no luck in Southampton? You must have just about exhausted the possibilities on the south coast."

"I have just about exhausted the possibilities everywhere," Nathan said gloomily. "There are one or two places in East Anglia, perhaps, but after that I must either start investigating the foreign ports or abandon the search altogether."

"That fellow you set to work through the shipping lists, has he—?"

Nathan gave a shake of his head. "Nothing, and I ask everywhere for a blond man of three and forty, formerly in the navy but there are none to be found. There is always some feature amiss — the hair is dark, or the eyes are green, or the fellow is not yet forty. And hardly a one who was ever in the navy. How is it that so few men quit the navy?"

"A career for life, I suppose," Harry said, with an indifferent lift of one shoulder. "Better financial prospects? A man can make his fortune in the navy. Shall we dine at the club this evening, since Mrs Pickles is not expecting you? But you will stay until Monday, I hope? You will not set out again on a Saturday and kick your heels at some dreadful inn on the Sabbath when you could be enjoying a fine shoulder of beef with me instead."

Nathan agreed to it, and the two men dressed for dinner and made their way to Brooks's for the evening. When they had finished their meal in the club's opulent dining room, and were lingering over the port, reluctant to move, Harry said, "You are very quiet, Nathan. Something bothering you?"

"A little, but there is nothing to be done about it."

"Come now, unburden yourself. You will feel better, even if the problem remains intractable."

Nathan gave a small laugh. "Well, then, there was a woman in Southampton— No, no, do not jump to any conclusions, I beg you, for you would be far out. A lady, I should say, for she is very much so. I never saw anyone so graceful in her movements, or so elegantly mannered. She could move in the highest circles in the land without disgrace."

"A paragon indeed! You are inspiring me to jump to some very particular conclusions. Is she beautiful?"

"I never saw a more beautiful woman."

"Aha!"

"No, no, you must not say *'Aha!'* in that suspicious way, for she is married, and my interest is not in that direction at all. My tastes have never leaned towards the cool and ladylike, as you well know, although I cannot imagine a man alive who would not admire her, as one might admire a great painting or an exquisite jewel. Her husband is away at sea, but she was so gracious as to answer my enquiries about Felix. She received me very kindly, and behaved with perfect correctness, and yet... her face sported the remains of several ugly bruises."

"What!"

"She had tried to hide them, of course. One about the throat was almost hidden by the ruff of her gown, and there was another concealed by the lace on her cap, only visible when she moved her head just so. But about her eye, the bruising could not be concealed. And there was just such a constraint in her voice when she spoke about her husband that I could not doubt the truth."

"Who is this man who beats his wife so?"

"He is a sea captain, a former naval captain."

"An officer! That is despicable," Harry said, in genuine shock.

"Exactly so. Yet what can I do? She is estranged from her own family, and from his too, it seems, and no one can interfere between husband and wife, if she makes no complaint against him. Such things occur amongst the lower orders who have not been brought up to the behaviour expected of a gentleman, but not amongst our class, one would hope."

"Some men treat their wives abominably," Harry said seriously, "yet they do not hit them. That is beyond the pale of acceptable behaviour towards a gently-born lady."

"Exactly!" Nathan cried. "Yet what is to be done? Nothing at all! Nothing to protect her from such abuse, nor encourage her to make a complaint to the constables."

"No, that would not help. Poor lady! I suppose she cannot leave the wretch?"

"She has nowhere to go — no family or friends, and to abandon the shelter of her husband's roof would put her beyond the reach of respectable society. Her future would be bleak indeed."

"No wonder you have been subdued, Nathan. Shall you return to Southampton?"

He gave a quick shake of the head. "It would do no good. However, I made sure that she had my card and I told her that she may call upon me if ever she has urgent need of a friend. If nothing else, I could provide her with a safe hiding place, and prevent her sliding into desperate actions. I can do no more, except to hope that it was a momentary lapse on her husband's part, and that he is now remorseful and wishing to make amends. Look, there is a fellow over there trying to attract your attention, Harry."

Harry turned his head to look, then quickly turned back again, whispering, "Oh Lord, it is Viscount Toller. Not my favourite person, but he has been uncommonly friendly towards me ever since I was so fortunate as to attract Lord Carrbridge's notice. I shall have to acknowledge him." In louder tones, he went on, "Ahoy there, Toller! Are you dining? Will you join us for port?"

Viscount Toller was a large man close to fifty and with foppish tendencies, an unfortunate combination. Nathan watched him approach with fascination, trying not to be dazzled by the array of diamond pins, rings and fobs, and the garish colours employed.

"Smethurst," the viscount said languidly, raising a quizzing glass to examine Nathan from head to foot. "And a friend. How delightful. From the northern wilds, I surmise."

"From Yorkshire, which is indeed in the north," Harry said. "I cannot say how wild it is."

"Very wild, I am perfectly sure. Will you introduce me?" Toller said.

"Of course. This is my very good friend Nathan Harbottle, from York. Nathan, Lord Toller."

Nathan rose and bowed. "How do you do, my lord," he murmured, before realising that Toller was standing transfixed.

"Harbottle? Are you by chance related to Felix Harbottle?"

A surge of hope shot through Nathan. "My cousin. You know him?"

"Knew him, long ago, but he disappeared. Have you any idea where he might be? I should very much like to see him again."

Nathan's excitement drained away as quickly as it had arrived. Nobody knew where Felix was. His cousin had vanished without trace.

~~~~~

Nell rose early on Saturday morning. If the winds and tides were favourable, the *Brig Minerva* could reach Southampton not long
~~~~~

after dawn, and she must be ready. Everything must be ready. She had only been sick once, and that was a good sign. She was calm, she must be calm. Her gown for the Sherrards' ball was laid out ready, and the weather was dry, so they would be able to walk the short distance to the Dolphin without any recriminations over the lack of a carriage. She must be calm.

She sat at the instrument in the morning room, not playing, for her hands shook too much, but allowing the thought of music to exert its soothing influence. Sooner or later, Jude would ask her to play, and she was glad to have this small piece of their former life. They could pretend, for a while, that everything was as it was, that they were still rich and happy, the disaster had never happened and they still loved each other as much as ever.

The knocking on the door was frantic. Then the bell, then the knocker again, even more peremptorily. Nell heard the sound of the door creaking open, then high, anxious voices.

A trickle of alarm ran through her, instantly stilled. Some domestic matter, perhaps, or something to do with the Lloyds. It could not be about Jude, for that would come from Mr Sherrard himself, or from Flack. The boy would bring a note — the tide was wrong or the winds, or there had been some problem with the cargo — written in Flack's firm hand, or Mr Sherrard's more rounded script. No, it could not be—

Steps on the stairs, feet thumping up and up, and then the morning room door was thrown open. Theresa Sherrard and Tilly Flack stood there, faces white and tear-streaked.

"Oh Nell!" Tilly cried. "It's gone down! The *Minerva* — it's gone, sunk like a stone. I'm so sorry."

4: The Day of The Sherrards' Ball

"There are survivors," Tilly added quickly. "There are known to be survivors, so we must hope for the best."

"When?" Nell croaked. "When did this happen?"

"Night before last, off the Cornish coast. Word just came in an hour ago. Julian and Barty are to go there at once."

It was as well that Nell was sitting down already, for her legs would not have supported her. Sunk? The *Minerva* sunk? "But how?" she whispered. "Was it stormy?"

It was Theresa Sherrard who answered. "No idea. Nell, we have to see other people... we cannot stay. That is all we know, truly. Julian is distraught. It is such a disaster — it could ruin us."

"Yes, I quite see—" Nell began, but the words caught in her throat.

"No, you don't," Theresa said harshly. "There was a *duke* on board. A *duke*. Your husband killed a duke."

So saying, she swept out of the room.

"Survivors," Tilly whispered. "He may be safe, Nell." Then she scuttled after her friend.

Nell had no idea whether she was talking about Jude or the duke. She was left wondering which she wanted most — Jude to be among the survivors or Jude to be drowned.

~~~~~

There was Louis to be told first, and then the Lloyds and the servants. If Jude were truly dead, who knew what would happen now? The house might have to be sold, for they would have only Nell's jointure to live upon. If it had been difficult enough to manage before, with Jude's salary, how impossible it would be on just her own money. A cottage somewhere, and a maid or two. She could probably not afford a manservant.

No, it was too soon for such thoughts. Jude may be one of the survivors. So she kept telling herself.

"Will Papa be home soon?" Louis said. "He will have to come on the stage from Cornwall. How long will that take?"

"Two or three days... less by the mail," she answered automatically.

An apartment in town might be more convenient, and they would only need three or four rooms... no, more, for they would have to find space for Maria and the girls, too. But Maria would cook, so they would only need a maid-of-all-work.

"He could ride... that would be quicker."

"Yes, it would."

"So he could be home in a day or two," Louis said happily.

She realised belatedly how he was thinking. "Oh, no dear, for he is the captain. He must stay with his ship."
~~~~~

"Oh." He thought about that. "He will be helping to rescue people, I expect, all the people who fell into the sea. Papa will be helping them get to shore."

"Yes, dear."

There would be something raised from selling the house. It would not be too bad. There might be something still in the bank, but would that come to her or...? It would depend on his will. The attorney would know.

"Will you still go?"

"Hmm? Go to what, Louis?"

"The ball tonight. I like to see you all dressed up, with jewels in your hair."

The Sherrards' ball. "No, dear. I cannot imagine anyone will want to dance tonight, and certainly not the Sherrards."

"Oh."

Becky tapped on the open door. "Madam? Do you want any breakfast?"

Food. A strange concept. She shook her head.

"Then may I take Master Louis to the kitchen? He'll want something to eat, I'm sure."

"Of course," she said vaguely, barely listening.

She could work, perhaps. Giving lessons on the pianoforte. She had played the harp at one time, too, although not very well. But what would she do, without Jude? How would she cope? Who would regulate her life and tell her what to do?

Survivors... there were survivors...

Herself and Louis, Maria, Lucy and Jane... a household of five. One maid-of-all-work. Becky would come with them, perhaps. Yes, Becky, and Maria to cook. They would manage.

Oh God! How would she manage?

Some minutes or hours later, she could not tell, Maria came back from the shipping office at the wharf.

"Nothing new," she said at once, before she had even removed her bonnet. "Except that it hit rocks along the coast just west of Trehowick. I have no idea where that is."

Nell pulled out the atlas, and for some time they pored over the many headlands and coves of Cornwall until they found Trehowick.

"If it ran onto the rocks, then it must be close to shore," Maria said. "There may be a great many survivors."

"Perhaps."

The two women stared at each other. They had been in this place before when the *Helen of Troy* had gone down, taking with it Maria's husband, Jude's wealth and all their hopes. First, the barest news — the ship is missing or sunk, but all may yet be well. There may be survivors. Then, after a few days of dwindling hope, the loss of life is accepted but at least the ship was insured, so there will be compensation and another ship. And finally, months and months later, the realisation that there was nothing left but a scramble for their own survival. But they *had* survived, and they would survive this, too. Surely they would survive.

"There was a duke on board," Maria said.

"So I heard," Nell said. Odd. Were there any dukes in Ireland? One, perhaps.

"He only became a duke a few months ago, and now he's dead. Poor man."

"Oh... I remember that. What was his name? I should remember it... I have met him, I think."

"No one knew the name. There are a great many people there, waiting for news. Poor Mr Weekes is quite beset. Mr Sherrard and Mr Flack have gone off in a chaise and four to Cornwall to see for themselves, so I do not suppose we will hear any more until they are on the spot, and have sent word back. It will be days. Nell, will you eat something? Or take a little wine? We have brought up that bottle of Madeira for Jude and it would be a shame to waste it."

"It will keep for years, if we take it back to the cellar," Nell said. "Do not open a bottle just for me."

"But you are so pale," Maria said. "Surely—"

"Falconbury!" Nell said. "That was his name. The Duke of Falconbury. Valmont. I only went there once, as quite a small girl, and it is the most amazing place… a veritable palace. It is supposed to be modelled on Versailles, but I could not say. Maria, what is it like to be a widow? Is it perpetually horrid or does the darkness lift, in time?"

"Oh, Nell!" She took Nell's hand and lifted it to her cheek. It was warm, Nell realised… her cheek was warm. That must mean that her hand was cold. "Let us be optimistic. There are survivors, and Jude may be one of them. I pray it may be so. Do not give up hope, dear, for you are not a widow yet."

"Yes. I am. There is no hope," she said flatly. "Jude is dead, I know it."

And yet there *was* hope… a little flare deep inside her. Relief, she realised. Relief that she would never again see that look on Jude's face, never again fear his return, never again have to bow her head and suffer the onslaught. Of words, at first, but then his fists. Such solid fists he had, thick and meaty and *heavy*. She shivered, and stood up abruptly. That was over now. She would never be afraid of a man again.

"I shall go and lie down for a while," she said. "Will you keep Louis occupied?"

"Of course, dear. I shall bring you some tea by and by."

She brightened. There was tea in the house! "Thank you, I should like that."

In her bedroom, her ball gown lay over a chair, with the shoes and gloves beside it. Methodically, she tidied them all away, then gazed into her wardrobe at the gowns and pelisses and bonnets.

"Black... I shall need something black."

She began to sort through the shelves.

~~~~~

Nathan was not at all pleased to have to stay an extra day.

"You cannot leave me to face Toller's family all alone," Harry had said plaintively. "I have to go, for his sister is married to one of the Bucknells, but it will be far more bearable with you there to share the amusement of the fellow's toad-eating. They are a rackety set — the whole Pascall family is rackety — but Edward is devious with it, and especially so since he came into the viscountcy. Do not try the ivories with him, or he will fleece you."

"Ah! Thank you for the advice. I will be careful. What about cards? Is he a sharp, too?"

"Not that I ever heard, but he is very, very good. You would be too, if you would pay a little more attention to the play, but on your usual form, Toller would relieve you of as much as you cared to lose. He lives well on his skill. He has not sixpence to his name otherwise, so it is a serious business with him."

"Pockets to let? No wonder he is an ivory-turner, then. With those outlandish clothes he wears, his tailor's bills must be
~~~~~

astronomical. Very well, I shall accompany you to dinner at this Lady Henry Bucknell's, and try not to lose my fortune to Toller."

Lady Henry Bucknell was almost as outlandish a dresser as her brother, but somehow her extravagant attire looked less grotesque on her comely form. She was small and plump and prettily coquettish, and Nathan was instantly drawn under her spell. She was just the sort of woman he liked to spend an evening with, and he got up a light flirtation with her in no time. She was delightfully responsive, with the result that he was invited to sit beside her at dinner, paying her increasingly extravagant compliments and enjoying her blushes and smiles and rather salacious gossip. In a few years time, when her early bloom had faded and she was just another matron wearing too much rouge and an over-decorated gown, he would have no interest in her at all, but for one otherwise dull evening in London, she was exactly to his taste.

He was so engrossed with his hostess that it was not until the ladies withdrew and he congregated with the men at the other end of the table that he discovered that a ship had sunk in the English Channel, taking with it England's newest duke.

"Six months he had the title, poor fellow," said one elderly member of the Bucknell clan. "Only seven and twenty, and his future wife waiting for him at home."

"But she will not be too despondent," someone else said. "She has a ready substitute in hand, and the younger boy was always the better bet. Very sound, is Randolph."

"What happened?" Nathan said. "Was there a storm that blew up unexpectedly?"

It was Toller who answered. "My cousin at the Admiralty says it was a calm night with good visibility, so they are suspecting poor navigation. Devil of a tragedy, though. Those brigs are generally solid little vessels, perfectly reliable and easy to sail. Only coming from Dublin, and that is hardly a great step."

Nathan's ears pricked. Dublin? "What was the name of the vessel?"

"No idea. Farquharson, you read the newspapers, what was it called, this brig?"

"Let me see..." He rummaged in a pocket, and pulled out a scrap of paper. "Trehowick... twenty six souls aboard her... three survivors... ah, here we are. The *Brig Minerva.*"

The *Brig Minerva.* Commanded by Captain Jude Caldicott. Who might, even now, be lying at the bottom of the sea. He would never hit his wife again.

But on the other hand, there were three survivors...

~~~~~

"Only three?" Nell said, looking up from the stitches she was unpicking.

"So Mr Weekes said," Maria said. "Three survivors, and one is Mr Blackwell, the Second Mate, and one is the Kibble boy."

"And the third?"

"Not yet known, but a man, not a boy. He is injured and too ill to be talked to, but Mr Blackwell is to go to identify him. I think, my dear Nell, we must be prepared for the worst."

"I am already prepared," Nell said. "Would you be so good as to hold the end of this strip of lace? It is much easier to see the stitches that hold it in place that way."

"Are you truly intending to dye this gown? It would be much better to buy a length of bombazine, if it should be necessary."
~~~~~

"Oh, I shall do that as well, but I must have more than one gown, Maria. Imagine how it would look if I wear the same gown every day."

"But you will go nowhere, Nell. No one will think the worse of you for having only one mourning gown, just at first. Once you start to go about the town again, that will be the time to extend your wardrobe."

"But I must have something to *do!"* Nell cried, fully aware that she sounded on the verge of hysteria. "I must be busy, my hands must be busy for that prevents me from thinking quite so much."

"Of course, dear," Maria said, sitting down beside her at the worktable and giving her a quick hug. "But let us not do anything precipitate — no dyeing, or expensive purchases of bombazine — until we know the worst."

"Maria, I know the worst," she said heavily. "He is dead, and there is an end to it. I enter the state of widowhood, and my life is over."

"No!" Maria said fiercely. "One part of your life is over, perhaps, but— Nell, I tell you truly, in friendship, which permits me to speak to you with a freedom you would not allow to others, that you are better off without him. No, do not protest, for you know it to be so. He has been the focus of your life for nine years, and you cannot imagine a life without him, but if he is gone, then you are free again. Free to be yourself, and not this timid creature you have become. Free to marry again, perhaps."

"Never!" Nell cried, horrified. Then, more quietly, she said, "I shall never marry again. *Never."*

"Well, that's as may be, but you still have your life to live out as best you can. You have Louis to think about now."

"Yes." Nell straightened her spine. "Louis... I must think about Louis. But first I must get all the lace off this gown so that it can be dyed. It will take the dye very well, I feel, for it is such a plain colour. One cannot dye patterns at all, for the pattern always shows through and just think how unsuitable for deep mourning! But this is so plain that, once the lace is off, it will take the dye beautifully. And my velvet pelisse... that might be dyed, as well. I shall need a pelisse in a month or two, when I start to go about a little."

"Yes, dear," Maria said sadly.

It was three more days before word came, the news that set all to rest. The third survivor was a passenger, a clerk called Ellsworthy. Everyone else on board was lost to the sea.

Nell was indeed a widow.

5: Condolences (March)

"I have two pounds three shillings and fourpence," Nell said despairingly. "No, here is another farthing, so two pounds three shillings and fourpence farthing, to last us until Lady Day. Another month, and then at least I shall have the Lloyds' rent, but I have no idea how far that will stretch. Jude always dealt with that sort of thing."

"Oh dear," Maria said. "Is there nothing else beyond the rent money? No other income?"

"My settlement," Nell said slowly. "Fifteen thousand pounds was settled on me, but I have no idea how to get the income from it, or how much it would be. What am I to do, Maria?"

"You must talk to Mr Vessey at the bank. He is such a pleasant man, and *so* kind to me after John died. Even before John's affairs were settled, he was so good as to advance some money from the account, and he arranged my little annuity for me. I am certain he will do the same for you."

"Will you come with me? I… I have never entered a bank before."

"Of course, dear."

"Thank you," Nell whispered.

The bank was not quite so terrifying as her imagination had made it. Once she had passed through its portal into the cool, high-ceilinged interior, and an underling had rushed forward to attend to her, and lead her across the chequered marble floor to Mr Vessey's inner sanctum, she was able to breathe and hold her head high. She was Miss Godney of Daveney Hall again, and Mr Vessey, however imposing he or his premises might be, was no more than a servant, managing her money in order to provide her with funds when she needed them.

This happy notion lasted a mere two minutes, until greetings had been exchanged, condolences offered and chairs arranged, and Nell had explained her predicament.

"I should love to help, my dear madam," Mr Vessey said brightly, "but there is no money in your husband's account."

"No money?" Nell croaked, her spirits plummeting.

"Less than none, in point of fact," the banker said, with an incongruously cheerful smile. "The account is in debit to the amount of twenty seven pounds."

"In debit?" Nell replied, stupefied.

"To the amount of twenty seven pounds, yes," Mr Vessey said, the smile widening. "But have no fear, dear madam. We will not expect repayment until the quarter end."

"Quarter end..."

"Indeed. When the other repayment falls due."

"The other repayment?"

"For the mortgage on the house. You did not know? Oh dear me." And he laughed. He actually laughed.

"But what am I to do?" she whispered.

"You need an attorney," he said. Then he laughed again.

The attorney did not laugh, which was a mercy, but his advice was no more reassuring, for all that.

"It is... *awkward*," Mr Pierce said, peering at her over his thick spectacles. "Very awkward. There are *procedures*, you understand, Mrs Caldicott. Processes to be followed. There is no *body*, do you see? No *body*. When one has a body, one knows that a man is dead. There is a funeral. A funeral, Mrs Caldicott. Then the will may be read, and the estate wound up and the bequests handed out. Do you see?"

"I do see, yes, but I must have money to live upon, Mr Pierce. The settlement made upon me at the time of my marriage is my own money, and I should be able to draw upon it, regardless of the presence or absence of my husband's body."

"I know nothing of your marriage settlement, Mrs Caldicott. There is no mention of it in your husband's will, so one must presume that—"

"No mention of it?"

"Not a word. Was it a large settlement?"

"Fifteen thousand pounds."

"Ah!" He steepled his hands together, and smiled. "Then there will be a trust of some sort, the capital bound up so that your husband could only enjoy the interest, do you see? Your father would have arranged it so. You should apply to him for information, Mrs Caldicott."

"My father is dead, Mr Pierce. My older brother has Daveney Hall now."

"Your brother is Sir James Godney?" She nodded. "Then you must apply to your brother, do you see? Apply to your brother, Mrs Caldicott."

"My brother," she repeated stupidly, wondering how on earth she could apply to a man she had not seen or heard from for nine years. "We are... not on good terms since my marriage."

"Ah. But nevertheless, he must be consulted now. After all, your husband appointed him as your son's guardian."

~~~~~

MARCH

Nathan made his plans calmly, without haste. Everything must be orderly, carefully arranged so as to avoid unexpected mishaps as far as possible. He did not, therefore, rush off to Southampton the very day after Lady Henry's dinner. Instead, he spent the day writing ahead to the inns on his route to ensure a change of horses would be available when he needed them, writing to Yorkshire to apprise his aunt of his change of plans, and calling in at Weston's to collect the coat he had ordered on his previous stay in the capital. He spent one night on the road, to be certain of arriving in Southampton early in the morning of his second day of travel. Having secured a room at the Dolphin Hotel, he then went directly to East Street and lifted the crepe-wrapped knocker.

The same neat maid answered the door, her face pale under the cap. Becky, was it?

"Good morning, Becky. Is your mistress at home?"

"Oh, no, sir. No, that she ain't. Isn't."

"I understand that she may not be receiving callers, under the circumstances, but—"

"No. She ain't here at all, sir. Gone away, sir."

"Ah." A moment's thought brought to mind the black-haired friend. "Is Mrs Delanoy at home?"

"I... don't know, sir."
~~~~~

"Would you be so good as to ask her if she would favour me with just a few minutes of her time? If she is busy in the kitchen, I am quite happy to see her there."

She giggled at that, and bobbed a curtsy. "Please to wait, sir," she said, directing him to a chair in the hall, before scuttling away to the nether parts of the house.

He walked about, examining a pair of cheap candelabra and an ornate silver salver on the console, and then adjusting his neckcloth in the mirror above it. It was an odd thing, but his neckcloth never stayed quite as he liked it. He was not vain, and he would love to be able to set himself straight for the day and then not think about his appearance again, but somehow it never quite worked out that way. A neckcloth was such an important part of a gentleman's attire that he felt drawn to check on its state whenever he passed a mirror, and then there was always some rearrangement to be done.

A girlish voice floated down the stairs. "Oh! Oh, is that Mr Harbottle?"

He turned, to see the lodger delicately descending, her skirts lifted just enough to display richly embroidered slippers and a pair of well-turned ankles.

"It is indeed," he answered, making her only a small bow, for they had not yet been formally introduced.

"You will remember me, I am sure. We met when you called on Nell Caldicott before. I am Mrs Gwilliam Lloyd. Are you here to see Nell? She is not here. You heard about her husband, I suppose?"

"Indeed. I came to pay my condolences."

"She has gone to her brother for help. That husband of hers left her in something of a pickle." She giggled, one hand covering her mouth. "Poor Nell! Although Mr Lloyd says that she is better off without him, but not if she is to be poor. Even more poor, I should say, for they never seemed to have any money. Some men are just feckless, aren't they? But she is one of the Godneys of Daveney Hall, so I daresay she will never starve, her and that scrawny son of hers. Such an ill-favoured child!"

"I thought him a pleasant boy," Nathan said, seething at such disparagement of the Caldicotts. "A little thin, perhaps, but such quickness of mind! He will do well, I am sure."

She tittered, and looked at him from beneath her lashes. "Oh, I say nothing against him, nothing at all, for he has never been taught any better, but Nell... so superior, and her husband nothing but a common sailor. In such cases, a woman should not give herself airs, should she? It merely sets people's backs up. Everyone say so, that she thinks herself too grand for Southampton society, just because her father was a baronet."

That was too much for Nathan. "It is not everyone who is capable of appreciating the more refined manners of those raised in the upper levels of society," he said. "Mrs Caldicott is far superior to any other person I have met in this town." And then, just in case she should be too stupid to take the point, he added firmly, "*Far* superior."

She flushed, and was about to retort when she saw Mrs Delanoy standing outside the baize door. With a huff of annoyance and a swirl of skirts, she flounced back up the stairs without another word.

Mrs Delanoy laughed. "Oh, excellent, sir! I have not enjoyed a put down so much in years. Will you step into the kitchen for a moment? I have a cake that must go into the hot oven right away."

So Nathan stepped into the kitchen, and sat for an hour eating Bath buns fresh from the oven and drinking his own tea and talking to Mrs Delanoy as she and her daughters moved efficiently about, preparing the dinner. He learnt that the house was mortgaged, but Nell had a settlement of fifteen thousand pounds.

"That's a good sum, sir, isn't it?" Mrs Delanoy said. "She'll be comfortably off with that, and her brother will take care of Louis' education, since he's his guardian."

He was reassured. Nevertheless, when he returned to his hotel, he wrote a long letter to Nell, offering his deepest sympathy for her tragic loss, and assuring her that he remained her friend, that he would be delighted to offer any assistance she might need and that any correspondence from her would receive his earliest attention. He then visited the bank to ensure that there would be no foreclosure on the mortgage without notifying him. Only then did he make his departure from Southampton.

~~~~~

Nell had forgotten just how long the Daveney Hall driveway was. As she peered through the gates, it meandered away through the trees and vanished into the gloom beneath them. The house was out of sight. If she were in a snug carriage, with a warm brick to her feet and rugs about her, it would be no distance, but on foot, on a bitterly cold March afternoon, with a sprinkling of snow lying, and Louis already exhausted, it would be a long, slow crawl.

She jangled the bell beside the gate, and waited. After a few minutes, an elderly man emerged from the lodge and peered at her through bushy eyebrows. The eyebrows shot upwards. "Miss Nell?" he said disbelievingly. "Surely it can't be!"

"Hello, Tom. How are you?"

"It *is* you! Lord bless me, come inside at once, Miss Nell. This wind's bitter. And never tell me this is your boy?" He fiddled with the side gate, throwing it open for them to pass through.
~~~~~

"Yes, this is Louis. This is Tom Grainger, Louis, the gamekeeper here."

"Nay, not any more, Miss Nell. My boy Robbie's gamekeeper now, although I help out a bit. Keep him straight, you know."

"Robbie? I always thought it would be Andy who would take over from you."

A shadow crossed his face. "Aye, so did we all, but he went off to fight the French six years ago last autumn, and never came home. Well now, Miss Nell and Master Louis, come you inside and sit by the fire for a bit. Dolly'll be thrilled to see you. We talk about you often and often, so we do, wondering how you're getting on. Come away in."

Nell had no objection to a sit by the fire to warm them up, and maybe one of Dolly's famous rock cakes. It was pleasant to be fussed over like a child, and their kindness was balm to her lowered spirits, especially when they realised she wore black.

"Aye, the sea's a cruel way for a man to earn his bread," Tom said, when she had explained.

"So how did you get here, Miss Nell?" Dolly asked, as she ladled hot soup into bowls for them. "A post chaise would have taken you to the door, not dropped you at the gates, and there be no stage coach along this road."

"We were dropped at Otterbourne," Nell said, not quite liking to admit that she could not even afford the common stage, and their first ride was a wagon of fish barrels. "Then Will Horrocks gave us a lift."

"What, you rode on a farm cart!" Tom said. "Well, now, that's not right for a Godney of Daveney Hall."

Dolly eyed her sadly. "Poor dears. Tom, you go and get out the dog cart for Miss Nell and Master Louis. No need to walk up that long drive," she added, patting Nell's hand sympathetically.

Nell was too grateful to mind them knowing how poor she was.

Warm, rested and filled with soup, the ride to the front door was sharply cold, but mercifully brief. With a wave of thanks to Tom, Nell and Louis climbed the many steps to the porticoed front door. Louis was silent, as he had been for many days now, ever since he had finally understood that Papa would not be coming home. Nell left him to his thoughts. Her own worries crowded in upon her too closely for her to have much energy to spare for her son. He had brought only one book with him, the history of naval battles given to him by Mr Harbottle, which he had read over and over again. It was squeezed into the top of the portmanteau for easy retrieval when there was a moment spare. It was his greatest comfort, and she blessed the happy thought that had induced Mr Harbottle, a complete stranger to them, to buy such a gift. She wished she could tell him how much pleasure it gave Louis.

On the top step, she halted. Never before had she been obliged to knock like a casual caller. Like Mrs Sangster, perhaps, rapping imperiously with the head of her cane, or Lady Toogood, with three quick taps — rat-tat-tat, always the same — or the Miss Caudreys, timidly, struggling with the heavy knocker. What kind of caller would Nell be? Imperious or timid?

She was not obliged to decide, for the high door opened, and a strange butler looked out at her. "Yes, madam?" he said haughtily.

For a moment Nell was disoriented. Had she mistaken the house? Had James moved away without her knowing? But common sense reasserted itself. Farlow must be elsewhere, and this fellow, however much he looked like a butler, must be only a footman.

"Where is Farlow?" she said, the thought being uppermost in her mind.

"Gone, madam. I am butler here now."

"And Mrs Farlow?"

"Also gone. May I help you, madam?"

"Oh." That made it awkward. Farlow would have known her instantly, just as Tom and Dolly Grainger had, but now she had to introduce herself, like a stranger. "I am Mrs Caldicott, sister to Sir James. Is he at home?"

"I am not sure, madam. Do you have a card?"

Now that was plain rude. "I do not need a card to see my own brother," she said sharply. "Go at once and tell him his sister and nephew are here! And do not dare to shut the door in my face!" she added, seeing him about to do exactly that. She marched past him into the hall, Louis firmly held in one hand, and the portmanteau in the other. "We will sit on the bench beside the fire and warm ourselves while you inform your master of our arrival. The footman lurking there will ensure we do not steal the candlesticks. Oh — Luke Grainger? Can it be? Good heavens, you were this big the last time I saw you!" She waved a hand vaguely at knee height, laughing.

As the butler departed in stately resentment, the footman crept out from his hiding place behind a suit of armour. "I'm second footman now," he said shyly. "Your face looks familiar..."

"Your ma and pa recognised me at once, Luke. I was Nell Godney in those days. Mrs Caldicott now."

"Miss Nell?" His face lit up. "Have you come home at last?"

If Nell had been the type to cry, that remark would have done the job. As it was, she was powerfully affected by the desire to *'come home'*. Not to be Miss Godney again, for those days were gone for ever, but to come to Daveney Hall just occasionally — a week or two every year, perhaps — and be part of the family again, to *belong*. Sometimes the effort of being a lady without any support and even without money was just too much for her.

But she could not hope for such an outcome. "Not… not permanently, no. Just for a night or two."

"Nell?"

She rose, knowing his voice at once. "James." He was older, of course, but she had expected that. The promising young man of three and twenty had become the solid and rather coarse-featured baronet of two and thirty. His clothes were fashionable but ill-suited to his rounded belly and spindly legs. He had always been indolent, preferring his own fireside to more energetic pursuits, but clearly such tendencies had become settled in him now.

"It *is* you, but what—?"

He looked at her with bewilderment, and she could hardly blame him. She had left Daveney Hall nine years ago for the parish church, never to return, or so her father had sworn. Yet here she was.

He must have registered her blacks, for he said, "Your husband?"

"Dead. His ship went down."

"Oh. I am very sorry for it, but what are you doing here?"

"I need your help with my financial affairs, that is all. Once everything is sorted out, I shall be gone from here, you may be sure."

"What? You want to stay here? That is impossible, you must know that. You are no longer a Godney, Nell. You have no claim on me."

"No, but—"

"It is no good, Nell. You will have to go. I cannot imagine why you thought— But it is impossible. You cannot be admitted. Harper, pray escort my sister from the premises."

6: Daveney Hall

Nell straightened herself to her full height, which was considerable. She was tall enough, in any event, to look her brother in the eye. "I am ashamed of you, James Godney! Is this how you treat someone who comes to you for help? Would you turn away even a stranger without an ounce of Christian charity?"

"You cannot stay here!" he said desperately. "I am quite happy to talk to you, Nell, but not under this roof."

"Very well. We will stay with the Graingers at the lodge, and you may explain to everyone of your acquaintance why your own sister had to seek shelter from the gamekeeper and his wife."

James licked his lips, his eyes skittering over the impassive forms of Harper and Luke Grainger and another footman hovering in the shadows. If there was one thing he liked above all others, even above the comfort of his own armchair before his own fire, it was the good opinion of his neighbours, as Nell knew perfectly well.

"One night?" he suggested tentatively.

"Two at most," she said, trying not to show how relieved she was.

"Of course. Harper, tell Mrs Millington that Mrs Caldicott will be staying for the night… or two nights. She may prepare the blue room in the north wing. Nell, take your coat off and come into the library."

She and Louis divested themselves of hats and gloves and coats, and followed James meekly across the hall, their steps echoing in the vast emptiness, its extravagant proportions topped by a glass dome four storeys above them. Louis clung to her hand with painful intensity, keeping his head low. He had never been into such a large house, where everything was built to a grandiose scale. To a child as puny as Louis, the marble pillars must seem to stretch away into the sky. The stairs, wide enough for twelve to walk abreast, and the stone fireplace which burned half a tree at Christmas, would be quite overwhelming to his child's mind.

"This is where I grew up, Louis," she said, with what she hoped was a reassuring smile. "It may be very big, but it is still a family home. Uncle James used to slide down those banisters when he was your age, and you cannot imagine how wonderful a place it is to play hide and seek."

He gave her a watery smile, but James turned with a frown and said, "What an idea you will give the boy of me, Nell! Once I did that, just once, and will anyone let me forget it?"

"Oh, do try not to be so stuffy, James," she said lightly, and he laughed, his face softening for a moment and reminding her of his light-hearted younger self. He had assumed the mantle of the baronetcy at far too early an age, and it sat uneasily on his shoulders.

He threw open the carved door and ushered them through. In their father's day, the library had been little used, for he had preferred a cosier room in the east wing, but James loved books, so he had claimed the library as his domain. Nell had almost forgotten just how imposing it was, two storeys high and crammed with the avid collecting of many generations of Godneys.

Louis stopped dead, letting go of her hand for almost the first time in two days. As he gazed, awe-struck, at the thousands upon thousands of books crammed into the shelves, he uttered a low growl deep in his throat, animal-like, which slowly rose to become a wail. Then—

"Books!" he shrieked, setting off at a run towards the nearest case. He stopped, both hands pressed against the glass doors, his eyes wide with desire. "Books," he whispered. *"Books!"*

James laughed, looking enquiringly at Nell. "Has he never seen books before?"

"Of course, but never so many. I doubt he realised there were so many books in the whole world. I have only the few that were my own, and we cannot afford the subscription to the circulating library. He loves to read, even more than you, James."

"Cannot afford—?" He looked puzzled, but turned instead to the easier information. "Loves to read, does he? Well, Louis, would you like to choose a book now?"

Thrilled by such generosity, Louis could only nod.

"What would you like to read? Shall I find you something with pictures?"

"Have you anything about the Battle of Minorca? My book only says *'Following the disastrous loss at Minorca, after which Admiral Byng was executed by firing squad...'* so I should like to know what happened, if you please."

James's eyebrows rose, but he answered the question seriously. "I always felt Byng was harshly dealt with, but you may read about it if you will. Let me see... the Seven Years' War will be down here... hmm... ah, this one is fairly general, but covers that period. Oh, here we are. *'The Seven Years' War, the Battle of Minorca and the Disgrace of John Byng'* That is exactly what you want. And here is another about the whole war, in three volumes. You may take them to that desk by the window, for the light is very good there."

With only a quick nod, Louis set off, balancing the heavy books carefully.

"We shall not have another word out of him now," Nell said. "If you have meals brought to him, he will likely stay at his post for ever."

"Well, that will not do," James said sulkily. "I cannot imagine what you were thinking, Nell, to come here like this, when you could have written."

"I have written before and received no reply, but this time I must have answers."

"How could I reply, when Papa forbade any contact with you? Julia will not like it," he added fretfully.

"This is your house now, James," she said gently. "*You* are master here, not Papa and certainly not Julia."

"Do you still dislike her?" he said, in resentful tones. "You were always against her, right from the start."

"I neither like nor dislike her," Nell said, with asperity. "I thought Nora would have made you the better wife, that was all, but I have long since stopped caring about the matter. You have made your choice, and must live with the consequences every day, just as I do."

His eyebrows lifted at this frankness. "Do you ever regret it, Nell?" he said, and there again was the indecisive young man who had dithered for years over Nora but had, in the end, succumbed to Julia's greater determination. Yes, Nora would have been a much better choice. "Do you never feel that things would have been different if—"

"There is no point," she said briskly. For the second time that day, she felt herself on the verge of tears, and that would never do. She would need all her wits about her when Julia returned.

They sat side by side on an ornate sofa, which was a hundred years old at least. In Nell's day, the fine silk covering had worn so thin that no one was allowed to sit on it, but since then it had been recovered in a less elegant fabric. Probably Julia's doing, Nell decided. The dilapidated state of the furnishings had always offended Julia, but the family never noticed, being accustomed to it, or simply accepting it as part of the antiquity of the house. The relics of the past were to be preserved, if possible, or if a thing had to be repaired, it should be done in so delicate a manner that no one would ever be able to tell the difference. How like Julia to use some brash modern fabric that was entirely at odds with the rest of the house.

"Whatever happened to the Farlows?" Nell said. "They have been here for ever. I never imagined they would leave."

"Oh..." He looked embarrassed. "They did not quite suit Julia's notions. She has some very particular ideas... and she must be allowed to choose her own servants, you know. Mrs Jayne has gone, too. We have a man cook, now, and some very elaborate dishes. Our dinners are very much sought after. Oh... we dine at seven these days, so you need not rush to change."

"My dear James, I have no intention of dining with you. I shall eat in my room."

"Nonsense! You were always the liveliest company at dinner, Nell. I have so missed your wit."

"I have brought no evening gowns, and I am hardly likely to be good company, with my husband barely two weeks' dead."

He snatched up her hand from her lap, and pressed a kiss against it. "Forgive me, Nell! You are so composed that... one forgets. I cannot imagine how you must be feeling, and you have come here all alone, knowing—"

"Knowing that I am not welcome?"

There was no one else in the room apart from the absorbed Louis, but James lowered his voice to reply. "You *are* welcome here, Nell. I wish you could stay longer, and Jack will be very sorry to have missed you, but he is not down from Oxford until Easter. He has talked of you often, you know, even in Papa's presence."

Before she had time to absorb the implications of this, the door burst open and Julia strode in, magnificent in her wrath. When she spoke, however, her voice was icily calm. "I am astonished that you should come to this place as if you belonged here." Julia never shouted, and her tone was never less than perfectly under control. Nevertheless, she quivered with righteous indignation.

Nell rose. "Hello, Julia. How are you?"

Like James, Julia had gained a little weight, which the present fashion for high-waisted, narrow-skirted gowns did nothing to flatter, and even her best friends could not think her clothes elegant. Everything she wore, however, from the delicately curled feathers on her bonnet to the exquisite stitchery on her kid boots, was of the finest quality, which Nell could only admire and envy.

Julia ignored Nell, turning instead to her husband. "What is she doing here, Sir James? I thought—"

Nell could not help laughing. "Really, Julia! *Sir James?* When you have known him since the day you were born, and spent every summer chasing him around the garden like a petticoated puppy?"

She coloured, but lifted her chin defiantly. "He was not then a baronet," she said stiffly.

That brought another laugh. "He is much the same James as he always was, although a little more...*cuddly* than he used to be," she said, poking him in the waistcoat. "You are feeding him too well, Julia, and forgetting to chase him out of the house from time to time. He will sit in his chair with a book from dawn to dusk if you let him."

James laughed, not in the least offended. Julia, however, was offended on his behalf.

"I think he looks rather splendid," she said huffily, which made even James roll his eyes. "You should have more respect, and to me, too. I am Lady Godney to you, Nell. But this is hardly to the point," she went on. "I do not know what Sir James was about to admit you, but you will have to leave at once."

"If we are to be formal, Lady Godney, then in courtesy you should address me as Mrs Caldicott," Nell said gently, which made Julia turn such a violent shade of puce that she was surely in danger of exploding. Hastily, Nell went on, "I am here only to ask James for his advice about my financial affairs, since he is the head of the family now and my nearest male relative. I shall be gone as soon as that is done, I assure you, and will stay in my room with Louis at all other times."

"Louis?"

"Her son, Julia," James said. "Surely you remember? He is eight years of age now, and a great reader." He remembered his age! There was even a hint of pride in his voice, which brought a little bubble of warmth to Nell's heart. James gestured to the table where Louis read steadily on, quite oblivious to the tensions in the room, or even aware, perhaps, that there were any other people in the world, lost as he was in the stirring events of fifty years ago.

Julia noticed him for the first time. "You brought the child here?" she said incredulously. "Oh, no, no, no! I cannot have such a...

such an appalling influence anywhere near dear Charlotte and Augusta."

Nell was consumed by laughter again. To name both their daughters after Princess Charlotte Augusta of Wales had always struck her as a great piece of presumption. Before she could recover her composure, James intervened.

"You are ungracious, Julia, to speak so of a boy of whom you know nothing."

"I know only that he is the son of a common seaman, and therefore no worthy companion for the daughters of a baronet."

"You place yourself on too high a form sometimes," he said crossly. "Caldicott was a captain, and not a common seaman. Louis is my nephew and has just lost his father, which I trust will weigh with you and enable you to deal with him compassionately for the short time he is here."

She huffed a breath, and Nell thought she would have liked to argue the point, but perhaps she felt it beneath her dignity. Whatever the reason, she gave a little lift of one shoulder. "It matters not to me. Let him stay, by all means. Clearly my wishes are of no account in my own house."

"The house is mine," James growled, and Nell recognised the abrupt switch from mere surliness to anger. Julia saw it too, for she raised her hands, as if in surrender.

"It is only for a night or two," Nell said hastily. "Louis will stay in my room, I assure you, and not go anywhere near the nursery."

"Two nights would be... tolerable," Julia said. "But no more than that, Nell. After that you must both go."

"Certainly." Some mischievous spirit rose in Nell's breast, for she added innocently, "But you will have plenty of time to get to know Louis later."

"How so?" Her eyes narrowed suspiciously.

"Why, because my husband named James as his guardian."

~~~~~

When Nell was shown to the room she was to occupy, she could not help smiling to herself. How typical of James to put her back in the room she had had as a child! It had been redecorated and was clearly intended for guests, but its position within the same wing as the nursery defined its original use. She could hardly blame James, for it had been her refuge from the world for almost the whole of her first sixteen years. Only when she had successfully navigated the treacherous waters of the season, made her curtsy in the Queen's drawing room and danced at Almack's had she been given a rather grander room at the front of the house. And within a few months, she had fallen from grace, married Jude and left Daveney Hall altogether.

She did not mind. The room was familiar, despite the expensive and rather garish new wallpaper. The cracked pane in the window, the drawer in the dressing table that needed to be pulled just so before it would open and the fire irons with dogs carved into the handles were just as they had always been. The maid making up the bed and the footman bringing coals were new to her — how many footmen did they have now? It seemed like dozens. Before long, however, familiar faces peeped round the door, with squeals of *'Miss Nell! Oh, Miss Nell!'* followed by hugs and tears and more hugs. Bella was first, the junior nursery maid in Nell's time, but now Julia's assistant lady's maid. Then Thelma, now a stately head housemaid, and finally Nurse, who had been at the Hall so long that her right name was forgotten, and she was known only as Nurse.

"You're far too thin, Miss Nell," she said severely. "You're not eating properly in that place you're at now. Seaports are dreadful unhealthy. And bless my soul, is this your boy? Well now, I never saw
~~~~~

a child more in need of some of my nursery dumplings. Stick to your ribs good and proper, they do."

Louis looked up briefly from his book, clearly decided this was just adult talk and therefore of no interest, and returned promptly to the drama of the Seven Years' War. Nell wondered how on earth the books were to be prised from his hands when they left, but that was a problem for another day.

"Has he met his cousins yet?" Nurse said, lowering her voice.

Nell shook her head. "Lady Godney does not wish them to become acquainted."

Nurse tutted, and rolled her eyes. "Too high in the instep by half, her ladyship is. Children have to have friends, and keeping them apart from their neighbours and even from their kin isn't going to make them any more ladylike, poor little mites. If they were boys, no doubt Sir James would have something to say about it, but with girls, he leaves it all to her."

"You should not speak against your mistress, Nurse," Nell said quietly. "I am sure she is a devoted mother, who is doing what she feels is best for her daughters."

Another tap on the door heralded the stiffly disapproving face of Makins, once a housemaid at Julia's former home, but now presumably her lady's maid. She carried several black gowns over one arm.

"Beg pardon, madam, but her ladyship sent these for you to wear at dinner. They might need a tuck here and there," she added, looking Nell up and down.

"Thank you, Makins, but I shall not be eating with the family," Nell said, although she looked longingly at the gowns. Silk! How glorious it would be to wear good silk again, in the latest style and not reworked a dozen times. Julia may not be the world's most elegant dresser, but she patronised the very best warehouses.

Makins sniffed, and withdrew huffily, deeply offended that her mistress's gracious offer should be so peremptorily rejected. Nell was left alone. Seeing Louis rubbing his eyes, she encouraged him to take his precious book to the bed, where even the excitement of the Seven Years' War could not keep him awake. She sat on by the fire, thrilled to the core by such a good blaze in the bedroom, and two full scuttles of coal at the side to keep it burning. Such luxury! She had taken it for granted when the Hall had been her home, but now she was grateful for any material comfort, however trivial.

For there was no other comfort to be had. Her husband was dead, and although she was relieved to be free from the hideous fear of his anger, he had still been her husband, the first and only man she had ever loved. She would miss him abominably, with his twinkling blue eyes, his wide smile when he first saw her after a voyage and his strong arms. So many memories of those arms — held out to her in love, holding her tight, stroking her face so gently or casually resting one hand on her hip as they lay in bed. She would never share her bed with a man again, and that was a grief to her as great as any other.

The quiet click of the door drew her back from the darkness of her thoughts.

"Nelly?"

"Come in, James, but speak low, for Louis is asleep at last."

"Poor little fellow! He looks very pale. So do you, but that is not surprising." He pulled a stool across to the fire and sat at Nell's feet. "Nelly, will you not join us for dinner? Having brought Julia grudgingly to admit the rightness of your claim to do so, I would not have my efforts wasted. Do come! One of the nursery maids will see to Louis, and I should so like you to be there. We are only family tonight, so you need not fear exposure to one of Julia's extravagant parties."

"Since you wish it, and if it will not distress Louis to be left, then I will do so," she said. "Besides, if you have managed to persuade Julia to admit to being wrong about anything at all, it would be churlish of me not to help you to gloat in your triumph."

He laughed, and again she was struck by how much younger he looked when amusement lit his face. "You see, that is what I have missed all these years! Julia has no sense of the absurd at all."

"No, or she would have to laugh at herself," Nell said, then was immediately mortified. "I beg your pardon, James, I should not speak so of Julia."

"You mean Lady Godney," he said, in mock severity, which made Nell laugh too. "Do not apologise, Nelly, for Julia is too pompous for words these days, and you would not speak so to her face."

"I should not speak so to *you*, either."

"Oh, believe me, I am fully aware of all Julia's faults. Now, do not misunderstand me, I am fond of her and content enough in my marriage. I chose her knowing perfectly well that it was not a love match, on either side. I envied you that, Nelly, did you know? You may have left under... difficult circumstances, but you and Caldicott were head over heels in love, and you have had nine blissful years together."

Nell could find no answer to that, so she merely smiled and said that she would see him at dinner, and tried not to think too much about those years of bliss. The bruises on her skin had healed well, but the bruises on her heart would never fade.

7: Demureness And Wickedness

James's idea of a family dinner was rather more extensive than Nell's. In addition to James, Julia and herself, she found the saloon also contained Julia's scrounging brother Alfred Rutherford, Mr Lumley, the parish clergyman, together with his sister and two sisters-in-law, as well as a stout girl of sixteen, who was a Rutherford cousin being polished up for her come out. There were also two lawyers visiting from London.

Nell knew and disliked Alfred Rutherford of old, and after making her greeting to him and finding herself intensively ogled by him through his quizzing glass, she moved promptly to the other end of the room where the clergyman and his family sat. She had not seen Mr Lumley since the day she and Jude had stood before him and plighted their troths, but she knew him for a kindly soul, who would be sympathetic and could be relied upon not to flirt with her.

"My dear Mrs Caldicott, what sad news! I am so very sorry to hear of your husband's tragic death," Mr Lumley said.

"Thank you, sir. How are you? And how is Mrs Lumley?"

"Ah, you do not know. I had the great misfortune to lose my very dear wife to the grippe seven years ago, so you see, I know exactly how you are feeling at this moment."

Nell doubted it, but she made all the right noises, and listened patiently as Mr Lumley related all the long-drawn-out details of his wife's final weeks and days and hours, with affecting descriptions of his own feelings at every stage of the process. Eventually, he said, "But tell me of your husband, Mrs Caldicott. He was lost at sea, I understand? What part of the great oceans saw his tragic end?"

"The Cornish coast, sir, somewhere near Trehowick."

The two lawyers, who were sitting nearby, exchanged glances. "Not the *Minerva?"* one of them said.

"It was indeed the *Brig Minerva* that my husband commanded," Nell said. "You have read the reports, perhaps?"

"Certainly," he said. "It is a name on everyone's lips just now. We have just come from Valmont, from His Grace the Duke of Falconbury's interment, for we had some dealings with his estates, and were required to be there to hear the will read."

Miss Lumley leaned forward to say, "The poor young duke! Such a great loss to the nation! And his poor brother, grieving yet obliged to assume his new position. How is His Grace bearing up?"

"As well as may be expected," the lawyer said. "However, he is not intending to claim the title just yet. He has made it known that he will remain as Lord Randolph Litherholm for the present, until it is absolutely certain that his brother has not married and sired an heir. He was in America for three years, so—"

"Oh, quite, quite!" Miss Lumley said, rather pink about the cheeks.

The lawyer looked thoughtfully at Nell. "So your husband commanded the *Minerva*, eh? Interesting. There will be questions asked, I make no doubt. Yes, questions will be asked."

"Let them be asked," Nell said stoutly. "Captain Caldicott was an experienced commander, trained in the Royal Navy, and I am certain nothing will be found amiss."

"Of course, of course," the lawyer said. "I am sure you have nothing to worry about, Mrs Caldicott."

Which naturally made her very worried indeed.

~~~~~

Despite Nell's misgivings, the evening was not as difficult as she had feared. Julia said nothing to her all evening, playing the effervescent society hostess to the two lawyers and Mr Lumley, all of whom were either inured to her gushing manners, or too polite to show any distaste. At dinner Nell was seated between one of the two lawyers and James, who were both considerate enough not to expect a new widow to engage in conversation. The lawyer applied himself to his plate as if he had seen no food for a week, and James was much occupied in instructing Julia's cousin in the finer points of society dining. Since he had grown up steeped in such conventions, and therefore had never been required to think about them before, his instructions were more confusing than helpful and the poor girl was constantly going wrong. Her cries of, "So sorry, Sir James!" punctuated the meal regularly.

Nell sat quietly, both enjoying herself and simultaneously berating herself for doing so, when Jude's poor body was even now resting in the churchyard at a remote village called Pendower in Cornwall. Unlike the Duke of Falconbury, Jude was not important enough or wealthy enough to justify the cost of bringing him home for burial. His worldly possessions, such as could be retrieved, were to be sent to her, but she could not imagine there was much to be sent, since the ship had sunk in the middle of the night. His nightshirt, perhaps. The ring he wore on a chain around his neck. Not much else.
~~~~~

Somehow, Jude seemed very far away now. Nell had not yet come to think of herself as a widow, and sitting there in the family dining parlour beside James, every plate and wine glass and spoon as familiar as her own hand, she slipped readily back into the rôle of daughter of the house. She was still too numb to be sociable, but it was enough to sit quietly and watch and listen. There was comfort, too, in the feel of silk about her — the barely-worn gown, the petticoat frothing around her feet, the luxury of brand new stockings again — it was shallow of her, but such trivial solaces were balm to her spirits. The food was too elaborate for her taste, but there was plenty of it and oh, the joy of good wine again!

When the ladies withdrew, she had the pleasure of seeing that the drawing room was exactly as it had always been. The saloon, where they had congregated before dinner, had been redone with surprising taste in the Chinese style. The dining room had also been refurbished, less successfully. But Julia's hand had not yet reached the drawing room, and the pianoforte — *her* pianoforte, for it had been a present for her fourteenth birthday — called to Nell from its dais at the far end of the room. After a quick visit to her room to assure herself that all was well with Louis, she obtained permission to play and sat down at the instrument.

At first she was too overcome to do more than run her fingers lightly over the keys, reminding herself of their cool beauty. Memories crowded in upon her — Mama in tears of happiness and Papa smiling proudly as she had performed for dinner guests. She must have been quite small then. The Italian singers she had played for at a musical evening who had called her *'magnifica bambina'*. The earl who had wanted to marry her at fourteen purely on account of her playing. And Jude... watching her with a smile on his face, always watching her. He had never taken his eyes off her, in those days. She had not seen such admiration in a man's eyes for years until she had seen an echo of it in Mr Harbottle recently.

Abruptly, she began to play, something fast and fierce, complicated enough to distract her mind from the past. Gradually, the mellow notes of the instrument wove their magic around her, and she slipped into that drifting state where she was one with the music, her fingers and the keys so entwined together that the whole melody had only to float into her head for it to appear in the air, a fully-formed piece of music. In such a dream-like state, she could play for hours, entirely unaware of her surroundings.

The gentlemen returned, tea was served and the card tables were set out, but Nell played on, barely conscious of what was happening in the rest of the room. It was only when she became aware of a pink-clad figure sitting quietly nearby that her fingers stilled at last.

"You play so well," the pink-clad figure breathed. Nell searched around in her mind for a name... Lucilla Rutherford, that was it. The young lady of sixteen who was preparing for her season in London.

"Thank you," Nell said, with a little smile. She herself was aware of her lack of practice on an instrument of such quality as this one, and again regretted that her own grand piano was sitting, unused and probably out of tune, in the Lloyds' side of her house. "Would you like to play something? I have been monopolising the instrument rather, and would be glad to listen to another performer."

"Oh, no, I could not, not after you! I play a little, but nothing like that. I quite see now why Cousin Julia was always so jealous of you, for you play ten times better than she ever did, and you are ten times more beautiful, too. No, no! It is true! Mama said so, and now that I have met you I can quite see what she meant. I remember Cousin Julia wearing that gown, but she never looked half so well in it as you do. Your husband must have been a wonderful man to win your heart, for I daresay you had innumerable suitors."

"Yes... I thought he was wonderful." Nell blinked away tears — such ridiculous sentimentality! Especially as it was so inappropriate, considering all things.

"Oh dear, I did not mean to distress you," Lucilla said. "My foolish mouth! Let us speak of other things. Did you have a season? Will you tell me about it? Is it a great deal of fun?"

"I enjoyed mine," Nell said, with a smile. "It can be very intense, however, if there are expectations placed upon you. Are you hoping to find a husband during yours?"

"Oh no, not at all! I have already found the man I mean to marry, although Papa dislikes it extremely. He is only a curate, you see, and not two pennies to his name at present, but he will find a living soon, I am certain of it. Papa says it must not even be thought about until he has a good income and..." She blushed a little and lowered her head shyly. "...and we have proved our love will last. It will, we are both certain of it. He is the kindest man alive, and wishes me to have my season so that I may enjoy myself and see a little of the world before settling down. Is that not generous of him? So I am to have my season, and I am so looking forward to it, although it will not be until next year, or possibly the year after if I cannot learn to be demure, Mama says. I am not sure if I can manage that! I have never been the demure type, not like you. You are so composed and so beautifully mannered that I cannot imagine why Cousin Julia warned me away from you. She said you are very wicked, but you are not, are you? No one so beautiful could possibly be wicked."

"Oh, if only one could tell by a person's appearance!" Nell said. "But you will find, when you go to London, that a beautiful exterior can hide a wicked heart, and a man of honour may hide behind a most unprepossessing exterior. It is often so, and therefore you must be guided by those wiser than you, Miss Rutherford."

"Oh, but I can tell for myself. I am a very good judge of character, though I am so young."

"Yet you think I am not wicked, but I am, I assure you."

"No!" she said robustly, eyes wide. "It is not possible." Then after a moment's thought, she added in a whisper, "Whatever did you do?"

"I married against my father's wishes," Nell said quietly. "I was seventeen, and the man I loved was thirty and not in the least suitable for a baronet's daughter, or so Papa said. He forbade me from seeing him. But I was not at all demure in those days and would not listen, so... I made it happen, and was thrown out of the family as a consequence. This is the first time I have returned here in nine years, and I am not at all welcome, I assure you. It is very uncomfortable to be cut off from one's family, and although I shall never regret marrying Captain Caldicott, I regret that it caused a breach with my family."

Lucilla looked at her, eyes round at these revelations. "But how did you manage it? Make it happen, I mean... what did you *do?*"

Nell laughed. "I should not tell you, but you are a sensible girl and perhaps my words will prevent you from making a mistake. Miss Rutherford, I did the thing that unmarried young ladies should never, ever do, and was thereby ruined and required to marry at once."

The eyes widened even more. "Ohhhh...!" Lucilla breathed.

"Precisely," Nell said crisply. "So be a good girl and do as your father bids you and wait patiently for your curate. There is a time and a place for spirited behaviour, but until you are wed, demureness has the upper hand, I should say."

~~~~~
~~~~~

Nell waited patiently all the next day for a summons to the library to talk to James, but he was closeted away with the lawyers. They seldom ventured away from London, but having been drawn to Hampshire for the funeral of the Duke of Falconbury, they were taking the opportunity to talk also with their other client in the county. Each time she enquired, she was told that Sir James was engaged and was not to be disturbed.

So she and Louis sat in their room, Louis reading and Nell staring gloomily out of the window. It was fortunate that it was wet, or she would have been tempted to go out for a walk and revisit all her favourite parts of the gardens, and that would have done her no good at all. There had been many happy times, it was true, but so many places now were coloured by memories of Jude. The gazebo where he had first offered her his arm. The rose walk where he had gazed at her with fire in his eyes, and told her that he would never forget the way she looked that day. The folly on the hill where he had first kissed her. And then there was the summer house where she had crept out to meet him that night and thus sealed her fate. Good memories, but clouded by time and later events. She did not regret what she had done, but her life would have been very different if she had obeyed her father and stayed in her bed that night.

After a while, Louis stealthily edged nearer to her post on the window seat, and nudged her arm.

"Look," he said, holding a book out to her, opened at the flyleaf. It was the book that had been given to him by Mr Harbottle, and on the leaf she read, *'To Louis Caldicott, with every good wish from his friend, Nathan Harbottle'.*

"He inscribed it — how thoughtful!" she said, her spirits lifting a little. "He is a kind man."

"And my friend," Louis said proudly. "He says so. I wish I could see him again."

"Do you?"

"Mm. I would like to say thank you. Properly."

"You could write to him," Nell said. "Should you like that? We could write to him now, if you wish. The escritoire has everything we need, for Uncle James has plenty of paper and ink and quills and sealing wax." Seeing his anxious face, and knowing that he had never written with a pen, she added, "You could tell me what you want to say, and I could write it for you, if you like. Then you need only sign your name at the bottom. I shall be your scribe."

He nodded, and she sat down, prepared her pen and drew a sheet of paper from the drawer. A whole sheet, fresh and new and of the best quality — such luxury. "Now, we must put where we are first, Daveney Hall, and then today's date, like so... and then the salutation. Now, what would you like to say?"

He spoke and she wrote, and although it was not perhaps the best composed letter she had ever read, it was heartfelt and would, she was sure, bring a smile to Mr Harbottle's handsome face. She smiled herself as she imagined him opening it, realising who had sent it and then perhaps chuckling at one or two phrases. Yes, it must please him.

She had only just sent the letter off with one of the footmen when there was a tap on the door, and James's head appeared. "Ah, there you are. I have another book for Louis, which I thought of only an hour ago. Another perspective on Byng, you see."

Louis whisked it from his hands with a hasty, "Thank you, sir!" and ran across to the desk to read it at once.

"Clever boy, that one," James said. "He will do well at Winchester."

"Winchester? You have decided on his schooling already?"

James looked at her in surprise. "Where else? All the Godney boys go to Winchester."

"Oh." That was good, she supposed. He had accepted his rôle as Louis' guardian without demur. Somehow, she had expected more resistance. A lesser school, certainly. Julia would not like the idea of a sailor's son being educated at the same establishment as the sons of the baronets of Daveney Hall. "James, have you the leisure to talk to me now? I have no wish to try Julia's patience by extending my stay, and I only need a little of your time."

His face shifted, and she saw the reluctance there. However, he nodded. "The lawyers are still going through papers in my library, so come through to the tower."

After arranging for a nursemaid to keep watch over Louis, Nell followed her brother along corridors, down a service stair, past the old buttery and through to what was known as the Tudor wing. It was probably not so old as that, but it was certainly the oldest part of the house and, unlike most of it, had never been remodelled to bring it into the nineteenth century, or even the eighteenth. It was full of solid oak furniture, gloomy paintings and dark wood panelling, and Nell had never much liked it. At one corner, however, was the suite of rooms which had traditionally been allocated to the heir to the baronetcy. Here James had lived from the age of twelve, with his own dining room, parlour and study, with several bedrooms above to house visiting friends.

Nell was amused to find that the study had a good fire going, and a homely feel from the books and newspapers scattered about, even though James had appropriated the library ever since his father's death.

"You still use this room, then?"

He gave a rueful smile. "It is my refuge. No one else is allowed in here, except by invitation."

"I am honoured," Nell said, although wondering what need James had for a refuge. Hiding from his wife, maybe.

"Now then, Nell, say what you have come here to say, although I am not sure what advice I might offer," he said tetchily. "I have no financial expertise."

"My need is more for legal advice than financial," she said.

"Then you need a solicitor."

"I have talked to my attorney, and he directed me to you. It is nothing complicated, James. I only wish to know how I may access my settlement, or jointure, as I suppose it is now."

"Settlement?" He looked bewildered.

"My fifteen thousand pounds. There is no record of the details in Southampton, and so my attorney presumed it must be held in some sort of trust fund, drawn up by Papa. You must know something of it, or else you can find out for me from the family solicitors."

"Settlement," James said heavily. "Oh, Nell... did your husband never talk to you about this?"

"Not... not a word," she said, filled with a dreadful foreboding. "Tell me at once, James, for I must know where it is."

He sighed, looked down at his hands, then at her, then down at his hands again. "Nelly dear, there is no settlement. There was never a settlement. It was always in Papa's gift and... and he chose not to settle anything on you."

"Nothing?"

He shook his head. "I am so very sorry."

8: Financial Matters

Anger boiled up inside her.

"Why would he do that?" Nell cried, pacing restlessly around the room. James's study was not a large room, so ten paces brought her to one wall, and another ten paces brought her back again. "Fifteen thousand pounds — that was always the arrangement. It was *mine*, Jamie! It was promised to me!"

"I know and I always thought it harsh, but Papa was implacable on the point."

"Did he *want* me to be destitute? I thought he loved me."

"He wanted only your happiness, Nelly, and he loved you more than you know. He doted on you. You broke his heart, you know. He could not forgive you… I had never seen him so distraught. Betrayal… that was the word he used, over and over. His only daughter, so beautiful, so clever, so much the lady. He had never a word of praise for *me*, but you — you were perfect in his eyes. He was so proud of you, Nelly. He was going to make a great match for you, and you betrayed him, throwing yourself away on a nobody. Besides—" He broke off, chewing his lip worriedly.

"Besides what?" He poured brandy into two glasses, and pushed one into her hand. "James, I do not—"

"Drink," he said, his voice gruff. "Sit and drink and I will tell you what happened."

Obediently she sat on the nearest chair and sipped the brandy. It burned its way down her throat and she pulled a face. It was so long since she had taken anything of the sort that she was no longer accustomed.

James pulled a chair near hers and sat facing her. "Nelly, you must not take umbrage at any of this, for it was all done in your best interests. You were only seventeen, after all, and barely out. You knew nothing of the world. So when Caldicott turned up and started making up to you and you seemed to return his regard, naturally Papa made enquiries. He was friendly with the Sherrards and the Kenricks and the Brockenhursts, but none of them seemed to know much about him. Family in Ireland, Royal Navy — that was all anyone could say of him. No proper connections at all. So Papa asked about. Well, no one knew of any Caldicotts in Ireland, for a start, so we tried at the Admiralty. Papa has one or two friends there. Nelly, there was no Judas Caldicott in the navy, ever."

"What!"

"It is true. No trace of any such person, and those people keep very accurate records. So Papa determined that he was a scheming, lying fortune hunter, sent him packing and forbade you from seeing him. Well, we know how that turned out. There had to be a marriage, and Papa said at once that he would give his permission, but he was determined that Caldicott would not have your fifteen thousand. At first he refused to give him a penny piece, but Caldicott argued that he needed some money to provide you with a house. Eventually, Papa yielded. He gave him three thousand pounds free of all conditions, if he would marry you and take you away and ensure that he never saw either of you again."

"Jude was no fortune hunter!" she cried. "He *loved* me!"

"Oh yes! No one could possibly doubt his affection for you, or yours for him, but that does not make it sensible, Nelly. Papa said... he had to protect the family, the estate. If Caldicott had your fifteen thousand in his hands, perhaps he would throw over his work and pretend to be a gentleman and get into difficulties and then he would be coming to Papa for help. It was necessary to make a complete break, to prevent any drain on the estate."

"Then I have nothing," she whispered. "No jointure. I am destitute."

"You still have the house, presumably?"

"Mortgaged."

"A pension from his employer? Insurance on Caldicott's life? Savings in the bank?"

She shook her head.

"There must be *something!"* James said, a note of desperation in his voice. "What of the three thousand? What of his ship? He owned his own ship, and it was comforting to think that one day he would have a whole fleet and be very rich and you would live in some style. It comforted *me*, anyway."

"Indeed he owned his own ship, and after we married, he bought a second ship— Oh! He must have used the three thousand pounds, of course. After the house was bought and furnished, there would have been something left over. I always wondered... So he used the remains of the three thousand pounds to buy another ship, much larger, taking out a loan to do so. He commanded the *Helen of Troy* himself, and he engaged another captain, Captain Delanoy, for the *Rosy Dawn*. But then... but then..."

She stopped. Even now, it was impossible to talk about.

"It sank," she said bluntly. "Jude lost everything, and he was forced to take employment with Mr Sherrard, and... we sold a few things, took in lodgers, we managed."

"Was it not insured?" James said. "Ships are usually insured, are they not?"

"The insurance would not pay out, so you see..."

"Oh, Nelly! No wonder you are gone so abominably thin! And the boy, too. You said you could not even afford the subscription to the circulating library. Has it been dreadful?" Again tears prickled, but she blinked them away. "Have you nothing at all?"

She forced a smile. "Oh, there will be something. Perhaps when the house is sold and the debts paid off, there will be some money left. I will talk to the attorney again. I am sure there will be something. Or I can find work... if I did not have Louis, I could easily find employment as... as a governess or some such. I could teach the pianoforte, perhaps. We shall not starve."

"My sister working for a living!" James exploded. "It is unthinkable! You are a Godney, after all. Fifteen thousand pounds would have given you a comfortable income."

"Would it?"

"Invested in the funds at three or four per cent — what would that be?"

She worked it out in her head. "Oh. Five or six hundred a year. That is... not much, I suppose, but something. Well, there is no use thinking of it, since I do not have it."

"Yes, but—"

"I shall manage, James. You need not fear that I shall be asking for your charity."

"Nor could I provide it," he said heavily. "Papa made me promise… when he was ill the last time, he made me promise never to give you money or a home, for the good of the estate. He was terrified of depleting the family fortune, of leaving the next generation worse off, and he never trusted my judgement in financial matters. Well, I admit that is not my strong suit. I gave my word willingly, for it made him easy at the end. Not for one moment did I imagine that you would ever need such aid. If I had but known— But your letters… you always seemed so contented. There was never a hint—"

"Do not distress yourself, James," Nell said gently. "I could not bring myself to reveal our difficulties. It was too shaming, so I restricted myself to reports of Louis' progress, or to congratulate you on your marriage or the births of your daughters."

"Oh yes, our daughters," he said, and she could not mistake the note of bitterness in his voice.

"Two daughters and no son, is that it?" she said softly. When he made no reply, she went on, "We cannot ordain these matters. It is as God wills it."

"No, it is as *Julia* wills it," he snapped. "After Augusta, she was exhausted, she told me. There was nothing truly amiss, you understand, and the physician assured me there was no reason not to— But she said she needed time to recover. Well, I knew she hated the whole business of babies, from beginning to end, so I understood her reluctance, and I am not an unreasonable man, I hope. I gave her time to recover, but Nelly, four years is a very long time for a wife to keep her bedroom door locked. I do not care so very much about a son, for there is Jack, after all, but I should like a little affection from her now and then. That is not too much to ask, is it?"

Nell was torn between amusement and exasperation. "You are too easy-going a husband altogether. Tell her the bedroom door is to be open to you or you will break it down."

"Break it down!" he said, scandalised. "Good God, Nelly, what would the servants think!"

"What do they think of a husband who meekly allows his wife to rule the roost? Who cares what they think, anyway? Well, if you will not break down the door, and perhaps that is just a little melodramatic, stop her allowance. Refuse her the use of the carriage. Refuse to entertain. Does she like to go to London? Make her spend the spring in Harrogate instead."

He laughed. "She would be apoplectic! Besides, I do not like to... to insist on my rights, not when she hates it so much."

"I suppose you are right. Well then, you could just take a mistress."

He was silent for such a long time that she wondered if he had already done so. "I confess I have considered it," he said at last. "Papa had someone in Winchester, did you know?" She shook her head. "He left her money and a house in his will. But it seems so... so *final.* As if I am giving up on my marriage altogether, and I am not quite ready for that." He heaved a great sigh. "Oh, Nelly, one sets out with such high hopes, but the reality is never quite so perfect."

"Real life is very far from perfect, as I am discovering," she said sadly. "So — no settlement. No money at all. What am I to do, Jamie?"

"I have not the least idea," he said.

~~~~~

Nell's second evening at Daveney Hall was only marginally easier. The lawyers had departed in a post-chaise, and the clergyman's family were not there, but Lucilla and Alfred Rutherford had been
~~~~~

joined by three more of Julia's female relatives. Nell barely remembered them, and her efforts to repair this deficiency were treated in a desultory manner. After a few sympathetic noises regarding her widowhood, they drifted away to Julia's side. The four of them spent the rest of the evening giggling together like a pack of schoolroom chits.

When the ladies withdrew to the drawing room, Nell settled down at the instrument again. Lucilla had disappeared, but Julia and her flock whispered together at the far side of the room, occasionally bursting into most inelegant laughter. Judging by the looks thrown her way, Nell supposed she was the butt of their humour. The thought gave her no pain. She had never expected sympathy from Julia, and so was not disappointed.

Lost in her own thoughts, she played by rote. James had given her so much to think about. No settlement, only three thousand pounds which was long gone, since there was nothing in the bank. No jointure, no annuity, no income of any sort. No house, possibly, which meant no rent from lodgers. Nor was any of that her father's fault. He had expected her husband to provide for her, and he had, for a while, until it all went wrong. And that wasn't his fault, either. She knew where the blame lay.

Behind all the money difficulties lay a greater grief. Jude had lied to her, lied to everyone. He had claimed a naval history that was fabricated out of thin air. None of it was true. And if he had lied about that, what else might he have lied about? It was a betrayal of the worst kind, for he was not the man she had thought he was. There was a great swathe of his life which was a complete mystery. If he had not been in the navy from the ages of twelve to three and twenty, where had he been? What had he done? She felt that she had not truly known her husband at all. He was a Judas indeed.

After a while, Julia and her friends crept towards the pianoforte. Nell at once jumped up and curtsied respectfully. There was no point in setting Julia's back up unnecessarily, and, after all, she did outrank Nell.

"You do not feel it inappropriate to perform publicly so soon after your husband's death?" one of them said, and the others tittered.

"Not at all," Nell said. "Music is a great solace, is it not?"

"I am far too busy to find the time to practise," Julia said. "It must be easier for you, Nell, with a much smaller house and only one child to care for." Nell thought of the troops of servants managing Julia's house and children, and did not bother replying, so Julia went on, "Did you have a satisfactory talk with Sir James? His understanding of money is not strong, and I often have to give him a hint myself, but his advice was useful to you, I trust."

"We had an interesting discussion," Nell said neutrally.

Julia was not quite sure how to answer that, but while she hesitated, one of her friends chirped, "How kind Sir James is to offer help to his sister in her time of need. Such a generous brother!"

That was too much for Julia. "Nell is here for advice only. She cannot expect any other kind of help, for Sir James has his own family to consider first. Our expenses are considerable."

Nell looked at Julia's elaborate gown and abundance of jewels, and believed it. She could not resist saying, "I imagine they are, with so many new footmen. The tax on manservants is ridiculous now."

Julia laughed, a brittle sound. "Pooh, manservants are nothing! It is the upkeep of the London house and the season, and the entertaining that is expected of us. I do not care for it myself, but a baronet has a position to maintain, after all."

"Such a sacrifice, all those balls and routs," Nell murmured sweetly. "But how fortunate it is that you have only daughters, Lady Godney. Sons are *so* expensive, with schooling and then Oxford, and clubs and curricles and hunters and gaming and heaven knows what, whereas daughters need only a governess. I congratulate you."

Julia made no reply, but she looked askance at Nell as if she suspected some sly reproach but could not quite make it out. One of the others, brighter than she was, smothered a laugh, and then, perhaps embarrassed by her own lapse of manners, rushed to say, "You are indeed fortunate, Julia dear, for Sir James is such a generous and doting husband."

That brought a smile to Julia's face. "Indeed he is, for he is forever giving me little gifts, but *you* take the prize there, I am certain. Such a magnificent phaeton and pair Henry bought you."

"Oh, yes, yes," she simpered. "I had only to drop the merest hint, and off he went at once to buy it for me. But I think Sarah's rubies must be the best present a man could give his wife. Such a magnificent set. Her husband is surely the most generous man alive."

There was a murmur of agreement at this, none of the ladies able to claim a gift superior to the rubies. Nell had nothing to contribute to the discussion, but it amused her all the same, although it was disappointing to discover that Julia was every bit as shallow as she had always been. Marriage had not mellowed her.

"But we should not talk about husbands in front of Mrs Caldicott," said one of them with greater delicacy than the others. "It is not kind to make comparisons in this way in front of a widow."

"No, indeed," Julia said smugly. "Comparisons are odious, especially when *we* have so much and poor Nell is alone in the world."

"Do not concern yourselves about me," Nell said. "I may be alone now, but I have had the incomparable joy of years with a husband who adored me, and whom I adored in my turn."

That silenced them. Julia stalked away, pretending not to be annoyed, and the others scuttled after her. Nell returned to her music, but for once it did not bring her the tranquillity she sought. Jude was not the only one who had been untruthful. Oh, the lies she had told over the years! Or rather, not lies, but so many things unsaid. There had been years of joy with Jude, it was true, until the disaster had overwhelmed them. Even in the joyful years, there had been... arguments, difficulties, slammed doors, followed by huffy silences and hurtful remarks, but always they had reconciled their differences with kisses and sweet love. Until the disaster. Then they had hurtled with terrifying speed into anger and violence and *fear*. So much fear. She still felt it sometimes when she woke shaking in the mornings, before she remembered that she was free from that now.

But she was not free from all fear, for now there was another anxiety. How on earth were they to live? Would they have anything left at all, after their possessions had been sold? Perhaps she and Maria and their children would have to survive on Maria's tiny annuity, sharing a rat-infested garret and scavenging from pigswill buckets. She shivered, and her fingers slowed on the keys. No, she would not let that happen. She would find a way. She had to. But she could not think how it might be done.

Later that evening, after she had gone to bed, there was a tentative tap on the door. It opened, and candlelight spilt into the room.

"Nelly? Are you awake?"

She pulled a robe around her — another grudging gift from Julia's sumptuous wardrobe — and slipped out of the door. James stood in the corridor, wearing only his nightshirt, robe and nightcap, carrying a wavering candle.

"I had a thought," James said, and she thought he looked rather smug. "I am not much good with money, but I keep Landon for all that sort of thing. You must remember old Landon — very clever fellow. Keeps all my money straight, anyway."

"Oh, not Julia, then?" Nell said innocently.

"Julia? I should think not! Money is men's work, Nell. Anyway, I took the liberty of mentioning your situation to Landon — I was sure you would not mind — and he has come up with a whole list of avenues you might pursue... or your solicitor, you know. He will have it all written up for you before you leave in the morning. And he said — and this is the clever part, Nell — that although I may not give you money or property, since I promised Papa, I may use my influence in your favour, do you see? So he is to write letters for you to take to the bank and anywhere else they may be useful, asking them to give you every assistance at this difficult time, and so on and so forth. And then I shall sign them. That is bound to weigh with them, is it not? Oh, and he said another thing that I had not thought about at all. He said, *'Your sister is not a Godney any longer, but she is a Caldicott, and so is her son. Therefore, she will be able to turn to her husband's family for aid.'* That is a good thought, is it not? You will have a family about you, and you will not need to come here again. Indeed, it is better if you do not. Julia does not like it above half, and I do not like it when she is unsettled. And now I shall leave you to sleep, Nelly. Good night."

He hastened away down the corridor, the candle wavering into the distance and then vanishing, leaving her in the dark. She groped her way back to bed by the glow of the fire's last embers, trying not to disturb the sleeping Louis. Then she lay motionless in the dark, trying to work out how on earth she was supposed to ask the

Caldicotts for aid, when she had no idea where they lived or anything about them. Somewhere in Ireland, that was all she knew.

And if Jude had lied about being in the navy, perhaps he had lied about his family, too.

9: Past And Future

Nell and Louis arrived back in Southampton in greater style than they had left it, in the sumptuous comfort of one of the Daveney Hall carriages, complete with four horses, two coachmen and two footmen on the back. James was prohibited by his deathbed promise and his own scruples from giving Nell money or property, but the estimable Mr Landon had pointed out that this did not preclude the giving of books, unwanted items of apparel, joints of meat, cheeses, jars of preserves and pound cakes. The carriage, therefore, was laden to the roof, and the passengers in more cheerful spirits than might have been expected, given their circumstances.

Half the street came out to see such a splendid equipage arrive, and the other half no doubt watched from behind the curtains. The footmen carried their prizes into the house, and then, giving them her last coins as vails, Nell watched the carriage roll away down the street until it turned the corner and vanished from view. Only then did she go inside and shut the door.

Maria stood in the hall, gazing at the mountain of boxes, packages and hampers. “You have made it up with him, then?” she said, with a hopeful smile.

Nell pulled a rueful face. “Not exactly. Let us get everything put away, and then I shall tell you all.”

The whole household fell to, falling on the gifts with cries of joy, and swiftly finding a home for everything. Even Lydia Lloyd emerged to watch and pass comments and get in the way. Eventually it was done, and with Louis in his room with his precious books, the Lloyds in their own apartment again and everyone else in the kitchen drinking tea and anticipating an excellent dinner, Nell retrieved a bottle of Madeira and a box of bon-bons and took Maria off to the morning room.

“We will have a decent fire, for once,” Nell said, heaping coals onto the flames. “There. Now let us eat and drink and be cheerful while we may, for this largesse will be gone in a week, and then we shall be destitute.”

“Is it truly as bad as that?” Nell nodded. “What of your settlement?”

“There is not a penny piece. Papa gave Jude three thousand pounds to spend as he would, which I would guess was lost with the *Helen of Troy*. I have nothing.”

Maria was silent for a long moment. It was one of the greatest joys of their friendship, that she asked no foolish questions. Anyone else would have said at once, *‘What will you do? Where will you go? How will you manage?’*, none of which Nell could answer. But Maria said nothing. Instead she got up and retrieved a paper from a drawer.

“Perhaps this will cheer you a little.”

A letter, on good quality paper, with an unusual seal. Nell turned it over and over in her hands. “Who is it from? It was hand-delivered, so it must have been a local man. Oh — not the bank! Please tell me it is not from the bank.”

Maria smiled. "Not the bank. I said it would cheer you, remember? Open it, and you will find out."

She broke the seal and unfolded the paper.

'Dolphin Hotel, 7th March 18—, Mrs Caldicott, I cannot express my great sorrow on hearing the tragic news of the loss of the Minerva *and the almost certain demise of your husband. Pray allow me to offer my condolences to you and to Master Caldicott, inadequate as they may be to your immeasurable grief. I came at once to discover if I might be of any service to you, however slight, in so difficult a time. Finding you gone to the consoling bosom of your family, I acknowledge that you are in the best of hands and will now receive all the comfort you need, as well as material help for your untimely change in circumstances. My services being unnecessary, I shall depart, but be assured that you may recall me to your charming town at any time, should you have need of a friend or adviser. A letter to me at York will receive the earliest attention and my speedy arrival at your door. If it should suit you better, you may come to York and I shall show you my own charming town, and the sites of much history that would interest Louis. With my heartfelt prayers for you and your son, I remain, madam, your well-wisher and friend, Nathan Harbottle.'*

"Mr Harbottle!" she said in astonishment. "He has been here?"

"Oh, yes! He came the day after you left, in a great deal of agitation, very concerned for you, but much relieved to hear that you were at Daveney Hall. *'The breach was not so great then,'* he said, more than once. And I told him — and do not be angry, for it was only what you told me yourself, and he was so worried about you — I told him about your settlement, Nell. I did not know, then—"

"Nor did I." Nell laughed. "It is ironic, is it not? My brother will not lift a finger to help me, yet a complete stranger tears about the country on my behalf."

"Oh, but Nell! He was so taken with you, nothing could be like it. He brought tea for you... oh, and he ordered paper and quills and ink to be delivered here for you, from that little shop in French Street, for he wanted to be sure that you could write to him if you needed to, he said. The box is in the cupboard over there. He is so thoughtful and kind, and now that you are widowed, he no doubt thinks—"

"Then he had better think again," she said savagely. "I cannot have a high opinion of the understanding of a man who pursues such a course on so flimsy a foundation. He saw me for half an hour with you, and an hour the following day, and that is not a solid basis for anything beyond the most casual acquaintance. What would happen if I were to call upon him for aid, friendly or otherwise? Why, it would raise all manner of speculation and expectation. No, I shall not take up his offer... generous though it is," she added in an undertone. For there was something appealing about turning to a man for help, and placing all her problems in male hands. She had never been brought up to make her own way in the world, and the prospect of doing so now was overwhelming. What on earth was she to do? She was paralysed with indecision.

Maria, however, was not. Having been told of Mr Landon's list of suggested courses of action and the letters signed by James, she exhorted Nell to put these to good use.

"There is no use in sitting in the house drinking tea and lamenting the situation," Maria said firmly. "You were not used to be so passive, Nell. You were a high-spirited creature when I first knew you. Were you subdued like this at Daveney Hall?"

"Not so much," Nell confessed. "It was a little like being young again. I felt... livelier, even though there were so many memories of Jude. But here..." She shivered. "Here I sit and wait, because that was what I did. I was always waiting."

Waiting for Jude to come home. Waiting for him to go away again. And worst of all, waiting for his anger to rise, for the inevitable quarrel, for his fists. She had learnt in the most wretched fashion that standing up to his rage only inflamed him, so she had hoped that docility would appease him, but it never did.

Maria understood, though. "It is this house, of course." She hugged Nell, and then said briskly, "Shall we start with the bank? Mr Vessey is such an agreeable man, and so helpful. Nothing would be more beneficial for you just now than to place all your worries in the hands of such a man."

So they went to the bank again and showed Mr Vessey the letter from James, which seemed to have the desired effect.

"Not the least need for concern in the world, Mrs Caldicott," the man said airily. "Delighted to oblige Sir James. I had not previously realised that you were a *Godney*. No, there will be no difficulty about the mortgage or the deficit in your late husband's account. Take your time to settle your affairs, Mrs Caldicott. Take all the time in the world." He laughed merrily, but Nell saw that it was just his way, and was not offended by his lightness.

Next they went to the attorney and he too was most amenable. "Anything I can do to help, my dear Mrs Caldicott. As soon as the *paperwork* arrives from Cornwall, confirming the *demise* of your late husband, the will may be read, do you see? As soon as Mr Sherrard returns, we can proceed, but I can set your mind at rest on one point, in that the will leaves *everything* to your son. He is the *heir*, do you see? So the house and everything in it belongs to him, with my good self as trustee, and Sir James Godney as the boy's guardian. So that is all most *satisfactory*, do you see?"

Nell was not sure about satisfactory, but it was certainly reassuring. They were not facing imminent homelessness, and that was something, but she still had no income, apart from the modest rent the Lloyds paid, and no obvious way to obtain any.

She sat down with Maria one morning to work out what they might do, and how they might economise.

"If we turn off Becky and the boy, that would save us a little," Maria said.

"I suppose it has to be Becky," Nell said slowly. "She is the most expensive servant we have. It is a pity, though. She keeps the place so clean. And Dick is useful for carrying things. Tilda is unwilling to lift anything, and she is not safe near anything breakable."

"My girls will help," Maria said. "Jane has a light hand for dusting, so she can do the parlour work, and we can all help beat carpets and so on." She frowned. "I suppose I could find work elsewhere as a cook, for I am sure you would give me a good reference. That would leave you without anyone to take charge of the kitchen, though, and the Lloyds are paying for meals, so that is no good. However, Lucy is twelve now, so she is old enough to go into service, and she will send some of her wages home, I am sure."

"This is dreadful," Nell said. "Your girls should still be at their slates, not working for a living."

"It is what most people have to do," Maria said mildly. "Those of us brought up surrounded by servants have had it easy. Besides, for all your gloom when you returned from Daveney Hall, we are not yet destitute. We have some money enough to live upon. Not a lot, but enough."

"Is it enough?" Nell said slowly. "There is the mortgage on the house, which will have to be addressed at some point. Mr Vessey is very generous but sooner or later we shall have to do something about it. And it is almost Lady Day, so all the bills will come in, and I have no money to pay them. Already I have had two bills presented to me — three guineas owed to Jude's bootmaker, and twenty guineas to a solicitor in Portsmouth. Twenty guineas!"

"Why did Jude have a solicitor in Portsmouth?" Maria said.

"I have not the least idea. Well, I cannot pay it, so it will go in the drawer with the other bills, and it can stay there for now, until I can find some way to get more money. I doubt there will be any to spare, even if we never drink tea again. I shall have to earn something, too. But what can I do, Maria? All sorts of ideas float through my head but none of them seem possible. I cannot be a governess or companion, for how could I leave Louis behind?"

"No, you have to stay here," Maria said. "Oh dear, this is so difficult! Money is a matter best dealt with by men. Could you not ask that charming Mr Harbottle for assistance? I am sure he would be very willing—"

"Maria, I could not possibly ask a virtual stranger to help me financially. It would place me under the most awkward kind of obligation. I suppose I could offer lessons upon the pianoforte. *'Mrs Caldicott, a respectable widow, offers instruction in performance at all levels, including singing.'* There! That might work."

Maria nodded eagerly. "Oh yes! But instead of a respectable widow, you should describe yourself as the former Miss Godney of Daveney Hall. Your brother is a baronet, my dear, so take advantage of that."

"I am only the relict of the late Captain Judas Caldicott now," Nell said sadly.

Judas... what had his parents been thinking of, to give him such an ill-omened name? And yet he had lived up to it, for had he not betrayed her, by lying about his time in the navy? And he had betrayed her in other ways, too. A husband should protect his wife from harm, not inflict it upon her.

Oh Jude... so much loved, once. So loving, once. What had happened to them, those young lovers? Gone. Gone for ever.

~~~~~

Mr Sherrard looked drawn and grey, seeming to have aged twenty years overnight. He had returned from Cornwall bearing the belongings of all those who had perished on the *Brig Minerva*, excepting only the Duke of Falconbury. A sad journey he must have had of it, his carriage laden with twenty two small parcels.

"It is not much to show for a man's life," he said grimly, looking at Jude's parcel as it sat on the morning room table. "I am sorry his mortal remains could not be returned to you, Mrs Caldicott, but with so many dead... and the difficulties of travel at this time of year... you understand, I am sure. But I saw him into the ground at Pendower. I saw all of them into the ground."

He closed his eyes for a moment, pressing thumb and forefinger against the lids.

"I understand," Nell said, feeling that she ought to offer some condolences but quite unable to do so. Everything to do with Jude had faded into the past. It was as if she had crossed a threshold at the moment he died, and now he had drifted away from her. While he lived, all her thoughts, her hopes, her fears had centred around him. But now that he was gone, he was not quite real any longer, and her mind was bent into more practical channels. Where would they find more money? How would they live? Dear God, how would they survive on so little?

"Five days on the road," he said, half to himself, "and the weather filthy for most of it. I shall have to go back for the inquiry, too." He looked at her searchingly. "You appreciate that there must be an official inquiry, both for the insurance company and for the satisfaction of the new Duke of Falconbury?"
~~~~~

"Of course."

"And that... difficult questions will be asked? About your husband?"

She was silent. Of Jude's seamanship, she had no doubts at all, for Mr Sherrard had always praised his abilities, and had not hesitated to offer him employment when the *Helen of Troy* had foundered. His worth as a captain was beyond dispute. But on other matters...

Mr Sherrard licked his lips. "Mrs Caldicott, were you aware that... that there might be some doubt about your late husband's career in His Majesty's Navy?"

So that was the problem. "I have heard rumours, but I cannot say—"

"No, no, of course! I do not suggest— But questions will be asked, unfortunately, and with the death of the duke... there is a great interest in the matter, which would not normally be the case. I would not normally mention such things, but I felt you should be prepared."

"Thank you. That was thoughtful of you, sir."

He looked at her worriedly. "Are you all right, Mrs Caldicott? You seem... very composed. Very calm."

"I am perfectly all right." Then, because he seemed to expect something more, she added, "I am not the type of person to fall into hysteria, Mr Sherrard."

"No, of course you are not." He rose, as if to leave, and she rose from her seat also. If only he would go away! She could not sit and make polite conversation, not any more. She had her survival to think about, which was of far greater significance than Jude's career, and whether he had ever been in the navy or not.

"Oh, I almost forgot," he said, fishing in a pocket and producing a brightly coloured object. "There. You had better have that."

She took it automatically. A purse. "What is this?"

"Captain Caldicott's salary for this quarter, paid up to Lady Day. And his bonus."

"Oh." She stared at it stupidly, suddenly aware of the weight of it. Coins! Money. "His salary. Thank you."

"You had better check that it is correct."

"Check that—? Oh, you wish me to... to count it? Now?"

"If you please. And then sign my book to say that you have received it."

"Oh. I see." She felt disoriented, adrift. A salary? Money? But it could not be very much. Enough to pay the butcher, perhaps. But Mr Sherrard was waiting for her, so she slid the rings to open the purse, and tipped the contents onto the table.

So many coins, that was her first thought. A small roll of paper money, and a great many coins.

"Oh, but..." She stopped, shaking her head. "This is too much."

"No, look, ten notes at ten pounds apiece, all from Mr Vessey's bank, and thirty sovereigns, since the bonus is fifty pounds. It would normally be a great deal more, but... there was no profit from this last stage of the voyage. One hundred and thirty pounds. Do you see that, Mrs Caldicott?"

"I do, but— Is this usual? Eighty pounds is one quarter's salary?"

"It is."

"He told me eighty pounds a year."

"You must have mistaken his meaning." He smiled benignly at her. "Eighty a quarter, and twice as much as that in bonuses, usually, or more. Your husband was so clever, Mrs Caldicott, always shaving off a day here or there, or turning aside to pick up an extra cargo. Or a passenger, sometimes. It was his idea to stay an extra day or two in Dublin to persuade the duke to travel on the *Minerva.* His grace would have got the packet otherwise, but he would have been more comfortable on the brig. Well, *that* did not turn to our advantage, but in general I made a great profit from his skills, and I recompensed him accordingly. In fact, it always surprised me that he had not enough saved by now to afford another ship of his own."

She was too bemused to say a word.

He patted her hand benignly. "Ah, you ladies are unused to dealing with large sums, I daresay. A few pounds here and there to buy furbelows. That is as it should be, naturally. It is for men to take charge of money, in a well-regulated world. But you will grow accustomed to such matters, and you will have your annuity, of course."

"Annuity?" she said, feeling very stupid.

"Naturally there will be an annuity. The insurance money should cover it, so long as— But we will not consider that possibility."

"What possibility, Mr Sherrard?"

He looked uncomfortable again. "Well, the inquiry, you see. If there should be any blame attaching— But I am certain Captain Caldicott was not negligent in any duty where the safety of his ship was concerned. There is no need to worry, I am sure. It is only that... where there is a duke involved... the authorities do take a close interest in the affair. And if they find any deficiency in the command of the ship, then there will be no insurance payment, and we shall all be sunk, Mrs Caldicott. Indeed, we shall all be sunk. Now, if you will just sign my book."

He produced a small box with writing things and prepared a pen, then opened a small notebook. Numbly, Nell signed where he pointed, he packed everything away and took his leave. Long after he had gone, Nell sat unmoving, the heaps of coins and notes still lying on the table, staring at nothing, entirely dumbfounded. Jude had been earning many times as much as she had thought.

Had her husband told her the truth about anything?

10: Secrets And Lies (April)

Nathan lounged in the bathtub in front of a blazing fire, soaking away the miseries of the journey to London. A decorated screen shielded him from the slightest untoward draft. On a stool within easy reach sat a large glass of brandy. Beyond the screen, his valet was humming a slightly off-key tune as he went about his business, unpacking and laying out shaving gear and clean clothes for his master. Later that day, there was the prospect of an excellent dinner and good company, for Harry's new cook was to tempt their appetites. A couple of Harry's friends had been invited, and afterwards there would be cards and gossip and, eventually, a decent night's sleep. Nathan never slept well in hotels, and there was not an inn in England that was tolerably comfortable, to his mind.

The door opened, and Harry's voice boomed, "Good Lord, Nathan, are you not clean enough yet? That water must be stone cold." He peeped round the edge of the screen, and tutted at his friend.

Nathan lay back with his eyes closed. "This bath is so comfortable, and Packard is keeping me amply supplied with hot water."

"You can talk as well as soak, I suppose. Come on now, there's a good fellow, and tell me all about your mission of comfort to your widow lady, and why you are back so soon."

"I cannot conduct a rational conversation while naked, Harry," Nathan said in the mildest of tones. "Can it not wait until evening?"

"It can *not* wait until evening, for Lord Toller will be here then."

"Ugh. Why did you invite him? I thought you disliked the man."

"So I do, but he stood me a dinner at Watier's the other day, and since I had already invited Bonar and Wright for tonight, and you were gone out of town, I asked Toller so we had a four. He has just this minute sent his acceptance. If you get dressed quickly, we shall have an hour or so to talk before changing for dinner. There are letters for you, too."

"Oh, very well, very well," Nathan said, with a sigh indicative of long suffering, sitting up and sloshing water over the side of the tub.

Dried, shaved and dressed, he made his way downstairs to Harry's study, where a good fire burned and a sideboard was laden with an array of liquid refreshments likely to tempt the jaded palates of London gentlemen.

"Help yourself," Harry said genially, folding away the newspaper he had been reading. "Although I do not advise the Canary. It was a present from Toller, so it might be poisoned."

Nathan laughed, unstoppered the decanter and sniffed the wine suspiciously. "I shall be your wine taster," he said, pouring himself a little. "Better that I should be poisoned than you."

"I do not see that at all," Harry said indignantly. "I have three younger brothers jostling for my place, whereas you are the last of your immediate line, and possibly the last of your cousin's line, too, if Felix cannot be found. But tell me of this widow of whom you are so enamoured."

Nathan sighed. "As has been repeatedly pointed out to you, there is nothing of that sort involved."

"And as has been repeatedly pointed out to *you*, my friend, chasing all over the country after a beautiful young woman is not a convincing sign of impartiality. But you are back sooner than anticipated. Did she send you packing?"

"Not at all, for she was not there. She is gone to her brother, Sir James Godney."

"Hmm. I know him a little. But was there not some estrangement? He will not want her back, surely?"

"In such cases it is usually the husband who creates the insuperable obstacle. Now that he is gone, I imagine there will be no further difficulties. Besides, she has a settlement, although..." He frowned, working out numbers in his head. "It does not add up. Fifteen thousand she had, seemingly, and the husband had paid employment and they had lodgers paying rent, yet they could not even afford tea. That does not seem right, somehow."

"One never knows what sort of debts a man may have," Harry said easily. "A man who appears to have a comfortable income may be living in penury, while a man one knows to be dished lives as high as a duke. Like Toller, for instance. His sister told me precisely what his income is, yet he is never short of the readies. It is very odd."

"Toller is a sharp, though, is he not? He may be living solely on his winnings at the table."

"Possibly. Never seems to mind losing, though. One can usually tell when a fellow positively *has* to win. No, I have no idea how he manages it. There are those who say he has other sources of income, not quite as legitimate as rents from tenant farms or winnings from White's, but who knows?"

"What, is he a highwayman in his free time? Or is it smuggling? That is still lucrative, so I hear."

Harry laughed, and shrugged. "Who can say? Whatever the case, I do not care for the fellow, and he is very encroaching. After this evening, I intend to avoid him as far as possible. Oh — I have not given you your letters." He jumped up, and went to his desk. "Here — one from your cousin's wife, two from your aunt, one from Henny... oh, and one from Meg."

He could not avoid looking conscious as he spoke Meg's name. Nathan would normally tease him about it, but now he was too distracted by his letters.

"Two from Aunt Amelie? That is not like her. And Cousin Jessica does not write often." He broke the seals, one after another and quickly scanned them. "Ah... William is very poorly."

"Worse than before?"

"Considerably so. Aunt Amelie worries about his every cough, but if Cousin Jessica is alarmed, then it must be serious indeed. I shall have to go up to Yorkshire as soon as may be." He pulled out his pocket watch. "If I write at once to the posting inns, can your man have them at the post office before six? Otherwise I shall have to delay another day."

Harry checked his own watch. "You know, if you scramble, you might make Charing Cross in time for the mail coach this evening."

"Scramble?" Nathan said, in horror. "I *never* scramble, Harry. Something important is always forgotten in the rush, and then things go wrong. Travelling in such a way is anathema to me."

"Well, write your letters, then. If you leave early tomorrow travelling post with a team, you might make it in two days, with luck. Lord, Nathan, I hope he is all right."

"When these letters were written, he was not expected to see another Sabbath," Nathan said grimly. "This makes the search for Felix of the utmost importance. If William dies and we cannot find the heir, then we are cast into the greatest uncertainty."

"Is everything entailed?" Harry said.

"Everything," Nathan said. "It is a damnable position to be in. Nothing can be done until he is found, or is known beyond doubt to be dead."

"Perhaps another advertisement might work? Or, if your cousin dies, Felix might see the notice in the newspaper?"

But Nathan could see no cause for optimism. If Felix had hidden himself so successfully for twenty years, he was hardly likely to emerge now.

The evening was long and tedious. After writing his letters and instructing his valet on the change of plan, there was nothing to do but dress for dinner and attempt to be sociable. Under other circumstances Nathan would have enjoyed the company, for Harry's friends Bonar and Wright were lively wits, and Viscount Toller was at least interesting, having an ear for the latest *on dit*. He had a cynical and rather jaded view of the world, always thinking the worst of everyone, and Nathan disliked him cordially, even though he had not poisoned the Canary. Even so, he could not resist asking him about the *Minerva* as they sat over their port, for if anyone would know the latest news, it would be Toller.

"Is there any more news about that sinking in Cornwall?" he said. "The one that took Falconbury with it?"

Toller's eyes glimmered as they turned to him. "Have an interest, do you, Harbottle?"

"The ship was out of Southampton and I was there very recently looking for Felix, so naturally I am concerned," he said neutrally. "I have met some of the families of those on board."

"Ah," Toller said. Nathan had the feeling that he knew perfectly well that there was something more to his interest, but propriety held him back from enquiring directly. "The investigation into the sinking is turning up some curious... oh, let us say anomalies. The captain was supposed to be a former navy man, but the Admiralty have no record of the fellow at all. May not have been properly qualified. Not to mention, it was a clear night with not the least hint of bad weather. No reason for it to sink, none at all. And the duke on board... makes one wonder, eh?"

"Wonder what, precisely?" Harry said, his voice clipped.

Toller waved a hand airily. "Oh, this and that, Smethurst. This and that. Such a coincidence that the very ship bearing the duke home at last should founder, and he a man ill-suited to the position, as all agree. Yet there is his brother, ready and willing... one might almost say *eager*... to step into his brother's honours. Already manages the estates. And there is a lady promised to the new duke — no doubt he has his eye on her, too. Oh yes, it makes one wonder."

"Yet he is not planning to claim the title yet," Harry said, a hint of asperity in his tone. "That does not seem so eager to me."

"Well, naturally he will not rush forward," Toller said, laughing. "That would be very bad form. But he is very pleased with himself, you may be sure."

Disgusted, Nathan turned the subject, and tried very hard not to think about poor Mrs Caldicott, whose husband's wickedness had blighted her life while he lived, and seemed likely to blight it even further now that he was dead. He had lied about his naval career, he had hit his lovely wife — what else might he have done?

When it was his turn to sit out at whist, Nathan found himself distracted by a rather vulgar diamond ring that Toller wore. It flashed and winked as he shuffled and dealt, and Nathan was reminded that his income was small. He watched Toller covertly and listened more carefully to his conversation, assessing his expenditure. He talked glibly of his hunters, his travelling chaise and his curricle with two sets of matched horses. He clearly had his clothes made by a very expensive tailor, and every piece of jewellery he wore, from his neckcloth pin to the row of fobs at his waist, from the rings on his manicured fingers to his snuff box, and even the pocket watch he examined occasionally, was adorned with diamonds. This latter item was new, he told them when Bonar admired it.

"I like variety," Toller said languidly. "Nothing is more fatal to the spirits than familiarity. I must have novelty in all things."

"We all enjoy novelty, when we can afford it," Nathan said wryly.

Toller merely smiled enigmatically.

Nathan was glad when the evening was over. The next day he would begin the long journey back to Yorkshire, and who knew what he might find there? A miraculous recovery or a house in mourning?

Whatever the case, Felix must be found. The matter was now become of the utmost urgency.

~~~~~

APRIL

Nell stared at the paper before her uncomprehendingly. She could see no mistake in her numbers or her addition, yet the answers gave her no satisfaction. She set down her pen with a sigh, and poured herself more tea, cradling the cup as she sipped.

She had the morning room to herself, for once. Maria had taken the girls across the Itchen to visit a friend, and Louis was contentedly
~~~~~

reading through the pile of books James had given him, or rereading, for he had been through them once already and had now begun again.

Nell was wrestling with the question of finances. She had never in her life had more than a few coins in her reticule, for Jude had dealt with all such matters. He had settled with the tradesmen, paid the servants and collected the rent from the Lloyds and Maria. Then he wrote it all into the household accounts. When they had had the whole house, Jude had kept them locked away in the big desk in his study downstairs, and latterly, after that room had been given over to Mr Lloyd, he had used a small desk in their bedroom, and kept the account books locked in a box under the bed. She had no key to it, however. One day she would get someone to break the lock so that she could open it, but not yet. She was not ready to face anything else that Jude had kept hidden from her. There had been enough secrets revealed lately.

But the mystery of Jude's salary was one that she must resolve, if only for her own peace of mind. She had never known his income before the disaster, but there had always been enough, in those days. If she had wanted a new gown or a fan, usually he would smile and say, "Of course! How much would you like?" Occasionally, he had said, "Can it wait until next quarter? I am at low water just now." But he had never refused her, and there had always been tea, and coals for the fire.

After the disaster, he had come home one day and said, "Sherrard has offered me work, commanding the *Minerva*. I shall have to take it, I suppose. No alternative. It is not much, but we can economise a bit."

"Can we?" she had said dubiously, never having been called upon to do so before. "How much will we be obliged to economise?"

"A great deal," he had said. "I shall only have eighty pounds a year, and perhaps as much again in bonuses."

Eighty pounds a year. She was sure he had said it was per year. To Nell, whose father had grumbled about managing on an income of four thousand pounds a year, it had seemed an unimaginably small amount of money. That was when she had suggested taking in lodgers and some of the gloom had lifted from Jude's face.

"That would help, yes," he said. "What a clever wife you are! We shall manage, you know. It is only a temporary setback. I shall be on my feet again in no time."

Eighty pounds a year, and as much again in bonuses. One hundred and sixty pounds a year. The numbers ran round and round in her head like so many rats in the attic, so that they filled her waking mind and she even dreamt about them.

Because that was exactly what they had been spending. Now that Lady Day had come and gone, and the tradesmen had presented their bills, she could see exactly what their expenses had been for the past year. One hundred and fifty six pounds, four shillings and sixpence halfpenny. Without tea or new clothes or a subscription to the circulating library, they were keeping within their income.

Except that it was not their *full* income. Jude himself had earned four times as much as that, and perhaps more, and then there was the Lloyds' rent. They should have had an income close to a thousand pounds, and even Nell, untutored as she was in living costs, knew that a man could live as a gentleman on such a sum. Or even on half as much. The living at Bishopswood Cromby was worth five hundred a year, she knew, yet the Lumleys managed well enough on it. Mr Lumley even kept an old cob for riding about on, and they had three servants and a man for the garden, and plenty of tea.

It was too much to accept with any degree of equanimity. After all that Nell had suffered over the past few years, all Jude's rages if she spent too much or, even worse, if she spent too little and the meat was stringy or the wine watery, she could not believe how much they could have had. She jumped up and paced the room, back and forth, back and forth, her anger as bright as the sun. How dared he! How dared he keep her in abject poverty? How dared he rage at her for the smallest unnecessary expense and deprive her even of tea! How dared he lie to her, and lie again! Was anything he had told her true?

Such thoughts brought the bad memories flooding back. Every meal she had been in agitation, in case some trivial deficiency set him off. The soup was not salty enough — could they not afford salt? Or the wine was not to his taste, or the joint, or there were no nuts. Then there were the occasions when he had sat down at his little desk in the bedroom to work out his accounts.

That was the worst time. It would be quiet for an hour, maybe two, and then he would emerge with two or three bills in his hand. "What does this mean?" he would say. Or, "Why have we spent so much on butter... or currants... or cheese?" And she would try to explain... the hot weather... the dampness in the cellar... but haltingly, stumbling over her words. And he would storm out of the house, slamming every door he passed through, to find a tavern or tap room. Then she would wait, sick with terror, for him to return home. Sometimes he came home a little drunk, but repentant and affectionate. And sometimes... not.

She leaned her head against the wall, shaking, her arms wrapped across her stomach. Even now it lurched in fear, just from the memory. He is dead, she told herself, he is in a Cornish churchyard, and he can never hurt me again. But still she shook from head to toe.

Maria found her there, some time later, although whether hours or minutes Nell could not say, and led her gently to a chair.

"You would feel better for a good cry," Maria said. "It does no good to keep everything inside you like this, and not have a proper outlet. I have not seen one tear from you, and Nell, that is not usual when a woman loses her husband, whatever the circumstances."

"I never cry," Nell whispered. "But I cannot think, and that is the worst part. I have to think what to do and I cannot! My mind will not work."

"Give it time," Maria said. "You have to grieve, Nell. Your life has changed, and it takes time to adjust. Let yourself grieve."

"How do I do that?"

"You will find a way."

Maria hugged her tightly, but Nell could not respond. She could not move. She was frozen in place, like a waterfall in winter, an illusion of movement captured in solid ice. She appeared to be a living, breathing person but inside her heart was nothing but ice.

11: A Day In Portsmouth

Nathan wished a thousand times over that he had caught the mail coach from London. A post-chaise and four should have made the journey easily in three days, or perhaps two if he were lucky with changes and weather. In the event, luck had deserted him entirely. He suffered every conceivable kind of delay, with every part of the vehicle breaking at some stage, and the horses falling into a great variety of afflictions, such that he could hardly proceed for ten miles without some mishap. They did not overturn, which was the only mercy afforded them, and the whole journey took six days from start to finish, driving him into a frenzy of impatience. He hated unforeseen mishaps with a passion. Order... he must have order and calm, and this journey had none of either.

But he was in time. His cousin lingered on, and had even rallied a little.

"We have a new physician attending him," his cousin's wife Jessica told Nathan. "Not that we have any complaint about Dr Sykes, for he has always been extremely thorough which is *so* reassuring, do you not agree? However, we thought it advisable to have another opinion, and Dr Hay so impressed me with that business with the footman last year. Fixed him up when no one else had the least idea what to do for him, and we all thought the arm would have to come off. Hay is terribly modern, of course, and he brings his sister with him, which I cannot quite like, but there is no doubt that William is at greater ease now, and therefore Mama is, too."

"I have heard of Hay," Nathan said. "He has an excellent reputation."

"Oh, indeed. Everyone speaks most highly of him, and his hospital is doing such good work. Even Mama likes him, despite all his new ideas. He is distantly connected to the Bucknells, and therefore to Mama."

"Is he not married to one of the Marfords?"

"Lady Harriet, sister to the present Marquess of Carrbridge. Mama likes that, too, of course. She does like a man to have *connections.*"

Nathan chuckled, knowing of his aunt's fondness for the nobility. But then she was a duke's daughter herself, so it was hardly surprising if she preferred her own kind.

He went to see his cousin first, and was shocked by what he saw. William's skin was grey, and he lay motionless, every breath a rattle deep in his chest. He was asleep, but it did not seem like a natural sleep. Such a healthy, vigorous man he had been, but his chest had always been a weakness. Another man could take a chill and shake it off in a few days, but William would decline into fever and heart-rending bouts of coughing, and be bed-ridden for weeks. Then he would have years of perfect health before being felled by another chill. Yet this did not seem like his usual malady, and perhaps even Dr Hay's modern methods could not save him this time.

Aunt Amelie was in her usual chair by the fire in the saloon, protected from the strength of the flames by a screen of exquisite tapestry work, the product of her own, much younger, fingers. She sat upright, as always, her back never touching the padding on the chair, despite her advanced years. Five sons she had brought into the world, only to see three of them leave it before her, and now a fourth hovered on the brink. Only Felix remained, if he still lived.

"Ah, Nathan!" she said when he greeted her. "We were worried that you might have encountered some mischief on the roads. You must take care, for all our dependence is on you now."

Now that he had arrived safely, the grievances of the roads seemed of less moment, so he said, "A few delays, but nothing too serious. Besides, the difficulties of the journey are greatly to our advantage. What would the world come to if one could travel into Yorkshire without a single problem, eh? Why, we should be overrun with the curious and the idle, the inns would be full, the streets would be impassable and one would not be able to hire a postilion for a king's ransom."

She did not laugh — Aunt Amelie felt it beneath her dignity to laugh — but her lips moved slightly upwards in what, in lesser mortals, might be called a smile.

"What do you think of him?" she said. "He cannot last much longer, I am sure."

"William is not well, certainly, but he has recovered from positions almost as dire as this before. You despaired of him five years ago, do you recall? And yet he was entirely well again within a month. Consider, too, that the weather improves every day. Nothing is so conducive towards health as a spell of warm weather and sunshine."

"Moss says there is rain coming, and an easterly wind."

Nathan laughed. "Moss is an excellent lady's maid, Aunt, but I do not consider her much of an expert on the weather. Let her advise you on velvet and lace, but do not let her predict the weather. On my journey north, every ostler and tapboy told the same tale — warmer weather is on the way."

"Well, if you prefer to listen to ostlers and tapboys and other riffraff... But tell me at once — have you heard any word of Felix?"

"I have not," Nathan said. "Harry thinks we should advertise again, and I must say—"

"Harry Smethurst!" she said disparagingly. "I have nothing against him, for his family has been in Yorkshire longer than ours, but I would not take advice from him or his father. You could find better friends if you set your mind to it, Nathan. You should have gone to Oxford, as all the Harbottles do. You would have made a very good sort of friend there."

"I enjoyed Edinburgh, and I must take issue with you regarding Harry. No one could have a better friend."

"Hmpf," she said, not at all convinced. "A Squire's son?"

"You are a grumpy old lady," he said, planting an affectionate kiss on her lace-capped head. "Harry is a splendid fellow, and I will not hear a word said against him. But what of Felix? Shall I advertise again? Perhaps more explicitly this time?"

"If you think it necessary, although it is humiliating to confess that we have no idea where he is."

"It was the family which rejected him, remember?" Nathan said gently. "Felix wanted your forgiveness."

"I shall never forgive him, never!" she said, her voice strident. "What he did was unforgivable. But he is William's heir, so he must come home now, he must! Nathan, what are we to do if we cannot find him? The position is so... so *awkward!*"

"We will survive," he said easily. "William has arranged everything so that I have the power to manage the estate, so there will be no difficulty in that way."

"But the uncertainty, Nathan! I hate uncertainty."

"As do we all, but we will manage," he said. "We will pursue every avenue to find him, but if we fail, there are legal processes to have him declared dead. While that is going on, I shall have the management of the estate. There is nothing to worry about, aunt, nothing at all."

"Hmpf. You will have to marry," she said, her eye brightening. "A wife and a nursery full of children, that is what we need. One of the Grayling girls. Lady Anne or—"

"Oh no, not this again! I shall marry when I am ready, aunt — when I find the right woman," he said, smiling at her. "And it will not necessarily be a duke's daughter."

"Well, do not leave it too late, will you? At least tell me that you are thinking about it."

"I am thinking about it."

And instantly his mind's eye was filled with the vision of a certain widow, the most beautiful woman he had ever seen. How foolish, for she was not at all the sort of woman he liked, not a cosy, convivial armful, with flirtatious eyes. But she was extraordinarily beautiful... and her serenity was balm to his spirits.

~~~~~

Nell was in no rush to settle the routine household bills, for now that she had Jude's salary, there was enough money in the locked drawer in her dressing table to settle all of them whenever it suited her. Instead, she spent a little money on herself — a length of bombazine, and some black ribbons and buttons. She might be in mourning, but she need not wear rags.

However, one bill in particular nagged at her like an aching tooth — the solicitor in Portsmouth who presented his compliments to Mrs Caldicott, and would be obliged if she would settle the
~~~~~

outstanding amount on her late husband's account with them to the sum of twenty guineas.

Why would Jude engage a solicitor in Portsmouth? It was a puzzle, but there was only one way to find the answer.

"I shall be out all day tomorrow," Nell said one evening at dinner. "I am going to Portsmouth with Mrs Flack. Her carriage will be here at eight o'clock."

"Are you to visit Admiral and Mrs Flack too?" Lydia said.

"No, I have business in the town."

"Business? What business?" Lydia's voice was high with surprise.

"Private business," Nell said firmly.

"May I come too, Mama?" Louis said, and she saw the anxiety in his eyes.

Poor Louis! He had never seemed to be troubled by the family's difficulties, but then he had always slept through the worst of the rows. He went to bed straight after dinner and nothing woke him before morning. Sometimes he had awoken to find his mother injured and his father gone, but everyone explained it as an accident and he seemed to accept that. He was, perhaps, a little inclined to cling to Nell. If she went out, he would insist on accompanying her, often holding her hand painfully tight. He was terrified that she might have an accident, she supposed. He could not know that the danger of that particular type of accident was now gone.

"Very well, but you must be on your best behaviour. You may take a book to read."

She had considered travelling on the stage, but Tilly Flack went every week to spend the day with her brother-in-law, the Admiral, and allow her two daughters to play with their cousins, so Nell had no compunction in begging for a lift. Unlike Lydia, Tilly was too polite to enquire as to the nature of Nell's business in Portsmouth, so they passed the journey agreeably, and Nell's spirits rose with every mile further from Southampton.

Tilly shared one piece of good news — the formal inquiry in London into the *Minerva's* foundering had concluded that it was most likely the result of faulty navigational maps. Local men reported that the particular rock which had been the brig's undoing was an especially treacherous one, frequently hidden below the surface of the water, and not marked on older maps. Mr Sherrard confessed that, although he obtained updated maps frequently, and all the others he had checked marked the rock, he could not be absolutely certain that there were not older maps in use aboard the vessels of his fleet. Mr Blackwell, the Second Mate, who had commanded the helm at the time, was adamant that he had been following the prescribed course to the very best of his ability, and that no rock was marked on the maps he had seen. The deck boy had been asleep until the collision had woken him, and Mr Ellsworthy, the passenger who had also been on deck, was still too injured to attend the inquiry and besides remembered nothing at all, and so Mr Blackwell's version of events prevailed, and no blame was attached to Captain Caldicott.

So Nell was let down in the centre of Portsmouth in cheerful spirits. She had on her new gown of black bombazine, a reworked bonnet with splendid black ribbons, and her best pelisse. The latter was a little too warm for the day, but she did not regard the discomfort for the pleasure of knowing she looked well. Or as well as a new widow might be expected to look. Two gentlemen watched her pass by with open admiration, and that too gave her pleasure, even as she chided herself for her vanity.

Mr Blake's office lay in a discreet side street, one of a row of well-kept terraced houses, some of them taken up by expensive shops — a milliner, two mantua-makers and a boot maker. One house appeared to be an exclusive gentlemen's club. Mr Blake's establishment looked no different from the other residential houses, except for a small brass plaque beside the door. *'Gideon Blake, Solicitor'* was all it said. Nell rang the bell, gave her name to the smartly dressed manservant who answered and was admitted without question, since she had written ahead to announce her visit.

With Louis and his book happily ensconced in an outer office with the clerks and a jar of sugared almonds, Mr Blake received Nell in the sort of book room that would not have disgraced a lord's London residence. The plush carpets, the highly polished wood and gleaming silver, and the cases of leather-bound volumes bespoke a life of elegance, and an army of well-trained housemaids armed with feather dusters.

"Mrs Caldicott." He was a dapper little man, perfectly fitted to his surroundings. Not ostentatiously fashionable, but quietly and expensively well dressed. "Pray sit down. May I offer my deepest condolences for your recent sorrowful bereavement. How may I be of service to you?"

Nell was not accustomed to matters of business or finance, and in other circumstances such conversations would reduce her to quivering indecision. This opulent room, however, was exactly the environment in which she had been raised, and Mr Blake reminded her of one of her father's stewards from many years ago. He was, therefore, only a servant and she was Miss Godney of Daveney Hall, who knew exactly how to deal with servants — politely, but firmly.

"You sent me this bill, Mr Blake. I should like to know the meaning of it."

He took it from her, but without looking at it. "This, madam, is the bill for services rendered to your late husband by myself and my employees." He gazed back at her complacently.

"I rather gathered as much, Mr Blake," she said, sweetly. "What I should like to know is what precisely those services were."

"Ah, such details are confidential, madam," he said smugly. "They must remain secret between lawyer and client, as I am sure you will appreciate."

"Your client is dead."

"Regrettably that does not affect the position."

"Does it not? I am sure *you* will appreciate, Mr Blake, that I cannot sensibly pay a bill for who knows what, without a full reckoning of activities undertaken, expenses incurred and so forth. Why, anybody could send me such a bill, could they not? A man could present a bill to me, and claim that it is for services provided to my late husband, and perhaps no such services were ever provided."

Mr Blake's face did not change, and his tone was urbane. "You cannot mean to suggest that this bill is false?"

"Not at all, Mr Blake. No indeed, I am sure it is all perfectly correct. I merely point out that, without further information, I have no way to distinguish one bill from another, the true from the false. If my butcher presents me with a bill, why then I know perfectly well that I have eaten beef, so there is no difficulty and I will pay the bill without hesitation. But a bill such as this—"

"I understand you," he said, his smooth composure not slipping in the slightest. "Very well. I can perhaps tell you that Captain Caldicott's instructions involved the transfer of sums of money. *Discreet* transfer, if you understand me."

Sums of money! "How much money?" she said sharply.

"Mrs Caldicott, you cannot expect—"

She got to her feet and whisked the bill out of his hand. "Good day to you, Mr Blake."

He jumped up too. “Now, let us not be hasty. I am sure we—”

“How much?”

“Two hundred pounds each quarter day.”

“Where to?”

He licked his lips, then sighed. “An attorney in London. I do not know where it goes after that, believe me.”

London. Two hundred pounds every quarter.

“How long has this been going on?” she said.

“Sixteen years.”

For a moment, the world spun and Nell wondered if she were about to swoon. Instead she sat down again, very slowly. As if in a dream, she opened her reticule and pulled out the small purse that contained twenty guineas. Wordlessly she handed it over. In equal silence he counted the coins, took the bill from her, inked *‘Paid in full’* across it, sanded it and handed it back. Still in silence, she folded it, pushed it into her reticule, rose and made for the door.

Mr Blake rushed ahead to open it for her. “I am very sorry,” he said quietly.

Nell walked past him without another word. What was there to say? There was only one reason for a man to send regular sums of money in great secrecy.

Jude had had a mistress.

~~~~~

Nell drifted through the days, hardly knowing one day from another except for the regular arrival of the Sabbath. Easter came and went, and she barely noticed. All she could think about was that Jude had maintained a mistress somewhere, and had kept Nell and Louis in poverty so that *she* might live in comfort. Most of his income had gone to her, while Nell had suffered without tea, and had suffered in
~~~~~

other ways too. How... how *degrading* to be so unimportant in his life.

One day at breakfast, Maria said to her, "I am going to take Lucy and Jane down to the Beach for a walk beside the river. Why not come with us? And Louis too."

"I do not think—" Nell began.

"It would do you so much good to get out of the house," Maria rushed on. "Lord, Nell, you sit here day after day, doing nothing, seeing no one, going nowhere. It would do you the world of good just to see the sun and stretch your legs for a while. You will fade away to nothing if you do not make an effort. Please come."

And because it was easier to give in than to contest the point, she went. They walked down the High Street, Maria and the girls racing ahead then stopping at every shop window, while Nell drifted along behind them, Louis gripping her hand with painful intensity. He felt as she did, in his way, this strange disorientation, where the world looked and behaved the same, and yet everything was different. She was a widow, and Louis was fatherless, and Jude had had a mistress, and nothing would ever be the same again. All her certainty — the *only* certainty in her life — that Jude had loved her and only her, despite everything, was turned to dust and blown away, and now there was nothing left. She was an empty husk, all the life and energy sucked out of her by the man who had lied about everything. She had given him all she had to give, and he had betrayed her.

By the time they had passed through the God's House Gate and onto the Beach, the warmth of the sun and the benevolence of the soft breeze had begun to have their effect. She began to look about her, to notice the other people strolling about, to see the waters of the Itchen rolling past, to smell the familiar aromas of the river — of fish and salt and seaweed and a certain tang in the air that woke her at last from her deep slumber.

Maria and the three children scavenged along the shore for the sort of items of interest that river and tide were sure to throw out, while Nell sat gazing out of the water at the ferry and the shore beyond, her mind clear for the first time in weeks. She knew at last what she must do. Jude's betrayals were in the past. He was dead, and could not hurt her any more — not just physically, but in other ways. What did it matter that he had had a mistress, or that he had impoverished his lawful family to support her? The past had floated away downstream and need not concern her. She must look to the future now, her future and that of her son.

To set the past entirely to rest, she must force herself to take command of her life. She would look at Jude's clothes and see what could be adapted for Louis, and what could be sold. She must find a way to open the locked box under the bed. She must obtain a proper accounting of the mortgage from Mr Vessey, and determine how she might repay it.

It would be stating the case too strongly to say that all her confusion had evaporated, but she felt more alert and enthusiastic than she had for an age. For years, perhaps. As soon as she returned to the house, she would make a list of what needed to be done and then... then she would do it. She would learn to manage for herself. She could do it... she was not helpless, for she was Miss Godney of Daveney Hall—

But that was not true. She was neither a Godney of Daveney Hall nor a wife. She was Nell Caldicott, widow and mother, and her life was for her alone to make now.

12: Benefactors

Nell walked back up the High Street in better spirits than at any time since Jude's death… no, before that. She had been dull and listless for so long, but no more. She would make herself a pot of tea, and then she would begin taking command of her life.

The door opened to them even before they had reached it, and Becky's anxious face peeped out.

"Please, madam, and I hope I did right, but there's three gen'lemen to see you on a matter of business, lawyers, they are, and I put them in the dinin' room. Didn't seem right to take them up to the mornin' room, not with you not in the house, and it being business and all, and Mr Lloyd has the study, so I thought—"

"That is perfectly all right, Becky," Nell said, as they gained the hall. "But who are they?"

Wordlessly the maid held out a card. *'P Willerton-Forbes, of Markham, Willerton-Forbes and Browning, Gray's Inn, London'*, Nell read.

"I expect they are sent by my brother," she said, untying the ribbons on her bonnet. "I shall see them in the dining room."

"Do you wish me to be present?" Maria said. "Chaperonage?"

"It is not necessary for a discussion with lawyers. Louis, will you take my bonnet and gloves up to my room, if you please? Becky, please wait in the hall, in case I should need you."

Her assured manner was such that they obeyed her unquestioningly. She could dither for days or weeks about financial matters, yet at a moment's notice she could assume all the self-confidence of rank. Lawyers did not dismay her after her meeting with Mr Blake in Portsmouth, for nothing they said could be as shocking. She lifted her chin, opened the door and entered the dining room.

They were nothing like lawyers, that was her first impression. One man of ostentatiously fashionable style, another wearing the flamboyant colours of the Four-Horse Club, a sword at his side, and one in plain black, carrying a writing box. He was a secretary, but it was hard to see the lawyer in either of the others.

"Good morning, gentlemen," Nell said.

They turned, and the fashionable one stepped forward. "Mrs Caldicott?" She nodded. "Thank you for receiving us. Allow me to introduce myself. Pettigrew Willerton-Forbes. My father is the Earl of Morpeth. This gentleman is Captain Michael Edgerton, formerly of the East India Company Army, and this is James Neate, my secretary."

"Did my brother send you?" Nell said.

"We are not here for any family matter," Mr Willerton-Forbes said. "It is to do with the *Brig Minerva*."

Her stomach twisted in sudden fear. "The inquiry? I thought it was over."

"Indeed it is, Mrs Caldicott. I assure you our business is a more pleasant one."

"Then pray be seated, gentlemen." She took a chair in the centre of one side of the dining table. Willerton-Forbes sat down opposite her, and Neate placed himself at the far end of the table. He opened his writing box and laid out a notebook and pencil. Edgerton, meanwhile, did not sit, but lounged against the wall behind Willerton-Forbes.

"First of all," Willerton-Forbes said, "may I deal with the preliminaries? You are Mrs Caldicott, widow of Captain Judas Caldicott, commander of the *Brig Minerva?"*

"I am."

"Your maiden name, Mrs Caldicott?"

"Godney. I was Miss Helen Godney."

"And your father is—?"

"My father was Sir Lewis Godney of Daveney Hall. He died four years ago. My brother James is the baronet now."

Neate's pencil moved swiftly across the paper, taking everything down.

"Do you have your marriage lines, Mrs Caldicott?"

She was aware of a shiver of fear. Her marriage lines? An odd request.

There was a pause while she dispatched Becky for the box in her dressing table drawer which held all her important papers — her sketches of Mama and Papa, one of Jack as a baby and many of Louis, the few letters from friends since her marriage, the three letters Jude had sent her and her marriage lines. Willerton-Forbes examined the latter with interest.

"St Peter's at Bishopswood Cromby — that is your parish church at Daveney Hall, I take it? And the officiating minister, Mr George Lumley?"

"He is still there. Mr Willerton-Forbes, is there some question about my marriage?"

"Not at all, Mrs Caldicott, not at all. We are just collating all the relevant facts in order to determine that you are, in fact, the next of kin of Captain Judas Caldicott."

"And have you so determined?" she said, puzzled but also amused now.

"Indeed we have. In which case, I am now in a position to reveal to you a matter of great advantage to you."

"I am glad to hear it, for I have been short of matters of advantage to me lately," Nell said.

Willerton-Forbes nodded, his expression sympathetic. "I am sure you have, Mrs Caldicott. So let me keep you in suspense no longer. There is a person — let us call this person the Benefactor, for want of any other name — who has been greatly distressed by the events surrounding the *Brig Minerva.* Therefore the Benefactor has decreed that every survivor of the tragedy, and the next of kin of every person lost in the foundering, shall receive the sum of one thousand pounds, free of all constraints or restrictions."

"A thousand pounds?" Nell said, staring at him. "That is... a prodigious sum." What could she not do with a thousand pounds? Settle all Jude's debts, for one thing. Or invest it for... she worked the numbers swiftly in her head. Thirty or forty pounds a year. A useful increase in her income. And yet... free of all constraints? Was such liberality possible?

"It is indeed a generous amount. My very pleasant task is to dispense this largesse to all those qualified to receive it."

"A pleasant task indeed," she said. "One thousand pounds apiece? This Benefactor must be a very rich man."

"Or woman, perhaps," Willerton-Forbes said cautiously.

"You do not know?"

"I know nothing of the Benefactor, and nor does my head of chambers. But then I do not need to know who pays me in order to perform my appointed task, Mrs Caldicott."

Perhaps her head was full of Jude's mysteries, for she said, "But you must wonder, Mr Willerton-Forbes."

He smiled and steepled his hands. "Naturally I wonder, but all that matters is that I follow my instructions to the letter. I must tell you that I am empowered to make the gift available in whatever manner best suits you. I may place it in a bank account on your behalf, or invest it in the funds for you, or buy property or goods, if you should wish that. But if you wish to receive it as a roll of notes, then that is permitted, too."

"Oh. I do not know..."

"Naturally you do not, for this has come as a surprise to you, or I may even say it is a shock. A happy one, but a shock, nevertheless. Naturally you can make no decisions immediately. We will return in a few days to talk further with you on the subject, but you may take all the time you need to reach a decision. You may also request us to carry out any other tasks or offer advice on any subject which may arise as a consequence of your bereavement. That too is a charge laid upon us by the Benefactor."

"Any advice? Any tasks?"

"We are authorised to offer you whatever help you may stand in need of at this difficult time in your life, Mrs Caldicott."

She took a breath to speak, then released it again. Mr Willerton-Forbes watched her attentively, his eyes not straying from her face. Captain Edgerton watched her too from his post by the wall, one foot bent to rest against the wainscot. Mr Neate's pencil wrote on, then he stopped writing and lifted his head to gaze at her.

A laugh burst out of her. "That is the most ridiculous story I have ever heard! A thousand pounds? For everyone from the duke's brother down to Tom Kibble? Preposterous!"

Mr Willerton-Forbes' smile widened. "What is so ridiculous about it, Mrs Caldicott?"

"That any man — or woman — of sound mind would give away so much money. There were six and twenty persons aboard the *Minerva* when it sank, Mr Willerton-Forbes. Why would anyone give away six and twenty thousand pounds, and so indiscriminately?"

"The Benefactor's intent is charitable," Mr Willerton-Forbes said.

"That is a vast amount of charitable intent," Nell said, with another laugh. "Depend upon it, either the Benefactor is quite mad, or there is some other purpose behind the gifts, or—"

"Or?"

"Or there is no Benefactor at all. You will forgive me, gentlemen, but I have more important things to do than to listen to such taradiddles."

She swept out of the room, still laughing, but this time at the astonished expressions on their faces. It was the first time she had laughed properly since Jude's death. Even before that, there had been few moments of unalloyed amusement in recent years. Her light mood carried her upstairs, but the morning room was empty. Up again, and she found Louis sprawled on his bed, a book open, but his eyes were heavy after so much exercise on the Beach. Perhaps he would sleep.

Her own room was at the back of the house, where they had moved after the disaster, since the best bedrooms had to be given over to the Lloyds. It was small and gloomy, and even Jude's efforts at painting the walls a paler colour could not bring light and warmth to a room that had only one narrow window facing north. It contained but little furniture — the bed, a tiny closet to one side of the fireplace, a small desk and chair, and her dressing table, the only item of furniture she had insisted on keeping, since it had come from Daveney Hall. It was the only link now to her former life.

As she entered the room, all her buoyancy evaporated instantly. So many memories, and none of them good. There was grief here, and anger, and fear — so much fear! The furniture, the bed linen, the very walls exuded it, so that it washed over her, sapping her energy, whenever she entered. It was like a sponge which had soaked up all the misery of the last five years until it was so sodden that the excess seeped out unbidden. When she left the house, her spirits rose up and up, and when she returned they sank again, the small happinesses of the day leached out of her by this reservoir of pain. And it was all centred here, in this room.

Yet there was nowhere else, unless she crept off to sleep in the attic like a servant, and that she would not do. She was a woman of six and twenty, not a child, she was a mother and had been a wife, and she was mistress of her own household. She would not be cowed!

Taking a deep breath, then another, she sat down at the desk. Jude's desk. Her desk, now. She looked into the drawers, opened the lid and examined inside. A few scraps of paper, a couple of dried-up pens, an inkwell and a half-used bottle of ink. Two or three pencils, a sand shaker and a box of pounce. Sealing wax, string, a knife. Nothing else.

Well, that would not do. She threw away all that was unusable, then went downstairs and fetched some of her own supplies, the gift from Mr Harbottle. That was a good memory to add to the desk, a complete stranger who had taken an interest in her and had showed her a great deal of unsolicited kindness. He was a benefactor, too, like this supposed person handing out a thousand pounds apiece to relatives of the *Minerva* victims. There truly were people in the world who were unstintingly generous. After that, she collected up all the outstanding bills, and arranged them in piles on the desk. Then she sat down to count her money, and to determine how best to settle all her accounts.

She had not been working for long when the room's chill atmosphere began to make her shiver. There was no fire laid, for they had never been able to afford the luxury, so she went to the closet to find her thick shawl, the one Becky's mother had knitted for her that first winter after the disaster, when she had never seemed able to get warm. It was not elegant, but the colours were gentle, heathery tones and it was blissfully cosy. As she wrapped it around her shoulders, her foot brushed against something that made a crinkling sound.

The parcel containing Jude's clothes. She had tossed it into the closet, and there it had lain ever since, unopened and unregarded. Now she picked it up and walked across to the bed. *'Possessions of Captain Jude Caldicott'*, read the label. Could she bear to see the pathetic few rags that were all that remained of her husband? Yesterday, perhaps, she would have left the parcel where it lay, but today— today was different. It was only a nightshirt, after all.

She sat down on the bed, and carefully unpicked the knot so that the string might be kept. Then, with shaking hands she pulled aside the paper.

There was a shirt, it was true. She also found a waistcoat, some drawers, breeches and stockings. No boots, for he must have been in bed, but it was rather touching that he had not undressed. Was that usual on board ship? Did everyone sleep in their regular clothes, and only remove their boots? Or was this something unique to Jude, the captain always ready to be summoned in case of mishap? Except that he had not been summoned. The ship had hit the hidden rock and sunk almost at once. There had been no time to wake the captain, for his body had been found still in his bunk. The duke had been retrieved first, and then the captain. She had a vision of him sleeping peacefully on his side, his thick, blond hair in disorder, his face calm. How many times had she watched him sleep, eyes closed, the lashes lying against his cheeks? In the early years, her heart had ached with love for him, but latterly—

She would not think about that. As she picked up the shirt, it was stiff with salt. All Jude's clothes came home salt-encrusted, but this was something more, the feel of a shirt that had lain beneath the waves for a while. Everything was the same. One by one she examined each item, tried to remember Jude wearing it and failed. Then she put each into the basket for laundry.

All except the waistcoat. There was a heaviness about it that spoke of weighty objects in the pockets. She withdrew his pocket watch first, with his initials on the back. *'JC'*, engraved in an elaborately curled script. The silver had tarnished, and it had stopped at twenty minutes past three. That might be sold, perhaps. Some coins in another pocket. The new, practical Nell counted them — two pounds three shillings and sevenpence — added them to the piles on the desk and noted the amount on the paper. Then, more methodically, she went through the rest of the pockets. First, she came across the ring on a long metal chain that he had worn inside his shirt. It was his seal, with a design of a bag of money. *'Judas's thirty pieces of silver,'* he had told her. She slipped the chain over her head and tucked it under her gown.

Finally, she found the cameo portrait of her that Jude had had made not long after they married — *'So I shall always have you next to my heart, wherever I travel,'* he had said, and so it was, even now, carefully tucked into an inside pocket. How could she ever have doubted his love? She had seen the way he looked at her, the tenderness in his voice and his hands, the sincerity when he had told her she was his own dear love, that he had never loved anyone but her. Whoever his mistress might be, it was Nell he had loved, at least in the early days. Those first years together, when everything had gone well, then he had loved her truly. The cameo, kept next to his heart even as he slept, proved it beyond doubt. He had promised to sit for his own cameo for Nell to keep next to her heart, but somehow he never had, and now she had no image of him except the one in her mind.

That could be remedied. Impulsively she went downstairs to retrieve her box of charcoals from the morning room, and one of her last few sheets of drawing paper. After looking in on the sleeping Louis, she returned to her room, cleared the desk of bills and money, and settled to her task. It was not easy to draw a man who was not there. She had a thousand images of him in her head, but they seemed ephemeral, skittering away from her as soon as she tried to focus on them. For every memory of a happy, smiling, *loving* Jude there was another, harsher, vision that drove it away. How could she capture Jude as she wanted to remember him? He had been a loving husband only part of the time, and latterly hardly at all.

But as a father... he had always been a loving father. He had never been angry with Louis, or even impatient. His face had always softened as he looked at him. *'He reminds me of myself as a boy,'* he had said once. *'Oh, not in looks, and certainly not in brains, for I was never clever, but in little mannerisms. The sound of his voice, that little cough sometimes when he wants your attention but dislikes interrupting. The way he can do things just as well with either hand. The way he throws dice up in the air and catches them again.'* And she had laughed and said, yes, she had noticed that. The remembrance made her smile.

So she went through to Louis' room, and sat on the floor beside the bed while he slept, the only room in the house not tainted by Jude's rages. There she drew her only portrait of her dead husband. When she had finished, she tucked it away in the box in her dressing table drawer, and heaved a sigh of satisfaction, feeling that, in some strange sense, Jude had been laid to rest now. Her bedroom still oppressed her, and perhaps always would, but she felt a little lighter of heart.

She picked up the waistcoat, intending to take it down to Becky to be cleaned, for it was in good condition, and could be sold if the salt could be got off it. There was still a heaviness about it. She sat down again, and once more went through the pockets. Nothing. But her fingers could feel something solid through the lining, so she examined the pockets more closely, and found a concealed pocket within another one. When she tipped it up, out slithered a metal key.

The key to Jude's locked box under the bed. Did she dare open it and rummage through his most private possessions? What might she find in there? She had discovered enough secrets in Jude's life already, and she was very sure she wanted no more. But the household account books were in there, and those she did need. She would do it! She would know the worst of her husband. Before she could change her mind, she dragged the box out from under the bed, unlocked it and threw up the lid.

There were the account books in a neat pile, strapped together. But on top of the pile, tucked under the strap, was a letter, written in a hand she did not recognise, and sealed with an unfamiliar seal.

It was addressed to *'AB, Percharden House, Sagborough, West Riding of Yorkshire'*.

Who was *'AB'?* She knew of no one by those initials, nor did she know of anyone living in Sagborough. It was a puzzle.

The rest of the box contained only Jude's naval uniform — another puzzle, for if he had never been in the navy, why did he have the uniform of a captain in his possession? — and a small notebook in which were meticulously recorded the payments of two hundred pounds, which began more than twenty years ago and ceased at Christmas last. On the first page was inscribed: *'Payments to EP.'*

Now she knew that Jude's mistress had the initials *'EP'*.

13: An Unexpected Visitor

With Jude's salary in her possession, Nell spent two days visiting all the shops and warehouses and suppliers patronised by the family and settling the bills. Everywhere she went, she was greeted with undisguised delight. "So happy to see you out and about again," they said with wide smiles. "So very sorry to hear of Captain Caldicott's demise, but now we have the pleasure of *your* visits to look forward to." And in every shop, she was given a little parcel of ribbons or sultanas or a jar of beeswax. "In gratitude for your custom," they said, with many bows.

"You did not give my husband such a gift when he settled up with you," she said to the grocer, as she thanked him for the little packet of tea.

"Ah, no," he admitted. "But it is different with a gentleman, is it not?"

"Is it?"

"Oh, indeed. A gentleman will often question the bill in the greatest detail. The flour was not of the usual standard. The butter became rancid very quickly. And so on. A gentleman sees it as a matter of business, naturally. So there were adjustments to be made, you see. But a lady— ah, a lady is very different. So happy to see you looking so *well*, Mrs Caldicott," the grocer added. "And such wonderful news about this Benefactor. A thousand pounds! What a princely sum!"

"Indeed it is," she murmured.

"There is to be a service of thanksgiving at St Michael's for his benevolence," the grocer said.

"Or hers," Nell said.

"Hmm? Oh, oh yes, indeed."

As so often when she went out, Louis insisted on accompanying her, which resulted in his pockets filling up with small, sweet items. He did not normally have much of an appetite, but he had a sweet tooth, and exhibited an unaccustomed bounce in his step as they returned home.

"Why is there a man sitting on our steps?" he said as they drew near.

"I am more curious to know why he is drinking a cup of tea there," Nell said, bemused.

"Who is he?"

"I have not the least idea."

The man jumped up as they drew near, setting his cup and saucer carefully on the step. "There you are!" he cried, smiling broadly at Nell. "And this must be Louis. I am very pleased to meet you at last."

"But who are you?" Louis said, with all the directness of youth.

The man laughed. "Your mama knows."

For a moment Nell floundered. A young man of seventeen or eighteen years of age, tall, well-formed and with the sort of handsome countenance and easy manners as would please any young lady of similar age. Well dressed, although more for comfort than fashion. Hands with delicate, slender fingers that... that she recognised!

"Jack? *Jack!* Is it truly you? You were Louis' age when last I saw you. Oh, *Jack!"*

It was as well that he had put down his tea cup, for she hurled herself at him, throwing her arms as far round him as she could reach, scattering parcels in all directions. He scooped her up in a great bear hug, and then swung her off her feet and spun her round.

"How are you, sis? Lord, you have got so thin and peaky looking."

"And you have got—" She stopped, trying to catch her breath. "Great Heavens, Jack, you are so big! How you have grown!"

"True. Children do that, you know. Turn your back for nine years, and they shoot up like weeds."

"So they do," she said, beaming at him. "Louis, this is your Uncle Jack Godney, my younger brother."

"How do you do, sir," Louis said politely, making him a bow. Jack swept off his hat and made a sweeping bow in return.

"But what are you doing drinking tea on my doorstep?" Nell said. "You always went your own way, but that is eccentric, even by your standards."

That brought another easy laugh. "Ah well, I am instructed, on pain of some terrible penalty, not to cross your threshold. Now normally James's prohibitions would not trouble me greatly, but he knows me of old, and made me swear that I would not — on the Bible, no less! No ordinary swearing, this! And so here I am, sitting upon but *not* crossing your threshold, according to my given word. Your maid was so very kind as to supply me with refreshments while I awaited your return." He turned and beamed genially at Becky, hovering just inside the front door. She blushed, and bobbed a distracted curtsy. Jack had always been possessed of a casual charm, even as a boy, but clearly that power was not one whit diminished in the adult.

“I am astonished that James allowed you to come here at all,” Nell said.

“He did not want to, I assure you, but I told him I was coming whether he approved or not, and that if he tried to prevent me I should burn the house down around his stubborn ears. He was sufficiently in doubt of the outcome not to put it to the test.” He gurgled with merriment. “James is so easy to lead by the nose. Papa was much harder to gull. But we cannot talk on the street. Is there an inn where we may be comfortable?”

“The Dolphin Hotel, just round the corner.”

“Then let us leave your purchases with your charming maid, and go there directly.” The blushing Becky helped him to gather all the fallen packages, then watched them go from the top of the steps.

It was a full year since Nell had been inside the Dolphin Hotel to attend the Sherrards’ ball, and she had never been a regular patron. Nevertheless, she was recognised the instant she walked in. Jack secured a private room for them, ordered food and drink with great liberality and sat down opposite her with a huge grin on his face. Nell thought her own grin must almost match his. After her cold reception at Daveney Hall, she had never expected further notice from her family, but she had forgotten that Jack had always done as he pleased.

Louis watched his uncle with wide, unblinking eyes, not sure what to make of this previously unknown uncle. Nell had never talked much to him about his kin, for it had seemed cruel to talk about people he would never meet. Now in the space of a few weeks, he had met a whole swathe of relations.

"Jack, I cannot tell you how happy it makes me that you have come here to see me," Nell said. "I never expected it. I guessed you must be down from Oxford for Easter, but I never thought to see you here."

"Naturally, your gratitude is very pleasing," he said, " but in this case it is a trifle misplaced. It is not on your account that I came to Southampton. I am here because of Master Louis."

"Louis!" she cried. "What is your interest in Louis? Or is it to do with James's guardianship?"

"Not that, no. Something occurred a few days ago that caused all of us at the Hall a vast deal of puzzlement. A letter arrived for Louis from Yorkshire, and very expensive it was to receive, coming such a distance, and it is more than one sheet of paper, as well. Great was the curiosity aroused in more than one breast as to who might be writing to Louis from such a place, and why it was sent to Daveney Hall and not here. I determined to come here at once to discover all, and it is only because James's inquisitiveness is greater than his desire to disown you that I was permitted to come. So there you have it. Can you guess who your correspondent might be, young man?"

"I expect it is from Mr Harbottle," Louis said. "My friend," he added proudly.

"Your friend Mr Harbottle, eh?" Jack said, eyeing him with interest. "Does your friend write often?"

"He wrote to Mama, but he has never written to me before."

"Oh!" Jack said, eyebrows lifting. "He wrote to Mama, did he? Is he a friend of hers, too?"

"Yes," Louis said. "He gave her tea and he gave me a book."

"Did he, indeed?" Jack said, and now there was a definite quizzical look in his eye.

"Now, do not be making anything of it, Jack," Nell said. "He was in Southampton looking for a cousin of his, missing for a number of years. As the cousin was a naval captain, he was asking everyone who might have known him. Since Jude was away, he talked to me in his stead. He gave us some small gifts in gratitude for our hospitality, that was all, and Louis wrote him a letter of thanks while we were at Daveney Hall. Naturally he wrote back to that address."

"But he has written to you as well as to Louis?"

She frowned. "Really, Jack, you have no business to question me on such matters. Papa cast me out of the family, and James is determined to continue the tradition, so none of you have the least right to concern yourself in my affairs."

"I beg your pardon, Nelly. It was impertinent of me. Please forgive me."

And he made her a little bow, accompanied by a smile of such sweetness that she could not help laughing.

"Oh, you! As if anyone could be cross with you for long. But truly, there is nothing to make you anxious in Mr Harbottle's attentions. He visited twice as part of his enquiries, and then left town. When he heard about the *Minerva*, he came back to see if there might be any assistance he could offer. Finding me gone to the Hall, he left me a note, that was all there was to it. I daresay we shall never meet again."

To her surprise, the thought made her sad. Such a pleasant man, with so much admiration in his eyes. Not that such a matter was of any importance, yet… it had made her feel alive again, not this sad shell of a woman she had become. A friend… how she had needed a friend. Not Maria, who hugged her and cared for her when she was hurt but was just as timid as Nell was. No, she needed a strong friend, one who was unreservedly on her side, who could stand beside her against the hostile world. James would not fulfil that role, and Jack could not, but Mr Harbottle perhaps could. He wanted to, he had made that clear. What had he said? *'I remain your well-wisher and friend'*. He wanted to see her again, too. *'A letter to me at York will receive the earliest attention and my speedy arrival at your door. If it should suit you better, you may come to York and I shall show you my own charming town.'* York. Somewhere that was not Daveney Hall, not London, not Southampton. Somewhere with no memories at all. How she yearned for a place with no memories.

Jack waved a letter at her. "You had better read it first, Nelly."

She scanned the direction, and recognised the handwriting. "No, Louis may read it in perfect safety. It is indeed from Mr Harbottle, and he would say nothing inappropriate. Here you are, Louis."

Eagerly, he broke the seal, unfolded the two sheets and began to read.

Jack watched her with a raised eyebrow, but made no comment, although she guessed what he was thinking. "You feel that I put too great a trust in a man only very slightly known to me?"

"Only you may judge that," he said slowly. "I have never met him, and know nothing of him. He is a gentleman, presumably."

It was not couched as a question, but she answered it anyway. "He is. He has spent two years looking for his cousin, which he could scarcely do if he had some occupation constraining him, and his manners were very pleasing, very proper. Is your letter interesting, Louis?"

He nodded. "He is telling me about the York Minister."

"Who is the York Minister?"

"It is not a person, it is a place he went to at Easter."

"Ah. York *Minster*. A church... or cathedral, perhaps. A very fine building, and a wonderful place to attend Easter services, I should imagine."

"Here it is," Louis said. *"'The cathedral church of Saint Peter.'* He says the singing from the choir was as fine as any he had heard anywhere, and he wished you had been there to enjoy it, Mama, because he knows how much you like music and... and...I cannot quite read this part where it is folded."

Jack whisked it from his hand before Nell could protest. *"'It would have given me the greatest pleasure to share the experience with one who could appreciate the finer points of the performance and could express the same in words far better than my pedestrian efforts. I can say only that I found the occasion deeply moving and that is a sadly inadequate description.'* Hmm. Only very slightly known to you," he murmured, with a wry glance at Nell.

"Stop it!" she said, slapping his arm playfully. "Ah, Jack, how good it is to see you! But I suppose James will not allow you to come again?"

"I fear he will not. But Nelly, there are only three more years until I am of age and come into my inheritance from Great-uncle Gordon. Then I shall live at Dunstan Manor, and you shall come and keep house for me, and James will not be able to prevent it. Can you manage until then, do you think? I know you have not a great deal of money."

For a moment, hope rose up like a swelling tide. Three years! In three years she would be rescued from the misery of counting pennies and shivering over unlit fires. But just as quickly common sense reasserted itself. "What, and have you cut off from James and the rest of the family too? No, I could not allow it. Besides, in time you will find yourself a pretty wife, who will not want your widowed older sister in the house, so I should have to move on again. Jack, I have a house of my own, enough money to live upon, if I am very careful, and my own life to lead. I am glad that Louis will get the education he deserves, but for myself, it is better if I am not dependent on your charity."

"As you wish," he said easily. "The offer will remain open, and once I am free of James's restrictions, I may come and see you whenever I like, and you may visit me at Dunstan. I shall certainly be able to send you money — fifty or a hundred a year. And who knows, perhaps you will not need my help at all by then. Perhaps you will be married to your admirer from York."

"What nonsense!" Nell said, robustly. She waited until Louis was engrossed in his letter again before adding in a lower tone, "Do not say such things, especially before Louis. I shall never marry again, Jack, and so I must learn to live on my widow's mite."

He nodded, and patted her hand in ready sympathy. "Of course. At least your mite will be a comfortable one, since you will have an additional thousand pounds from this mysterious Benefactor. That is a great gift to bestow."

Nell only laughed.

~~~~~

The lawyer came again, naturally. Lawyers had, among many disagreeable traits, the habit of persistence, although in this case it was very much to Nell's advantage. They met in the dining room again, and this time Mr Willerton-Forbes placed a roll of notes on the table.

"One thousand pounds," he said. "These notes will be acceptable at any of the town's three banks. Does this convince you of the Benefactor's existence, Mrs Caldicott?"

"Oh, yes!" she said, picking up the roll, and feeling the solidity of it. "This is convincing evidence indeed, sir. You must think me
~~~~~

quite mad, but indeed it sounded ridiculous to my ears. I had spent the weeks since my husband's death seeing desperate poverty bearing down on me, so when you came along and offered me a thousand pounds without conditions… it seemed far too good to be true. Since then, of course, I have heard of many others who have received the Benefactor's munificence, so I have come to acknowledge that I was mistaken. Happily so, in this case."

"So you will accept your share of that munificence?"

"Most willingly. What must I do with it? It is too much to keep in my stocking drawer."

"Such a sum is best deposited with a bank, Mrs Caldicott, and at once, if I may suggest. Now that the Benefactor's purpose has been revealed, there are persons of ill-intent who are watching all those eligible to receive the gift, looking for an opportunity to prey upon them. If you wish to deposit your bounty in a bank, we will accompany you there at once. We need fear nothing when Captain Edgerton is with us."

So it was that Nell found herself sitting once more in Mr Vessey's bank, and this time the meeting was far more agreeable. Madeira was poured, she was congratulated on her unexpected acquisition of wealth, the roll of money was rushed away to be secured in the vaults and a clerk wrote out the record of the transaction.

"And now you will wish to settle your husband's debts, Mrs Caldicott," Mr Vessey said, with a rumble of laughter. "Start afresh. Clean sheet. Et cetera."

"This gift is for Mrs Caldicott alone," Mr Willerton-Forbes said. "There is no need—"

"It is quite all right," Nell said. "This money is for me to do with as I please, is it not?"

"Indeed it is."

"Then it pleases me to settle my husband's debts. You gave me a reckoning of the outstanding mortgage, Mr Vessey, so you may take that amount, and the twenty seven pounds the account is in debit."

"Most gracious," Mr Vessey said, "but there is also the matter of interest." He laughed, his whole body quivering with merriment.

Mr Willerton-Forbes raised an eyebrow, and looked as if he would speak, but Nell forestalled him.

"You said nothing to me of interest, Mr Vessey, therefore I shall pay none. You may take the amount we agreed, or nothing. The choice is yours."

Mr Vessey opened his mouth, then closed it again. "Thank you, Mrs Caldicott. I shall take the principal amount, plus the twenty seven pounds."

He did not laugh.

"You are a lady of formidable courage," Mr Willerton-Forbes said, as he and the captain accompanied Nell home again. "Mr Vessey struck me as an unpleasant, encroaching sort of fellow, and I very much enjoyed your put down of him."

"Such men look at me and see only a timid, impoverished widow," she said. "At such times, I remember that I was once a Godney of Daveney Hall, and that strengthens my resolve not to be browbeaten. I may not be rich or of any importance in the world, but I am respectable and God-fearing, and therefore entitled to be treated honourably by everyone, even bankers."

And even her husband, she realised, with a sudden spurt of anger. Especially her husband.

14: A Journey North (May)

MAY

Nell's money worries were at an end. With the residue from the Benefactor's thousand pounds, the modest annuity Mr Sherrard had arranged for her, Maria's annuity and the rent from the Lloyds, she found herself with an income of almost two hundred pounds a year. She had discovered some waste in their expenditure which might save a little money, too, and she could still take pupils for music lessons to make a few extra pounds, if she wished. There would be no need to do without tea in the foreseeable future.

No sooner had the service of thanksgiving been held in gratitude for the benevolence of the Benefactor than alarming tales began to circulate concerning the recipients of the gifts. The widow of the *Minerva*'s carpenter had been burgled, although the thieves had not discovered the hiding place of her money. The cook's mother had been defrauded of twenty pounds by a man who came to her door and said her husband had owed him money. Mr Blackwell, the Second Mate of the *Minerva*, who by the greatest good fortune had survived his ship's foundering, had been attacked outside his house by ruffians in broad daylight. Everyone had suddenly acquired a great many friends, and long-lost relations had decided to visit, to congratulate the recipient in person. Nell's household was not exempt, for Maria had found a complete stranger in her kitchen, rifling through cupboards and drawers.

"As if anyone would keep a thousand pounds in my knife drawer," she said, roused to righteous ire. "It is all in the bank, I told him. There is not a farthing of it here. He just *grinned* at me, like an idiot, so I went for him with my mixing spoon. Pity it wasn't the rolling pin or the carving knife, but the spoon was what I had in my hand. Still, he will not be back in a hurry."

"Just as well it was not the carving knife," Nell said. "I should not like you to be sent to the Assizes for murder."

Maria only giggled. She was beginning to be more bold, just as Nell was, and perhaps for the same reason. Jude's unpredictable moods had affected everyone in the household. Maria was more adventurous with her dishes at dinner, now that she had a slightly larger budget to work with. She had even suggested offering meals to paying customers.

"Mr Lloyd has some friends for cards two or three times a week, and he would like to offer them a good supper — something tasty, you know what men are like," Maria told Nell. "It would be no trouble, in fact I should enjoy it, and we should make a little extra money from it. What do you think?"

"I do not quite know what to think," Nell said. "I am not sure about opening up as a chop-house."

"Oh, no, no, no," Maria said. "Nothing like that. A few very select friends of Mr Lloyd's, that is all. A modest supper of lightness and delicacy, very refined, and a bottle or two of a decent claret, nothing too elaborate. We could make a few shillings a week on the business."

"Let me consider it," Nell said.

Lessons were over one day, but the spring weather was so fine that Nell could not bear to be indoors. She had a new pelisse, too, in fine merino wool, which was just the thing to wear for a walk beside the river. She could consider Maria's proposal, and try to distract herself from the mysteries of Jude's life. Louis insisted on going, too, but she never minded his company.

However, as she opened the front door, Nell found Mr Willerton-Forbes coming up the steps, with Captain Edgerton two paces behind. Having established that she was pleasure bound and not rushing off on an errand, they begged leave to accompany her. As they walked down the High Street, Mr Willerton-Forbes made polite conversation with Nell, while Captain Edgerton devoted himself to the task of entertaining Louis with increasingly outrageous tales of his time in the East India Company Army.

"He is very inventive," Nell said in an undertone to Mr Willerton-Forbes. "Is any of that true?"

"All of it," Willerton-Forbes said, with a smile. "Captain Edgerton has led a very colourful life. Or perhaps he has the knack of attracting colourful characters about him. The Tiger Blythe of whom he now speaks is perfectly real and a very charming lady, despite all the shooting of elephants and tigers. I have met her myself, for she is now Lady Humphrey Marford."

"A week ago I would have disbelieved every word," Nell said. "The world is a strange place, Mr Willerton-Forbes."

When they had passed beyond the town's walls and reached the area known as the Beach, Captain Edgerton took Louis to the river's edge while Mr Willerton-Forbes and Nell walked along the path a little higher up.

"You wished to speak to me on some matter, Mr Willerton-Forbes?" Nell said. "I had thought our business was concluded, and most satisfactorily."

"Indeed it was, but events have occurred... You will have heard, I daresay, of the problems which have arisen for those who have received gifts from the Benefactor. We are doing all we can to help by making it widely known that these large sums of money are safely in the vaults of the various banks, but there is still an assumption that the recipients will have more money about them than before. I imagine you have more coins in your reticule at this moment than would have been the case a month or two ago, is it not so?"

She nodded ruefully. It warmed her heart to walk about with several pounds in her purse, just as she used to, years ago.

"Exactly so," he said. "Since you are well known in the town, that makes you prey to every rogue and pickpocket for miles about. Nor do you have a man on hand to protect you. My advice, therefore, is to leave Southampton until the fuss has died down. Do you have anywhere you might go? A relation or friend who would take you in for a while?"

"Leave Southampton?" That was unexpected, yet she could see the sense in it. But where could she go? "I have no friends beyond this town, not any more." Even as she spoke the words, she thought of Mr Harbottle, but that would not do. She could hardly stay with a single gentleman. "And my family... no, that will not be possible, either. My brother has chosen to follow our late father's decision to pretend that I was never born, and there is no one else I could turn to."

"Ah. That is a pity. Yet you visited your brother recently, I understand? He sent you home laden with gifts. Or perhaps my information is faulty. One hears rumours, but sometimes they are far from the truth."

"No, it is true, but he is bound by a deathbed promise to Papa. When we parted, he told me never to return, but to seek out my husband's family if I need aid. How I am to do *that* I cannot imagine," she added in sudden bitterness. "They live in Ireland, but I have no direction for them, no idea even of the town where they might be situated. It is impossible."

"Your husband was a gentleman, I understand? Everyone speaks of him so, and at the inquiry into the sinking of the *Minerva*—"

"You were there?"

"I have read the reports," Willerton-Forbes said. "He was described as a gentleman and a ship owner at one time, but one who had come down in the world. There was some difficulty in tracing his naval record, but he was widely acknowledged as a fine seaman. All those who had sailed under his command spoke of him in the highest terms. And if he was a gentleman, there should be no difficulty in tracing his family in Ireland."

Nell hesitated, but there was something about Mr Willerton-Forbes which invited confidences. "He was certainly a gentleman, although he seldom talked of his family or his own history. Indeed, his whole life is shrouded in mystery, Mr Willerton-Forbes, and it is the most painful shock to me how little I knew him. He possesses a naval uniform, yet he was never in the navy. We were in desperate financial straits, yet he supported a mistress to the sum of eight hundred pounds a year. He loved me, of that I am certain, and yet... yet he was not kind to me."

"I have heard something of that," Willerton-Forbes said softly. "Yet he was raised as a gentleman."

"Of that I am sure. Once or twice he mentioned the house where he grew up. It had a ballroom, or perhaps a saloon or gallery that might be used in such a way. He liked to see a lady in a ball gown, he said, for it reminded him of his mama. The house was smaller than Daveney Hall, he told me once, and the library a great deal smaller, but it was more elegant, with greater symmetry."

"Then it should be an easy matter to find the family. Should you wish us to make enquiries? I believe Captain Edgerton has acquaintances there. He has acquaintances everywhere, which is very useful. It is part of our remit to assist the beneficiaries in whatever way we can."

"That would be excessively kind, and I should be very much obliged to you," she said. "I do not believe we shall require any assistance from them now that I have money in hand, but I should like Louis to know his kin. As for leaving Southampton—" Abruptly, she knew where she would go. She stopped, and turned to face the lawyer with a smile. "I shall go to Yorkshire. Louis wishes to see the cathedral at York, I have a letter to deliver, and I have a friend there. An acquaintance, anyway."

"A letter to deliver?" the lawyer said, chuckling. "You do not trust the mail?"

"It was in a locked box under the bed," Nell said, "along with my husband's fraudulent naval uniform and the record of his payments to his mistress. All the things he wanted to hide from me. I should very much like to know my husband's connection to this unknown person in Yorkshire, who has the initials *'AB'*."

"It would be my pleasure to help you to plan your journey, Mrs Caldicott. And I approve of your choice. Yorkshire is a great distance from Southampton. You should be perfectly safe there."

~~~~~

The journey was long, but it was neither arduous nor tedious. Mr Willerton-Forbes, through the agency of the Benefactor, arranged
~~~~~

for them to travel post up to London. They had the company of another *Minerva* widow as far as Guildford, where she and her three daughters were to stay with her sister. After that, Nell and Louis travelled on alone. Louis had never journeyed so far before, and Nell not for many years, so every mile brought new delights for them to enjoy, new vistas to feast their eyes upon, villages and small towns, rivers and woods and rolling hills, all in the finest spring greenery.

London was as it always was — big, noisy and foul-smelling, filled with the chaos of busy streets and vast numbers of inhabitants rushing here and there on business too important to care much about the arrival of one widow and her young son. Even so, the liveliness was exhilarating to Nell after her quiet life in Southampton. They were met in Holborn by one of Mr Willerton-Forbes' lawyer colleagues and his wife, who escorted them to Charing Cross where they were to stay overnight before leaving for the north.

"There has been a small change of plan, Mrs Caldicott," the lawyer said. "There is a client of ours, a widow like yourself, who is going to Yorkshire also, travelling post. She would be delighted to have company on the journey. I took the liberty of accepting the offer on your behalf. She is a most agreeable lady, and it will be a great deal more comfortable for you to travel post than by the stage. Mrs Young will defray all the expenses of the horses and postilions, so you will only have your inn costs to find."

Nell envisioned an elderly woman, perhaps maternal enough to take an interest in Louis, but otherwise not likely to be good company. She was startled to discover that Mrs Young was a rather pretty woman of four or five and twenty, and determined to enjoy her widowhood to the utmost.

"I was a good and dutiful wife for seven years, and never went anywhere or saw anyone, so now I shall make up for lost time," she said, with a gurgle of merriment. "You can do so, too, if you wish.

Was your husband horrid? Henry was not exactly horrid, for he quite doted on me and gave me so many jewels and gowns, anything I wanted, nothing was ever like it! Still, it is not pleasant, being married, is it? A wife must do as her husband bids her, whether she wishes it or not. We are better off without them."

Such a declaration pressed Nell's conscience powerfully. In part, she could not help but agree with it. She was better off without Jude's rages, his violence against her. But she could only regret the loss of her loving husband. For four years, until the disaster overwhelmed them, Jude had loved her passionately and she him, and nothing could ever replace that. Then there was Louis, who had lost his father — how would that affect him in the years to come? Would a fine education compensate for the lack?

But there was no time for introspection, for Mrs Young rattled on at a great pace. She told Nell that she had an ample jointure and had declined the offer of a dower house, choosing instead to spend her time staying with one relative or another, and moving on whenever she felt like it.

"Or when they grow tired of me," she said, laughing. "But there is always another aunt or cousin or great-uncle to visit. Lord, how I love visiting! But I shall be glad to get back to Yorkshire again. The moors are so beautiful at this time of year. So delightful, and empty of people. I am very tired of people, Mrs Caldicott. I have been in the metropolis for more than a month, and it feels like forever. I am quite worn out by it. So now I am going to my sister-in-law, who lives in a tiny village in the North Riding, and very peaceful it will be, too. But there, I daresay that I shall be tired of being peaceful in a few weeks and shall long for the excitement of the town." She laughed heartily at the thought. "But I do wish I had some acquaintance or other in Bath. I have never been there, and I long to go. I know no one there I might stay with, however. It is most unfortunate."

All this and much more she told Nell before they had even reached Barnet, and she chattered on unstoppably as the carriage rolled along the road to the north. Still, she was inoffensive and required no response from Nell, for which she was grateful. As the lawyer had predicted, it was a more comfortable journey than the stage, with a fresh team waiting at every change and an excellent dinner provided at their overnight stops. Mrs Young's own lady's maid, a rather stiff woman of above forty, attended to Nell as well, and would accept no vails, being, as she explained, excessively well paid already.

Mrs Young was very happy to make a small detour to Sagborough.

"Oh, Sagborough! That is where I used to live! Just fancy you going there — such a coincidence. Do you have many acquaintances in the town?"

"No one," Nell said, then, to deflect any further questions, she added, "I have business in the town, to do with my late husband's affairs. We shall only stay for one night, and then go on to York to see the historic sites."

"Oh, attorneys and such like, I suppose. Such matters are most disagreeable. You must stay at the Carrbridge Arms, for that is quite the best establishment in Sagborough. Do not go to the King's Head, it is far too rowdy there."

The Carrbridge Arms looked to be no better and no worse than any other inn, and not noticeably different from the King's Head which they had passed earlier on the main street. However, Mrs Young alighted and was immediately recognised and treated with great deference by the various servants who emerged to attend them.

"You must provide Mrs Caldicott with every comfort, Wainwright," she said to the innkeeper. "Your best room, and not one of those looking out to the yard, for they are far too noisy. Mrs Caldicott is my particular friend, so I expect you to pay her every attention, do you hear? Well, my dear, I must leave you here, for I have some distance yet to travel today. Wainwright and Mrs Wainwright will take good care of you, only do not eat the fish except on Fridays and Saturdays, for the fish barge only comes once a week and it will not keep, not in this warm weather. Mrs Wainwright's game pie is to be recommended, however. Quite famous locally for her game pies, is Mrs Wainwright. Oh, just one more thing before I go..."

There were several more things, in point of fact, but eventually she was got back into the carriage and driven away. Despite the lengthy farewell, when Nell and Louis had had something to eat and had settled into their room overlooking a narrow field and a canal, it was still only an hour after noon.

"What do you say to a walk, young man?" Nell said to Louis. "You have slept in the carriage the whole way, so if you tell me you are tired, I shall not believe you. Shall we go and find Percharden House?"

Louis nodded.

15: A House In Mourning

A maid set them in the right direction, and Nell and Louis began walking. Sagborough was not a prepossessing town. It had no ancient edifices or monuments to admire, no great boulevards or parks or palaces to boast of. Beside the canal and along the York road clustered warehouses and small manufactories and craft shops, in the centre were several fine churches, a number of better houses and the principal shops, but the western edge of the town was quieter, the larger buildings giving way to well-kept smaller properties with leafy gardens, orchards and fields. Before long, they came to a high wall on one side and, a little further on, a pair of gates, the gatepost bearing the words *'Percharden House'*.

Nell opened the gate and they entered the grounds. The drive strode away from them in a straight line, with pairs of trees marching either side of it in regimented precision. Heaven forfend that a tree should droop out of alignment or fail to grow at the exact angle required. In the far distance, a glimpse of grey stone could be discerned.

Louis sighed.

"Not much further now," Nell said cheerfully. Her spirits always rose when she ventured onto such properties. Such places were where she had been raised, and where she felt most at home. She was always Miss Godney of Daveney Hall at such times.

Louis held tight to her hand as they walked. Abruptly, he stopped.

"Chicken!" he cried, pointing through the trees to a lawned area. "Blue chicken!"

Nell laughed out loud. "That, Louis, is a peacock. Do you see his long tail? If he were to lift it up, you would see how beautiful it is. Is he not a lovely colour? Your Grandmama had a ballgown once that was just that colour. It was magnificent. I do not think he is inclined to show us his tail. Shall we walk on?"

They emerged from the tree-lined drive to find the house immediately before them. It was everything that Daveney Hall was not. Instead of mellow stone and ancient irregularity, Percharden House was austerely modern, a single long building in grey stone, and to Nell's eyes, very plain. But Louis gazed upon it with awe.

"It is straight," he said. "A straight house. I like it."

It was true that everything about it was constructed on straight lines. Even the approach to the house, so often arranged as a circle for the convenience of carriages, was here a square edged with rigid topiary. Hand in hand, Nell and Louis crossed the open expanse of raked gravel, finding themselves dwarfed by the vast columns flanking the steps to the entrance, the pediment several storeys above them.

It was only when they had tramped up the many steps to reach the door that Nell realised that the knocker was swathed in crepe, indicative of a recent death in the family.

While she stood, uncertain whether to retreat at once, the huge mahogany door opened. A very tall butler gazed down at her.

"Good day, madam. Please come in."

Momentarily lost for words, Nell entered the house, Louis still clinging to her hand. The entrance hall was every bit as grandiose as the portico, and although Nell considered it starkly plain, Louis stared around him with apparent pleasure.

"I beg your pardon," Nell said to the butler. "I had not realised the house was in mourning, or I should never have intruded upon the family's grief."

The butler was too well-trained to show any surprise, but he said, "You are not here, then, to offer condolences?" No doubt he had been confused by Nell's widow's blacks, and assumed she was a family member.

"I am not." She hesitated. It was impossible now to call upon the residents of the house and enquire into the meaning of the letter and why it was amongst Jude's things, but she could not sensibly withhold it from the intended recipient. "My only object was to deliver this letter," she said, producing it from her reticule and handing it to the butler.

At once, his impassive demeanour gave way, and he uttered a cry of astonishment. "Oh! Her ladyship has been awaiting this most anxiously. You must give it to her yourself, madam."

"Impossible! I cannot disturb a lady in mourning, not when I am wholly unconnected with the family."

"No, no, you must," he said eagerly. "It will cheer her tremendously. Please — let me take you to her. She will wish to thank you personally."

Nell could not easily refuse, and perhaps there would be a cup of tea offered, which would be most refreshing after her walk. She inclined her head in acquiescence, and the butler led them into a large room leading directly off the hall. It was, like the rest of the house, starkly rectangular and decorated with subdued simplicity, nor did the furnishings soften the severity of the effect, for the chairs and sofas were arranged with great regularity into squares.

"Straight," Louis muttered under his breath, and Nell could only agree.

The butler crossed the room to the massive hearth, where a fire burned despite the warmth of the day. "The letter has arrived, my lady," he said, his excitement evident. "A little late, but it is here."

The object of his address was a very elderly lady, richly garbed in black twilled sarsenet. She was quite wizened and frail, yet she sat rigidly upright in her chair. "The letter? At last!" The butler handed it to her and she turned it over and over, feeling the seal, then running her fingers over the direction, as if she could scarcely believe her eyes. "Read it to me, Craven. Read it at once."

Nell and Louis stood, unregarded, near the door, still hand in hand, Louis gazing about him with avid curiosity, while Nell watched the little drama taking place beside the fire. This letter was long awaited? That was unexpected.

The butler took the letter from the old lady, broke the seal and unfolded it. *'My dearest AB, There is snow today. After weeks of balmy days with the illusion of spring, now we are plunged back into winter again. God is teasing us, is He not? He gives us snowdrops and daffodils and primroses and catkins all over the bushes, and then He blasts them all with icy winds and buries them in snow. Even the rivers are trimmed with ice, and all the roofs sport great icicles like crystal daggers waiting for the butcher's boy to pass beneath before they drop, silently lethal. But as soon as the sun emerges, they drip-drip-drip, the drops falling from the sky like diamonds. I should like to gather them up where they fall and make a chain of them for you to wear about your neck, but as soon as I reach for them, they are gone. Life is like that, is it not? One may have the most beautiful, precious object in one's hand, and cherish it above all things, and yet it may still be broken or tarnished or lost. Men are careless creatures, and often we destroy the very thing we love above all others, and then everything changes. The warm days of summer give way to the icy blasts of winter, which will, in their turn, eventually yield to spring again. Only one thing never changes, and that is the affection of your ever loving son, Felix."*

Felix! How strange to hear that name again, and in such different circumstances, although... was it possible that this was the same Felix Harbottle whom Mr Nathan Harbottle had been seeking? The one who wrote but once a year to his mother, and always from a different port? Perhaps it was supposed to be Southampton this year. It was too confusing, to have two disparate worlds collide in this unforeseen way.

The old lady laughed in delight, and clapped her hands excitedly. "He never fails me, Craven. The mail may be erratic but Felix never fails me."

"This did not come by the mail, my lady. It was delivered by hand. The lady who brought it is here now." He waved Nell forward imperiously. "This is the lady."

"Come nearer, pray," the old lady said, peering vaguely in Nell's direction. It was only as she drew closer that Nell realised that the eyes that gazed out from the wrinkled face were sightless. That must be why the furniture was arranged with such angular precision, to present fewer obstacles. "May I ask to whom I am indebted for the service of bringing my son's letter to me?"

"I am Mrs Caldicott, my lady, from Southampton, the widow of Captain Jude Caldicott." She curtsied, and Louis, still holding her hand, bowed. "The letter was found among my late husband's possessions, and as my son and I needed to leave Southampton for a while, I thought to bring the letter here and see if I may discover my husband's connection to your family."

"From Southampton? And your husband is a captain in the navy?"

"His command was mercantile, not military, my lady."

"Nevertheless, I believe there is no mystery regarding your husband's connection to my son. Felix has been severed from his family for more than twenty years now, but every year, around the time of my birthday in April, he writes to me to reassure me that he is still alive. Every letter arrives from a different port, and clearly Southampton was the chosen port this year. Felix gave the letter into your husband's care, to be taken to the post at the appropriate date. That was not done, since your husband died. When did he die?"

"February, my lady. May I ask... is your son the same Felix who was sought by Mr Nathan Harbottle?"

"You know Nathan? Ah, he was in Southampton recently, was he not?"

"He was. Then you are a Harbottle too!" Nell cried. "You are Lady... something Harbottle?"

The old lady laughed. "Did you truly travel all the way from Southampton without knowing to whom you were to deliver this letter? But then it is addressed only to *'AB'*, is it not? My initials, written into all my books, and so Felix always addressed me. *'Dearest AB,'* he always called me. Lady Amelie Bucknell I was born, but now I am Lady Harbottle. The Dowager Lady Harbottle, that is, for my daughter-in-law is Lady Harbottle also. Wait— Did you say your name is Caldicott?"

"It is, my lady."

"Then you are the lady of whom Nathan spoke, of whom he was so anxious, the one whose husband—" She stopped abruptly. "Mrs Caldicott, please sit down... in this chair close beside me, if you would be so good, for then I can see you just a little — the outline of your face, splashes of colour. Ah, now I see your widow's weeds, just like mine. You have lost a husband recently and I my oldest son just a week ago today. He was buried two days ago, the very last of my sons, excepting only Felix. Five sons I brought into the world, and only one now remains to me. We are alike in our mourning, are we not?"

Nell had to smile at the comparison, she in her cheap bombazine and Lady Harbottle in the finest silk.

"Craven, bring some refreshments for Mrs Caldicott." As the butler crept away, Lady Harbottle started suddenly. "There is someone else here." She moved her head this way and that, trying to see.

"This is Louis, my son. He is eight years old."

Louis bowed again.

"He was so quiet I did not realise he was in the room. Children are not usually so soundless. Come nearer, child. Nearer still, so that my ancient eyes may see you. Ah, there you are. Young man, there are some interesting objects in the glass case near the leftmost window. You may examine them and commit to memory all that you see there. Then you may tell me what you have observed."

Louis looked to Nell for permission. She nodded and he scampered away.

"Now, Mrs Caldicott—" Lady Harbottle began, but before she could continue, the door opened and another woman in black entered the room. Nell jumped to her feet.

"Mama! Craven tells me you have received your letter at last." She was tall and long-limbed, an attractive woman in middle age. Nell guessed her to be not much above forty.

"Ah, Jessica, do come and meet my most surprising visitor, who has brought my letter to me all the way from Southampton. This is Mrs Jude Caldicott."

"Caldicott!"

"My daughter in law, Lady Harbottle, Mrs Caldicott."

Nell curtsied low, but the younger Lady Harbottle exclaimed, "Are you Nathan's Mrs Caldicott? Surely it cannot be!"

"I did indeed meet Mr Nathan Harbottle in Southampton," Nell said, and explained again how the letter had come into her possession.

"But what an extraordinary coincidence, is it not?" the younger Lady Harbottle said. "That the very person Nathan spoke of, who knows nothing at all of Felix, should be the very means of bringing your letter to you, Mama."

"Not a coincidence at all," the dowager said. "Nathan has talked to everyone who might ever have known Felix. It is hardly a surprise that one of them should turn out to have this year's letter."

Louis reappeared at Nell's elbow, tugging frantically at her sleeve. "What is it, Louis?" she whispered.

"Are you finished, young man?" the dowager said. "Come here, and tell me all that you saw in the glass case. I wager you will not remember all of them."

"I can," Louis said. "There was a very long feather, a blue egg in a nest, a weasel, a wooden tube with holes in it, a pocket watch, a ring with a red stone, a pair of dice, one black with white spots and one white with black spots, a wooden box, a small metal box and a very old book that belonged to the first baronet."

"Well!" the dowager said. "You have an excellent memory, Louis. The wooden tube is a flute carved by the first baronet, and the book was his psalter, but how did you know it belonged to him?"

"I read the sign beside it, although it was hard to read some of the letters," Louis said. "Books are easier to read."

"So they are, for the letters are printed. You are a very clever boy, to read so well at your age. Perhaps you would like to read to me later?"

"Yes, please, but..." He tugged Nell's sleeve again. "Mama, there is a picture of Papa on the wall."

"Of Papa? Louis, how can that be?"

"It is, it is! It is Papa! Come and see!"

The younger Lady Harbottle rose from her seat and held out a hand to Louis. "Will you show me, Louis?" He nodded and trustingly took her hand.

Nell followed them across the room. On the wall behind the glass case hung a number of miniatures, no doubt recording the features of Harbottles through the generations. They all three peered at the one that Louis pointed out.

"It is rather like," Nell said. "It is hard to tell with the wig."

"That is Great-uncle Matthew," Lady Harbottle said. "Rather a character, by all accounts. He was the second son, and swore he would never marry unless he was obliged to in order to secure the succession. Kept a string of mistresses, but he never did marry. Became a famous judge, eventually. Is that not so, Mama?"

"Infamous, more like," the dowager said, with a throaty laugh. "Liked to hang everyone brought before him, and thought that was too good a punishment for most of them. There is a larger portrait in the gallery, Jessica. Take Mrs Caldicott to see that. Louis, will you stay with me? Perhaps you could read to me for a while — there is a book on the table just there."

Louis rushed eagerly for the book, so Nell judged he would not object to being left behind. She followed the younger Lady Harbottle out of the room.

"Your son is very obliging to stay with an old lady when he had much rather be exploring, I am sure," she said to Nell.

"If there is a book involved, he is perfectly amenable," Nell said. "The difficulty will be separating him from it later."

Lady Harbottle laughed. "He is a lovely boy. So well mannered! How lucky you are to have a child! William and I were never blessed, although we were twenty years married." She sighed with sentimental fervour. "How I should have loved to have a child or two. A son for William, and a daughter for me — that is what I hoped for. But there, it was not to be. Here we are."

She led the way across the room to another door. A footman rushed to open it for them, and they passed into the gallery. Nell had expected the usual long, narrow room, but to her mind this was more like a ballroom, being almost as wide as it was long. Tables, globes and groupings of chairs filled the centre of the room, but with the minimum of effort, the floor could be cleared to leave room for fifty or sixty couples without crowding. A large balcony above the centre of the room provided for an orchestra, and doors along the wall suggested the possibility of smaller rooms for supper or cards. Above the whole arched a magnificent curved roof, seemingly supported by sturdy pillars set into the walls. It was, like the whole house, unembellished but imbued with an austere beauty.

"What a lovely room!" Nell said, swamped by an overwhelming urge to sweep away all the impedimenta and dance her way down the length of it.

"Do you think so?" Lady Harbottle said. "It always makes me cross. Such a waste of space! We could have had three serviceable rooms out of this, with doors to open up if we wished to entertain, but as it is we never find a reason to sit in here." She stopped abruptly. "*Found*, I should say. I keep forgetting that he is dead."

Impulsively, Nell laid a hand on her arm. "I know. It is hard to adjust to widowhood."

"It is, indeed it is," Lady Harbottle said in a whisper, tears sparkling in her eyes. "In William's case, we had some warning of it, and a little time to prepare ourselves, but your case is harder, I feel. Nathan was so shocked when he heard of it. He wrote to us in great distress. The sea is so fickle, calm one moment and a tempest the next. Our sailors are brave men, whether they keep the French from our shores, or bring us oranges and cotton. Come, let me show you Great-uncle Matthew in his full glory."

The man who stared down haughtily at Nell was every inch the aristocrat. From his carefully contrived powdered wig to his buckled shoes, from the elaborate embroidery fringing his coat to the quantity of lace at wrists and throat, he looked exactly what he was — a man of wealth and power. But the resemblance to Jude was striking.

"He *is* like my husband," Nell said. "Taller, perhaps, and wider, especially about the waist, but the face... the eyes are very like, and the nose, too. Not so much the mouth. If I passed him in the street wearing modern clothing, I should certainly look twice, but I should not be fooled for long."

"Is it possible that there is... how shall I put this? Some *connection,* let us say, between your husband and Matthew Harbottle? An irregular connection, perhaps, for he is reputed to have left remembrances in any number of otherwise respectable families."

"I cannot say," Nell said. "My husband's family came from Ireland, so it seems unlikely, but who knows? These things do happen. But that would be a great coincidence, would it not? I do not trust coincidences, Lady Harbottle."

"No, indeed, but sometimes they do occur. The letter from Felix, for instance."

Nell nodded, remembering Mrs Young, a random traveller who had lived in the very town for which Nell was bound. "True, and all I know of my husband is what he has told me himself. Since his death I have discovered that he concealed much from me, so perhaps this is another part of his history which he forgot to mention. Poor Jude! His memory was excessively deficient, it seems."

Lady Harbottle laughed again. "You take it lightly, and that encourages me to hope that my spirits, too, will rise in time. Life will not always feel so bleak as it does now. Mrs Caldicott, may I ask what your plans are? You did not come all this way solely to bring Mama her letter, I feel sure."

"Circumstances oblige me to leave Southampton for a little while, and the letter suggested a visit to Yorkshire, of whose beauties I have heard much."

"Perhaps then, if you have no other arrangements in place, you would be so kind as to stay here for a while, and bear us company in our grief."

"The kindness is all on your side, Lady Harbottle, but I could not possibly encroach during your mourning. I shall go to York and see the sights until it is possible for me to return home."

"Please stay! You would be doing us the greatest favour," Lady Harbottle said. "You cannot imagine anything sadder than two bereaved women in this great empty house, with nothing to fill our days. We may not go out for this first month, but with you and your son, we should have to rouse ourselves from our melancholy. You understand our feelings just now as no one else can, and Mama is so taken with Louis already. I have not seen her so animated for a long time. And I… I should dearly like to have a child in the house for a little while. Can you understand? I have so much love inside me for a child, yet I have never had an opportunity to express it. Will you allow me to do so, just for a little while?"

"It is true that a child gives one purpose as nothing else can," Nell said softly, remembering that it was Louis who had brought her back from despair after her illness. "If Louis would like it, and Lady Harbottle agrees, then we should be delighted to stay for a time, if we can be of service to you."

"You are generous indeed. Perhaps your presence will distract Mama from fretting over Felix. Let us go back to the saloon, for Craven will have brought refreshments by now."

"Mr Nathan Harbottle will find his cousin, I am sure," Nell said, as they walked back down the gallery. "He seems determined to leave no stone unturned in his search."

"Oh, yes! Nathan is very determined and very methodical, but Felix has hidden himself well enough for these sixteen years past. And if he cannot be found, then I do not know what will become of us, for everything is entailed and, with William gone, Felix is now the heir to both the estate and the baronetcy. He *must* be found. It is imperative."

16: Two Gentlemen

Nell and Louis were given a fine room with a prospect over the formal gardens, laid out in rigid squares of low hedges and topiary. Their box had been brought from the inn, and all their clothes had been pressed, neatly folded and put away. A bed for Louis had been made up in the dressing room, but Nell asked for a truckle bed to be brought into her room.

"He will sleep better if he is close to me," she told Lady Harbottle, who showed them to their room. "Shall you mind if he takes breakfast and dinner with me, too? It is what he is used to, and—"

"Of course. We have no nursery staff, so that is for the best anyway. We dine at five, and Mama and I always dress, but you need not, if you do not wish. It will only be the three of us... four of us, I should say," she added with a smile at Louis. "Ah, how delightful to have a child in the house!" She sighed again, her smile turning wistful. Nell sincerely pitied her.

While the maids brought in the truckle bed and made it up, and Louis investigated every drawer and closet in the two rooms, Nell looked about her with satisfaction. She had forced herself not to repine at the loss of the life she had been brought up to, and even during the painful years of bare survival, without even the comfort of tea, she had tried very hard not to be discontented with her lot. She had chosen it, after all, and the mistakes and the blame had been entirely hers. Yet there was something glorious in finding herself once more in such a place. It was wrong of her, and naturally it was only a temporary respite, but it felt so much like home. The large rooms, the army of silent servants, the luxury everywhere — so little considered as she grew up, yet of so much moment to her now.

Her resentment against her father simmered still. He it was who had turned his back on his only daughter, who had shut her out of his life so thoroughly and so implacably that even after his death her brother could not mend the breach. He had seen it as protecting the family from the predations of a fortune hunter, but Jude had never once suggested asking her family for aid, even when they had faced financial ruin, and it would have been the greatest comfort in her trials to know that her father still cared for her. Just to visit now and then would have been the most wonderful boon. How ironic that her own family rejected her utterly, even now, yet the Harbottles, who knew nothing of her, offered her the open hand of friendship. Such wonderful people. She would do her utmost to be a helpful guest while she stayed with them.

Admonishing herself briskly for falling into maudlin introspection, she chose one of her two evening gowns and prepared to enjoy her stay at Percharden House, however brief it might be.

Dinner was enlivened by Louis' presence. After discovering that both the Lady Harbottles were fluent in Italian, he plied them with questions in his own halting version of the language, and thus extended his vocabulary dramatically. The ladies seemed to enjoy the exercise, and Nell found she had little to do except to remind him to eat occasionally.

Having put him to bed after dinner and left him in the charge of a young housemaid, who assured him she had five younger brothers and knew exactly how to take care of him, Nell returned to the saloon. To her surprise, the dowager was seated at the pianoforte, her fingers moving with great confidence over the keys as she played a gentle air.

She stopped, resting her hands in her lap, at the sound of the door closing. "Is that you, Mrs Caldicott? Do come and sit beside me. Jessica is engaged in a most complicated part of her embroidery and will not be good company until she has completed the rose in its entirety." Nell did as she was bid, as Lady Harbottle went on at once, "You are surprised to find me able to play when I can barely see the instrument, never mind the keys?"

"I was at first, I confess, but a lifelong player may be so familiar with the keys that the melody almost plays itself."

The dowager chuckled. "Indeed. It is my blessed comfort, especially now, so I make no apology for playing with my son not yet cold in his grave."

"So it is with me, also," Nell said, "although I have not such a magnificent instrument available to me."

"Then if you will assist me to your chair, Mrs Caldicott, you may give me the pleasure of listening to another performer for a change."

Oh, the delight of a fine instrument! Unlike her stay at Daveney Hall, there were no sad memories or worries here to affect her pleasure in the music. She was free of her husband's rages, she had enough money to live upon and she was a guest of two people who offered her only kindness. For tonight at least, she would be happy.

And so she played, mostly from memory, and only slower, gentler pieces in keeping with the mood of a house in mourning, but it was a great joy to her. Every time she stopped, the dowager urged her to continue and so she played for the whole evening. Only when the dowager nodded off in her chair did the party break up and retreat to bed.

~~~~~

Nathan was still dressing at his house in York when the letter from Jessica arrived, marked *'Urgent'*, the word underlined three times. The housekeeper had been so flustered by such an imperious command that she had brought it to him at once.

"Oh, Lord, this cannot be good news," he said to Packard, ripping it open.

But it was. Felix's letter had arrived, brought by Mrs Caldicott personally all the way from Southampton. *'I persuaded her to stay for a while,'* Jessica wrote. *'I knew you would want to see her again, and far better that she stays with us than in York. Less talk that way. Besides, she has her son with her, the most delightful child. I plan to smother him with affection while he is here.'*

He laughed out loud, so startling Packard that he dropped the coat he was holding.

"Excellent! Here, give me that coat. I can put it on myself. You go and tell William I shall want the carriage in an hour, and I shall want you to take Mr Smethurst a note just as soon as I have written it. Off you go now. Run, run!"

It was a little more than an hour, but in the end the carriage was ready, Harry was collected from his lodgings round the corner and the two set off for Sagborough. In the carriage, Harry read Jessica's note.

"You see, she understands you well enough, and she is making it easy for you to court her."

"It would be shocking indeed to court a widow of only three months' standing," Nathan said, too cheerful to be cross with Harry.
~~~~~

Soon he would see her again, and admire her cool beauty and her mannered elegance. Even though she was not at all the sort of woman he preferred, it would be a pleasure to be reacquainted with her and observe whether the strain in her pale face had lifted at all, now that her husband was at the bottom of the sea.

"So why are we rushing off to see her with such indecent haste?" Harry said, with a wry smile. "I had to bolt my breakfast, I would have you know, and I am not accustomed to such reckless starts to my day. But then, what does food matter when I am to meet the acclaimed beauty of Southampton? I am sure she is worth the sacrifice of a second slice of plum cake."

"You may tell me when you have met her," Nathan said complacently. "I am confident that you will not consider yourself hard done by."

Craven received them with a smile. "The ladies will be very happy to see you, Mr Nathan, and Mr Smethurst also. Their ladyships have been sadly pulled these last few days. There is a guest staying just now, a widow with a young son, and that has cheered the ladies tremendously. They are all in the blue parlour this morning."

Nathan would have been astonished if they were anywhere else. They were always in the blue parlour until noon, after which the dowager rested for an hour and then liked to sit in the formality of the saloon until it was time to dress for dinner. She also liked to have all her visitors announced, even one so familiar as Nathan, so he and Harry meekly followed Craven to the blue parlour.

"Mr Nathan Harbottle and Mr Harry Smethurst, milady," Craven intoned.

Eagerly, Nathan scanned the room for Mrs Caldicott. His aunt... Jessica... the boy... where was she? Ah, there she was, watching him, her face expressionless. Black suited her, that was his first thought.

She had looked elegant in Southampton in her plain morning gowns, but in the deep black of widowhood her alabaster skin was accentuated, and her lace cap framed her delicate features to perfection. As his eyes met hers, he could feel a huge grin spreading across his face. She blushed slightly and lowered her eyes demurely.

Jessica came forward to take his hands and kiss his cheek. "Nathan! What a delightful surprise," she said, just as if she had not written to urge him to come. "And Harry, too. How kind of you to visit us in our seclusion. Nathan, you will find some old friends here today."

"So I see," he said, his eyes drinking in the sight of Mrs Caldicott. But first, he must talk to his aunt. "Aunt Amelie, how are you?"

"Still here," she said, "and that is all that can be hoped for at my age. Have you heard? My letter from Felix has arrived."

"So I understand. Did he say aught of interest? Such as where he is?"

She laughed. "It was all about snow and ice. Very Felix. He was ever an oddity." She laughed. "Have you made any more progress in your search?"

"I have been too much occupied with my role as executor of William's estate to have leisure for the search. There has been no response as yet to the new advertisements."

She grunted, and shook her head. "Foolish idea! As if he would answer an advertisement now, after all these years."

It was an old argument, and he said no more. If Felix had seen the advertisement, he would know that his older brother was now dead, and the family feud with it. As the new baronet, Felix could order his life as he chose, without reference to anyone else. It might well be an inducement for him to return, and it would be just like him to simply turn up on the doorstep without prior warning. Every morning Nathan woke wondering if today would be the day when his stubborn cousin would finally come home. Each night so far he had retired to bed disappointed, but he still had hope. So long as Felix lived and breathed and wrote to his mother, there was hope.

Nathan moved away to allow Harry to make his greetings to Aunt Amelie, which she turned aside with the briefest of courtesies. Ah well, she would never alter. If she disliked a person, there was no changing her mind.

He found Louis watching him with the unblinking gaze of youth. “Well, young man, and how are you? Enjoying Yorkshire?”

Louis executed a rather elegant bow, clearly learnt from his oh-so-elegant mother. “I am well, thank you, sir, and I like Yorkshire very much, although I have not seen very much of it yet because I slept in the carriage and we have not gone out anywhere yet, not even into the garden.”

“These are easy difficulties to resolve. Perhaps, when everyone has got all the talking out of the way, we may persuade your mama to take a turn about the garden with us. And on another day, because ladies like notice of such affairs so that they may decide which gown and bonnet to wear, we might ask Lady Harbottle if we may borrow the barouche and all of us go for a little drive. Should you like that?”

He nodded, and since Harry came nearer to make Louis’ acquaintance, Nathan was free to turn to the lady herself. She had risen as they entered the room, and then waited patiently to greet him. She was still a little flushed, he thought, but perhaps that was his fault for displaying so openly how pleased he was to see her. He hoped he had his countenance under better control now.

"Mrs Caldicott!" he said, bowing. "I cannot tell you how happy I was to receive Jessica's letter, and discover that you had ventured into our fair county. How are you?"

She dipped a graceful curtsy. "I thank you, sir, I am very well."

"Indeed, you look as if Yorkshire agrees with you."

That made her laugh. "I believe it does, sir. And you are well yourself?"

"I am in excellent health, I thank you. But how wonderful this is, to meet again so unexpectedly. I had not thought you would be able to leave Southampton for some time. It gives me the opportunity to convey to you in person how grieved I was to hear of your husband's tragic end. So many fine men are lost to the sea, and yet how bravely they venture forth despite the risks."

She lowered her eyes, but he could not tell whether she was distressed or embarrassed by his words. It seemed somewhat false of him to express sorrow for the death of her husband when in reality he was glad that she was reprieved from the nightmare of matrimonial violence.

"You are very kind, sir," she said in a low voice. "I was advised to leave Southampton for a while, and your letter inspired us with a wish to see York and the Minster."

That raised so many questions! Why had she been advised to leave home, and by whom? Her brother, presumably, but had he also paid the cost? Travelling was expensive. But all he said was, "I had thought you settled with your brother."

She looked up at him, her face suddenly alight with merriment. "I, the reprobate, sully the corridors of Godney Hall? Never!"

His breath caught in his throat. Heavens, she was so beautiful, and when she looked at him in that playful, teasing way…

Luckily, she noticed nothing, for she went on, "Your letter to Louis caused great consternation, Mr Harbottle. James was so desperate to find out who could possibly be writing to a boy of eight that he dispatched my younger brother to find out."

"Jack," Nathan said.

"Yes." She tipped her head to one side in puzzlement. "Did I mention him to you?"

"No, I looked the Godneys up in the baronetage," he said, with a wide grin.

She laughed out loud at that. "Oh, of course! So Jack was allowed to deliver the letter, but forbidden from crossing the threshold into my house of shame. I found him sitting on the front step with a cup of tea."

"An enterprising gentleman," Nathan said, noticing just how her eyes sparkled when she was amused. "Which school does he attend?"

"He is at Oxford already. He went up a year early. Mr Harbottle, I do believe your friend is trying to attract your attention."

Nathan turned, to see Harry loitering nearby, waggling his fingers at him.

"Ah, I expect he wishes to make your acquaintance, but I do not recommend it, Mrs Caldicott. He is a thoroughly disreputable fellow whose behaviour on a Sunday is quite unforgivable. Can you believe it, he only attends church twice, when I know for a certainty that there are three services each Sabbath, and when he returns home he refuses to read sermons, insists on mutton for dinner, when his companions would prefer goose, and spends the evening declaiming from the works of William Shakespeare, while marching up and down the drawing room with the book in his hand. It is a fearsome sight, I assure you."

Mrs Caldicott laughed. "He sounds splendid, and I should very much like to make his acquaintance."

"There you are, Nathan," Harry said in a loud whisper. "Some people appreciate my worth."

"Very well, madam, but on your own head be it if he proceeds to bore you with Henry V. Mrs Caldicott, may I present to you my oldest and dearest friend, Mr Harry Smethurst, who is the son of Squire Smethurst of Highley Manor and also a Member of Parliament. Harry, this is Mrs Caldicott, of whom I have spoken."

She dipped an elegant curtsy to him. "I am very pleased to make the acquaintance of anyone who values Mr Shakespeare," Mrs Caldicott said. "There are some stirring speeches in his work which must inspire your own speeches in the House, Mr Smethurst."

"Oh, I do not aspire to such a level of oratory as that," he said. "Workmanlike and plain, that is all that may be said of my speeches to date."

"Perhaps I am mistaken," she said, "but is Parliament not in session at the moment?"

"Indeed it is, but my father was ill and I was summoned north. He was on the mend before I arrived, but then Nathan's cousin died, and so I stayed to attend the funeral, and glad I am that I did so, for it gives me the opportunity to meet you at last, Mrs Caldicott. Nathan has talked of you so much."

"Has he so?" she said, arching her eyebrows in surprise, and turning her clear blue eyes on Nathan. "Has he told you how very kind he has been towards us? I am the more grateful because my brother is unable to heal the family estrangement my marriage caused. Poor James! He cannot go against our father's wishes in the matter, and so his hands are tied."

Nathan was shocked. She had left her brother's house, then, without receiving any assistance from him at all. What about her jointure? Was she still so impoverished that she could not afford tea? Yet her mourning gown was of good quality, newly made, and she had travelled all the way to Yorkshire, which was not cheap. She could not be penniless. And then he wondered just why he took such a close interest in the lady. She exerted a powerful fascination for him.

He had no time for further conversation with her, however, for Jessica called them to gather around the dowager, and the talk became more general for an hour or so, until it was time for the old lady's midday rest.

"Well, Louis," Nathan said, after his aunt had left on the arm of her footman, "have you seen the library yet?" Wordlessly he shook his head, but his eyes glittered with excitement. "Come then. Mrs Caldicott, have you been shown around the house yet? No? Then let us all go."

Jessica was quite willing to show them around, through the saloon, then the dining room and music room, and finally the library. There was no fire, but the shutters were open and vases of delphiniums and roses added colour.

Louis stood, revolving slowly around.

"What do you think?" Nathan said.

"It is not as big as Daveney Hall."

"Oh. Is the Daveney Hall library a great deal bigger?"

He considered that carefully. "Ten times bigger."

"That is very big indeed," Nathan said gravely. "Would you say that is an accurate assessment, Mrs Caldicott?"

"I would, sir. The Daveney Hall library is about the size of the gallery here."

Jessica laughed. "Your family must read a great deal, Mrs Caldicott. But come, Louis, let us find you some books to read. You tell me what you would like to read about, I shall find the right case and Mr Smethurst will climb the ladder to retrieve the volume, if necessary. You must never go up the ladder yourself, you understand? Nathan, why do you not show Mrs Caldicott the rest of the house? I am sure the Italian room would please her."

A burst of pleasure washed over him. He turned to her and bowed, offering his arm, although half expecting her to find some excuse to refuse such an obvious attempt to throw them together. To his delight, she smiled her acceptance, placed her hand on his arm and allowed him to lead her out of the room.

17: Conversations

Nathan had thought Mrs Caldicott might be embarrassed by their unexpected tête-à-tête, but she was not a lady to be discomposed by any situation.

As soon as they had left the library, she said, "Lady Harbottle has a romantic nature, I think, who sees a young widow and cannot resist pairing her off with the most eligible man in sight. I fear she is wasting her efforts on me. At only three months widowed, I cannot begin to consider such possibilities. In fact, I very strongly suspect I shall never marry again, so you are perfectly safe with me, Mr Harbottle." Without waiting for a reply, she went on, "This is a very fine house, so far as I am able to judge. So very well laid out, and with every modern convenience. Oh, what room is this?"

He could only admire her deftness in turning aside the awkwardness of the situation. "This is my cousin William's study." The room was in darkness, but he opened some of the shutters. The room looked odd to him now, with no fire burning in the grate, no dogs lolling about, no William in the leather chair behind the desk, spectacles perched on the end of his nose.

"How very tidy," she said.

"This is exactly how he left it. I have removed a few important papers, but otherwise nothing has been disturbed."

"What a methodical man he must have been. Was he very elderly?"

"He was not yet sixty, and should have had many more years of life left to him," Nathan said quietly, feeling oddly emotional, as he had not felt even in the immediate aftermath of William's death. "Such a pity he and Jessica had no children or we should not now be in this dreadful position. Yet who would have thought it? Five brothers should have secured the succession more than adequately, but William had no children at all, Andrew and his son both died, Walter never married and James had only daughters. And no one knows about Felix."

She moved to the wall where he had pinned his map of Great Britain and his list of ports, most of them neatly crossed out.

"Your investigations," she said. "I see that you are a methodical man, too, Mr Harbottle. What happens if your cousin cannot be found? He can be declared dead eventually, can he not? That happens when a ship is lost at sea and the men aboard are presumed to have drowned."

"True, and for the estate, perhaps, that can be done, although I can administer it in the interim, so there is no difficulty with that. But the baronetcy is not so simple. The Master of Rolls will want clear proof that Felix is dead and left no legitimate heirs before the title can be given elsewhere, and that is almost impossible to provide."

"Who is the next heir after Felix? Perhaps he has secretly had him killed in order to inherit," she said teasingly.

He laughed. "I can tell you definitively that he has not done so. Firstly, because in order to inherit, he must demonstrate that Felix is dead, and he cannot do that if he murders his rival in secret and hides the body. And secondly, because I am the next in line, and I believe I would remember if I had murdered anyone. Although if Felix ever does turn up, I may very well be tempted to murder him for leading us such a dance. Shall we move on to the billiard room?"

The billiard room being of little interest to Mrs Caldicott, and having seen the breakfast room and blue parlour already, they came quite soon to the Italian room. It was the only part of the house that Nathan strongly disliked, for it was entirely marble, hand selected by the third baronet in Italy and imported at vast expense, then installed to his specific design. The floor, the several wide pillars and even the walls were marble, and the ceiling was painted to resemble marble. It was a work of art, and yet he was entirely unmoved by it.

"It feels very cold, does it not?" Mrs Caldicott said. "In the heat of an Italian summer, such a cool room would be a delight, but it is out of keeping with England, in my opinion. I prefer warm wood and glowing colours."

"Then we are in accord," he said, absurdly pleased to find their opinions so exactly in line.

They came then to the gallery, and at once she spun away from him, arms out. "This room is glorious," she cried, spinning round again, her skirts swirling about her feet. "It makes me want to dance."

"Did you dance a great deal in Southampton?" he said, watching her move through the steps of the cotillion with an imaginary group of dancers. He burned to know everything about her.

"Not as much as I should have liked." She made a change of footwork. "When we were first there..." Another change. "...we went to all the assemblies, and a few..." She curtsied gracefully to her invisible partner. "...private balls, too, but later..." Her face changed, and the animation dropped from her. For a moment, he had been privileged to glimpse a different woman, but now all her cool composure was back. "Later, either Jude was at sea or I was... unwell, and so we never went anywhere, except to his employer's ball once a year."

Unwell. That was an interesting word for it. "Were you often unwell?" he asked, keeping his tone blandly neutral.

"Not often, but..." She trailed off, her face showing traces of strain again. But she took a deep breath and composed herself, before saying brightly, "Ah, there is Great-uncle Matthew, who looks so like my late husband. Lady Harbottle thinks there may have been some irregularity in my husband's ancestry to account for it. Great-uncle was a man with an eye for the ladies, seemingly."

"Was he now? Jessica knows more about the family than I do, even though she is the newest member of it. She married William only after his brothers had scattered to the four winds, so she missed all the scandals, even Felix's. Everything she knows is hearsay, but she takes an avid interest in it. If there is anything you wish to know about the Harbottles, you may ask her."

"I do not imagine I shall be here long enough to delve into family history," she murmured.

The thought pierced him to the core. Of course she would not stay long. She would go back to Southampton, and he would be tied to Yorkshire by the needs of the estate, and unable to find an excuse to see her again. But he could at least make the most of her time in the north.

"Mrs Caldicott, I wonder if I might be so bold as to invite you and Louis to my house in York for a short visit? Aunt Amelie and Jessica will not be attending church for some weeks yet, and I should love to have your company for services in the Minster, perhaps on Sunday next. My sister would be delighted to—"

"Oh, do you have a sister? I had no idea! Do tell me about her." She sat on an overstuffed sofa, and looked at him expectantly.

He took the chair next to the sofa. "Meg is my half-sister, two years older than I. She was born in the West Indies, and her mother died on the voyage home. My father settled in Edinburgh and married again almost immediately, but my mother died shortly after I was born. At that point, my father decided that the Good Lord did not wish him to be married, so he gave up the practice for good."

She gave a little laugh, but said, "And she is not married, your sister?"

"No, although she has had suitors enough. She keeps house for me, and would be delighted to welcome you to York. Will you come?"

"I should very much like to, but the invitation should come from your sister and we are not acquainted. Perhaps if you were to bring her here so that she might meet me?"

"That is impossible. Aunt Amelie greatly dislikes Meg, and she is not welcome here."

Mrs Caldicott raised her eyebrows, but said only, "The Dowager Lady Harbottle has some strong opinions. She dislikes your friend, I think, whereas she has been kindness itself to me and to Louis."

"Harry is only the son of the Squire, whereas you are a lady through and through. Your father is a baronet, Mrs Caldicott. Good breeding always shows, my aunt says." He imitated his aunt's querulous voice perfectly.

They both laughed, and he thought how pleasant it was to sit and talk to her in this comfortable way. When he spoke, she listened with an intent expression on her face, and when it was her turn, her mobile hands moved this way and that, gesturing, drawing elegant shapes in the air. A few stray curls fell from below her cap and lay about her slender neck. When she talked with animation, they danced about here and there like brown butterflies. The urge to reach out and touch them, to run his fingers over those dancing locks, was almost overwhelming. Yet when she was still, so were the curls, waiting motionless for her to come alive again. When he had seen her in Southampton, they had been mostly still. Today, they danced with delight, just as she did.

"I am so glad that we are still friends, Mr Harbottle," she said, taking him by surprise.

"Why should we not be?"

"No reason at all, for my part, but I was afraid that you would think it encroaching of me to come scampering up to Yorkshire, invading your home territory. That, however, is quite your own fault for writing so evocatively of York Minster. When we were obliged to leave Southampton suddenly, your letter and the letter from Felix conspired to put Yorkshire at the forefront of my mind."

There it was again, the need to leave Southampton. When he asked, she said that there had been money given to the next of kin of those lost in the *Minerva*, and it had caused some difficulty. Yes, he had heard of the Benefactor, and the troubles, for the newspapers had been full of the subject.

Shortly afterwards she suggested that they re-join the others. He was content to do so. All his main concerns had been addressed. She was no longer poor, she was in Yorkshire and she was his friend. For the moment, he wanted nothing more.

~~~~~

"Come on, admit it, Nathan. You are head over heels in love with her," Harry said, as the carriage made its way back to York.
~~~~~

"I admit to no such thing," Nathan said complacently. "Just because a man admires a lady and enjoys her company does not mean he is about to hurtle into matrimony."

"There can be no hurtling, not when she is still in full mourning, but I wager matrimony will come into it sooner or later."

Nathan shook his head. "You are quite wrong. I like her very well, I confess, but it is more a fascination with some exotic species, as in a menagerie. I have never met anyone quite like her, and so I wish to find out everything about her, and what makes her the way she is. But cool, composed ladies have never been my type. I do not like my women reserved, Harry. They must needs have energy and liveliness and *passion*. I want a woman who will wake me at dawn to run barefoot through the dewy meadow. I want a woman who will love me so deeply that she will never leave my side. I want a woman who will sing and laugh and dance for joy..." For an instant his mind's eye was filled with the image of Mrs Caldicott spinning round in the gallery. Yes, she had danced with joy then, but only for the briefest moment. He went on quickly, "And she must *weep*. Can you imagine her weeping, or even the slightest bit discomposed? Passion, you see, Harry. I must have passion, and Mrs Caldicott is not the passionate type."

"Barefoot through dewy meadows? Sounds dashed uncomfortable to me. Seriously, Nathan, have a care, for the lady if not for yourself. You make your preference for her company very obvious, and it is clear that she likes you too. In time, she may come to believe that—"

"No, no!" Nathan said. "There is no danger, I assure you. I offered her friendship at a time when she was very much in need of a friend. A gentleman friend, that is. She has a female friend, but that is not the same, is it? Otherwise, she had no one apart from her husband. I wanted her to know that she had someone she could turn to if… if ever her life became unbearable. But now the scoundrel is gone, and she will make a new life for herself. She has made it very clear that she is not looking for another husband."

"Not now, perhaps, but in the future she may feel differently."

"Mrs Caldicott and I understand each other very well, Harry. Neither of us wishes to marry in the slightest. *You* are the one who should be giving consideration to the question of matrimony, now that you have good prospects in your career."

"I have given consideration to the question," Harry said shortly.

His tone was worryingly brusque, and Nathan thought it wise to let the subject drop.

~~~~~

Nell could not have imagined, in the immediate aftermath of Jude's death, that just three months later she could be so contented. Her money worries were resolved for the moment, she had congenial company, Louis was happy and letters from Maria assured her that all was well at home and her little scheme for gentlemen's suppers was working out to everyone's benefit. Only one occurrence marred Nell's pleasure, and that was a letter received from Mr Willerton-Forbes. Captain Edgerton had made exhaustive enquiries of his Irish acquaintances, and all agreed that there was no family of note in that country by the name of Caldicott.

'Capt. E. Is very willing to travel to Ireland to pursue his enquiries amongst the less prominent families, if that would be of help," the lawyer wrote. *'Such a family could not be of any material assistance to you, but it might comfort you to know of their existence."*

Such news threw Nell into gloom. She no longer needed direct aid from Jude's family, and she had no wish to discover that he had originated with a clan of poor farmers and had thoroughly misled the
~~~~~

world regarding his origins. There had been enough shocking discoveries since his death, and she had no inclination for more. Accordingly, she wrote to Mr Willerton-Forbes to express her gratitude, but to declare herself satisfied with the results of Captain Edgerton's enquiries and to desire him not to pursue them further.

In every other way, however, life was more than satisfactory. Within two days of their arrival at Percharden House, the younger Lady Harbottle had thrown a troop of industrious housemaids at the long abandoned schoolroom, and created a miniature paradise for Louis. There were books galore, and although many of them were too simple for him, he read them all with great glee. There were chalk boards and globes and an abacus, which fascinated him, when Mr Harbottle had shown him how to use it. Nell wished she had thought to provide him with one before. There were toys, too, of a kind which made Nell nostalgic for her own childhood but which Louis had never encountered before.

Now everything was made available to him, and a schoolroom routine established. Before noon, Nell and Lady Harbottle were to share teaching duties, Nell instructing Louis in reading, writing, ciphering and music, while Lady Harbottle taught him Italian, French, Latin and Greek, at all of which she was fluent. At noon, Louis was to rest in his room for an hour. There were times allotted for walks in the garden, too, or on the covered terrace if it should happen to be raining, and a time each day when he would read to the dowager.

Whenever Nell protested, or talked vaguely of moving on, Lady Harbottle would say, "Oh, but you cannot leave just yet. Why, you have only just arrived. We are so enjoying your company, and Louis is a delightful boy. You can stay another week or two, surely?"

"You are all kindness, Lady Harbottle."

"Do, please, call me Jessica. And may I call you Nell? I look upon you quite as a friend already."

"I should be honoured," she murmured, although it puzzled her. There was more than matchmaking behind Jessica's affability. Was it because of Louis? Her affection for him was obvious, and he basked in her constant devotion, his attachment to her growing with every day that passed.

These arrangements gave Nell a great deal more spare time than previously. Often she found her way to the music room, where there was a pianoforte almost as fine as the one in the saloon for her to practise upon, as well as a clavichord, a spinet and two harps. With paper and ink always at her disposal, she wrote often to Maria, and encouraged Louis to write to James, now that he was the boy's guardian. In the evenings, after Louis and the dowager had gone to bed, she would read a book while Jessica worked at her complicated embroidery, the two sitting in companionable silence. Hour by hour, day by day, her contentment grew. It was, in some queer way, as if she had come home.

Then there was Mr Nathan Harbottle, who somehow found a reason to visit every day, bringing papers for Lady Harbottle to sign, or looking for a particular document from Sir William's study. He would usually stay for the whole day, seeking Nell out for quiet conversations, or walks in the garden, sometimes with Louis and sometimes just the two of them. She was careful not to make more of it than friendship. There was admiration in his eyes, it was true, but that did not mean anything, and besides, she had made it as plain as could be that a second husband was not in her future.

One day they were walking in the gardens, strolling sedately up and down the rigidly straight paths, while Louis raced along the cross paths to intersect with their route before tearing off again.

"Oh, for the energy of youth!" she said, shaking her head. "If only I had so much myself."

"But consider how tedious it would be if the urge to run everywhere never left one. The streets would be full of people tearing about in the most distracting fashion, and no one would stay still long enough to conduct a rational conversation."

"True, but a ball would be the most entertaining spectacle," she said. "Just imagine if everyone leapt and twirled and bounced so enthusiastically. I should love to be able to dance all night and not feel the least bit tired. Whereas today a simple walk at a snail's pace has exhausted me. Shall we sit down on that bench for a rest?"

He agreed to it, and for a while they sat in silence, watching Louis run about, while a couple of gardeners worked in the distance, and a pair of orange butterflies danced together in fluttering harmony. There was a pool with a tinkling fountain playing. Nell felt as if she could sit there for ever, listening to its gentle music.

"I have brought you a letter from Meg," he said eventually. "Will you read it?"

"Of course."

"And consider the invitation it contains?"

"I shall consider it carefully, and very likely accept."

"Even though you have not been introduced?"

Nell laughed. "Even then. It would be perverse of me to insist upon an introduction first when we cannot easily meet. As to any other concerns I might have had about staying with a single man and his unmarried sister, I asked Jessica about it, and she said that your sister lives with a pair of formidable matrons who are the epitome of respectability, and I need have no scruples about staying under your roof with them. The word *'dragons'* was used, as I recall."

"Ah yes. The two Macs. Mrs MacMorran and Miss MacKinnon. They were Meg's governesses, many years ago, and now they bring an air of respectability to our ramshackle household." He added in a whisper, "They are dreadfully strict, and do not scruple to express their opinions of any lapse in propriety in the most robust terms."

"I look forward to making their acquaintance, and shall try to be on my best behaviour so as not to incur their censure," Nell said. Then, on impulse, she added, "Everyone in your family is so kind to us, Mr Harbottle. I am quite at a loss to understand it, when we are complete strangers."

He was silent for such a long time that she began to wonder if she had said something to offend him. But then he sighed. "May I speak plainly, Mrs Caldicott?" She nodded her assent. "When I first met you, I could not help but notice that..." He stopped, taking a deep breath before ploughing on. "Forgive me, but there were signs that your husband did not treat you kindly. It was beyond my power to remedy, but... it made me angry that someone like you — a *lady*, a person of refinement and good breeding — should be dealt with in such a way. I regret to say that my anger still burned when I returned home, and I spilt my thoughts to many people. All Jessica's sympathy was aroused, and when you arrived here by chance, naturally she took you to her heart. My sister desires to meet you for the same reason. Believe me when I say that only an earnest care for your welfare drove me to reveal your secret to my family. I wished with all my heart that I could do something to alleviate your suffering."

"But you did," Nell said quietly. "You brought me tea, and a book for Louis, and you offered us your friendship. You cannot imagine how much those gifts meant to me. To both of us."

"If only there had been more I could do! You should not have had to suffer so!"

"But I should," she whispered. "Who else should suffer but myself? It was my punishment, and a just one, for it was all my fault. Everything that happened, all the evil that befell us — the blame was entirely mine."

He looked shocked. His face was so expressive that he could never dissemble. Before he could speak, however, Louis came running up.

"Mama! Come and see. There are fish in the pool."

They both rose to follow him. As he ran off again, Mr Harbottle whispered fiercely, "It was *not your fault!*"

But it was.

18: A Visit To York

Nell had one more member of the immediate Harbottle family to meet. Mrs John Drabble was the dowager's only daughter, and a widow of some years' standing. She was a bustling woman with a loud voice and a straightforward approach that was not ill-mannered but bordered on brusque. While Jessica was occupied with Louis, Mrs Drabble took Nell out into the garden for a little exercise and a lot of gossipy chatter.

"Widowhood is not easy," she told Nell, "but the sable cloud turns forth her silver lining, as the poem goes, and so you will discover, my dear, if you have not already. One loses a beloved husband, but one regains *oneself*, if you understand me. The days of standing in a man's shadow are over. And there are other benefits... I loved John dearly and I miss him still, but if he had lived I should have been knee-deep in children. A dozen, at least. As it was, the four who survived were more than enough for me to manage after he died. But they are all settled now, the boys in good careers and the girls advantageously married, and so I am quite at leisure to meddle in everyone else's lives." She laughed at her own wit, with a merry, musical chuckle that was infectious, and made it quite impossible to dislike her. "How long were you married, Mrs Caldicott?"

"Nine years."

"Oh. You are so young I had thought it must be less. Why, you must have been barely out of the schoolroom."

"I was seventeen, and I had had my season in London already."

"Ah, that is something, at least. One does not quite like to see a girl move directly from schoolroom to altar. It is unseemly, in my opinion, and not in the least necessary. If a woman is to be a helpmeet and companion to a man of sense, then she ought to have a little experience of the world. I was nineteen when I married and that was young enough, for I knew nothing. But I had eleven good years with John, and Jessica almost twenty with William. Jessica does not know it yet, but she is free at last. William was a good sort of man, but he had no imagination. He was the only one of us who dutifully married to please Mama and Papa's notions of an appropriate match. Andrew, James and I all married beneath us, and Walter never married at all." She laughed again, then went on more seriously, "Did your parents have the same sort of high-flown ideas for their offspring, Mrs Caldicott?"

"Papa did. My marriage caused an irreconcilable estrangement." Nell felt no need to offer any reasons for the breach.

"Mine too," Mrs Drabble said, laughing again. "However, when John died, my brother accepted me back into the family fold."

"Whereas mine did not," Nell said, trying not to sound bitter. "Papa made him swear a solemn oath."

"Ah," Mrs Drabble said, shaking her head. "So much family pride, instead of family affection. I do not think William wanted to acknowledge me, but I had returned to Sagborough and we moved in the same circles. It would have looked very odd for him to cut his own sister. However, he never forgave me for my marriage, nor Felix for what he did."

This made Nell deeply curious, but it would have been impolite to ask directly what dreadful offence Felix had committed. Fortunately, Mrs Drabble was not a secretive woman.

"Did anyone tell you about Felix's catastrophe? Probably not, for Mama never mentions it, and Jessica was not even here then. Felix is the youngest of us by quite a margin — six years younger than I am. Mama was five and forty when he turned up, quite unexpectedly and not entirely welcome, by all accounts. But he was a charming child who could wind everyone around his little finger, especially Mama. He was dreadfully spoilt, needless to say, and he quickly learnt that if he should be denied a wanted treat, he need only make a great fuss to produce a more favourable outcome. You may imagine how the rest of us liked *that!* We were good and did as we were told and were not even praised for it, and he screamed and kicked and yelled and was given whatever he wanted. Heavens, but he had some rages! He pushed a footman down the stairs once and broke his arm, poor fellow, and the nursemaids had a dreadful time with him. Mama could never deny him anything he wanted, and then all would be sunshine again. He never learnt self-restraint or generosity, but he did imbibe some sense of the family honour, which only made it all the worse when the crisis came."

Nell was too interested now for polite dissembling. "Whatever did he do?"

Mrs Drabble laughed once more. "He married the housemaid."

"No!"

"Indeed he did. He said nobly that he had dishonoured her and therefore, as a gentleman, he was obliged to marry her. There was the most almighty fuss about it, as you can imagine."

"Oh yes! I have never heard of a gentleman marrying a servant before."

"It is simply not done. In such circumstances, one pays the girl off, sets her up in a little cottage somewhere, or perhaps marries her hastily to one of the gardeners, or the gamekeeper's son. One does one's duty by her, but as for marrying her... well!"

"It is an unkindness to the girl, I should think," Nell said thoughtfully. "To take her into society and expect her to know how to go on — she would be quite at a loss. Nor would she be accepted, either, not if people knew her origins. Society can be very harsh. I wonder how happy such a marriage could ever be, with so great a disparity of rank and education. Was it a love match?"

"Not that I could tell. I suspect that Eliza seduced him, anticipating a purse of sovereigns for her trouble, and she got a husband instead, but one cut off from his family. It was not much of a bargain on either side. And then a few months later, she died."

"In childbed?"

"Nothing so mundane," Mrs Drabble said, with her attractive laugh. "She fell from a high balcony at night. Very strange. Then Felix wrote a long, pleading letter to Papa, asking to be forgiven, but Papa would not, naturally. *'As ye sow, so shall ye reap,'* he thundered. When Papa died, Felix wrote again, but Mama was implacable and William did not feel he could go against her wishes in the matter. After that, Felix never contacted the family again, except for that one letter a year to Mama. We only found out by chance, through a mutual acquaintance, that he had left the navy. It is all very tragic, and Mama would be very glad to receive him back into the family fold now."

"Especially tragic for the poor housemaid," Nell said. "I wonder how she came to fall."

"Do you know, I have always wondered about that. There was no notice in the paper, or anything of the sort. Perhaps Felix realised his mistake and quietly settled her in the country somewhere so that he could return to the family. When that failed… who knows? He seems to have disappeared himself. Poor Nathan has been trying to trace him for two years, ever since Andrew died and Felix became the heir, but with no success. Personally, I think he must be dead."

"But the letters to the Dowager Lady Harbottle," Nell protested. "Surely that proves he is still alive?"

"Those letters are very odd," Mrs Drabble said. "They are so vague, they could have been written at any time. Years ago, perhaps."

"Except that the paper is fresh, and the ink has not faded or discoloured," Nell said.

Mrs Drabble brightened. "That is very true! How clever you are! So he must still be alive, and perhaps, now that William is dead, he will just walk through the front door one day. And who would recognise him after more than twenty years? Hardly any of the servants from those days remain, Mama is practically blind and Jessica and Nathan never met him."

"You would know him," Nell said. "He was your brother, so you would know him again."

"Would I?" she said. "After all this time? He must have changed a great deal. But there is no one else, that much is certain. I am the only one who might conceivably be able to identify Felix, and he fades in my mind with every year that passes. If he is to come home, he must do it soon, or not at all."

~~~~~

Nell was both glad and sorry when the day came to move to York to visit Mr Harbottle and his sister. She looked forward to it, of course, but she also felt it a pity to interrupt Louis' growing attachment to Jessica. Her affection for him had been fixed from the first moment
~~~~~

she set eyes on him, but Louis was more cautious. Nell was very willing to encourage the friendship, but they could not stay at Percharden House for ever, and each day away from Jessica's calming presence in the schoolroom was a loss. Jessica managed to drag Louis away from his books better than anyone else, taking him on long, rambling walks through the woods surrounding the gardens to collect leaves and flowers and all manner of interesting objects, which they pressed or painted or arranged in vases.

But to York they were to go. Jessica had lent Nell her own maid, a somewhat formidable woman of fifty or so, whose presence as chaperon would allow Mr Harbottle to accompany Nell and Louis in the carriage.

"Not that I need a chaperon, at my advanced years," Nell had said gaily, when this point was first raised.

"A lady can never be too careful," Mr Harbottle had said severely.

So a chaperon she would have, and in truth she was very glad to have the use of a maid of her own, to arrange her hair just the way she liked.

Having had a long spell of fine, dry weather, on the appointed day it rained steadily and very little could be seen from the carriage. Mr Harbottle did his best to point out features of interest as they passed by, but Nell soon gave it up.

"We shall see it on the way home," she said, and then wondered at herself, to be thinking of Percharden House as home. Two weeks they had been there, that was all, and yet already she felt an ease such as she had not felt for some years, even in her own house in Southampton.

"You like Yorkshire, I think, Mrs Caldicott," was all Mr Harbottle said, but he smiled at her in that lazy way he had, so that his eyes twinkled charmingly, and she could not resist smiling back.

He turned his attention back to Louis, and she watched the two of them as they talked and peered out of the rain-streaked windows of the carriage. Louis was still pale and far too thin for his age, but she thought his face had a little more fullness about it. Or perhaps it was just the animation he so often displayed now. In Southampton, he had been very subdued, unnaturally so, she now realised. Why had she never noticed that before? Because she had been so caught up in her own worries, of course. Her dread of Jude coming home. Her worse dread when he did. The relief when he went away again. She had had little energy to spare for her son. So many hours she had spent with him, yet he had rarely had her full attention. She had encouraged him to read early so that he could amuse himself, and had kept him at home with her when she had retreated into her shell. How often had she packed him off to bed, supposedly to rest, so that she could be alone with her misery? Now, with Jessica to dote on him, and the dowager to be read to, and Mr Harbottle to explain the exact manner of chopping down a tree, or driving a team of horses, suddenly it felt as if he had a whole family around him. As if *she* had a whole family, and how comforting that was.

When she turned her gaze to Mr Harbottle, she realised with a start just how familiar his features had become. The angular jaw, the lips that curved so readily into a smile, hair the colour of pale honey, his powerful legs... The modern fashion for clinging breeches or pantaloons was not kind to men with spindly thighs or knobbly knees or bow legs, but Mr Harbottle looked very well in such styles... very well indeed, and for all she was in mourning and not in the least on the lookout for a husband, she could appreciate a fine figure in a man.

The narrow streets of York brought much to interest the occupants of the carriage, with many fine churches besides the cathedral, the old city walls and a great many shops everywhere. Davygate was in the heart of the city, the houses being of some antiquity. Mr Harbottle's house boasted a narrow frontage, and looked far too small to house the number of people already contained within it, let alone visitors, but as soon as the front door was opened by a footman, Nell could see that the interior stretched away into the distance.

Several servants emerged to assist with luggage, as Mr Harbottle jumped down from the carriage, lifted Louis to the ground and then offered his hand to Nell to assist her to alight. She took it, aware of a ripple of pleasure at having a gentleman available for such courtesies, and also having a carriage from which to be handed down. Jude had never been able to afford such a luxury, even in their days of affluence.

As she gazed up at the house — was it four storeys high? — a figure in vivid blue silk trimmed with black ribbons shot out of the front door, heedless of the rain. "Here you are at last! What kept you?"

"No introductions on the street, Meg," Mr Harbottle said, although he was smiling. "Let Mrs Caldicott get out of this rain first."

"Of course, of course. Goodness, it is wetter than I had realised. Do come inside, and let me look at you properly." Then, tucking her arm through Nell's in the friendliest manner imaginable, she pulled her into the house.

Nell had supposed, when she had given the matter any thought at all, that Mr Harbottle's sister would be rather like him — possessed of blonde good looks, a pleasingly courteous manner and a pronounced air of fashion. Meg Harbottle had none of those things. She had the dark skin of a mulatto, that was the first surprise.

Although Nell knew Miss Harbottle had originated in the West Indies, she had not suspected that her mother's ancestry was anything other than British. Then there was her gown, which was plain to the point of asceticism. And this bouncing, lively creature was nothing at all like her restrained and gentlemanly brother.

"Oh, I see what you mean, Nat!" Miss Harbottle cried, as soon as Nell had set foot over the threshold. "She *is* the most beautiful creature in the world. He has told us so much about you, Mrs Caldicott, you cannot imagine. We have all longed to meet you to judge for ourselves, but it is all true, every word."

Mr Harbottle raised his eyebrows. "Really, Meg! Must you embarrass me so thoroughly by revealing all my private disclosures."

"You do not mind, do you?" Miss Harbottle said to Nell. "You must be used to gentlemen saying how beautiful you are."

"No lady ever minds a compliment," Nell said, smiling.

Mr Harbottle gave a self-conscious little shrug, but said only, "Mrs Caldicott, this is my wild sister, Meg. I trust you will forgive her for her impertinence, since no one has ever managed to rein in her tendency to say whatever comes into her head."

Miss Harbottle tutted at this. "My brother would have you believe that I have no tact at all, but I assure you I know perfectly well when to hold my tongue. Oh, but you poor thing, still in full mourning. I have set aside my blacks for Cousin William already, except for ribbons and gloves, but you have months yet to suffer."

"I do not regard it as a suffering to display my loss to the world," Nell said, a little affronted.

"Oh, but—" Miss Harbottle began, but then, with a quick glance at her brother, said brightly, "Come upstairs, do, and meet the others."

The others turned out to be four in number — Mr Smethurst, two identical elderly ladies whom Nell had no trouble identifying as the dragons, and a child clutching a doll.

"You know Mr Smethurst, of course," Miss Harbottle said breezily. "These are the two Macs, Mrs MacMorran and Miss MacKinnon. We call them Mrs Mac and Miss Mac. And this is Miss Henrietta Wilson, Nathan's ward, or Henny, for short. Everyone, this is Mrs Caldicott. Oh, and Master Louis Caldicott."

Nell made her curtsies and began her polite greetings, but all the time her eyes were drawn to the girl with the doll. Henrietta Wilson, a previously unmentioned ward of Mr Harbottle's. She was around ten years of age, and she was everything that Nell had expected Meg to be, with fair hair falling down her back, and features that reminded her forcibly of Mr Harbottle. A ward? Or a natural child? It was a common device, a convenient way of keeping a small mistake within the family, but without public censure. However, she could not ask about it directly.

The afternoon passed pleasantly. Louis and Henny, although each rather suspicious of the other, were easily drawn into a game of spillikins with the two Macs. Nell sat sipping tea, an excellent Pekoe, and talking quietly to Mr Harbottle, while Miss Harbottle and Mr Smethurst joked and teased each other like old friends. Nell had not been in the house five minutes before she realised that Harry Smethurst was deep in love with Meg Harbottle. It was there in the way his eyes followed her all the time, in the way his animation dropped away if she left the room or even turned away from him. He paid her no compliments and bantered with her as if they were brother and sister, but he was sick with longing.

And yet... what was there to stop them? If the lady was not in love, she certainly liked him well enough. But perhaps there were financial difficulties, or his father might be against the match. She could not imagine that Mr Harbottle would raise any objections to his half-sister marrying his best friend, and anyway, she was of age.

When she dressed for dinner, she had a new gown to wear, loaned by Jessica — *'I ordered far too many, and it would look a vast deal better on you'* — and Quinn arranged her hair in a different style, which was quite the latest thing in London, she assured Nell. There was nothing like a new gown and a stylish new hair arrangement to make a woman feel alive again, she discovered. Or perhaps it was the company. Meg was vivacious, Harry was witty, the two Macs were droll and even Nell was induced to relate a story of one of her partners at Almack's who had walked like a duck, with his chest forwards and his rear rather more rearwards than was customary, owing to some misfortune with his corsets. Meg roared with laughter.

"Why, Mrs Caldicott, you are not at all the serene lady Nat described. You are quite wicked!"

And Nell was so at ease that she answered at once, "So I am, very wicked indeed." Then she saw Louis watching her, eyes wide, unsure of her. "I am so wicked that I wake little boys at night to make them cry and then—"

"Then?" he whispered, his wide eyes suggesting he was not quite sure how the sentence would end.

"Then I tickle them and tickle them until they scream for mercy." His face dissolved into smiles. "Are you going to finish that syllabub, young man, because it is time you were away to your bed."

Later, Nell played while Meg sang, and then Meg played alone. She was a little careless with the notes, but the performance was so spirited that no one could imagine anything wanting. Harry watched her in open admiration. The two Macs, working side by side on their tatting, listened respectfully. And Nathan...

As he had all evening, Nathan watched Nell, a little smile on his lips, his eyes warm with affection. Yes, affection, she decided. Nothing more than that. He was a warm-hearted man whose goodwill spilt over onto everyone around him, including her. Such a kind, open-handed man! She could never thank him enough for all his generosity. Yet his whole family was the same. Such lovely people.

She wondered what Jessica and the dowager were engaged in that evening. Jessica bent over her embroidery, no doubt, calling for extra candles as the evening light dimmed. The dowager would be at the instrument, her fingers running expertly over the keys.

Then her thoughts turned to Southampton. What would Maria be doing now? Preparing supper, perhaps, for some of Mr Lloyd's gentleman friends. The scheme was going well, according to the letters. Nell could picture her in the kitchen with Lucy and Jane, the three of them weaving this way and that about the room in a domestic version of the cotillion, only holding pans and bowls instead of fans and reticules. And Tilda... she had forgotten Tilda. She would be in the scullery. Becky and Dick would be preparing the dining room. She had not thought a great deal about any of them for an age, but now she had an urge to rush away and write to Maria, a long, newsy letter instead of the formal little notes she had sent so far. And James. She should write again to James, with more details of her situation. Had he come to some arrangement with Julia yet? Now that she thought of it, she burned to know. Why had she not wondered long since?

She had been too wrapped up in herself, drowning in her own misery. Everything else had no substance, faded and far away. Like the memory of Jude. Faded like an old tapestry.

Once, a lifetime ago, when Nell had been forbidden from seeing Jude and was sent to her room in disgrace, he had climbed over the wall into the grounds of Daveney Hall and stood, a lonely figure, on the edge of the shrubbery. For hours he stayed there watching her window as the summer sun sank slowly down the sky. He never moved an inch, but gradually, oh so slowly, the colours leached away from him until he grew shadowy and grey, and then utterly dark, so dark that not all her straining could make him out. And then she had wept, for he was gone from her life, gone for ever, faded away to nothingness by the implacably setting sun.

But then, the miracle had happened. The moon had risen and there he still was, a little paler, a little colourless but still her own Jude. No darkness could take him from her. His memory would fade, but he would never leave her. She would always have his love.

Or so she had believed, then. For years she had believed it. Even after the disaster, she had told herself that he still loved her, despite everything... that he was still her own beloved Jude. How many times had he told her so, in his repentant, tearful moments? But he had betrayed her. He was Judas indeed, for he had lied to her and mistreated her, he had hurt her with words and fists until she was consumed with anguish and pain, and that was not love.

She had learnt not to weep, not to argue, not to disobey. She had learnt not to cry out. She had survived by freezing her heart. But now, the spring sunshine was melting the icicles that imprisoned her. For the first time in years, she felt an interest in someone other than herself. She *cared* about people again. Her heart was thawing at last.

19: Intimacy (June)

Nathan had dismissed his valet and was ready for bed, but not yet under the covers. How could he possibly sleep on such a night? Instead, he sat beside the open window, the scent of roses and jasmine rising up from their tiny patch of garden far below, listening to the night sounds of the town. From the streets came the sounds of revellers passing by or the occasional rumble of a carriage, and from open windows he caught distant threads of music or bursts of laughter. Everyone was happy this night, and Nathan most of all.

A tap on the door was instantly followed by a mop of dark curls and Meg's beaming face. "I knew you would not be in bed yet. May I come in?"

Since she instantly bustled in and shut the door firmly behind her, he merely laughed. He was used to Meg's ways.

"Well, you were quite wrong about her, you know," she said, heaving his dressing chair nearer to his seat, and arranging the skirts of her night robe daintily about her ankles as she sat.

"In what way was I wrong? She is beautiful..."

"True."

"... and ladylike..."

"Indeed."

"... and perfectly composed on every occasion."

"Oh yes! But you did not tell me she has such a *wicked* sense of humour. She will fit in perfectly with this family. When am I to wish you joy?"

He heaved a dramatic sigh. "You are as bad as Harry. He is forever wanting to wish me joy, too. Have I not explained a hundred times that she has no desire for another husband, and who can wonder at it, after the last one? Nor do I want to risk my heart again, Meg."

"Your heart was lost to her long ago, if you want my opinion..."

"Which I do not."

"...and you *must* marry, Nathan, you absolutely must. Whatever will happen to Papa's fortune if you have no heir?"

"You and Henny will be very rich women one day, that is what will happen. Now do not tease me about Mrs Caldicott, Meg, or I shall be obliged to enquire about Harry, and you know how that will end."

Her face fell. "I *do* know," she said softly, "and I wish you would not make a fuss about it, Nathan. Harry must decide what is best for himself, and I would not make him a good wife, you know that. I am quite resigned to it. All I wish is that—"

Nathan reached out and stroked her cheek gently. "What do you wish, sister dear?"

She jumped to her feet, wrapping her arms about herself. "That he would just get on and *do it!* Find himself a charming little society wife who will do the pretty to his political comrades and give him a quiver full of little Harrys."

"Why could you not be that charming society wife?" Nathan said. "That is the part I cannot understand. Who is better suited to be a political hostess than you?"

"Me? A mulatto, and one, moreover, who says the first thing that comes into her head? It would be a disaster. I should only be a hindrance to his advancement, and he knows it, or he would have married me long since. But I am determined not to regret him. If he does not love me well enough to set the world at naught for me, then I am well rid of him, say I. He will not break *my* heart, you may depend upon it."

And so saying, she turned in a swirl of silk and strode out of the room.

~~~~~

Sunday brought a walk to the Minster through the rain, a long sermon made all the more tedious by sitting in wet clothes, followed by another rainy walk home. There was much grumbling from some of the company, but Nathan was too happy to mind a little rain. Who cared tuppence for rain when there was Nell to walk beside and to talk to and to watch surreptitiously?

"It is a fine building — very fine indeed," she said when pressed to give an opinion, "but I am not convinced the sermon was worth journeying all the way from Southampton to hear."

They were all glad to dry off over breakfast. Since the rain was relentless, they eschewed the Eucharist in favour of reading sermons. Harry and Meg took it in turns to read, while the two Macs and the children listened quietly.

Nell attempted to sketch the Minster while it was fresh in her mind, an enterprise soon abandoned as too difficult. "I have no eye for architecture," she said sadly.

As she slipped the sketchbook back into its bag, Nathan glimpsed a number of other sketches tucked away. "May I look?" he said.
~~~~~

"Of course. Most of them are years old, for I draw very little now."

Faces. They were almost all faces, mainly children. "Will you tell me who all these people are? Oh, this is Louis, is it not?"

"These here are all Louis. That one is my brother Jack as a baby. Mama and Papa. More of Louis. Oh, this is Daveney Hall... and this. Louis again."

"And this one?" he said gently, for he guessed the answer.

"That is Jude. I drew it after his death, for remembrance. He would never sit for me when he was alive. When we first married, he had me sit for a cameo, so that he could take it with him on his voyages. He was supposed to sit for one too, for me to keep, but he never did. So I drew a picture of him as I remembered him."

"He was a fine, handsome fellow," Nathan said, but inside he raged to look at the smiling, happy face of the man who had hurt her. She nodded, but said nothing and he could not read her face. To fill the silence, he said, "I suppose the cameo of you is at the bottom of the English Channel now."

"No, it was in his waistcoat pocket when they found him. He always carried it there, next to his heart, so he said." There was a brittle note to her voice as she spoke. "His clothes were sent back to me, with everything from his pockets. This is his ring, you see? And the cameo."

She wore the ring on a chain around her neck, invisible under her high-necked gown. He gave it a cursory glance, but it was not of any artistic merit, being plain gold embossed with some kind of emblem — a bag, perhaps. He turned to the cameo she produced from her reticule. She kept it in a tiny velvet pouch to preserve its delicate beauty, and it was undoubtedly worth preserving. There she was to the life, captured in miniature in two square inches of painstakingly carved ivory. It was beautiful, but he could not see it without thinking of the man who sentimentally carried his wife's image next to his heart when he was away and then came home and beat the living woman black and blue.

"It is a good likeness," he said, with difficulty, for his throat was unaccountably tight.

"Jude thought so too," she said, her voice subdued.

The noise from the rest of the room suggested that the children were becoming restless. The two Macs whisked them away for milk and cakes, followed by naps, and as the company now gathered into one group, there was no further opportunity for private conversation. Nathan was rather glad of it, for it gave him a chance to compose himself and to wonder why he was so unsettled by the actions of a man who was now dead.

That night was only the second dinner he had shared with Nell, and again he claimed the pleasure of sitting beside her. If she had always looked entirely the lady in her day gowns, in evening dress she was magnificent. Black silk with black lace and a single black ribbon in her hair were all the ornamentation she allowed herself, with not a bit of jewellery apart from her wedding ring, but Nathan was almost speechless with admiration. It was as well that the table did not depend upon him for conversation, for he said next to nothing, but sat watching her. He could scarcely take his eyes off her.

But she was not silent. He had to agree with Meg that the cool, composed and reserved lady had flown away. In her place was a vivacious and quick-witted woman who could tell an amusing anecdote or argue point for point with Harry, and yet was never unkind or in any way overstepping the bounds of ladylike behaviour. Occasionally, some casual remark would distress her — Harry mentioned the dead Duke of Falconbury once, and that was enough. Then she would grow quiet for a while, the conversation swirling around her until she felt able to join in again. But no one was so impolite as to remark upon it, and she recovered each time.

After dinner, she insisted on hearing Harry reciting Shakespeare, and although the two Macs twittered a bit — *'Nothing too unseemly, dear Mrs Caldicott, not on a Sunday'* — Henry V was deemed suitable. Nathan had to admit that Harry was a fine orator, and the original could hardly have been more stirring. Harry stood before the fireplace, his voice echoing around the room, holding them spellbound.

'Once more unto the breach, dear friends, once more;

Or close the wall up with our English dead.

In peace there's nothing so becomes a man

As modest stillness and humility:

But when the blast of war blows in our ears,

Then imitate the action of the tiger;

Stiffen the sinews, summon up the blood,

Disguise fair nature with hard-favour'd rage.'

When he had drawn to a close, there was a stunned silence until Nathan jumped to his feet. "Give me a *sword*, someone, and let me have at these surly Frenchmen. God for Harry, England, and Saint George!"

They all laughed, and Nell laughed too and gazed at him with something in her eyes. Something that was not cool or composed, and he could not be at all sure it was even ladylike.

His breath caught. The world faded to nothingness and there was only Nell, Nell with her shimmering blue eyes fixed on him, and a smile playing on her lips. Those *eyes...* as blue as the ocean and as deep. A man could drown in those eyes.

Drown...

An infelicitous word, under the circumstances, but perhaps he *was* drowning. He was certainly out of his depth. Oh Lord, were Meg and Harry right? Was he falling in love?

~~~~~

JUNE

Nathan found some excuse to visit Percharden House every day after Nell and Louis returned there. Sometimes he rode, sometimes he went in the carriage, and often there would be some little gift — a wooden horse for Louis, some marzipan for the ladies, a new piece of sheet music for Nell. Some days he hardly saw her, but one day he found her out in the garden all alone, sketching the house.

"No Louis today?"

"Jessica has taken him into town to procure new pantaloons for him."

He had nothing to say about pantaloons, so he peered instead at her drawing.

"Your eye for architecture is improving," he said, pushing her discarded bonnet and shawl aside, and sitting down on the bench beside her.

She laughed. "Ah, but it is so much easier when the object is directly before me. In York, I had seen the Minster only briefly and through a downpour, and it is not easy to study a building in such conditions. Has it stopped raining in York yet?"

"Days ago, just as it did here."

"Indeed? You astonish me. I thought it always rained in York. It is a rational conclusion, since I have never seen York when it is *not* raining."
~~~~~

That made him laugh. “You must come again when the sun shines, which it does with tolerable frequency,” he said, smiling at her. Was he smiling too much? He rather thought he was.

“I should very much like to. Have I told you how much I enjoyed my stay at your house, Mr Harbottle?”

“About a dozen times. Thirteen, now. And Meg and I enjoyed your visit too.”

“And Henny? Was she put out to find her family home invaded by a pestilential boy?”

“Henny is never put out by anything,” he said, his voice softening as he thought of her. “She is a delightful child.”

“She is, and so very like you.” She turned and smiled at him as she spoke, but there was no condemnation in her manner. She was surprisingly direct, but not judgemental. And then, in that deft way she had, she changed the subject. “Have you heard from Mr Smethurst yet? I trust he arrived safely in London.”

“He did.” He hesitated, but there was no point in pretence, and he wanted no secrets between them, so he went on, “You are right, of course. She is mine. A natural child. May I tell you about it? I should like you to know.”

She set down her sketching book and turned to face him fully. “I should be honoured by any confidences you wish to share with me, Mr Harbottle.”

So formal… If only she would call him by his name! He longed for such intimacy. Taking a long, slow breath, he said, “I was nineteen, and she was seventeen. So young, both of us. This happened in Edinburgh, so you would not know her, but her family was… *is* respectable. We had been acquainted for some time, so she was a good friend, but nothing more until that summer. Then, I do not quite know how it was, but one day everything changed. There was a pleasure excursion — a drive into the country, a picnic, you know the sort of thing. I was allowed to take her up in my curricle, and somehow, everything fell into place. We set out as friends, and we returned as lovers. My father approved, so I courted her openly. We never made any secret of it, and her mother made no demur, on the contrary, she encouraged us. Her father was away at the time, but we had no reason to doubt his approval. I made my declaration, she accepted me and it needed only her father's return for us to marry."

He paused, mesmerised by the intentness of Nell's gaze as she listened, rapt. Her face, normally so calm, showed interest but also solicitude, knowing how the story would end. With difficulty, he continued.

"As you will have guessed, he refused to give his blessing. She was too young, I was too young, there was another young man who would suit her better... he came up with a dozen excuses, but when I pressed him, he confessed that my father was too ramshackle a connection to admit to *his* oh-so-respectable family." Nathan could not keep the bitterness out of his tone. "Never mind that they were poor as well as respectable, never mind that I could bring money to the family, never mind that his daughter's happiness was at risk. He would not have it."

"Whatever was so ramshackle about your father?" Nell cried. "The brother of a baronet? His social position was unimpeachable, surely."

"True, but an English baronet is of little account in Scotland, and my father was deemed to have lax morals. There were rumours of a mistress, although I never knew the truth of that. There were also questions about Meg, and whether she was legitimate or not. We never found her mother's marriage lines. Even if the marriage had been valid, there were those who questioned my father's judgement in marrying such a person, and raising the offspring as a lady. In the *beau monde*, such things are of little account, but to my betrothed's father it was of greater import than the Harbottle name or money."

"Who could possibly object to Meg?" she said indignantly.

"Exactly!" he said, basking in the warmth of her approval. "But he did, and there was no persuading him. We did not need her father's permission to marry, not under Scotch law, so we pressed ahead with our plans, and of course we did not quite wait for the wedding. But he forestalled us. He sent his daughter away to a cousin in Cornwall, and there she stayed, even when her condition was discovered. That was a lesser shame than marrying me, it seems. In time, the whole family moved to England, and I never saw or heard from any of them again. Only the solicitor communicated with me, to ask for money for Henny, who had been fostered out. I told him that I was more than willing to fulfil my obligations, but I wanted the child with me, to be brought up as the gentleman's daughter that she is. She has been with me since she was a year old, and is the greatest delight to me. She brought me some comfort during the long years when I grieved for my lost love."

"That is a sad story," Nell said thoughtfully. "To separate two young people so deep in love, and without any serious reason for objection is very cruel. Whatever your father may have done, there was no blame attached to you. But did your betrothed never write to you, or try to return to your side?"

"I do not know what she may have tried, but she certainly never succeeded, and it is not so difficult to write a letter, surely? In all these years, surely she could have written, if only to tell me that she was well and content with her situation. It has torn me apart, imagining her suffering just as I did. If I had only known what became of her..." He stopped, voice quavering as the old emotions boiled up inside him. He rested his head on one hand, shading his eyes. "Forgive me..."

"No forgiveness is necessary," she said. To his surprise, she reached out and took his other hand in hers, gently stroking the back of it. "I am so very sorry, Nathan."

At her touch, a shiver rippled through him. Without gloves, the softness of her hands on his was as delicate as the touch of a moth's wing, but the effect was as intense as fire, making his heart thunderous and his breath ragged. He lifted his head but he could not — he *dared* not — look at her. Hoarsely, he said, "You do not, then, condemn me for what I did? For seducing her?"

"You were both young and lost in love and shortly to marry. The consequence of that is almost inevitable."

"But I should have had more restraint. I should have—"

"Hush." She placed one finger on his lips, sending another ripple through him, stronger than the last. "*'Should have'* will not pay the butcher, as my old nurse used to say. What is done is done. You must not take all the blame upon yourself. The lady permitted it, after all, and it was her father who created the disaster. Implacable fathers cause so much tragedy."

"You understand," he said wonderingly, looking her in the eye at last. Gently, he raised her hand to his lips and kissed the back of it, the most feather-light, yet intimate, of kisses.

Her eyes widened a little, but she made no protest. Instead, to his astonishment, she smiled and said, "Of course I understand. Who better? For did I not do exactly as you did? And I too paid a dreadful price," she added in a low tone. "Mr Harbottle... Nathan... you have shared your history with me. May I repay the compliment and tell you my story?"

He could scarcely breathe. "I should be greatly honoured... Nell."

She nodded, and settled herself more comfortably on the bench, although she did not withdraw her hand from his, and began her tale.

20: Another Unexpected Visitor

Nathan sat, mesmerised, as she spoke, enchanted by this abrupt shift to intimacy. Her hand rested trustingly in his, and occasionally, when emotion overcame her, she squeezed it a little, as if to draw comfort from it.

She talked first of her meeting with her future husband. For her, too, it was a summer romance, and it drew to the same conclusion — a couple desperately in love and a father violently opposed to the match. Since they were subject to English law they could not marry without his consent, so Nell tried to force his hand, creeping out one moonlit night and offering her lover her virtue. She achieved her object but at a terrible cost — the loss of her family and even her dowry, as she discovered later.

For a time, they were happy. Louis was born, her husband's ships were doing well, there was money and society and a joy in life. But there were blacker moments, too, when her husband's true nature showed itself.

"Some business he wanted fell through at the last minute," she said, her voice faltering. "He flew into a rage. Even though his anger was not directed at me, it was frightening. But the storm blew over and we were in harmony again. Then the disaster happened..." Her voice trailed away to nothing, and the grief in her face was almost unbearable for Nathan to see.

"You do not need to speak of it if it distresses you," he said softly.

She straightened her back. "But I wish to. It is good for me, especially now that I know so much more about him. Or perhaps less." She smiled, then, and he kissed her hand again, although he knew not why. She did not object. "I was increasing again, and it was winter. We had had snow, and then even colder weather. Jude told me to stay at home, it was too icy underfoot, too dangerous... but he was a dreadful worrier when I was increasing, so I took no notice. Besides, there were some new bonnets in from London, and so..."

She stopped, withdrawing from his grasp and covering her face with trembling hands. Nathan was overcome with grief for her. He so badly wanted to hold her in his arms, as if he could shield her from the hurts of the world, but for her it was far too late. She had already seen the worst of man's evil.

"Bonnets!" she said abruptly, with a harsh laugh. "Such a trivial thing, but it destroyed us. My vanity destroyed us. I went out, I fell, I was carried home insensible. Jude was distraught." A long pause, but then she burst out, "Oh God, if only I had listened to him! We might have been happy yet. He might have been alive yet."

"Such regrets do no good," Nathan said fiercely. "You must not think that way. It is a tragedy to lose a baby, but—"

"Oh, but I did not, not then. No, I recovered well, but Jude... Jude had two ships then, a larger one which he commanded, and a smaller one, which John Delanoy captained. Jude had an important cargo coming up, very profitable, it would make us rich, he said. The next cargo was always the one to make us rich, yet somehow we never were. But because of the fall, he was too concerned about me to go, so he sent John instead and that was the true disaster."

"The ship sank?"

She nodded, eyes full of tears. "All hands were lost. The cargo was lost. Our chance of riches was lost. And the worst of it was that the insurers would not pay out. John was not properly qualified, they said, they had only insured the ship on condition that Jude captained it. He got virtually nothing. Far from making our fortune, we were ruined. That night—"

Again she stopped, and now the tears were flowing in earnest. Quite unable to help himself, he put one arm around her shoulders, and she leaned towards him trustingly.

"That night," she went on, her voice stronger, "he went out and got drunk. I had never seen him drunk before. I was in bed when he came home, and he was in such a rage. I tried to reason with him, but he yelled at me, screamed at me... and then he started hitting me. It was all my fault, he said. I had destroyed everything. He wished he had never married me, and on and on. I was trying to fight back but he was bigger and stronger than me. He kept hitting me, until I was on the floor and screaming in pain. And then... then..." She heaved a sobbing breath. "Then he kicked me in the stomach. *That* was when I lost the baby. Oh God, the blood! So much blood. I... I don't remember much after that. For weeks I was ill. The physician was afraid I might die, but I wished for death. Can you understand that?" She turned a tear-streaked face towards him. "It was wrong of me, but I... I felt I had nothing to live for. But Maria kept bringing Louis to see me, and eventually I realised that I *did* have a reason to live. Or to endure, anyway. Because we could never go back. Even if he never hit me again, I would always be afraid that he would."

"But he did," Nathan said.

"Oh yes. Five times, in all. That is not much, is it? Five times in three years. Most of the time he was almost like the man I married, loving and gentle, although the lack of money wore him down. He was always anxious about it, and especially so as the Quarter Days drew near. Then he would get restless and start grumbling that we ought to have more money, and it was all my fault for spending too much. Or it was my fault that the *Helen of Troy* went down and left us poor. It was always my fault, he said."

"It was *not* your fault!" Nathan hissed, too angry to be conciliatory. "It was not your fault that the ship went down or that the insurers would not pay. It was not your fault that an unqualified commander took that ship out. That was your husband's decision."

"True, but I must shoulder *some* of the blame. My foolish vanity triggered all the evils that later beset us. Vanity and disobedience. The disaster came about in part because I disobeyed my husband. I caused the breach with my family because I disobeyed my father. Everything that has gone wrong in my life is because I disobeyed. So I became the world's most dutiful wife. Everything Jude told me to do, I did without question. None of it helped. He would grow despondent and turn to drink, and then... sometimes..."

"Did you never think of laying a charge against him? Applying to your family for aid? Or leaving him?"

She shook her head, her curls brushing against his coat as she nestled in his arm. "I had too much pride to admit that anything was wrong. Besides, he was my husband," she said simply. "For better or for worse. We had had the better times, and I just had to endure the worse times until the better times came again. I was sure they would. If only I could be the perfect wife we would be happy again."

"Nothing you could possibly do would make him change," Nathan said. "I have seen his type before, and they never reform, never."

"I know," she said sadly, "but we were caught in an endless cycle by the time I came to understand that. I was a timid, fearful creature and he was... not the man I married. Or perhaps I should say, not the man I *thought* I had married. I had imagined that I knew him quite well. He had never talked a great deal about his earlier life before he moved to Southampton, but some men do not talk about themselves, do they? Perhaps his childhood had been unhappy, and the navy — I can understand that a man may not want to talk about war and battle and death once it is behind him. I never questioned any of it, never wondered *why* he never talked about such things. Now I know. Since his death, a great deal of his history has been shown to be a sham. He was not raised in Ireland, he was never in the navy and we were nothing like as poor as I had thought."

"Really? You could have afforded tea?"

That raised a small smile. "Tea! How I missed it. Even when it could be afforded, it was the very cheapest. We could have had tea, enough coal, new gowns, paper and ink, books... but we had none of that because Jude kept a mistress in London. She has been living in relative luxury while Louis and I scraped and patched and made do. When I opened the locked box under the bed, I found a book detailing payments going back more than twenty years to someone with the initials *'EP'*, of eight hundred pounds a year."

"That is a considerable sum." It was all he could think of to say, for the anger was rising up again, making him wish very strongly that Jude Caldicott were alive and standing before him at that moment, so that he could have the satisfaction of knocking him down.

"It is, and it should have been given to his wife, not his mistress." There was a long silence, and then, to his delight, she laid her head on his shoulder. In a small voice, she said, "He must have loved her very much."

"Did he go to London often?" Nathan said, in as neutral a tone as he could manage.

"Oh… I never heard him mention London. No, I think not. He always said he hated London, although he said a great many things that were not true. When he sailed, it was always westerly and then north. Never towards London."

"Then perhaps it was an old obligation," Nathan said. "A child to be supported, or promises made. I doubt he loved a mistress as much as he loved you."

"You are very good to say such things," she murmured, without moving her head from his shoulder. "You cannot know how much your kindness helped me when I was first widowed. Just knowing that you were willing to stand my friend was the greatest encouragement. I never needed to call upon that friendship, but it helped me to be strong and do what was needful, to stand up to bankers and lawyers — and my brother! It reassured me that there were still generous, compassionate people in the world."

Nathan was too overcome with emotion to speak a word.

After a pause, she went on, "I am sure that our present position is wildly improper, and the two Macs would be horrified to see us sitting thus, but I confess that your shoulder makes a most agreeable pillow. The sun is so warm that I might even drop off to sleep here."

He tried not to laugh for fear of joggling her, but he could not suppress a smile of pure satisfaction. "Sleep if you wish, Nell dear, for I am perfectly willing to sit here all day, if it please you."

"Thank you for listening to my ramblings."

"Thank you for allowing me the privilege of hearing them. Does it make you feel a little better, to have shared your story?"

She turned her head so that she was looking directly into his face, and her smile made his heart jump about alarmingly. "It does, and to have cried a little. That is the first time I have cried since—" A long pause, then she went on smoothly, "You are such a good friend to me, Nathan."

He held his breath. She was inches away from him, her countenance open and unafraid. Her lips were so close to his, so close... He had only to move forward the minutest amount... yet he dared not. Holding hands, putting an arm about her shoulder, allowing her to lean against him, sharing confidences — these were the province of a friend. But a kiss... that would change everything. Yet he was not sure he could resist her. Every second she gazed at him with those limpid blue eyes eroded his resolve.

He was saved by the sound of a carriage on the drive.

She jerked away from him at once. "I must go in. If the dowager is up from her rest, she will not want to meet visitors alone, and Jessica is out."

"Might this be Jessica's carriage returning?"

"She and Louis were on foot." She gathered up her scattered sketching things deftly, and pushed them hastily into a bag. With the end of her shawl, she wiped away the last traces of tears, and tied on her bonnet. "There! Do I look respectable?"

"You look perfect... perfectly presentable, as always."

He was rewarded with a smile, and a demure lowering of her eyes.

"Aunt Amelie may not want to receive callers so soon after her bereavement," Nathan said, as they set off to walk back to the house. "It is only a month, after all."

"That is time enough. We had the mayor's wife on Monday, and a viscountess on Tuesday, and Lord and Lady Gilbert Something yesterday."

"Lord Gilbert is brother to Harry's benefactor, Lord Carrbridge."

"Oh, I wish I had known that! I am so out of society that I have no idea who anybody is, these days. Oh — Lady Craston, that was the viscountess. She was very sweet, but so young. Having done it myself, I do not recommend girls dashing to the altar practically from the schoolroom. My goodness — that is a post chaise, with luggage on the back. Have you any idea who it might be?"

He frowned. "One of the cousins, I suppose, or perhaps the lawyers from London, although they would have written... Jessica did not mention any visitors?"

"No. Oh well, I daresay we shall find out soon enough. You will not run away just yet, will you? The dowager may need your support until Jessica returns."

"Of course."

The post chaise disappeared from their view as it neared the front of the house, while Nathan and Nell entered through a rear door and walked through the house to the hall. A man stood there, attired for travelling, and scowling as if he had been served watered wine. Nathan had never seen him before in his life. The stranger was young, only a little older than Nathan, but his clothes looked as if he had selected randomly from a selection of the latest fashions, but without consideration as to whether he looked well in them. Such peculiar colours, and nothing quite fitted as it should. He was an oddity, and from his attitude, Nathan decided at once that he was a pompous bore.

Nell, however, gasped when she saw him. "James? Whatever are you doing here?" She cast her bag of sketching things onto a marble-topped table, the contents spilling out in her haste, and rushed forward.

James? Her brother? Nathan felt his eyebrows rise in surprise.

"I wonder you have the gall to ask me such a question, sister," he said. "You must guess my purpose, I am sure, and very inconvenient it is too, to be trailing up to the wild north country on such an errand, and at the height of the season, too."

"I am sure it is," she said. She looked around, as if suddenly aware of the wooden faces of Craven and the footmen, standing about pretending they were not listening to every word. "Shall we go into the saloon, and you may tell me all about it? Craven, is the dowager up from her rest yet?"

"Not yet, madam. Shall I advise her of Sir James's arrival?"

"No need to disturb her, for my brother is no doubt here on family business. Come, James." She shepherded him into the saloon, and firmly shut the door on the interested servants. "There. Now, brother, you may tell me what strange start brings you here, for nobody asked you to come. I certainly did not."

The change of room did not disrupt the flow of bile in the slightest. "Ha! I believe you. My coming has put a spoke in your wheel, I make no doubt. I always knew you were incorrigible, Nell, but truly, to see you here, parading yourself about as if it were the most normal occurrence in the world, and pretending to wonder why I am here — it is the outside of enough. I swear you are the most troublesome sister that ever a man had."

"Really, James, I have not the least idea what bee you have now in your bonnet, but I do wish you had not come. It is most inconvenient, especially if you expect to be put up here."

"Put up here? I should think not indeed. No, I shall find myself rooms at an inn as soon as I have put some distance between myself and this place of evil. Julia was most distressed, I can tell you, most distressed, and she should not be subjected to such violent emotions, not at this time. Her condition is most delicate and—"

"Oh, James!" Nell said, suddenly beaming in pure delight. "Did you take my advice?"

Abruptly the bluster dropped away, and he looked boyishly embarrassed. "Oh, well… I did, as it happens. Told her that if she had still not recovered after four years, then I was taking her directly to Harrogate to take the waters to see if that had any effect. Worked like a charm." He laughed, waggling a finger at her. "You always were a clever little puss."

Nathan watched in silence, quite forgotten by the brother and sister, trying to piece together both the reason for Sir James to descend upon them and the sudden change of subject. The latter was something to do with his wife, and, he guessed, a return to the marital bed after four years. An odd sort of marriage, then, and a wife who was able to ride roughshod over her husband's wishes. But as for why he had come haring up to Yorkshire, he could not guess.

"But this is nothing to the point," Sir James said, resuming his offended baronet role without missing a beat. "Where is Louis?"

"Louis?" Nell said. "Oh, is this about your guardianship? Because you could have put it all in a letter, you know."

"I could *not* have put it in a letter! What good would that do? Really, Nell, you are positively hen-witted sometimes. Of course I had to come myself, despite the inconvenience. But you need not worry, for I have brought Nurse with me, so he will be well looked after until I can get him home."

"Home?" Nell said faintly.

"Yes, home to Daveney Hall. Truly, Nell, you could not imagine I would leave the boy here with *you*, did you? I am Louis' guardian after all, so I am taking him away to a proper home at once. Where is he?"

Nathan jumped forward just in time to catch Nell as her knees buckled and she fell, limp and insensible.

21: Despair

Nell came to herself with Nathan's concerned face bending over her. She was lying down on a sofa in the saloon, and somewhere in the distance were raised voices, anxious voices. Was that James amongst them? Then she remembered...

"No, no. You must not try to sit up, not yet," Nathan said. "Lie still. Someone has gone for smelling salts."

"But I must. If James—"

"Hush now." His voice was as soft as butter, and as soothing. "Later. Lie still for now."

"Sorry," she murmured. "So sorry... so foolish of me."

"It was a dreadful shock. I am not surprised you were overwhelmed for a moment."

The distant voices became louder for a moment, and then one familiar one rose above the others. "Stand aside, Master James, for goodness sake! Where is she? Where is my little lady? Ah, Miss Nell, well now, what a to-do! But I'll take care of you, never fear. I'll have you right as a trivet in no time."

Nurse! Even in her distress, the familiar scolding tones made Nell smile.

Nathan laughed. "Your nurse, or I am a Dutchman. I shall yield to her greater authority."

"Do not leave me!" Nell cried, in sudden panic.

His lazy smile both thrilled and reassured her. "I shall be right here, never fear."

And then Nurse was bending over her, feeling her brow, waving smelling salts under her nose so that she half choked, before pronouncing, "You'll do well enough, I daresay, if Master James would stop harassing you, my pet. I told him how it would be, but would he listen? Never did listen, even as a boy. Still doesn't listen, and never mind that he's a baronet. No, lie still, my pet. And where is my precious lamb?"

Interpreting this to be Louis, Nell said, "He has gone out with Lady Harbottle."

"Lady Harbottle?" James's scowling countenance appeared above Nurse's shoulder. "Who is Lady Harbottle?"

"The widow of Sir William Harbottle, whose house this is," Nell said.

"Oh." James threw a quick glance at Nathan.

"No, not my house."

"Ah." James became thoughtful. He was not a quick-witted man, and clearly this information surprised and puzzled him, but his precipitate arrival began to make some sense to Nell. Brushing aside Nurse's protests, she slid her legs to the floor and sat up. At once she felt better.

"James, shall I introduce you properly? This is Mr Nathan Harbottle of York, who is cousin to the late Sir William. My brother Sir James Godney, of Daveney Hall in Hampshire, who has jumped to some erroneous conclusions, I fear."

"Well, naturally I thought— Your letter said you were staying with a friend, and Louis' letter was *'Mr Harbottle this'* and *'Mr Harbottle that'* and *'Mama's friend Mr Harbottle...'* It was a natural assumption to make."

"The friend I am staying with is Lady Harbottle," Nell said gently.

"Even so, *he* is obviously running tame in the house, and you are still in full black, Nell. It is not seemly."

"Mr Harbottle is executor of Sir William's will, and manages the estate in the absence of the heir. He has every right to be here, James dear, and it is not for you to criticise my behaviour. You declined to offer me any aid, so you have no right at all to interfere in what I choose to do with my life."

James drew himself up a little, then said with cold disdain, "I do not care what *you* do, Nell. You are a grown woman and may be as wanton as you wish." This drew a gasp from Nurse. "But I have every right to look to the moral and spiritual welfare of my ward. You are clearly not a fit and proper person to have the care of a young child, and as soon as he returns to the house I shall remove him from the unsuitable company into which you have brought him."

Nell could feel the roaring in her ears, but she was determined not to swoon again. She took a deep breath, and then another. Nurse thrust the smelling salts under her nose, and she half choked again, but it brought her back to her senses.

"Well, really, Master James—" Nurse began, then subsided as Nathan shook his head at her.

"Sir James," Nathan began, "your concern for your ward is very proper, but perhaps you may wish to become better acquainted with Mrs Caldicott's present situation before you rush to tear a young boy from his mother's arms. I am sure you would agree that such a separation would be most distressing for the child, and one would want to be very sure of the necessity before taking such a step, which would also be disruptive to your own household."

"Well... as to that... given my wife's delicate health... and Louis is so quick that he would benefit greatly from a school..."

Nell shot to her feet. "*School!* He is eight years old, James. You cannot send him away to school."

Nathan rested a warning hand on her arm, the other held up in appeal to James, and cut in quickly, "There is much to discuss, but—"

The door opened, and Louis burst in. "Uncle James! Have you brought my book?" When James looked puzzled, he went on, "The second volume about the Peloponnesian Wars. I only brought volumes one and three away from Daveney Hall. I wrote to you, asking you to send it. Did you not receive my letter?"

Nathan burst out laughing. "I do not think your uncle came all this way just to bring you a missing book, young man. Where are your manners?"

"I beg your pardon, sir." Louis dropped into a respectful bow. "Good day, Uncle James. I trust you are well."

In the doorway, Jessica stood, still bonneted and gloved, taking in all that was going on. She would see Nell's distress, and Nurse with the smelling salts still in her hand, and the attitudes of the two men, James belligerent and Nathan with hands raised in appeasement. She might not know exactly what the problem was, but she would see very clearly that there was trouble.

"What a delightful surprise," she said now, stepping forward into the room. "Nell, I had no idea we were to expect the honour of a visit from your brother. Would you be so good as to introduce me?"

Nell made the introductions, then said pointedly, "Louis, why do you not take Nurse upstairs to show her the nursery here?"

"Oh, but—"

"You may talk to Uncle James later."

Nurse understood at once. "Yes, come along, little man. I'll wager the nursery here is just as grand as at Daveney Hall, isn't it? Do you have a hobby horse?"

"A rocking horse! That is much better than a hobby horse. It is just like riding a real horse. I wish I had a horse... or a pony. Then I could ride every day..."

Nurse closed the door as they left the room, cutting off his high voice. Nell's legs would hold her up no longer, and she plumped back down onto the sofa. It was Jessica who took charge, smoothly insisting that James should stay for a night or two, and sweeping him, despite his protests, out to the hall to organise luggage and rooms, and send footmen and maids scurrying about at her command, the perfect hostess. As she left, she murmured to Nathan, "You will stay for tonight too, I hope? Another gentleman..."

They were alone. Nell found herself shaking uncontrollably. At once Nathan was there, sitting beside her, one arm about her shoulders.

"Do not give way to despair. Shall we escape from this room? The dowager will be here at any moment, and I am not sure I can manage to explain your brother to her without the use of language unfitting for a lady's ears. Come."

He stood, holding out his hand to her. Obediently she took it, and followed him through the door to the dining room, then the music room. Finally they crept across the passageway to the study, where he settled her gently into a chair.

"There. Now we can be comfortable for a while. I have no doubt they will find us soon enough, but perhaps I shall have my temper under control by then. Is your brother always so obnoxious? Had you not been in the room, I should have smacked him on his pompous nose. Jessica was very quick on the uptake, though. I am not sure it will be comfortable to have him staying here, but it will perhaps prevent any precipitate action on his part."

All the while he was finding glasses and bottles from a cupboard and pouring measures of liquid into two glasses.

"Here," he said, pressing a glass into her trembling hands. "It is brandy, to help steady your nerves. Take a little sip. Careful... here, let me help you."

He wrapped his own hands around hers, helping her lift the glass to her lips. She took the tiniest sip, then another.

"Better?" he said, tilting his head to one side.

She could not imagine that anything would make her feel better, but she nodded anyway, cradling the glass in her hands. Were they shaking less now? She thought they might be.

"I must write a quick note to my valet to bring my things from York, so that I may stay tonight. Sit quietly for a minute and drink your brandy while I do that, and then we shall discuss what is to be done."

She nodded and sipped, and allowed the warmth of the drink to seep into her and calm her, while he scratched away with the pen, and then summoned a footman to dispatch his note. Nathan was such a wonderful support. She knew she was perfectly capable and could manage her own life, but at times of high stress it was such a relief to have a shoulder to lean on. And his shoulder was so delightfully comfortable.

His message sent, he sat beside her, took a long draught from his own glass, then said, "Now, you must not give up hope, for we have time to consider what can be done about James."

"Nothing can be done," she said bleakly. "He is Louis' guardian, he has the right in law."

"He has been named as guardian in your husband's will," Nathan said, "but that may be challenged in the Court of Chancery."

"James is a baronet. Who would deny him?"

"That is a good point, and will weigh with the Lord Chancellor, undoubtedly. But you are his mother and, despite your brother's opinion, of excellent character. I must say, Nell, I cannot approve of a man who immediately supposes the worst of his own sister. I am very sorry if this offends you, but I cannot like him."

Nell managed a weak smile at this sally. "Today I do not like him very much either, but I cannot fight him in court. How can I afford lawyers?"

"You cannot, but I can, and I wager that my pockets are deeper than your brother's. I shall certainly fight him to a standstill in court, if that is what is needed. However, you are quite right. It would take some doing to convince any judge that a widow of limited means, however respectable, is a better guardian for Louis than a wealthy baronet. For a girl, they might be content to leave her with you, but a judge will very likely consider that a boy will have better prospects with his uncle."

"Then it is hopeless!"

"Not entirely." He set his brandy glass down on a side table. "We may not be able to convince a judge, but perhaps we do not need to. All we need to do is to convince James. He has already realised his mistake in assuming this house to be mine, finding it instead occupied by the fearsomely respectable relict of a baronet."

Nell shook her head in anguish. "But that did not sway him! He still thinks me immoral, and considering my history—"

"That has nothing to do with it!" In one fluid movement, he knelt at her feet and took her hands in his. "Nell, your brother does not want Louis one bit, and his wife even less, by the sound of it. He is only acting from duty. If we can convince him that a court case would be uncertain of success, that you are a woman of impeccable virtue and that Louis would be better off staying here with you, I believe he would be very happy to give up the idea altogether. He will not want to put himself to the trouble of a public battle over Louis, I am sure."

"True, but... it is impossible! How can we convince him?"

"There is one way..."

"Is there? Truly? Tell me what I must do, Nathan, for I cannot see any way out of this."

He looked into her eyes, and said, "You could marry me."

The room spun. Nell stared at him, unable to comprehend.

"Marry me, Nell, and at once the problem goes away. Louis has a step-father who can give him everything James could, and his mother is demonstrated to be a virtuous matron, perfectly suited to raise her fatherless child. Even the Court of Chancery would very likely be convinced of the benefits of leaving Louis with you." A long pause. "Say something, Nell, for God's sake."

"I..." Her head felt stuffed full of cotton. She could not *think*. "I cannot..."

He tilted his head again. "Cannot decide, or cannot marry me?"

At that precise moment, a footman came in. Studiedly staring at a point on the far wall, and not at Nathan on his knees and holding Nell's hands, he intoned, "Beg pardon, madam, sir, but her ladyship requests your presence in the saloon. If convenient," he added as an afterthought.

"The dowager?" Nell said.

"Yes, madam."

"Then we must go to her at once." That was something that did not need to be thought about, that was not confusing or distressing or frightening. Yes, she must go to the dowager, and drink tea, and talk about the weather. Then she would feel better.

~~~~~

Nathan thought he had never endured such a difficult evening. Everyone in the house, servants included, was now aware of the nature of Sir James Godney's visit. Jessica was weepy, Nell was pale and silent, and Louis refused to be in the same room as his uncle. The man himself was surly, and Nathan was fighting a strong desire to knock the stuffing out of him. Only the dowager was serene as always, her pleasure in having another baronet in the house outweighing the awkwardness of the circumstances.

However, her near-blindness made dinner very slow. First every dish had to be described for her in great detail so that she could choose what to eat, and then her own footman would prepare some of the chosen foods in a manner which permitted her to eat unaided. Her independence was inspiring, but it made the meal very, very drawn out and conversation something of a trial. Fortunately, wine loosened Godney's tongue somewhat and Nathan was able to cajole him into a discussion of his journey north, and discuss the best inns to patronise on his return journey.

When the ladies withdrew, Nathan thought he might tackle Godney regarding Louis and perhaps hint at his own scheme — he could not say that he was betrothed to Nell, but he could suggest the possibility in a roundabout way. He was forestalled, finding himself
~~~~~

on the receiving end of detailed enquiries into his own position and that of the Harbottles in general. When the question of the heir came up, Nathan found himself describing his search for Felix.

"And he has been missing for twenty years?" Godney said.

"Not quite. He has been estranged from the family for twenty two years, but while he was in the navy we at least knew where he was. But when he left the navy, he vanished. That was sixteen years ago."

"How very awkward," Godney said. "The title will become dormant unless you can find out what became of him, and that is always a tragedy. How many baronets have there been?"

"Sir William was the sixth. But perhaps he will be the last."

"You are very calm about it. Is there any possibility of having him declared dead so that you may claim the honour?"

"Unlikely," Nathan said. "Nor would I wish to, if there remains the least possibility that my cousin is still alive, or has fathered a son."

"Good point," Godney said. "He could have married and produced a string of brats in his image by now. Devil of a coil, Harbottle."

He smirked in the most irritating fashion, as if smugly pleased with his own well-regulated baronetcy. Nathan's urge to wipe the complacency from his face was almost overwhelming.

And all he wanted to do was to take Nell away somewhere quiet and list for her all the reasons why she should marry him. He cursed the footman who had interrupted them, and stopped her from answering. He cursed the need to behave with propriety, to portray the outward calm of the well-mannered gentleman, when inside he was screaming, *'Marry me, marry me, marry me!'* His words had been the impulse of the moment, the sudden realisation that they could resolve the question of Louis' welfare in the simplest way possible. His heart had surged with joy, and now, as he waited for her answer, he knew that she held all his happiness in her hands. He wished she would marry him in love and joy, but if she would come to him as a way to save Louis, he would take her just as eagerly. He would have a lifetime to make her smile and teach her to love him. Or at least to allow him to love her. Yes, that would be enough.

All evening he had watched her, seeing the pale face and the lifeless eyes, guessing how much she must ache inside. Her fears must be tearing at her vitals. She had eaten nothing, drunk nothing. She was there but not there. He longed to take her in his arms, to have the *right* to hold her close and offer her what comfort he could, and his inability to do so was like a knife driving deep into him. But once or twice he had caught her looking at him with a thoughtful expression on her face, as if she were considering his proposition. Please, please let her consider it. Please, please let her say yes, his dear, sweet Nell, so lovely and so many times hurt by the very men who should have given their lives to protect her.

But there was no opportunity to speak to her that night, and he retired to his room still roiling with waves of emotion — anger, despair, fear, love… and just a tiny shard of hope.

The next morning saw the four of them sitting down to a strained breakfast, Nell, Jessica, Godney and Nathan. The dowager was still in her room, and Louis had refused to leave the nursery. Jessica had recovered her spirits somewhat, and made polite conversation with Godney, successfully persuading him to stay for another night.

"Such a long journey back to Hampshire," she trilled. "So tiring travelling in the summer — so much dust! And all the inns full to bursting, and the meat going off in the heat. Quite unbearable. No, I insist upon you staying a little longer, Sir James, before setting out again."

And he, basking in her attentions, smiled and agreed that yes, travelling was unpleasant and it was *such* a long way to Hampshire, and then back to London to finish the season. Nathan thought of poor Louis, to be deposited at Daveney Hall with just the servants for company, while James and his delicately-situated wife disported themselves in London. It was unthinkable. Yet what could be done to dissuade him from the idea?

Godney's chair was facing the breakfast parlour windows, which overlooked the front drive. "You have a visitor," he said, through a mouthful of lamb chop.

"Who is it, Craven?" Jessica said.

Craven peered out. "It is Mrs Drabble, my lady."

"Oh, Barbara. Well, she is early today. My late husband's only sister, Sir James. A widow now."

Craven disappeared to admit her, their voices drifting in from the hall. Then a long silence, before Barbara came in, a sheet of paper in her hand.

"Where did this come from?" she said, bewilderment in her tone, as she held it up for them to see. One of Nell's drawings. "It was lying on the table in the hall."

"I drew it," Nell said. "It is of my husband."

"Your *husband?"* She stared at the drawing again, her expression one of complete confusion. "No... it cannot be."

"I assure you it is."

"But this... this is Felix."

22: A Face From The Past

Nell knew at once that it was true. It made complete sense. It was like an acrostic that one puzzled over for hours, and then the answer was simply there, entire and right. There was no record of Jude Caldicott's naval career because he had served as Felix Harbottle. There was no family in Ireland, because it was right there in Yorkshire. He had the letter from Felix in his box because he had written it himself, except...

"The script was different," she said, into the silence that had fallen. "The letter to Felix was not in Jude's hand."

It was Barbara who answered. "Felix could write with either hand. Not equally well, of course, for the right hand produced a fine, flowing script and the left only tiny, cramped lettering."

Nell nodded slowly. "I only ever saw him write with his left hand. Yes, tiny... cramped... that was it exactly."

Nathan was watching her anxiously. "Are you all right?" he said. "You are not feeling faint?"

She smiled. "No. This answers so many questions. It raises a few, too, but... it makes sense."

"It is wonderful!" Jessica burst out, tears pouring down her face, as she dabbed at them ineffectually with a tiny, lace-trimmed handkerchief. "Do you see what it means, Nell? Do you understand? It means that *Louis* is now the baronet, and this is his house... his home! He cannot leave here now!"

Nell looked at James, who was looking bemused. "I suppose... if this is true... this changes things somewhat, but I am still his appointed guardian."

"He must grow up to understand his responsibilities, with his family. His aunt and his grandmother," Nell said firmly.

"And his mother!" Jessica cried. "A child needs his mother, above all."

Nathan cut in smoothly, "We can discuss the ramifications in more detail later. The first thing to be done is to see if anyone else recognises Felix in this drawing. Jessica, are there any servants who were here then?"

"Marigold might remember... or old Ted, the coachman in those days."

"What about Mrs Wells?" Barbara said.

"She has always been in the kitchen," Jessica said. "She would never have been above stairs to see the family."

"Felix was often down there," Barbara said. "Especially when his father had sent him to bed with no supper."

And so it proved. Old Ted could not say for certain, and Marigold the housemaid thought it was rather like the previous vicar, but Mrs Wells gasped in delight when she saw the drawing.

"That's him to the life, milady, just like him. A bit older, like, but exactly him. Oh, milady, have you found him? Is Master Felix coming home at last?"

"No, Mrs Wells," Jessica said sadly. "He is not coming home."

Nell was glad that the task of telling the dowager the news did not fall to her. They waited for her in the saloon since the blue parlour, with its informal female atmosphere, was not considered a solemn enough setting to tell a lady of the dowager's advanced years that her youngest and last son was almost certainly lost for ever. As soon as she appeared on her footman's arm, Nathan brought her in and told her that Felix had been masquerading as Jude Caldicott for years.

The dowager displayed no open grief. "He is dead, then," she said, in a flat tone. "He died on that ship that sank and his bones rot in the sea."

"He is buried in the churchyard near to where the *Minerva* sank," Nell said. "A village called Pendower. He had a Christian burial."

"Ah. That is good," the dowager said. "That is something, at least." Her face softened suddenly. "And he had a son. An heir. We have found the next baronet."

"Only if it can be proved," Nathan said firmly. "Aunt Amelie, can you think of anything that might enable Nell to say definitively that her husband was Felix? Some birthmark or scar, perhaps?"

"No birthmark. He was perfect, a perfect little boy. Scars... I do not remember any."

"Did he have any possessions that might have identified him? William and Andrew both wore rings with the Harbottle crest on them. Did Felix have one, too?"

"All the boys had such a ring," she said.

"Nell, did Jude—?"

"Not with the Harbottle crest." She glanced at the fireplace which bore the engraved crest on the lintel. "He had a different ring..." She pulled it out from where it lay, hidden beneath her high-necked gown — the ring on its long chain, smooth under her fingers, and warm from its hiding place next to her body. "He used to seal his letters with it and he never wore it, but it is a ring."

"Felix's seal had a pair of dice upon it," the dowager said. "For luck. That is what his name means."

"Jude's seal is a bag," Nell said. "The thirty pieces of silver Judas was paid, or so he always said."

"Ha!" the duchess said. "That is Felix's seal. Give it to me."

Nell handed it over, and the dowager felt the ring with her fingers. Then with a sudden twisting movement of her fingers, she smiled. "Yes, this was Felix's."

When she handed it back, the ring showed two dice. "It changes?" Nell said wonderingly.

"He had it specially made," the dowager said. "Dice for his gambling luck, and bags of money for his investment luck. When he was feeling reckless, he gambled and then he used the seal with dice. When he was being sensible, he used the bags of money. He was always... mercurial. He had a pocket watch, too, that he inherited from an uncle."

"Jude's pocket watch had his own initials on it," Nell said. "*'JC'* for Jude Caldicott."

"Jeremiah Coales. Do you remember Uncle Jeremiah, Barbara? Left Felix one hundred pounds and his pocket watch."

Nell took a deep breath. "Then... then it is true," she whispered. "Jude truly was Felix Harbottle."

Nathan reached across from his chair and touched the back of her hand very, very lightly. "This is all circumstantial. We will need to prove all of this beyond any shadow of a doubt before we can be secure. But I do believe we have at last found Felix."

"And the answer to all the mysteries of my husband," Nell said.

But Nathan's face was shadowed, as if he was troubled.

~~~~~

While Nell and Jessica went off to the nursery to tell Louis of the dramatic change in his fortunes, and Barbara sat with the dowager, Nathan bore Sir James away to the male retreat of William's study and poured him a generous measure of Madeira.

"There is a newspaper in the drawer over there," he said. "No, not that one, the next one along."

"You keep the newspaper in a drawer? Whatever for?"

"My cousin was a very tidy man. He liked everything just so, and nothing lying around. If a book should be misaligned, he fretted dreadfully. The servants still follow his orders. You will not mind if I begin making lists? I shall have a great deal to do to get this matter settled."

"Shall you be able to? Supposing this is even true, of course, and not some convenient fiction."

Nathan was preparing a pen, and these words made his fingers curl tightly around the knife. Good grief, but the fellow was irritating! He breathed deeply, carefully set down the quill and knife, and turned to face the baronet. "It would have been a great deal more *convenient* to find it out two years ago, when Felix was first looked for in earnest," he said through clenched teeth. "It would have been a great deal more *convenient* if he were still alive to swear to his own identity. I cannot imagine how you think we might have contrived this *'convenient fiction'*."

Godney smirked. "Oh, come now, Harbottle! You must think me a fool. You met Nell in Southampton, did you not? I daresay you cooked it up between you. A husband of the right age and background — what could be more perfect? It is a little inconvenient
~~~~~

that the fellow is dead, but it can still be done. A fortuitous discovery of a letter, no doubt, confirming all. The old retainers to swear to the likeness of Nell's drawing. I dare say you gave her the ring on the chain for the Dowager Lady Harbottle to recognise. Very convincing. And now, I suppose, you will marry my sister to gain access to the fortune."

Nathan laughed. "You have a twisted mind, Godney, if you think that would be a sensible way of proceeding. If I wished to gain access to the fortune, I have only to prove that Felix is dead without issue, for I am next in line. In fact, I already have access to it, for my cousin left me with the power to manage everything as I see fit. If I were a different sort of man, and I had not already a much larger fortune of my own, it might be a temptation, I concede."

Godney eyed him speculatively. "Larger fortune, eh?"

"West Indies," Nathan said, not feeling any obligation to elaborate.

"Ah." Godney lost interest, picked up the newspaper and began to read, and Nathan was able to return to his lists.

Some time later, when Godney had long since grown bored and wandered off, there was a tap on the door, followed at once by Nell and a footman bearing a tray of tea things.

"Should you like some tea?" she said. "If not, will you mind if I have some, and drink it in here with you? I shall not disturb your work."

"I am very happy to be disturbed, I assure you, and to have some tea."

For a few minutes there was silence as the footman arranged the tea things, and Nell poured. She remembered how he liked his tea, he noticed, and the thought pleased him to an absurd degree.

When the footman had withdrawn, she said, "Thank you for letting me escape for a little while. Your aunt wishes to tell me how perfect Felix was, but her version of his character does not quite match my memories of my husband, and I have no wish to quarrel with her. But I thought James was here with you. Where did he go to?"

"Jumped in the lake, I hope. Is he always this obnoxious? Thinking the worst of people?"

She smiled. "Oh, yes. Julia is worse. If James has a book in his hand, and nothing requiring him to move from his chair, then he is perfectly contented, whereas Julia is *never* contented, and sometimes I think she is downright malicious. I am very thankful I do not have to live with her, for we should be pulling caps within a day."

"This is the lady of the excessively long recovery time?"

She giggled in a most unladylike fashion, almost choking on her tea. "I could not possibly say, although it does seem as though they have resolved their difficulties."

"Then he should be considerably less grumpy," Nathan said firmly.

This time she did choke on her tea. "You are very bad," she whispered. "Poor James! He does rather set himself up as a figure of fun, but then he was always stuffy, even as a child. Not high in the instep, as Julia is, but pompous, like a much older man."

Such pleasantries were delightful, and Nathan was relieved beyond measure that his clumsily executed proposal had not created any constraint between them, but he had no wish to waste his precious time with her talking about her annoying brother, so he said, "How did Louis take the news of his elevation in rank?"

"Well, I did not mention the baronetcy to him. Jessica and I decided that it would distress him too greatly if it all falls through. I told him only that it seems likely that his father was actually Felix Harbottle, which makes him a Harbottle too. He is delighted to discover that Jessica is his aunt. Furthermore, he finds it wildly exciting that his father was pretending to be someone else, and has decided that he was probably on some secret mission for the government. He will work it out soon enough about the title, or one of the servants will let it slip, but he understands it may be hard to prove, now that Jude is dead. But not impossible, I hope?"

He shook his head. "Not impossible, no, but it will need a great deal more evidence than we have so far. I cannot believe that Felix was so lost to all that he owed his family as not to make some provision for this eventuality. He read the newspapers, I assume, so he would have known that the last brother standing between him and the baronetcy had died. He must have realised that he was the heir, and that he would have to show himself eventually, when William died."

"But he died before Sir William. He did not know the time or place of his own death," she said.

"None of us do," Nathan said. "That is why we write wills, to ensure a tidy transition. There was nothing untoward in his will, presumably?"

"Nothing. He left everything to Louis, apart from a few small bequests to his fellows on the *Minerva*, most of whom are also dead."

"And there was nothing odd amongst his effects? No letters, papers, documents, apart from the letter to Aunt Amelie?"

She shook her head. "I did not look very thoroughly, however."

"I shall have to go and check. There may be a false bottom or a hidden drawer or a box under the floorboards with all his papers. There has to be *something* that connects Felix Harbottle to Jude

Caldicott, something that will convince the Master of the Rolls. And then, once that has been proved, I shall also need to prove that Felix had legitimate issue."

"There is no difficulty there," she said. "We were married in the parish church at Bishopswood Cromby by Mr George Lumley, an ordained clergyman, in the presence of my father and brother and most of the village. I have my marriage lines to prove it. Louis' birth was registered in Southampton."

"Nevertheless, I shall have to go to these places and check the registers. There is Felix's change of name, too. We must hope that was executed in some official manner. Nell, it is an imposition, I know, and I have no right to ask it of you, but this will be a great deal easier to accomplish if you are with me. I have no authority to investigate Jude or your marriage or Louis' birth, and although you can write me letters authorising me to act on your behalf, there may still be those who refuse to assist me."

"You want me to go with you?"

"If you are willing."

"With Louis?"

"I do not think it would be wise for Louis to be party to our investigations," he said cautiously. "He is too young to understand it all. However, if we can persuade his uncle to agree to it, I believe he would be perfectly happy to stay here with Jessica."

He paused, watching her face. It pleased him that she did not immediately say no. Instead, she considered it carefully, thoughtfully, her lovely face serious. Her cheeks were a little plumper these days, he thought, and it suited her. It was always a pleasure to sit and look at her, but the intimacy which had grown between them made the watching all the sweeter. So he watched and waited as she thought it through.

Her head lifted. "Would it be quite proper? The two of us travelling together, I mean... even though we are... cousins by marriage."

He broke into laughter. "So we are! But I had not intended us to travel alone. I shall find you some fearsomely starchy lady's maid who will share your room and guard your virtue, and my valet will lock me in at night to forestall any nocturnal wanderings."

"I am not afraid of what you might do, only of what the world might say. However, the starchy lady's maid would suffice to protect my reputation, such as it is. If Louis is permitted to stay with Jessica and is happy with that arrangement, then I shall willingly accompany you, but you will appreciate that his welfare must come first."

His unruly heart surged in delight at the glorious prospect opening up before him — weeks, perhaps, in her enchanting company. What more could any man wish for?

There was just one small difficulty...

"Nell, there is one point in all this that we must consider, no matter how painful. If we are to make our investigations into your husband, there is the possibility that we may discover even more unhappy truths about him. That we may end up a great deal worse than before."

"It is difficult to believe it could be any worse. Oh, but... you suspect something?" She sat a little straighter on her chair, and set down the tea cup she had been cradling. "This sounds very ominous."

"I hope I am wrong about this, but it must be considered."

Nodding, she said, "Very well. I am prepared for the worst. Tell me what you suspect."

"You are aware, perhaps, that Felix was married when he was very young — only one and twenty."

"The housemaid. Mrs Drabble told me all about it, that she fell to her death and— Oh."

Nathan could see her abrupt realisation. Her face paled.

"She said..." She stopped, caught her breath, ploughed on. "She said there was some suspicion that she had *not* died, that he had simply got tired of her and... Oh God! Perhaps she is still alive? Perhaps she has a son? A *legal* son, and Louis is—" Her breath grew ragged and she covered her mouth with her hand, eyes closed.

"That is what we must find out, with some urgency," he said, in his gentlest tones.

She jumped to her feet, and paced across the room and back. "No, I cannot believe it! Jude would never have married bigamously, no. He would not have done such a thing, not to me. He *loved* me, Nathan, he did!"

"I am very sure of it. But if we are right about this, then something drove Felix to abandon his real name and leave his past behind so thoroughly that no one could find him. Who was he hiding from? Could it have been his wife?"

"I *cannot* believe it," she said stubbornly.

"Then who are all those payments to, Nell? Eight hundred pounds a year, for more than twenty years... enough to support a wife, surely."

"*'EP'*," she whispered. "Was that the housemaid's name?"

"Her name was Eliza," he said. "His wife's name was Eliza."

23: A Journey South

Nathan spent one more night at Percharden House, working subtly but steadily towards eroding Godney's plans for Louis. After a second night of good food, good wine and gentle persuasion, Godney had been brought to concede, albeit rather ungraciously, that the home of the widow of a baronet was a perfectly proper place for Louis to stay, whether or not she turned out to be his aunt. Louis himself was happy for his mother to leave him there for a while with the besotted Jessica. No child ever minded being spoilt, and besides, Louis was clever enough to have worked out that the Percharden House library was now *his* library, and all the books therein, and was determined to read every last one of them.

Reluctantly, Nathan returned to York to plan the journey south. It would be more complicated with Nell, but vastly more pleasurable. When he arrived home, there was such a great deal for him to tell Meg and the two Macs that the discussion of it carried them through dinner and the whole evening. Even that was not enough for Meg, who came through to his room to continue the conversation. After a while, her chatter slowed.

"So, brother, are you going to tell me the parts you have left out?"

"What makes you think there is anything left out?"

"Because you are as miserable as a ten-hour sermon, that is why, and considering you will be spending weeks on the road with your beloved, you should be in alt."

He was sitting on the window seat, his long legs stretched out before him, but it was not a question that could be answered in so casual a pose. He swivelled round to face her.

"I offered for her, Meg."

"Ohhhh... finally! But she rejected you."

"No."

"She... accepted you?"

"No. We were interrupted, but it is immaterial now. I offered for her as a way to keep her miserable brother away from Louis, and now that the boy is a baronet, there is no need for such protection." He leaned forward, elbows on knees, and looked studiedly at his feet. "I had her in my hands, Meg. She was considering it, and she would have done it, too, for Louis' sake."

"So... your offer was merely the unselfish gesture of a friend? Is that what you are trying to convince yourself?"

He shook his head with a rueful smile. "No. I have finally seen the truth in my own heart. My offer was made on impulse, but at that instant, as I spoke the words, I understood at last how much she means to me. I know she does not love me, and perhaps she never will, but I would have made her happy. We would have had years and years for me to make her happy, and give her the wonderful life she deserves and that her husband failed to give her. And now I have to smile and pretend it makes no difference and inside I am hurting. It hurts so much. I *want her* so much. I hate being a gentleman, Meg. I hate it. Having to be restrained and polite and... and not touch her. I cannot bear the thought of never touching her again." He took a ragged breath. "Forgive me. I should not burden you with things you cannot understand."

"Oh but I can," she said in a low voice. "I understand better than you know."

"Harry?"

"Harry. But I have too much pride to let him see how much he affects me. You will survive this, just as I do, by taking each day as it comes. And I bring you good news, brother. You want a starchy maid to accompany Nell, and you shall have one. You may take Carlotta."

"Your own maid? But how will you manage?"

"I cannot, of course, so I shall have to come with you." She gurgled with merriment. "This will be so much fun!"

~~~~~

Nell had travelled but little in her life. Childhood visits to relations, meaning dreary hours confined in the old travelling coach with Nurse. The journey to London, her senses assaulted with every new sight and sound and smell, and feeling sick with excitement. The short journey from the church to Southampton with Jude, delirious with happiness. And finally, her strange flight to Yorkshire, bewildered and grieving. She had never yet travelled with two good friends, who beguiled every mile with diversion of one sort or another. At least, Meg beguiled every mile. Nathan started the day cheerful, then fell into silence, fingers tapping his knee impatiently, until the first change of horses was accomplished, repeating the pattern as the hours passed.

"He becomes fretful when he travels, in case of mishap," Meg said. "Take no notice of him, for there is nothing to be done to relieve his anxiety. He will be better once we arrive."

It was Meg, therefore, who maintained a stream of anecdotes and observations, and cajoled Nell out of her gloom.
~~~~~

She was undeniably gloomy. For the first time in eight years, there was no Louis at her side, sitting next to her at table, his hand firmly in hers when they walked, or leaning against her when they sat together. Sometimes when she walked, her hand stretched out to reach for him, only to remember with a pang of sorrow that he was far away. It had hurt that he was so excited to stay with Aunt Jessica and Grandmama, but then he had never before had relations who wanted him and loved him and smiled whenever he entered a room. His father sometimes, when he was at home, but mostly it had been just Nell, and a child needed more than his mother. He needed a whole family of relations.

There was another cause for her gloom, too, because Nathan had asked her to marry him. It was only because of Louis, she knew that, and it had been couched in practical terms and not at all romantic, but still, she had seen the light in his eyes, and could recognise the eagerness in his voice, in the way he leaned forward as he spoke. His motives were not entirely altruistic.

Marriage... she shivered even at the thought of it. For Louis' sake, perhaps, she might have considered it, but for herself? She never wanted another husband, never! She had lived the last few years in darkness, and now that she was finally catching glimpses of sunshine, there was nothing on earth that could make her surrender it again. Besides, would she really want to marry Nathan, knowing that she would always be second best? He would never forget his first love, just as Nell would never forget Jude, even though neither love had brought lasting happiness.

And yet, when he looked at her with such admiration in his eyes, her resolve weakened. To be loved, as she once had been, to be cherished again would be so glorious. Then there was his wealth. It should not matter, she scolded herself, but inside she yearned to be rich again, to buy a new gown whenever she wanted one, and have a carriage at her disposal. One could live without much money, but life was a great deal more pleasant when one had more of it.

And yet... could she trust him? How could she ever trust a man again?

It was too difficult to think about, so she pushed the subject to the back of her mind and hoped that Nathan would not mention it again.

Nathan did not, but Meg had no such inhibitions. At the first overnight stop, as soon as her very prim maid had readied them for bed and withdrawn, Meg pushed back the covers and sat up in bed.

"Now, Nell, we can have a comfortable coze," she said.

Never having had a sister, Nell was unused to having her repose disrupted by a whirlwind like Meg. "Can we?"

"Yes, for we are cousins, are we not? We have hours and hours before we have to be up and about again, and what else is there to do?"

"Sleep?" Nell suggested tentatively.

Meg laughed uproariously at such a cowardly attitude. "Nonsense! You may sleep in the carriage tomorrow if you wish. You cannot imagine how much I have longed to have a good friend of my own age."

Nell resigned herself to the inevitable and sat up too. "I am sure you have many friends."

"Once, I did," Meg said, a hint of a shadow crossing her face. "In Edinburgh I had a great many friends, but one by one they married and disappeared from my life. Then we moved to York and somehow, I do not know why it should be so, but it is more difficult to make friends when one is an outsider."

"How old were you when you left Edinburgh?" Nell said, interested despite her wish for sleep.

"Five and twenty."

"Ah. Too old to mix with the newly out, but with nothing in common with the matrons."

"True," Meg said with a sigh. "I have made friends of a sort, but none with whom I may be intimate. Not like a sister. I always longed for a sister. I daresay you did, too."

Nell chuckled. "I was too vain to want any rival in the family. Perhaps a younger sister would not be so bad, but an older sister would be a dreadful burden. To be always second — or third, or fourth! Imagine how wearisome."

"But *we* could be like sisters," Meg said eagerly. "We could even be sisters in truth. Are you going to marry him?"

Nell did not have to ask which *him* she had in mind. "It is unlikely," she said cautiously.

"But he is so much in love with you, and—" Meg stopped, bit her lip and then went on more slowly, "He would be good to you, Nell. He would treat you well and..."

"Not like Jude, you mean," Nell said bitterly.

"Oh Nell, I so much want you to be happy. I want *both* of you to be happy."

Nell closed her eyes. How difficult it was to explain! To an outsider, it must seem so simple — her husband had hurt her, so she must be glad to be rid of him and happy to be sought by another man. In some ways she *was* glad to be rid of Jude and the ever-present fear of what he might do. But she had loved him for a long time, deeply and passionately, and could not lightly set aside the memory of the good times or the erosion of the happy marriage that she had once set down as certain. Her sense of loss was almost as great as her sense of release.

Not equal to the task of explaining what she did not fully understand herself, she said only, "Who among us truly knows what it is to be happy? Or what would make one happy? I do not know myself what would make *me* happy, not any more. Life seems so straightforward when one is seventeen, but as one grows older and sees more of the world, so it seems that people everywhere are always unhappy, always discontented and wanting something that is not within reach. The sea took my husband from me only four months ago, Meg. He was not the perfect husband I had hoped for, but we shared many good years, we had a son together, and I am not yet ready to let go of his memory, or begin to think about the future."

Meg hugged her and begged her pardon and after no more than another hour or so of chatter, finally allowed her to sleep.

~~~~~

Nathan was awake very early the next morning. Travelling always made him restless, with the noise, the constant motion and the fretting over every little detail. He wished he could see a journey the way Meg did, as a glorious adventure, an experience to be revelled in to the utmost, without the least care in the world, but he could not. He would not sleep or eat well or be free from anxiety until they reached their destination.

This particular journey, however, had one particular compensation, and she, too, was up early. He had not long settled in their private parlour to begin his lists for the day, a pot of coffee at his elbow, when Nell appeared. Even in her unadorned black travelling gown, her hair pinned into a simple knot, she was as beautiful and elegant as ever, brightening the day and bringing a lift to his heart.
~~~~~

"Good morning! Did you sleep well?" he said, his pleasure at seeing her bringing a smile to his lips.

"As well as I ever sleep at an inn, which is to say, not well at all. It is not the inn's fault, however, for I never was in a more comfortable one in my life."

"I never sleep much when I travel, either," he said. "Then I doze in the carriage and get a crick in my neck and my head aches abominably, which throws me quite out of temper, and makes me fractious with ostlers and tapboys and chamber maids."

She smiled, but shook her head. "I cannot imagine you fractious with anyone. I beg your pardon... you are hard at work, and I am disturbing you."

"Oh, I am only writing lists. I am always writing lists. Planning, you see. Everything orderly. The whole journey is planned to a nicety, no detail too small to be thought of. That way, we suffer no delays. Shall I order some fresh coffee for you? This pot will be cold by now."

She agreed to it, and as the servant brought a basket of buns as well, they sat companionably together, eating and drinking. He began several topics of conversation, but when she answered only in the briefest terms, he said, "You are very quiet today. Is there something worrying you?"

With a sigh, she said, "Only Louis. He has never been separated from me before, not for a single night. I only hope that he is not waking this morning missing me as much as I miss him."

"He is with Jessica," he said gently. "She will take good care of him, for she has enough mother's love for twenty children. It is a great tragedy that she had none of her own. She wanted to take Henny under her wing at one time, and I might have considered it, but William would not have it. Well, Aunt Amelie was the one who would not have it, I suppose, and he always followed her opinion."

"She is quite a high stickler," Nell said. Cautious words! How like her, not wanting to offend.

"Oh yes! And Henny is a natural child, after all," he said. "But there was a cousin — there were five daughters in the family and very little money. Jessica thought to take one of them off their hands, but Aunt Amelie would not have that, either. It was not right to raise children above their station, she said. I am very fond of Aunt Amelie, but it would have been better for William and Jessica if she could have gone to the dower house when Uncle Henry died. Unfortunately it was impossible, for her sight was already failing, even so long ago. She was there for a month, but she kept bumping into things and tripping over. After the third fall, William brought her back to Percharden House where she knows her way about, and there she has stayed."

"That is never a good idea, having the old mistress of the house still in residence," Nell said. "Although Jessica does seem to be very firmly in charge."

"Of domestic matters, yes, but Aunt Amelie ruled William, and Jessica never attempted to wean him away from his mama. Should you like to write to Louis? He will be interested to hear of your journey, and compare it with his own journey north."

"I thought to write when we get to London, but... is there somewhere here that takes in the post? This is only a small village."

"The other inn. I should be happy to take your letter there, and see it safely handed over."

So she thanked him and fetched her writing box, wherein he recognised his own gift of paper and quills. Although Nathan continued to work on his lists, he watched her surreptitiously as she wrote two full sheets to Louis, the pen scratching away on the paper, then dipped in the ink pot, then scratching again, in a steady rhythm. She wrote rather fast, but neatly, the letters smoothly regular. When she had finished, he went out to the post office and by the time he returned, Meg was up, breakfast was set out, the carriage was ordered and all was a-bustle preparing for the second day of their travels.

Only one incident marred the otherwise perfect journey. Having both the travelling carriage and a luggage coach with them, and needing four horses for each, Nathan had carefully written ahead to ensure that each change of horses would be ready for them. However, they arrived at a busy coaching inn to discover that their two teams were on the point of being given to an earl instead and there were no more teams available that day. Yes, the innkeeper had received Nathan's letter and yes, he had understood the expected time of their arrival, but the earl was in urgent need, and he knew that Mr Harbottle, being such an amiable gentleman, would not mind.

Nathan minded very much. It threw all his careful preparations quite out of kilter. It was too late in the day to obtain more horses, and it did not suit him at all to stop for the night so soon, for that would make for a much longer day's travelling tomorrow. He would have to reconsider all his arrangements for the rest of the journey, and if there was one thing he disliked above any other, it was being required to alter arrangements at short notice.

There was only one thing to be done, and that was to persuade the earl to surrender any claim to the horses — *his* horses, as he already thought them. This was not as easy as it seemed. The earl, a large and florid-faced gentleman, accompanied by several stiff-necked ladies and an improbable number of footmen, coachmen, grooms, maids and postilions, was not inclined to give up the horses.

He needed them, he told Nathan, and the needs of a peer naturally took precedence over any mere commoner.

Being unable to summon a marquess or a duke to his aid to outrank the earl, Nathan set to work on the innkeeper instead, whose eyes glistened at the sight of the roll of soft wafted under his nose. He wavered, dithered and then called to the ostler to stop hitching the team to the earl's carriage.

The earl exploded. He berated in the loudest possible terms the innkeeper, the ostlers, Nathan and then the innkeeper again. When the innkeeper's wife rushed out to placate him with offers of wine and mutton stew, he yelled at her, too. Two passing coachmen and a small gaggle of townsfolk stopped to watch. The innkeeper dithered again, wringing his hands, but the prospect of so much money was too tempting. Nathan began counting notes into his hand. The earl took a step forward and raised his fists at Nathan, who pushed the whole roll into the innkeeper's hand and turned round to face the irate earl, fully prepared to defend himself.

Meg's small hand tugged at Nathan's sleeve, at first gently, then more urgently. "Nathan! *Nathan!* All this shouting... Nell is upset."

He broke away at once, dashing back to the carriage. Through the window, he saw Nell hunched up in the corner whimpering with distress, her face turned away from the open door and buried in the squabs. At that moment, the only thing in the world he wanted to do was to take her in his arms and hold her until her fears subsided. If only he could! But he had no right... and more than that, he doubted there was any comfort he could offer her that would help. The earl's raised voice — the raised *male* voice — had brought back all her fears of her husband. There was no man on earth who could assuage those fears, for her terror of men was still too deep-seated. No matter how much he loved her, he could not help her.

Nathan turned away from the carriage, and spoke quietly to the innkeeper. "His lordship may have the horses."

24: London

It took Nell the whole evening and much of the next day to recover her equanimity. It helped that Meg and Nathan neither fussed nor asked questions. Instead, they treated her exactly as usual, making no comment on her long silences or the way she toyed with her food, carrying the conversation between them and giving no sign, by word or expression, that they saw anything amiss. For the rest of the journey, Nathan tactfully sat on the box beside the coachman, and although she felt sure she would not have minded his presence inside the carriage, she was grateful for his forbearance.

By the time they drew into London, Nell was sufficiently recovered to look about her with eager anticipation. There was a pleasure in living in the quiet of the country, but the metropolis brought a very different kind of pleasure. The busy streets full of horses, carriages and wagons, the press of people thronging the pavements and the ever-present noise exhilarated her. London was exciting, and her only regret was that she was not to be there long. Three nights they would stay with Harry Smethurst, no more. Just enough time to enquire at the Admiralty for information about Felix's wife.

Harry's house was charmingly appointed. It was not large, but the rooms were well-proportioned and fitted out with great elegance. The visitors were shown into the drawing room to await their host.

"Mr Smethurst has the honour of entertaining the Marquess of Carrbridge," the footman, Withers, informed them with some pride. "His lordship is in the study at this very moment."

"Does Lord Carrbridge often call upon my friend?" Nathan said, in surprised tones.

"Not often, sir, but he occasionally finds it convenient to conduct private meetings here, rather than at Marford House or the House of Lords. May I fetch some tea for you?"

While they waited for the tea, as Meg flicked through the newspaper and Nathan adjusted his neckcloth in the mirror, Nell walked around the room admiring the accomplished hand of the Marchioness of Carrbridge in the decorations. The lady had exquisite taste, reflected in every item in the room, from the delicately wrought chandelier to the polished slate fireplace to the Turkish rugs on the floor. It was delightful.

Voices on the stairs were followed almost instantly by the door being thrown open to admit three gentlemen. Harry she knew, but the other two were unknown to her. The very handsome fellow with the fashionable attire and a patrician air she had no trouble identifying as the marquess. The thin-faced man in black she took to be an aide of some sort.

"Here you are, just at the hour expected!" Harry said, with a warm smile, his eyes lingering on Meg. "Lord Carrbridge has expressed a wish to make your acquaintance, if that is agreeable to you, Mrs Caldicott?"

"That would be a great honour," Nell murmured.

"Mrs Caldicott, Miss Harbottle, may I present to you my noble and most generous patron, Lord Carrbridge, and his secretary, Sir

Daniel Merton. My lord, Sir Daniel, may I present Mrs Caldicott of Southampton and Miss Harbottle of York."

After the exchange of bows and curtsies, Lord Carrbridge offered his condolences, which Nell thought very handsome of him. At least he did not mention the Duke of Falconbury! She was so tired of hearing about the poor duke, as if he had been the only man on board the *Minerva.*

Harry then introduced Nathan, and for some minutes the conversation was all of Yorkshire, for the marquess had his principal seat there.

Before they left, the marquess said brightly, "You must all come to dinner at Marford House tomorrow. Very informal, you know, only family, but Lady Carrbridge will want to meet you."

Nell demurred, but within an hour a letter had been delivered from the marchioness herself, making the invitation formal and expressing her hopes of their attendance in such terms that made even Nell hesitate.

"Oh, but you *must* go!" Meg cried. "For if you do not, then I must stay here and bear you company and think how infamous it would be to deprive me of such fun! I shall be excessively blue-devilled if you do not."

Nell did not feel she could well refuse and to Marford House, therefore, they were to go.

~~~~~

Nathan was not in the best of spirits. He had set out with such high hopes of a glorious time in Nell's company, their intimacy gradually deepening into something more than friendship. Perhaps there might even be a moment during their travels when he could raise the subject of marriage again. He would have to express himself more delicately than before, since there was not the same urgency of
~~~~~

losing Louis, and Nell was still in mourning, after all. But it could be hinted at, the subject raised, his own feelings made a little plainer.

But now it was impossible. It was clear that all her composure was no more than a veneer, and the fear that her husband had engendered in her still lay very close to the surface, and that was a dispiriting thought. It was not merely that he felt himself obliged to draw back a little, not seeking out her company at every opportunity. Nor was it that his hopes of pressing his suit upon her had receded somewhat.

No, his real fear was that her experience of one evil husband had soured her for matrimony altogether. She had said more than once that she had no wish to marry, and he had not believed her. He had assumed, in his arrogance, that patience and gentleness and ardent love, combined with the manifold benefits of the match, for Louis as well as herself, would eventually win her round. Now he was brought to acknowledge that it might not be so. He was not yet ready to give up all hope, but he could appreciate that he must proceed with the utmost caution, to avoid an outright rejection.

London helped. There were no bad memories there for any of them, and already they were forging new and illustrious connections that must surely please Nell. The Marquess of Carrbridge noticing them was a piece of the greatest condescension, and they could hardly have expected it. Nell had scruples about dining in unfamiliar company while in deep mourning, which was understandable, but a family dinner, even in so grand a family as the Marfords, must be unexceptionable.

Before that, however, there was a less agreeable task to be undertaken.

"I hope you will not mind, Nathan," Harry had said, rather sheepishly, "but Lord Toller has expressed a wish to see you while you are here, and since it is about Felix, I felt you would have no objection."

"On the contrary," Nathan said, "I should like to talk to him, too. He is on my list of those who knew Felix in his navy days, so he may have useful information."

"Excellent. He will be at White's this evening, so we can slip round there after dinner."

Toller loomed over them in his garish clothes, full of *bonhomie*. "Ah, there you are Smethurst, Harbottle. Been expecting you for some time. You there! Bring more brandy over here. Sit, both of you and tell me the news from the north. *Is* there any news from the north?"

"None at all," Nathan said promptly. "The Scots are peaceable, the weather is balmy, the sea is calm and the corn is ripening."

Toller laughed, but rather half-heartedly, as if he was unsure of Nathan's mood. Nathan was unsure of his own mood, in fact, disliking the fellow cordially and for no good reason that he could think of. For a few minutes they talked on indifferent subjects, before Toller said, "So, Harbottle, tell me — have you heard anything of that cousin of yours?"

"Nothing. In fact, I have reason to believe Felix may be dead."

"Dead... ah." Toller twirled his brandy glass thoughtfully.

"In fact, my visit to London is to establish if I can the circumstances of his wife's death, and determine if there might have been a son. That is a matter you may be able to help me with, since you knew Felix in those days, I understand?"

Toller was an expert card player, so he had his features under control. Nevertheless, Nathan thought a certain cautiousness crept into his expression.

"Knew him... a little, certainly."

"Did you know his wife?"

"Slightly. Very slightly."

"We heard little of Felix in those days, but he informed us that his wife had died. Did you know anything of that?"

Now there was definite wariness in Toller's countenance. "Knew of it, yes. She fell from a balcony, as I understand it. Seems a little morbid to be concerning yourself with such matters after all this time, Harbottle."

Nathan sipped his brandy thoughtfully. Was Toller trying to turn him away from such questions? Interesting. "The trouble is, my cousin Sir William Harbottle died recently without issue, leaving Felix the putative heir. He himself may be dead, but if he left a son—"

"Now that I can assure you of at once. There was no son. Eliza died before her child could be born."

Eliza. His slight acquaintance was such as to permit him to call her by her Christian name. "And he did not marry again, that you know of?"

"Lord, no! She was a shrew and a great trial to him, and he was glad to be rid of her. Nothing would induce him to marry again. Or so he said."

That made Nathan smile inwardly — Nell had changed his mind about that!

Toller went on, "So you have reason to believe him dead, do you?"

Nathan hesitated. He hated to discuss Nell with a relative stranger, but they had agreed that disseminating their suspicions as widely as possible could only be helpful. There must be someone who had information connecting Felix with Jude Caldicott. So he said, "We suspect that the captain of the brig that sank, the *Minerva*, may have been Felix. He went by the name of Jude Caldicott."

"At what port was the *Minerva* based?"

"Southampton."

"Ah..." Toller said pensively. "More brandy, gentlemen?"

~~~~~

The following day, Nathan went to the Admiralty. Since his enquiries concerned only Felix, and not his existence as Jude Caldicott, he left Harry and the ladies to fill the day as they chose. Knowing Meg, Nathan suspected that they would fill the day rather expensively.

He had, naturally, written ahead to the Admiralty, so he was led at once to the office of an Admiral Beckley, a ruddy-featured man of about five and forty.

"Felix Harbottle!" he said, after the greetings. "That is a name to conjure up memories. A fine fellow, as I recall him. But you enquire about his wife, as I understand it?"

"About Felix, too, if you have any recent knowledge of him."

"Alas, no. He left the navy some sixteen years ago, shortly after he was promoted to the rank of Captain, and nothing has been noted on his record since then."

"He did not marry again, to your knowledge?"

"He did not ask permission to do so, certainly, and his marriage was not such as to— Hmm. Were you much acquainted with his wife, Mr Harbottle?"

"Not at all. I never met either of them. She was a housemaid at my aunt's house, so I can only guess what sort of navy wife she made."

"A housemaid?" The admiral's neatly-trimmed eyebrows rose a fraction. "That does account for... certain irregularities in her behaviour. She was not the easiest person to live with, certainly, but Commander Harbottle must have been fond of her, for he was very
~~~~~

distressed by her death. To the question you posed in your letter, Mr Harbottle, yes, she is most certainly dead, and the child she carried with her also. The coroner was very thorough, and she was identified by your cousin and two others who knew her. She is most definitely dead. It was a rum business, though. Did you ever hear the details?"

"No, nothing at all except the bare facts," Nathan said. "I should be curious to know how a lady might fall from a balcony to her death."

The admiral sat back in his chair, resting his steepled hands against his lips as he pondered. "Commander and Mrs Harbottle, being very young still, had fallen in with rather a wild crowd. Well, our officers are trained to fight wars, and life aboard ship is very disciplined and rigorous, you understand, so when ashore they like to be... a little less restrained, shall we say. That particular night, there was a great deal of rum punch consumed, by the ladies as well as the gentlemen, and so matters became lively. Commander Harbottle had... a tempestuous relationship, let us say, with his wife, and they had quarrelled, loudly and publicly, earlier in the evening. Around two in the morning, the watch found her broken body beneath the balcony. Commander Harbottle was located, fast asleep in the marital bed, two hours later. The coroner deemed it a tragic accident."

Nathan frowned. The admiral's clipped tones and flat recitation of the facts suggested... he was not sure what they suggested, but it was unsettling. "Was there any question that it was *not* an accident? Was Felix suspected?"

"Those are... interesting questions," the admiral said carefully. "At the time, no doubt a great many rumours swirled about, but the coroner's report shows nothing of that, only the bald facts and the coroner's judgement. I reviewed the report again when I received your letter, and I can tell you that there is no stain on your cousin's record of any sort, and nothing transpired in the coroner's court to indicate otherwise. In fact, there was a witness found some days after the tragedy who had seen Commander Harbottle leave the house while his wife was alive and well."

"A witness?"

"A Mr Pascall. A *friend* of your cousin's." Now there was obvious disparagement in his tone.

"Admiral Beckley, I have reason to believe my cousin is dead, and whatever you say cannot harm him. Will you not speak plainly? You suspect some... deceit, perhaps?"

The admiral regarded him thoughtfully, then said, "As I have said, at the time there were a great many rumours, but the coroner attends only to facts. It was deemed a tragic accident, and your cousin left the navy with his record unblemished. I see no reason to delve any deeper. It cannot be of benefit to anyone."

A moment's reflection persuaded Nathan that he was right. He had come to establish that Felix's wife was dead, leaving no child, and he had achieved that object. Nothing more was needed.

Having furnished Nathan with the address of the place where the register of Eliza's death might be viewed, the admiral showed him out.

~~~~~

It was years since Nell had had such a pleasurable day. She and Meg had passed the whole morning indulging in the hedonistic delights of Oxford Street, Piccadilly and New Bond Street, while Harry looked on in affectionate amusement. They returned home laden with parcels — lengths of material, gloves, stockings, lace, scarves and even ear drops and bracelets. Although Nell had bought little for herself, Meg's enthusiasm was infectious, and Nell enjoyed the purchases almost as if they had been for herself.
~~~~~

She prepared for the evening with some eagerness. She had one of Jessica's unwanted gowns to wear, a charming shawl that Meg had insisted on buying for her and a new pair of silk stockings she had bought for herself. She would have liked new slippers, but she still had to be very careful with her money. When Carlotta had devised a new and very attractive coiffure for her, she felt buoyed up with happy anticipation. To be in company again! Such a pleasure.

Meg, however, was unaccountably nervous. "Will they be very grand, the marquess's relations?" she said, as they prepared for the evening in the bedroom they shared.

"I daresay," Nell said absently. "They always are, these noble families, but the marquess did not seem at all high in the instep."

"What is his wife like? She sounded very amiable in her letter."

"My dear Meg, I do not number marchionesses amongst my acquaintance! I am sure she is perfectly affable."

"To you, perhaps, but not to me," she said in a small voice. "How shall I go on in such company?"

"You have only to be friendly and unassuming, as you always are, and they cannot fail to be delighted with you."

"That is very easy for you to say, when you grew up amongst such people. Nell, I am terrified of doing anything to damage Harry's prospects. I do try to be ladylike, but it does not come naturally to me, as it does to you. What shall I do?"

Nell considered the question carefully. "When I was preparing for my come out and wondered how I would manage my curtsy in the Queen's Drawing Room, or a cotillion at Almack's, my governess used to say, *'Remember, you are the Grand Duchess Magnifica. You are the equal of anybody.'* I used to say it to myself as I dressed for the evening, or just before I entered a ballroom."

"The Grand Duchess Magnifica?" Meg said, disbelief on her face.

"It sounds silly, I know, but it really worked."

Marford House was every bit as magnificent as Nell had expected of such a noble and wealthy family as the Marfords. Having grown up in a household with an income of four thousand a year, and having recently learnt to manage on a great deal less, she looked about her with new eyes, counting the number of footman and candles, and wondering at the size of the fireplaces. Yet as they crossed the vast expanse of marble-tiled floor in the entrance hall, childish laughter drifted down from the upper floors, and when she gazed up at the massive staircase, two small faces peered through the balusters. She smiled and waved to them, and after a moment's hesitation they waved back. She liked to think of this palatial building as a family home, echoing to the high voices of children.

They were shown into the Chinese saloon, a room so large that a whole wing of Daveney Hall would fit into it. Nell was gazing intently at the glass-domed roof, knowing that she would have to describe it in detail to Louis, and wishing she had her sketchbook with her, when she became aware that Meg was shaking beside her.

"So many of them!" she whispered, in horrified tones. "And all of them grander than me."

The room was, indeed, filled with people, and for a moment the sea of silks and jewels and waving feathers was almost as impressive as the room itself. Even Nell quailed at the collected mass of the peerage. But then the sea solidified into individual faces — a young lady here, an old one with too much rouge there, a jolly-looking gentleman leaning against the mantel.

Nell straightened her spine. "They are only people, Meg," she said firmly. "They still snore and sneeze and sniff like everyone else."

"Yes, but… do they not terrify you?" she said, as the butler announced them.

"No, for tonight I am the Grand Duchess Magnifica, and so are you. Lift your chin and smile, for we are not intimidated by anyone."

"The Grand Duchess Magnifica," Meg whispered. Then, standing a little taller, "I am the Grand Duchess Magnifica, and I am the equal of anybody." She let out a breath, and gave Nell a tremulous smile. "Yes. Not intimidated. I am *not* intimidated."

25: Return To Southampton (July)

Nathan was not of a type to be overwhelmed by the imposing grandeur of the nobility. Like his father, he had never yearned to own a country estate or a majestic town house, and although he sometimes wished he might escape the bustle and noise and smell of York, and regretted that his dining room could only seat twelve, he had no desire at all to live in anything like Marford House. Nor did its size impress him. It was evidence that a previous marquess had been rich enough to build it, and the present one to maintain it, that was all.

He could see, though, that Meg felt oppressed by it, or perhaps it was the press of absurdly fashionable people filling the room, and every last one of them, so it seemed, a lord or lady of rank. Harry was less than his usual confident self, as well — a little nervous, constantly adjusting his sleeves, or pulling on one ear. Nell, of course, was quite at home. He smiled as he watched her chatting easily with a dowager in a strange trailing headdress edged with jewels.

The dinner was exactly as he had expected, abundant and extravagant, but the conversation was mostly less high-flown than he had anticipated. Once an elderly gentleman raised the issue of slavery in robust terms, asking Lord Carrbridge for his opinion on a point of abstruse detail, and Nathan was amused to see the marquess, for all his society polish, look suddenly panic-stricken and refer the questioner to Sir Daniel, as if he could not give an opinion without his secretary to tell him what his opinion should be. Generally, however, the talk was of children and servants and society *on dits*, and the tragedy of the young Duke of Falconbury, and how his brother had sent envoys to America to find out if the duke had perchance married while he was travelling there and sired an heir.

"Very proper," one of the elderly gentlemen said, and they all nodded and agreed that it was indeed very proper of his brother not to assume the dead man's mantle before all avenues had been explored.

Nathan could not often catch a glimpse of Nell once they were at table, for she sat on the same side that he did, but Meg was almost directly opposite him, between Sir Daniel and a garishly-attired brother of the marquess. He watched as she demurely cast her eyes downwards and made only brief answers at first, but by the time the second course had been set out, she was beginning to relax and the fellow with the violently-coloured waistcoat was seen laughing at her remarks.

"Who is that gentleman in the green and yellow striped waistcoat?" Nathan whispered to his neighbour.

"Lord Humphrey Marford," she whispered back. "A fine fellow, is he not? Be careful how you answer, Mr Harbottle, for I should not like you to say anything in disparagement of my husband."

"I should not dream of it, Lady Humphrey," he said. "I was only about to remark that he is getting on very well with my sister."

"It is difficult to imagine anyone not getting on well with her, Mr Harbottle. She seems a delightful lady, and I should like to get to know her better. Are you in town for long?"

"Another day only, and then we must go to Southampton."

"What a pity. But you are from York, I understand? Very well, I shall come and find you. Have you your card with you? Ah, thank you." Her eyes turned to Meg again. "A delightful lady. Quite wasted in York, I feel. Has she been much in town before this? I am sure I should have heard her mentioned, if so."

Nathan hesitated, but Lady Humphrey seemed genuinely interested. "Meg has always felt that she would not fit into the *beau monde*. She is not good *ton*."

"Because of the West Indian heritage? She will probably never marry a ducal heir, that is true, but then who would want to? Dreadfully stuffy, most of them. Still, there are plenty of younger sons who would be delighted to have such a beautiful and lively wife who is not just in the common way, and only the very highest sticklers would snub her. I am living proof that one may be outrageous and still get vouchers from Almack's. Have you ever been to Almack's? I went once, to please Humphrey, but it was excessively dull."

"Are you outrageous, Lady Humphrey?" Nathan said, intrigued. "I do hope so, for I have never met anyone outrageous before."

She laughed merrily and said, "I was positively infamous before my marriage, although I cannot think why, for I only sprang a man from gaol once, and the fellow I shot was only winged, after all. Nothing but a scratch, and he deserved far worse." Her eyes twinkled as she spoke, and Nathan was left hoping such tales were true, but rather afraid they were not.

It was Lady Carrbridge, however, who set the seal on the evening as she moved round the drawing room dispensing tea. “Will you be back in town next month, Mr Harbottle? We have our final ball of the season in two weeks. Mrs Caldicott will not care for such an event, I daresay, but I should love you and Miss Harbottle to be amongst our guests. Mr Smethurst will be invited, of course, and there are one or two young men I can call to mind who would be very happy to make Miss Harbottle’s acquaintance.”

“I cannot say if our business in Southampton will be concluded by then,” Nathan said neutrally.

“I shall send you cards anyway,” Lady Carrbridge said. “If you are here, you will be very welcome, I assure you.”

He thanked her with genuine gratitude, and resolved to leave the decision to Meg, but if she were minded to make a public appearance in London, it would be hard to find a better sponsor than the marchioness.

~~~~~

JULY

It was strange to be returning to Southampton after so many weeks away. Despite the cheery letters from Maria telling her that all was well, Nell was not quite sure what to expect. Was Maria’s optimistic tone a true reflection of circumstances, or was she sheltering her friend from grim news?

The journey was cheered, however, by the presence of Harry Smethurst. Since the Parliamentary session was almost at an end, Lord Carrbridge had suggested that his friends might enjoy his company and had given him fifty pounds to defray his expenses.

They planned to stay only a day or two, so all four of them would stay at the Dolphin Hotel, to minimise the disruption to Maria. The hotel was always busy, but when they arrived there was a
~~~~~

veritable frenzy of activity in preparation for an assembly that evening.

"There you are, Meg," Harry said. "And to think you were afraid Southampton would be very flat after the excitement of London, and now you have something to cast even Marford House into the shade. How can dining with the Marquess and Marchioness of Carrbridge compare with a public ball at a provincial sea port? Just think, if you are especially fortunate, you may be invited to stand up with a bellows-maker or a rat-catcher or an apothecary's apprentice."

"You do talk some nonsense, Harry," Meg said robustly. "I love a public ball, and shall have no objection to the apothecary's apprentice if he can dance. It will be glorious to stretch my legs after so many hours confined in a carriage. Sitting still is such a trial to one's endurance."

"I wish I could dance, too," Nell said wistfully. "We used to attend every assembly here for a while, and they were always great fun. Ah well, one day I shall be out of black."

Leaving the valets and Meg's maid to settle in at the Dolphin, the four walked round the corner to East Street, where Nell fished in her reticule for her door key. Before she could find it, the door was opened by a young footman she had never seen before.

"Who are you?" she said before she could stop herself.

"William, madam. Are you wishful to reserve a place?"

"Reserve a—?" She eyed him in astonishment. "Is Maria at home?"

"I shall enquire, madam. What name shall I give?"

Nell burst out laughing. "Good heavens, William, you are very new! Tell her that Mrs Caldicott is here."

His eyes widened. "Beg pardon, madam. Please to step inside while I fetch Mrs Delanoy."

She laughed again, for who could not laugh at being invited to enter one's own house? But a footman was unexpected. When had the household become grand enough or wealthy enough to afford to employ a footman? There had certainly been some changes in the short time she had been away.

They had only to wait a few minutes before Maria appeared, bustling up from the kitchen in her apron, as always, but the gown was a new one, Nell noticed, and her friend wore a rather fine lace-trimmed cap. The two exchanged hugs, Nathan was received with pleased recognition, and Meg and Harry were introduced. William the footman relieved them of hats and gloves and parasols and canes.

"Oh, Nell!" Maria cried, weeping all over her. "And so fine as you look! What a fetching gown — is it from London?"

"From Yorkshire, but it has had a little London polish applied to it. But... a footman, Maria?" Nell said. "You are getting very grand. Can we afford it?"

"Oh, yes! Our card evenings are doing very well, and a manservant adds so much style. We even have a waiting list for places now. Come on up to the drawing room, and let us have some tea."

"The *drawing* room?" Nell said, surprised.

"Oh, did I not mention it in my letters?" she said airily. "Mr Lloyd wished to use it for his card parties, which means we have to be in and out... and Lydia's mama is here from Wales, managing the household until Lydia's confinement, and she saw how silly it was not to use the rooms properly. Here we are."

Nell had almost forgotten how elegant her drawing room was. She had supervised the redecoration of it herself when she had first married, and although there was nothing extravagant about it, the room had an air of delicate good taste that pleased her greatly. It had been a great wrench to surrender it to Lydia Lloyd.

The pianoforte drew her with a powerful attraction. She sat down and ran her fingers over the keys, a smile of pure pleasure on her face. There was no time to play, however, for there was much news to exchange, and although most of it had been conveyed by letter, it was necessary to tell it all again, so that it might be exclaimed over to the proper degree.

"So Louis is the heir?" Maria said over and over. "He owns a great house? He is a *baronet?"*

"Only if we can prove his claim," Nathan said crisply. "That is why we are here, to look through Captain Caldicott's effects and see if there might be anything to link him to Felix Harbottle."

"Goodness," Maria said. "So you will have to live up there, Nell... in Yorkshire? With Louis?"

Nell heard the unspoken question, and answered gently, "Nothing is decided about that, but this house belongs to Louis too, and he will never throw you out, Maria. Besides, you seem to be managing very well without me."

"Oh yes, everything is going along swimmingly. We have your share of the proceeds tucked away in the safe. Mr Lloyd will get it for you when he returns from the vintner."

"My share of the proceeds?" Nell said, feeling stupid. "This is your business, not mine."

"But the house is yours," Maria said. "We could not operate without it. We charge five shillings for each seat, with a shilling for each of us — Mr Lloyd, for managing the card room and providing the wine, me for the supper, and you for providing the premises. Then a shilling goes to the player with the most fish at the end of the evening. You see? Very equitable."

"And the extra shilling?" Nathan said. "You said five shillings, and there are but four accounted for."

"To set aside for unforeseen circumstances," Maria said firmly. "We have thought of everything."

"And you are getting along well with the Lloyds?" Nell said carefully. "With Lydia?"

Maria laughed, and put down her cup. "Nell, Lydia is perfectly charming when you are not around."

Nell could not have been more astonished if Maria had slapped her.

"It is true," Maria said. "She was always so jealous of you."

"Of me? But why? She was the one with the money, the best of the house, the increasing family, the prospects."

"But you are a lady. Even when you were... *ill*, you were so composed, so ladylike. Like a queen, she said. You made her feel like a scullery maid in her own home."

"I was always perfectly civil to her," Nell protested.

"Precisely. But without you around, and with her mother here to take charge of all those tedious domestic details, like the children and the servants — why, she is perfectly affable. So you see, we are managing quite well without you."

They lingered over their tea, but there was no avoiding the moment Nell dreaded, when they had to go upstairs and begin the task of looking through Jude's things. Maria went back to her kitchen, but the rest of them trooped upstairs, all crowding into the tiny bedroom. Nell shivered as she looked around her at the familiar old furniture. The room looked so shabby to her eyes, and she was ashamed to have her friends see how she had lived. How she might still live, if Louis could not claim the baronetcy after all.

None of them made any comment on the room. Nathan said briskly, "Shall we start with the locked box?"

"It is under the bed," Nell said colourlessly.

"We will wait outside, so as not to crowd you," Meg said.

Nell unlocked the box, then sat on the dressing table stool while Nathan, on his knees, swiftly examined all the contents. From outside the open door came the murmur of low voices, Meg's high and excitable, Harry's lower and calmer, punctuated from time to time with gusts of laughter.

Nell could not decide how she felt. Numb, perhaps. For weeks she had been free — free of the past, free to be herself and to see the colour in the world, to enjoy friendship and music and beauty and the innate goodness of people. She had learnt to smile again, and even to laugh. But now, being once more in that room where all her terrors had originated, she was crushed. She was nothing.

"Ah!" Nathan said, with satisfaction. "The book with the payments to *'EP'*. Who was not Felix's wife, for her surname was Smith. So who was it? Or I should say, who *is* it, for she was receiving payments as recently as last Christmas. We shall need to find her, whoever she is."

"You believe, then, that it must be a woman?" Nell said in a small voice.

He turned to look at her. "Well... it is hard to see it being a man. Two hundred pounds every quarter — those are living expenses, the cost of a modest establishment. A woman, perhaps two living together, with a manservant, a cook and two or three maids. And a child, perhaps," he added gently. "A man would have no need to be supported by Felix, for he would have his own income or trade."

"Could it be a charitable organisation, perhaps?" she said. "An orphanage, say."

"It is possible. However, the initials and the secrecy suggest… other possibilities."

"A mistress," Nell said flatly.

"That is my guess, although there is always the possibility, however remote, that she is a legal wife. But whatever her status, she must be informed of Felix's death, and provision made for her and any children."

"Of course."

"There is nothing else in the box apart from various items of naval uniform," Nathan said. "Do I have your permission to check the pockets?"

She nodded, and he began to remove items one by one, carefully examining the seams and sleeves as well as any pockets. Almost at once he found a small silver case. "Felix's cards," he said with satisfaction, passing one to Nell. "That is very helpful."

Nell gazed at the small square of card with its neatly printed letters. *'Capt. Felix Harbottle, Royal Navy'* "This is proof, then. Jude truly was Felix."

"There is no longer any doubt of it in my mind," Nathan said. "However, this is still circumstantial. The strongest proof would be a letter written in Felix's own hand, or a sworn statement before a magistrate or some such. Aha! A letter! Perhaps this is— Oh."

His face puzzled, he passed it to Nell, who read, *'To The Reverend George Lumley or his successor, Bishopswood Cromby Parsonage, Hants.'*

"Why would Jude — or Felix — write to this Mr Lumley?" Nathan said. "Where is Bishopswood Cromby? Oh, I remember — it is by Daveney Hall."

"It is," Nell said. "Mr Lumley is the incumbent there, and he it was who officiated when Jude and I were married. As to why Jude would write to him, and a letter which would only be found after his own death, I cannot even hazard a guess."

"Hmm. *'...or his successor'.* It is not Mr Lumley himself who is the object, but the present incumbent. A church matter, then," Nathan said. "A bequest, perhaps, or a request for prayers to be said for him. Not relevant to our quest, but we must call at the church to check the marriage register, so we may hand over this letter then. We can do that on our way back to London."

"Mr Lumley will not be there. When Daveney Hall is closed up during the season, the Lumleys all go to stay with Mrs Lumley's sister. She lives along the coast — Eastbourne or Hastings, somewhere like that. Fresh air and sea bathing."

"Well, no matter. We are quite at leisure to wait upon their return. After all, I have been searching for Felix for two years, so a few more weeks is of little consequence. It is only the record of your marriage, after all, so there will be no surprises at Bishopswood Cromby. There is nothing more to be found in the box, and there is no sign of a false bottom or hidden compartment. It grows late. Let us go back to the Dolphin for tonight, and continue our searches tomorrow."

"Do you think there is anything more to be found?" Nell said.

"No," he said at once. "Anything of significance would have been in this box. However, we must make the effort, just in case."

"May I keep this?" she said, gazing at the calling card still in her hand.

"Of course," Nathan said. "The whole case is yours. Here..." He pressed it into her hands. "It is a fine piece of silver, with his initials on it, see? *'FCH'* — Felix Charles Harbottle."

"Thank you," she said, clutching it tightly, another symbol of the part of her husband's life that she had known nothing about.

That evening, they dined at the Dolphin Hotel, together with Maria and her daughters, Mr Lloyd, his wife and her mother, after which Lucy, Jane and the Lloyds returned to the house, and the others went off to dance and be happy. Nell sat in their private parlour pretending to write to Louis, and in reality listening to the music from the assembly room, her feet forlornly tapping out the steps, while at the same time feeling guilty for wishing she were dancing. Widowhood, she decided, was unexpectedly complicated.

26: To London Again

Nell slept badly that night, but she imputed it to the melancholy task of trawling through Jude's effects, combined with being woken by Meg returning from the ball, humming loudly, at some desperate hour of the night. After that, Nell had lain awake for hours, wondering what would happen if Louis' claim to the baronetcy could not be proved. Would they have to return to Southampton for good, and live again in the East Street house, with its vitality-sucking aura? Even if she could bear that, the prospect of struggling on a tiny income again and having to consider every penny spent was dispiriting. There was enough, and they would not starve, but for a few glorious weeks she had lived a different life, the life she was born to, and she had wallowed in the luxury. It would be hard indeed to give it up a second time.

The morning saw a return to East Street, while Nathan worked methodically through all Jude's clothes, the drawers of the small desk and his single shelf of books in the morning room. He had never been a great reader. Then he checked every piece of furniture for hidden drawers or false bottoms, and tapped methodically at walls and floorboards for secret hiding places. Finding nothing, they went to All Saints' Church to check the register for the record of Louis' birth. That done, Nathan said, "Shall we walk down to the river and stretch our legs a little?"

It was agreed, and so they walked slowly down the High Street, past their hotel and on down to the God's House Gate and the Beach beyond. Meg was not a person who ambled, so she and Harry tended to shoot ahead and then wait for Nell to catch up before shooting off again. Nathan was gentlemanly enough to adjust his pace to Nell's, talking easily of the shops they passed and the ball the previous night, unperturbed by her lack of response. He was such undemanding company, seeming to understand her feelings without the need for explanation. She always fell into this gloom when she had been in the East Street house. It horrified her now to recall that she had in the past spent weeks on end trapped there, unable to venture outside until her bruises had healed, and even when she was physically recovered, often too downhearted to leave the house. How had she survived? Yet somehow she had, curled up in her shell like a snail.

When they reached the Beach, Meg and Harry strode on, engrossed in each other, but Nathan suggested that he and Nell should sit on one of the many seats that were conveniently placed along the path. For a while they said nothing, watching the river roll swiftly by, and the clouds drifting overhead. Such a peaceful scene, and as always her gloom was gradually worn away by the charms of the vista.

"You are very quiet," Nathan said after a while. "Does it bring back bad memories, the house?"

She nodded, then said, "It is not only that. If it cannot be proved that Jude was Felix, then we shall have to return here to live on an income of only two hundred pounds a year. I know I should be grateful to have even that much, for many people have far less, and indeed I myself had less only a few weeks ago, but it still feels like poverty to me. It is so disheartening to be poor. One has neither the time nor the energy for anything beyond the merest necessities for survival. Every day becomes a battle between opposing needs. Shall we have beef today, or mutton again, or perhaps no meat at all? And if we buy meat, then the purchase of new shoes must be put off. One goes to church to pray, not for salvation and forgiveness, but for a mild winter, please God, so that the coal will last. It is miserable, utterly miserable."

"I can imagine," he said, and his voice was infused with sympathy. "I have never been poor, but I thank God every day for the comfort of wealth. It salves my conscience somewhat to try not to spend it frivolously, and to do a little good with it, where I can. But you do not need to be poor, Nell. Whatever the outcome of our quest, Jessica would be delighted to offer you and Louis a home for as long as you wish."

"And live on her charity? I think not."

"She would not see it so. She adores Louis already, and you would make an excellent companion for her. Aunt Amelie will not live for ever, after all. You would be giving charity far more than receiving it."

Nell said nothing, knowing it to be true, and yet she would still feel beholden.

"Alternatively, you could marry a rich man," he said in genial tones. She looked at him suspiciously, but his face was bland, and he was not even looking at her, but gazing out across the river. "You are young and beautiful and well-bred," he went on. "Plenty of men would be delighted to take you to wife. You would live as a lady, as you were born to do, and Louis would have a father again."

Still his tone was level, but she could not forget that he had already proposed to her once, albeit only in response to her desperation when she thought she would lose Louis. Was he thinking now of himself, or had he given up that idea?

Yet it was impossible, and if he had any idea of marriage in his head, it would be as well to disabuse him of the notion at once. "I do not wish to marry again," she said in a low voice.

"Oh, not yet, naturally," he began. "But when you are out of mourning—"

"Never!" she cried. "I shall never marry again."

His head spun round to look at her, and abruptly the easy tone was gone, his eyes afire as he gazed at her. "Never?" he said hoarsely. "You are too young to turn your back on matrimony entirely, Nell. You have had a difficult time, but—"

"Never," she said firmly.

He turned his head to watch the river again, but this time he sat rigidly, and she could hear his rapid breathing. For a long time they were both silent. Then he spoke, but so quietly that his words were almost inaudible.

"Nell, I had a bad experience, too. My heart was shattered by a woman who said she loved me, but then gave me up without the least struggle. I waited a long time for her to return to me... or to send me word, for I would have gone to her wherever she was. It was years before all hope of her was finally extinguished. I thought that wound would never heal, that I would never trust another woman. But I have finally come to see that the only way to heal a hurt is to risk being hurt again. It may be that you will one day come to feel that way, too. Not today, perhaps, and maybe only far in the future, but I hope... I truly hope, my dear friend, that eventually that day will come for you."

She could make no reply, for tears were very close to the surface. Poor Nathan, nursing his broken heart for so long! Even now, he was not entirely recovered, for he could not hide the emotion in his voice. He lapsed into silence too, so they sat, unspeaking, for a long time. Nell could not decide if it was a comfortable silence or not. She herself was not entirely easy with it, not quite sure whether his words constituted a declaration of sorts or were merely a general expression of optimism, and yet she felt his goodwill towards her. He would never hurt her.

Then she was shocked at the thought, for had she not been just as certain of Jude? She could never be sure that a man would not turn against her, just as her husband had. No matter how civilised the exterior, inside every man lurked a savage who might turn to violence at any moment, even kind, gentle Nathan. No man on earth was to be trusted. She must never put herself into the power of a man again, *never*.

After a while, Meg and Harry began to walk back towards them, and Nell could not help but smile to see them together, Meg bouncing with enthusiasm, hands waving as she talked, while Harry strolled on, hands behind his back. Meg's enthusiasm carried her forwards, so that she was obliged to spin round to face Harry, and then she would spin again, to put herself alongside him, in a dance of constant movement, while he ploughed steadily forwards. She was like an ever-changing melody, full of life and inspiration, while he had the constancy of rhythm. Yet together they were in perfect harmony, if they could but see it.

"Will they make a match of it yet, do you suppose?" Nell said, feeling herself to be rather daring in asking, but trusting that she was enough of a friend to risk it.

Nathan sighed. "I cannot say. They spent the whole evening together yesterday, and yet when we retired to our room, Harry could speak only of his fears for his own future if he marries her. He understands only too well that for a man with his career to make, the wrong choice of wife could be very damaging. Society can be very cruel to those it decides to disapprove."

"He is so much in love with her," Nell said wistfully.

"Love is not always enough," Nathan said, and there was a harsh tone to his voice that she had never heard before. "The poets say that love overcomes all difficulties, but that is not so. There are many obstacles that can keep two people apart, no matter how deep a love they share. Harry and Meg must have complete trust in each other and no regrets before they contemplate matrimony, for it is an irrevocable step. Who knows how long that may take, or whether it will ever be achieved?"

Nell could not argue the point, although it saddened her beyond measure.

~~~~~

They stayed four more nights in Southampton, as Nathan called on every friend of Jude's, and then on every bank and solicitor and attorney in the town, in case he had left a letter with any of them. Then it was the inns and taprooms, in search of a drunken half-believed confession. But there was nothing at all in Southampton to connect Jude Caldicott to Felix Harbottle, and finally he was obliged to give it up.

Was there enough evidence to convince the House of Lords? Impossible to say, but his hopes of finding conclusive proof were fading. There remained only the unknown woman in London, whether mistress or wife, who might have documents, letters or jewellery. Felix's ring was still missing, but he might well have left it with the woman he had supported for all these years. She alone now held the last possibility of proving the claim, but Nathan was not optimistic.
~~~~~

There remained only Nell's emotional farewells to her friends. She had left them in the spring with every intention of returning very soon, but now her home might well be at Percharden House, hundreds of miles from Southampton. She was not a woman who displayed her feelings openly, but she hugged Mrs Delanoy fiercely, and the girls too, and even some of the servants, and it was some time before Nathan could draw her away from the melancholy parting. He fervently hoped she would never return to the scene of so many unhappy episodes in her life.

One cause for cheer lightened the first stage of their journey, for Mr Lloyd had handed over Nell's share of the proceeds from the supper parties.

"Ten pounds!" Nell said repeatedly, in utter astonishment. "How can it possibly be so much?"

Nathan explained the prices charged, and her share of it, and gently pointed out that two such evenings every week would provide her with an income of seventy five pounds a year.

"They must be charging too much," she said firmly. "Five shillings a night — is that excessive?"

Nathan considered that. "It is not cheap, but in the true gaming houses, a man may lose as much as he pleases in a single night. Ten or fifty or five hundred pounds at once. In London, it might be thousands. Many men would play more often, perhaps, if they could guarantee not to lose more than a fixed amount. Yet here, for five shillings a participant enjoys a convivial evening and an excellent supper, and cannot lose more than his original stake, which is no more than the price of a pair of gloves. He need never fear to be swept away by the excitement of the moment. It is a sum a prudent man may set aside for his own pleasure. No, it is not excessive. Mr Lloyd told me they hope to increase to three evenings in some weeks," he added. "Your income could be more than a hundred pounds a year, although there is a modest increase in expenditure on coals and candles."

"One hundred! On top of two hundred! That is *three hundred pounds a year!* I shall be rich."

Nathan had laughed at that, thinking of his own eight thousand a year. "Not rich, perhaps," he said, "but not poor, either."

That left Nell speechless, and Nathan forbore to point out that her money from the supper evenings was trade and therefore not respectable to the *beau monde*. It gave him some satisfaction, though, that the enterprise was likely to be profitable enough, in the long term, to enable Mr Lloyd and Mrs Delanoy to buy the house outright, and therefore set Nell free of its malign influence for ever.

Their journey back to London took them first to Portsmouth, where Nathan and Harry visited the very expensive solicitor who had been sending two hundred pounds a quarter to a counterpart in London. He was at first reluctant to divulge the identity of the recipient, but between the transfer of a large roll of paper money, and a casual mention by Harry of his noble patron, he was induced to reveal it.

When they arrived in London they found a quantity of mail awaiting them. Leaving the two ladies to read their letters, therefore, Nathan and Harry made their way to visit the second solicitor, in order to find the address to which Jude's money had been transferred. Although Nathan was prepared with another roll of notes, this solicitor needed no persuasion once it had been explained that the gentleman sending the money was now believed to have died.

"Ah! Thought so, thought so indeed," he said. "Nothing on Lady Day, you see. Suspected something amiss."

"It is my fear that there might be a lady dependent on this money, and now in desperate straits," Nathan said. "If my cousin was responsible for her, then—"

"A lady..." the solicitor said thoughtfully. "Reason to believe it to be a lady, have you?"

"Only that it seemed a likely situation. When a young man begins paying regular sums in great secrecy, and continues to pay them over a number of years, it would be a natural supposition."

"Would be, would be indeed. Although... well, it may be so, and one would not wish a lady to suffer in such circumstances. No reason not to give you the name and address of the person to whom I delivered each package that arrived, no reason indeed."

He scratched away with a pen so badly made that Nathan itched to mend it for him. The resulting letters were almost illegible. By squinting at them, and slanting the paper to catch a little more light, he managed to make it out. *'Alfred Herbert, 25 Hill Street, Mayfair.'*

"Alfred Herbert?" he said, bemused. That was not at all what he had expected. "Is Mr Herbert a gentleman?"

The solicitor laughed. "Bless you, sir, no, although he works for one, I imagine. He is a valet, indeed."

"A *valet?* Then... may I ask... who is his employer?"

"Not the least idea," the solicitor said smugly. "No part of my brief to enquire, only to deliver the parcel as agreed. Herbert is the latest such recipient. His gentleman has employed several such valets over the sixteen years I have been called upon to deliver these...packages. Several such, indeed."

"Sixteen years..." Nathan mused. Yet the notebook showed payments as far back as twenty years ago. It was sixteen years ago that Felix had vanished from society, taken the name of Jude

Caldicott and settled in Southampton. For four years, then, he had made these payments in some other way.

The solicitor, although willing enough to reveal all, had no more information to offer. Nathan and Harry, without a word being spoken, turned their steps to Hill Street. Number Twenty Five was a double-fronted house in a terrace of similar houses, neither ostentatious nor run down.

Seeing a butcher's boy delivering at a nearby house, Nathan said to him, "Tell me, who lives at Number Twenty Five over there? A gentleman, is it? And a lady, perhaps?"

"Lor' no, sir! That's a lord, what lives there. A viscount. No lady, not as I ever 'eard."

"Does the viscount have a name?"

"'Course 'e do! Lord Toller, 'e be."

Nathan gave him sixpence and he and Harry walked on thoughtfully. Why on earth would Felix be sending eight hundred pounds a year to Lord Toller?

"Was he passing it on to someone else, on Felix's behalf?" Nathan said. "He had, after all, been a friend of Felix's at one time. Or an acquaintance, at least. Although... he does not seem like the sort of man to put himself out for anyone."

"No, he is all for himself," Harry said. "Undoubtedly the money was going into his own pocket."

"Then who is *'EP'?"*

"Edward Pascall," Harry said heavily. "That was Toller's name before his elevation to the peerage. There is no question about it, he is the person Felix has been paying all these years. So much money, Nathan! Why, Toller must have taken thousands from him over the years."

"Sixteen thousand," Nathan said grimly. "But why, when Felix could ill afford such a sum?"

"There is only one way to find out," Harry said grimly. "We shall just have to ask him."

27: A Ball At Marford House

The invitations to the Carrbridges' ball awaited them on their return to London. Nathan was not minded for it, and Nell would not even consider it, but Meg and Harry both wished to go, although for different reasons. Harry hoped to mingle with a number of influential political figures. Meg wanted to dance in the splendour of Marford House.

"You must come, Nat," she said, "for I cannot go without you, you know, and it will be such a wonderful sight. I shall never have such an opportunity again."

"We do not know many people," Nathan said. "I fear you will be doomed to spend much of the evening sitting watching everyone else dance. Do not expect me to stand up with you!"

She laughed gaily. "Now when have I ever embarrassed you so? Harry will dance with me, and after that I shall be content to watch, I assure you. I shall find one of Lord Carrbridge's fearsome aunts to chaperon me, and you may go off to the card room."

Having assured himself that Nell was content to spend the evening alone — "I am quite worn out with travelling, so I shall go to bed early, I dare say." — Nathan allowed himself to be persuaded to go. There was another reason for his surrender, too. Everyone of consequence who was still in town at this late stage in the season would be at Marford House, so there was a reasonable expectation of meeting Toller there. Then he could ask him directly why Felix had been paying him for all these years.

As their carriage drew near to Marford House that evening, Nathan was reminded of why he had avoided London society for so many years. The press of vehicles arriving was so great that they had to await their turn to alight, and then proceed slowly into the house, crowded about on all sides. There was another queue to deposit cloaks and hats, and then the slow procession through several saloons until the ballroom was reached, and finally another queue to greet their host and hostess before being released gratefully into a room already hot and airless.

Meg gazed around her, eyes wide with amazement. Nathan, too, admitted to some astonishment at the glory of the *beau monde* at play. The colour, the extravagance, the dazzling jewels, the constant movement was overwhelming. Harry whisked Meg into the nearest set, and Nathan was left to wander about, trying very hard not to be impressed by the brilliance of the room, and failing. How he wished that Nell were there to share the spectacle! She was used to high society, for she had grown up as a part of it.

He ambled here and there for some time before encountering anyone he knew, and when he did so, it was Nell's brother, not a person he particularly wished to meet. There was no avoiding the acquaintance, however, so he smiled and bowed and said everything that was proper.

"Is Nell here?" Godney said, as soon as the preliminary politenesses were got out of the way. "It is *highly* unsuitable for such a recent widow, and with her reputation—"

"Mrs Caldicott is not here," Nathan said coldly.

"Ah, good, good. She has not completely abandoned the proprieties, then."

"She is the most correct person I know," Nathan said with some heat, but trying very hard to rein in his temper. It would do no good to quarrel with Godney.

"Quite, quite," Godney said, eyeing him knowingly. "But she was invited, I take it? That is good, very good. The Carrbridges are such good *ton*, it must add to her consequence, even if she prefers not to be seen in society yet. Still, I should like to talk to her. Will she be in town for long, do you suppose? We should have left by now except for this invitation. Julia was wild to come here, for we are not well-acquainted with the Carrbridges, and rarely receive invitations. Ah, Julia my dear, may I present to you Mr Harbottle, Nell's friend from the north. My wife, Harbottle."

Nathan had noticed Lady Godney already, for although she had been engaged with a group of ladies some distance away, she had been watching him intently. Now her curiosity had drawn her to her husband's side, an insincere smile fixed to her face. She was not a great beauty, and dressed without much taste, but he supposed she would be accounted stylish. He could not help comparing her eye-wateringly mismatched furbelows and gushing society manners with Nell's quiet grace.

"Lady Carrbridge is *so* charming, is she not?" Lady Godney trilled. "And such a *superior* eye for decoration. When we were here on a previous occasion, I was so impressed with the Chinese Saloon that I begged for the name of the gentleman who had executed her ladyship's design, and commissioned him to do our own saloon in just that manner. We are quite delighted with it, are we not, my dear? But can you believe it, Mr Harbottle, Sir James will not allow me to have him back to refurbish the drawing room, for he says the cost was outrageous and another room is likely to bankrupt him. Foolish man," she said, smiling up at her husband.

Godney appeared not to want to talk about refurbishment, outrageously expensive or otherwise, for he turned to Nathan and said, "When you see Nell, tell her that although I am pleased that Lady Harbottle requires Louis to write to me every week, it disturbs me that he seems to do nothing but roam the countryside, collecting butterflies and beetles and such like. He even sends me drawings of some of them — beetles! What a thing to be sketching! Although his attempt at a likeness of a peacock showed some promise. Still, the boy should be at his desk, studying. But I have a plan in mind. Yesterday I met, quite by chance, an old tutor of mine, an excellent fellow and somewhat down on his luck, so he will be glad of the opportunity, you know. Greek, Latin... all that sort of thing. That is what Louis should be doing, not paddling about in pond water."

Nathan was torn between amusement and irritation. "I suppose Louis has always lived in a town, so having a whole estate to explore is exciting to him," he said in his mildest tones. "His letters to you reflect that, but Lady Harbottle is teaching him Greek and Latin and a great many other subjects, I assure you."

"But she is a woman," Godney said with unassailable logic. "What can women know of such matters? A tutor is what the boy needs. I shall see to it. And a drawing master, perhaps. As his guardian, the responsibility falls to me to ensure that he receives an education fit for his station in life."

Nathan had not much longer to maintain his hold on his temper, for Lady Godney soon saw a more promising acquaintance and veered off with an even wider smile, towing her husband behind her. Almost at once, Nathan spotted an object of his own interest, none other than Lord Toller. Deftly cutting a path through the crowds edging the ballroom, he reached his quarry just as he was about to disappear through a doorway.

"Lord Toller!" Nathan said. "Would you favour me with a moment of your time?"

"Ah... er, Harbottle, is it? Certainly, if it is indeed a moment, for you are keeping me from the card table. Unless you would like to play?"

"What is your game? Piquet?"

Toller gave a wolfish smile. "Shall we find a quiet table?"

In a very few minutes he had located a secluded corner of the card room, a pack of cards, a scoring marker and a decanter of claret. Nathan was no gamester, but he was quite happy to lose a few pounds to Toller if it gave him the information he wanted. Toller won the cut and dealt first. They played his deal and then Nathan's, with no conversation beyond the game, before Toller said languidly as he shuffled, "What was it you wished to talk to me about, Harbottle?"

Nathan was ready for him. "I merely wondered why it was that my cousin Felix was paying you eight hundred pounds a year."

Toller's hands stilled, and for the space of perhaps ten heartbeats he was motionless. Then, without a word, he dealt the cards, and they played another two deals before he answered. "Your cousin owed me some money. A debt of honour, you understand."

Nathan looked at him, amused. "Sixteen thousand pounds? That must have been quite a night. What was it, dice or cards?"

Again Toller lapsed into silence, and they finished the partie without a word spoken except the calls of the game, but Toller seemed distracted, and Nathan found himself with an easy victory.

"Shall we play again?" he said. "Perhaps for a little more this time."

Again Toller smiled, eyes gleaming. Both men added more coins onto the table. This time, Nathan won the cut, but before the first deal, he paused, cards in hand, and said, "Are you going to explain the debt of honour, Toller?"

Toller sighed. "I made him a loan. Not sixteen thousand, for I do not have such sums at my disposal, but seven thousand. We agreed that he would repay the principal over a period of years, but Harbottle insisted on paying me interest as well. That was no doing of mine, I assure you! When he vanished from society, he continued to make the payments. If I had been able to find him, I should have told him that the debt was long since repaid, but I could not."

Nathan tapped the pack of cards on the table as he pondered that. Was it plausible? Toller's face was, if not guileless, at least open. He looked Nathan in the eye, and seemed sincere enough. Yet he was such an expert card player that he must have learnt well enough how to dissemble. "What need had Felix for such a sum?"

"I did not enquire too closely," Toller said, and this time his answer was glib. "Something to do with his wife's death."

"Oh?" Nathan realised with a surge of excitement where else he had heard the name of Pascall recently. "You spoke at the coroner's court, did you not? You testified that Felix had left the building before his wife fell."

For the first time, Toller was visibly disconcerted. "Who told you that?"

"Admiral Beckley. It is all in the official report from the coroner."

Toller took a long sip of claret, then set his glass down carefully. Folding his arms, he said evenly, "I see I must tell you the whole story, and since your cousin is dead, it can do him no harm now. The truth is that Felix Harbottle killed his wife."

"What!"

"It is true. I saw him do it, for I was there on the balcony with Harbottle and his wife. They had quarrelled earlier in the evening, and he had been persuaded to step outside... take some air... cool down. Which he did, but later he returned and started up the quarrel again. She went out onto the balcony to escape his wrath, he followed her and the quarrel became violent. I had seen them go outside, and followed in a futile attempt to remonstrate with Harbottle. My efforts were in vain, for he pushed her a little too hard, and over she went."

"Good God! This is far worse than I had imagined," Nathan cried.

"It was quite unintentional, of course, and one does not wish a man to face execution for an accident of that nature," Toller said. "At the very least, he would have been cashiered. I did what I could to mitigate the results, by speaking for Harbottle at the coroner's court, and lending him what he needed. I had the impression he used it to bribe the right people to ensure the death was set down as accidental. Whatever he did with it seems to have been effective." He shrugged. "It was a long time ago, Harbottle. Old history. Are you playing, or not?"

Nathan nodded and dealt the cards. They played two more parties, and with fifty pounds lost to Toller, he felt free to quit the card room. If he had not talked to Admiral Beckley, he would have disbelieved Toller absolutely, but Beckley's suggestion of deceit and his discomfort with the idea of enquiring too deeply into the matter made Toller's version of events all too plausible. It also fitted with the history of violence against Nell. It was a sad story, and not one that Nell needed to be burdened with. It also extinguished the last hope of finding someone who could prove the connection between

Jude Caldicott and Felix. A mistress might have some knowledge of that matter, but clearly Toller was as much in the dark as anyone.

The first sight to greet him on his return to the ballroom was Meg, dancing with a young man some years younger than she was.

"Who is he?" he asked Harry, who was watching her with a wide smile on his face.

"A viscount... heir to an earldom, apparently. Her previous partner was merely the younger son of a baron. I must say, Lord Carrbridge is excessively well connected. I feel inadequate without a title. A mere Squire's son has no place here, I feel. Have you seen the crystal in the supper room? There is an ice sculpture of a swan, of all things, and there is to be roast peacock and peach ice cream. I have never tasted peach ice cream, have you? I was shooed out by a very grand footman, but I am looking forward to supper enormously. Oh, look over there! Heavens, have you ever seen anything as grotesque as that turban? She is a duchess, so I suppose she may wear what she pleases."

Nathan obediently looked, as the duchess sailed majestically past with a small entourage in her wake. As the last of them moved on and a small clear space opened up, it became possible to see several people standing against the walls. Nathan looked, then looked again and froze, standing as if transfixed.

"You all right, old fellow?" Harry said. "You look as if you have seen a ghost."

"I believe I have," he muttered, setting off determinedly across the room, his eyes never straying from his object.

At first, he was unsure. Could she have changed so much in only eleven years? The pleasantly soft curves had expanded in all directions, and her hair — her lovely auburn hair, so long and thick!

— had been clipped short all over her head, and wound about with ribbons and beads. And where had her beautiful smile vanished to?

She was engrossed in animated conversation with the man at her side, her expression clouded with displeasure. Her companion was some years her senior, and for a moment, Nathan thought it must be her father before realising his mistake. As he approached, she turned to him with a frown.

"Selena?" he said, although tentatively, for he was still not certain.

The frown deepened. "I do not believe we are acquainted, sir," she said, looking him up and down haughtily. But the voice — yes, it was her, beyond any doubt.

He huffed out a breath of pure surprise. How could she not know him? It was inconceivable, and so ridiculous that he laughed out loud. "Oh, we are very well acquainted, or we were once. Do you not recognise me, Selena?"

Slowly her expression changed to one of chagrin, her cheeks reddening slightly. "Oh… of course." Turning to the man beside her, she said, "It is very warm in here and I am so thirsty. Would you be so good as to fetch me some lemonade?"

His eyebrows snapped together in annoyance, and he threw Nathan a fulminating glance, but he was too gentlemanly to refuse a lady's request. Glowering at Nathan, he left.

"Goodness, Nathan, whatever are *you* doing here?" Before he could formulate a reply, she raced on in a low voice, "For Heavens sake, say nothing to my husband! He has not the least idea about you, and I do *not* want him to find out, do you understand?"

"Credit me with a little discretion, Selena."

"Oh… of course, I know you would not… But he would be so angry if he knew everything about me. It is so much better if a gentleman is not told such things, do you not agree? Honesty does not always pay. Well! Imagine meeting *you* here. You are the last person in the world I would have expected to be at a grand ball at Marford House. How did you wheedle an invitation?"

There was too much insult in her words for him to ignore. "Whatever happened to the charming girl I fell in love with?" he said, quite unable to keep the bitterness out of his tone. "Did you think of me at all, Selena? Did you ever think about what might have been, or about Henny?"

"Henny?"

"Henrietta. Your daughter. She is very well, thank you for asking. Growing up into a lovely young lady. Almost as pretty as her mother once was, but with better manners, I trust."

She coloured, but lifted her chin. "Why should I think about you, after you led me astray so appallingly? Why should I think about... about *her*, the proof of it? I wanted to forget everything that had happened, to put it all behind me and I have, Nathan, I have. I am respectable now. My husband is an Honourable, the son of a baron, and so long as his brother does not marry again... well, we have hopes. So I shall be a baroness and you will still be *nobody*."

"I wish you joy of your title, Selena. May it warm you when you grow old and care for you when you grow sick and cherish you when you are lonely, as I would have done."

He spun on his heel and stormed away, almost knocking over her hapless husband, returning at that moment with the unwanted lemonade. He strode through the crowds unseeingly, until someone grabbed his arm.

"No, no, no, you must not rush off like that!" Harry cried. "Tell me who she is, for pity's sake."

"A viper," he hissed. "A worm. A traitorous snake."

"Hmm. Not a friend, then."

"Ha! Definitely not a friend." Yet he had once loved her so intensely that he had felt life was not worth living without her. He had thought their love would sustain them for all eternity, yet it had not survived its first crisis. More slowly, he said, "She is *not* a friend. A friend would be pleased to see me, even after eleven years. A friend would have sent word to me, somehow. A friend would care about a man she once professed to love. Even when love dies, there is still *something*, surely?"

"Ah. *That* viper," Harry said. "Just fancy meeting her here, after all this time."

He waved an arm expansively at the brilliantly-lit room, and Nathan recalled with a jolt that he was standing in the middle of a crowded ballroom. It was hot and loud and the scent of the flowers arranged in urns around the room could not mask the aroma of many sweating bodies.

"I have to get out of here," he muttered. "Get some air, and cool off. Harry, you will not mind if I go for a walk, and Meg will not notice my absence, I am sure. I will be back in time to take her home."

"No need," Harry said easily. "I shall bring her home. She is not some schoolroom miss, and I can be trusted to keep to the line, I hope, for a five minute drive. You go home. You were not enjoying yourself anyway, were you?"

"You are the best friend a man could have," Nathan said with feeling.

With one last glance at Selena, now engaged in a fierce argument with her husband, he stole out of the ballroom and disappeared into the night.

28: After The Ball

For Nell the evening had passed slowly. She was determined to be productive, so there was a little reading, a little sewing, a letter to Louis, a little more reading, a letter to Maria. None of them were sufficient to distract her mind. Eventually she had succumbed to temptation and asked Withers to unlock the instrument for her. Only then, with music flowing through her, could she clear her mind sufficiently to allow her to consider her situation.

For Louis, she no longer had any concerns. His letters from Yorkshire had grown from brief, stiff summaries to effusive descriptions of his outings with Jessica. Walks through the woods, excursions to a pond, a drive out onto the moors and a visit to Henny in York had all featured. He was happy, she could tell. He asked her wistfully when she would be home, but he was neither lonely nor bored. Jessica's letters, while a little brisker, listed his progress in Latin, Greek, Italian and French. Louis had found a primer for Hebrew in the library, so he was learning that, too, and a tutor came twice a week to teach him history, especially the battles, which he found of great interest. He was greatly enthused by the armies of tin soldiers unearthed from the attics and was busy re-enacting the Peloponnesian Wars. She was looking about for someone to teach him astronomy, and would Nell mind if she bought him a telescope?

For Nell herself, life was more complicated, and most of the complication revolved around the person of Mr Nathan Harbottle. She liked him, of that there could be no doubt. As a friend, she enjoyed his company and was completely at ease with him. She felt she could talk to him about any subject that troubled her, and he would give her sensible advice, untainted by his own wishes, and without patronising her. So many men would smile in a supercilious way, and tell her not to worry about whatever it was. Even Jude had done so, telling her that some aspects of life were better left to men, but Nathan never did.

She could certainly appreciate his outward attractions, too. He was smoothly handsome, a fine figure of a man, and his blond hair, blue eyes and ready smile were immediately appealing. Even in her mourning, she could appreciate him. He reminded her somewhat of Jude, but that was no longer surprising, now that she knew them to be cousins.

No, it was not his good looks or his friendship that troubled her, it was that he had proposed to her. This was the point where her ruminations failed her. It would be wonderful to have enough money again, and to give Louis a father who would not go away for weeks on end, but what about herself? Did she want to marry him? For all that she had sworn to him that she would never marry again, there was something so appealing in handing all the worries of life over to a husband. She could focus her attentions on deciding which bonnet to wear, and whether to have beef or mutton for dinner, and if the under-housemaid was dusting the ornaments on the mantel properly. And yet surely there was more to life than bonnets and beef! Society, company, conversation — these were what she craved. Dancing and music, too. Nathan could give her all that, and more. Perhaps marriage to him would not be so terrible. He had always treated her as a rational creature, so perhaps he would continue to do so if she were his wife. Perhaps... if... That was the whole problem, that there was no knowing how it would be. Marriage was such a risk...

She had learnt in the harshest way possible that a man, even one who professed his unreserved and eternal love, could not be trusted. Her father had loved her and yet cast her out of the family when she displeased him. Her brother loved her and yet would not break her exile. Her husband had loved her and yet had lied to her and blamed her for all their misfortunes and even hit her. It was only now, with the distance of several months to give her perspective, that she could be properly outraged about his violence. How dared he treat her so! She had trusted him with her love, her life and all her hopes, and he had betrayed her utterly.

For a while, she paced around the room, too restless, too *angry* to sit and play the instrument. She was not a person who could sustain anger for long, however. Her good sense reasserted itself. Jude was dead, and could hurt her no more. Her father was dead, and there could be no reconciliation in the living world. But James... here she paused, for James still held great power over her, for he was Louis' guardian. He could take him away from her altogether and send him to school, and then she would be quite alone. Unless she married... unless she found a new guardian for Louis. And that brought her back to Nathan.

So her thoughts ran, round and round with no conclusions. At least her mourning protected her from needing to make a decision. She could not marry again for many months, so she could put the whole problem to the back of her mind. One day soon she would be settled somewhere, either at Percharden House or at Southampton, and then there would be leisure to consider the future, when she was not consumed by uncertainty or bombarded with new revelations about Jude's life.

She heard voices in the hall below, and her fingers stilled on the keys. Were they home already from the ball? It was still so early. That was not a good sign.

When the drawing room door opened, however, only Nathan entered. He stopped on the threshold, and she was shocked at his appearance, his expression drawn, his complexion ashen.

She jumped to her feet and almost ran across the room. "What is it? Are you ill?"

"No… no…" He seemed dazed. "Whatever are you doing still up at this hour? Did you get so lost in your music that you forgot to go to bed?"

"Is it late?" She looked at the clock — almost one in the morning. "Oh — I had no idea. But whatever has happened? You look very pale. May I pour you a glass of something? There is claret and port and sherry, I think. Or shall I send Withers for some brandy?"

"Thank you… brandy, I think."

She rang for Withers and gave the order, then gestured to a chair. "Sit down, for you look liable to fall down. Do you wish to talk about it, or must I sit in sympathetic silence, while in an agony of suspense?"

He gave a wry laugh. "I beg your pardon, but my past rose up to greet me tonight and it was rather a shock."

"Your past? Oh… not the lady you almost married? Henny's mother?"

He nodded. "Can you imagine how foolish I feel?" he said with a harsh little laugh. "For eleven years I have carried with me this image of a pretty creature, all smiles and glowing looks and delightful affection, and now I find she is grown fat and discontented, and is married to a man almost old enough to be her father, in the hope that he will make her a baroness one day. She did not even recognise me at first and has no interest in her own daughter. I imagined her suffering from the separation as I did, but so far from regretting me, she is astonished to find me respectable enough to be invited to Marford House. I almost wondered if she thought I had crept in through the servants' entrance."

Nell could not help smiling at his indignation. "I daresay that is how she excuses her actions to herself. You are not respectable and therefore she was right to give you up."

"No, no! Do not be so reasonable," he cried. "I am not minded to admit to any justice in her cause. She abandoned me to my suffering, without a word to set my mind at ease in all these years."

"That was very bad of her, but only consider her situation. She was with child — ruined in the eyes of the world, should it become known. Her father whisked her away from you, and only much later, perhaps, discovered the unhappy truth, with no time to make a recover. All they could do was to settle the child as discreetly as possible and make a fresh start in another town. Convincing the lady that you were not worthy of her was undoubtedly part of her family's strategy to ensure her compliance."

He said nothing, his head low. Impulsively, she crossed the room to sit beside him on the sofa, taking one of his hands in hers. "I am so sorry, Nathan. Have you been in love with her for all this time?"

At that, he raised his head, and she was shocked at the hopelessness she saw written there. "Oh, no, not that. I was very unhappy for a long while, it is true, but that is not what grieves me now. Nell, I waited for her. I saw myself as bound to her, and... I refused even to consider marrying elsewhere in case... in case she came back one day. There was an obligation, you see. We were betrothed, and she never released me."

"That was very honourable," Nell said. His hand rested motionless in hers, warm and heavy.

"Honourable! Ha!" He huffed a quick breath. "Perhaps that was it, but I suspect, if I am being honest, clinging to that old love was my way of protecting my heart from further hurt. Every woman I met was compared with my first love, and found wanting in some way."

"Ah, that is so true," Nell said, much struck. "No one can ever compare with the bliss of first love."

He turned to her with surprise in his eyes. "Do you truly believe that?"

"Indeed I do. There is an all-encompassing intensity to young love that cannot be recreated later. At seventeen, there is nothing in the world so important as the one true love, whereas at six and twenty one can see a score of other considerations to be taken into account."

He turned away from her in silence, and she worried that she had ventured onto dangerous ground. But he was her friend, and would not take offence, of that she was certain.

"It is true that the practical aspects assume a greater importance as one grows older," he said slowly, his voice soft. The flickering candles threw a gentle light onto his face. "I could not marry, for instance, without considering Henny's welfare, just as you must always have regard for Louis. But just because one is older and arguably wiser does not preclude the possibility of falling every bit as desperately in love as in the shining optimism of youth. It is worse, in a way, since one's youthful self cannot envisage the likelihood of loss or change or the effects of adversity, which are as clear as day to the older self."

Nell was too discomposed to answer him immediately. Desperately in love? Was this a declaration? Surely he no longer thought of marriage, after all she had said to him on the subject.

Withers came in just then with the brandy, and to cover her confusion, she quickly jumped up and crossed the room to the sideboard where he placed the tray.

"Thank you, Withers. I shall serve Mr Harbottle."

"Should you care for some supper, sir?" Withers said.

"Oh... that would be very kind. Thank you," Nathan said.

Nell poured two brandies, a large one for Nathan and a small one for herself. Nathan had risen as she had, and now he took his glass to stand beside the fire, unlit at this time of year. Nell resumed her seat on the sofa, and after a moment he sat again, but on a chair opposite her. She was glad of his tact, for his words had unsettled her and continued nearness would make it difficult for her to appear calm.

Perhaps he felt some discomposure too, for when he spoke again it was with an effort at brightness. "I am glad Withers suggested supper, for I left Marford House too early to taste the delights in store there."

Taking her cue, she said, "Was the ball enjoyable? I imagine it was rather a squeeze."

"It was. Your brother was there. I had the pleasure of being introduced to the never-contented Lady Godney," he said, which made Nell splutter over her brandy. "I am afraid that Sir James has devised another scheme for Louis' education — a retired tutor in Latin and Greek. He needs the money, apparently, so your brother is fulfilling two charitable missions in one endeavour."

Nell shook her head in exasperation. "I wish he would leave well alone! Louis has enough changes to which to become accustomed without inflicting an elderly tutor on him. Even if a tutor were wanted, he needs a young man, who can roam the countryside and play cricket with him."

"And teach him to ride and to shoot and to be a gentleman," Nathan said.

"You mean that he needs a father," she said softly.

"Not necessarily. A cousin would do just as well for most purposes, and that is a task I should be delighted to perform, as I am sure you are aware. But your brother is a problem which will not, I fear, go away. He wishes Louis to spend more time at his desk and less roaming the countryside. He feels also that women are inferior creatures to have the responsibility for educating his ward. He will be constantly interfering, and you will have to live with the perpetual threat of Louis being taken away from you."

"I do not know what I can do about that!" she cried, jumping up and sitting down again at once, so that he would not be obliged to stand. "James is his guardian, after all, and there is only one certain way to replace him, in law, and that is for me to marry again."

"Which you do not wish to do," he said at once.

"For myself, no, but for Louis..."

He smiled suddenly. "Yes! You would do it for your son, if not for yourself." But then he abruptly returned to seriousness. "But you should not be pushed into a situation distasteful to you by concern for your son or in fear of what your brother might do. Sir James is a strange fellow, to maintain the family feud after his father is long dead, and reject you absolutely even after all your troubles. You are his sister — his *only* sister — after all."

"James knows nothing of my troubles," she said. "I had to tell him of my desperate financial state when I was first widowed, but he believes me secure now. Indeed, I *am* secure, if not rich, even if it cannot be proved that Jude is Felix. As for the rest... the way Jude treated me latterly... I have never spoken of it to anyone but you and Maria. James thinks I was blissfully happy, no doubt."

"Perhaps if you were to tell him—"

She shuddered. "I could not. It is too shaming a thing to be confessed. One day, I shall be able to tell him of it, or Jack, perhaps, when he is older and it is a little further in the past. Louis must be told one day, as well. But not yet."

"If Sir James could be brought to understand all that you have suffered and how desperate you would be to lose Louis, he might be less inclined to interfere. Do you not think it might be worth a try?"

She took a deep breath, considered it, shuddered again. "I cannot."

"Then—"

Withers came in just then with a tray of cold meats, bread and fruit, and they waited in silence until he had withdrawn. Absentmindedly, Nell picked up an apple, then set it down again.

"I have a presumptuous suggestion to offer," Nathan said slowly, when they were alone again, but he looked conscious.

Her heart sank. Was he about to offer for her again? She had thought, after their conversation in Southampton, that no more would be said on that subject. He had offered for her in a moment of desperation, when she had swooned in despair at the prospect of losing Louis at once. But that threat had receded, and she presumed he had given up the idea. It had been a generous impulse, but he must have thought better of it. Even this evening he had said something... what were his words? *'You should not be pushed into a situation distasteful to you by concern for your son.'* Surely that meant he had given up the idea?

"If you do not like to speak to Sir James yourself, might I be permitted to speak to him on your behalf? To tell him all the wrongs that have been done to you, and your terror at the prospect of losing Louis. Such information might be more easily imparted by a friend, rather than by you."

His words took her breath away. "You would do that? You would speak to him for me?"

"If you permit me, I would. As your friend, there is nothing I would not do to make your life more comfortable. You will be easier in your mind if you are not in constant terror that Sir James will take a sudden whim, and whisk Louis away from you. If you will allow me the privilege, I should like to see if I cannot persuade him to agree to leave Louis entirely in your care, at least until he is of an age to go away to school."

"Nathan, you are such a good friend to me!" Her voice wobbled, for the tears were very near the surface. "Thank you! I do not know if you will be able to convince him — I am not sure that anyone can change his mind once he has fixed on a course — but if anyone can do it, you can."

29: The Parsonage

Nathan sent a note to Sir James the very next morning requesting the favour of an interview. He was rather surprised to receive a response almost at once, inviting him to call at four o'clock.

The Godneys' town house was a modest residence in a fashionable square, a compromise between the need to cut a dash in society and the need to rein in extravagance. As Nathan arrived, a line of barouches and stylish town carriages was drawn up outside, the vehicles disgorging an array of young ladies in muslin and demure straw hats, and their silk-clad and befeathered mamas, with just a sprinkling of young men in starched cravats and ostentatiously large hats. However, when Nathan handed in his card, the butler said, "Sir James is expecting you, sir," and led him away from the crowd into a somewhat disordered study.

"I shall inform Sir James of your arrival, sir," the butler said.

Left alone, Nathan amused himself by glancing at the desk, littered with opened letters, newspapers and books. On the tables, more books. On the floor, piles of books ten volumes high. The bookcase on one wall was crammed so full of books stuffed in anyhow that he doubted a single sheet of paper could be squeezed in there. In the bay window, a comfortable and well-worn armchair suggested that the baronet passed many pleasant hours there.

The door flew open, and Sir James Godney came in. "You are very prompt, Harbottle," he said. "Excellent."

For a moment, Nathan was too surprised to answer. He had seen Godney in a range of moods from sullen to grumpy to outraged, but he had never before seen him in sunny good humour, smiling broadly. He was not sure whether this presaged good or ill. "Thank you for seeing me so soon," he managed eventually.

"Oh, I am very grateful to you, I assure you," Godney said. "You are preserving me from the dreadful fate of attendance at one of Julia's hideous afternoon parties. So many of the best families have already left for the country, but the Marchioness of Carrbridge always holds an afternoon party for the daughters of cits and nabobs, and so Julia must do no less. But now, with you here, I have business to attend to and may lurk in here until the dressing gong. Madeira or Canary?"

"Madeira, thank you. I am very happy to be of service in so noble a cause. I am not enamoured of London society myself, so I have every sympathy with your wish to escape."

"Oh, I have no objection to *good* society. I will squire Julia to Marford House as often as she can get cards of invitation, but these daughters of merchants and bankers and nabobs... what is one to say to such people? I know nothing of their lives, nor they of mine. I have nothing in common with those whose fortunes all came from trade or India or the plantations."

"My own fortune came from the plantations," Nathan said mildly, accepting a glass of Madeira.

Godney looked askance at him, then said, "But you have sold out now, I take it?"

"My father sold out when he returned to these shores thirty years ago," he said easily. "It is all invested now, mostly in the Funds"

"Ah well, that is perfectly respectable, but you should get yourself a decent little estate somewhere. A house and park, and some good arable land, not too far from London... that would establish you very well. Then... perhaps a knighthood?"

"I have no desire for honours," Nathan said, amused. "I might consider an estate, if one should cross my path, but Yorkshire suits me very well."

"It is a long way from London."

"Which is precisely why I like it."

Godney grunted, pulled over a matching armchair to the one in the window, and gestured for Nathan to sit. "I daresay you want to talk about Nell."

"Mrs Caldicott, yes, amongst other things."

"Let me guess. You intend to offer for her, and so you apply to me as head of the family for approval."

Nathan laughed. "You would guess wrong. I have not come to talk about any marriage of mine, but Mrs Caldicott's, for there is much that you do not know about it. Have you ever wondered why I have taken such an interest in her?"

"She is a beautiful woman. Does any man need another reason?"

"Perhaps not, but she was a married woman when I first met her, and is still in mourning, so she is out of bounds to me. But the first time I saw her, she bore the tell-tale signs of bruises about her face."

Godney froze, his glass halfway to his lips. Carefully, for his hands shook slightly, he set it down on the nearest table, shifting a pile of books to do so. Then, his voice trembling, he said, "Do you mean to tell me that... that *scoundrel* hit her? Beat her?" Nathan nodded. "Dear God! But why did she not come to me? Or to my father?"

"Your father was probably dead by the time this happened. It was after his ship sank and they were suddenly poor."

"That is *damnable!"* Godney cried, jumping up. "The *blackguard!* I never liked him, never! Nor did Papa. He was a rotten fortune hunter, no good at all and— I beg your pardon, Harbottle. The fellow is your cousin."

"Pray do not apologise. I am heartily ashamed to acknowledge him as a part of the family, and believe me, I have called him far worse epithets. His behaviour was unconscionable."

"But why did she not come to me?" Godney said. "She must have known that I would never—" He stopped, picked up his wine glass again and took a long draught. "Of course she would *not* know," he said savagely. "Papa had broken all contact. I never even wrote to her, except for family happenings — births, marriages, deaths — and her letters were infrequent, too. Very formal. Besides, it is hardly something she would put in a letter. *'The weather is very fine just now and by the way, my husband beats me.'* Damnation! She had to suffer that all alone, at least until you came along. Do you know, Harbottle, I thought you were an encroaching meddler who had designs on my sister. I am happy to acknowledge that I was wrong about you."

Honesty compelled Nathan to say, "Not entirely wrong, I confess. I have admired Mrs Caldicott since the first day I met her, but she has always made it clear that the last thing she wants is another husband. One can understand such a view, naturally."

"Of course! After such a bad experience, she would be most reluctant to try again."

"Quite. But when you came haring up to Yorkshire threatening to take Louis away from her there and then, she was so distressed that I could think of no solution other than to offer her marriage. Fortunately, we were interrupted before she could answer, so—"

"Fortunately? Do you want to marry her or not?"

Nathan hesitated, but he had said too much now to withdraw. "I do, but only when she is willing for her own sake, and not just because she is desperate not to lose Louis."

"Hmmm." Godney frowned at him. "But you expect her to be willing, sooner or later?"

"I... hope, not expect. She might never be willing."

She might never be willing. As he spoke the words, he could no longer deny the truth of them. Nell had said, more than once, that she would never marry again, but he had not quite believed it. He was prepared to wait, naturally, for he had no wish to urge his suit on an unwilling recipient, but in his heart he had always been supremely confident that eventually he would win her. How could he not succeed, when he loved her so much? Yet his hopes and wishes had played him false. Now, for the first time, he had to acknowledge the dreadful prospect that she might truly prefer perpetual widowhood to his love. He might never be more than a friend to her.

He took a deep breath. Nell's happiness was too important for him to waver now. "I will not press her on the subject. She must be allowed to marry or not by her own desire, and not simply to provide Louis with a different guardian who would not send him away from his mother."

He watched Godney as he absorbed this information. "Louis is my ward in law," he said slowly. "I must do what I feel is best for him."

"Naturally, but given the upheavals in his life recently, what he needs most is a settled existence with his mother, and perhaps some assurances from you that he will not be sent off to school until he is a little older."

"I am not at all convinced that Lady Harbottle is experienced enough to teach a child as quick as Louis. He needs tutors, and a strict regime of lessons for every hour of the day."

"Certainly. You will find, if you discuss the matter with Lady Harbottle herself, that she already has such a regime, although she includes plenty of excursions around the estate for Louis' health. If you write to her, she will be very happy to explain her methods, and will naturally be pleased to listen to any suggestions for improvement you care to make."

Godney nodded vigorously. "Write to her… excellent idea. I shall do that. If I am satisfied with the structure of her teaching, then Louis may stay under her tutelage. And as for Nell and this *stupid* breach since her marriage…! I can at least set *that* right, and accept her back into the family fold. Julia will not like it, but when does Julia ever like anything? That should not stop me doing what is right, should it?"

"Indeed not," Nathan said gravely.

"I am glad we have had this talk, Harbottle," Godney said. "You will not rush away, I hope? Will you have another glass of Madeira? What do you think of this latest news from France, eh?"

With an inward sigh, Nathan settled down to entertain Godney until Lady Godney's party had broken up and it was safe for him to emerge from his refuge.

~~~~~

The following morning brought the Godneys in state to pay a formal morning call. Harry had gone off to do Parliamentary things, but Nell, Nathan and Meg received their visitors in the drawing room. Nathan could see at once that they were disconcerted by Meg, having seen her at the ball without realising who she was.

"Oh, your *half*-sister," Lady Godney said, rather disparagingly.

"A sister is still a sister, whether we share one parent or two," Nathan said evenly, relieved that Harry was not there to observe the insult. He might be dithering over marrying Meg, but he was her stoutest champion in the event of any perceived slight.

"Nothing is more important than family," Godney said, loud enough to startle everyone. "Miss Harbottle dazzled everyone at Marford House, and I am delighted to make her acquaintance."

Lady Godney threw him an odd look and seemed about to speak, but wisely refrained.

When it emerged that Nell, Nathan and Meg were about to travel to Hampshire to visit Mr Lumley, who lived within half a mile of Daveney Hall, Godney's face lit up. "Why, then you must all stay at Daveney Hall." Lady Godney gave a squeak of astonishment, but he ploughed on, "It would be our pleasure to have you as our guests. Would it not, Julia?"

Her mouth flapped open. "Sir James..."

"Of course it would. We can invite some of your old friends for dinner, Nell. The Mattocks and the Dimfords, for instance."

Nell laughed. "You are very kind, James, and we would be delighted to stay at the Hall, but there is no need to entertain on our account. I am still in full mourning, remember."

"Oh. Still, it will be a pleasure to have you at home again, Nelly." And he gave her a smile of genuine warmth, despite the frosty
~~~~~

expression on his wife's face. "We could all travel down together. That would be amusing, would it not? I am sure we should find somewhere to stop overnight with enough room for all of us, and at least we would have a decent number for whist. What do you say, eh, Harbottle?"

Nathan could find no answer but to smile and pretend to be pleased at the prospect of two days on the road with the Godneys.

When they had left, Nell turned to Nathan with merriment in her eyes. "Whatever you said to James, you have brought him round wonderfully. I never knew him so tractable before. Thank you!"

He made her a bow. "It was a pleasure. He is tolerable company after a few glasses of Madeira, or perhaps that is only when Lady Godney is not around. Even so, I am sorry to inflict him on you for the journey into Hampshire. I did not expect such condescension."

Nell laughed, "I would not mind for myself, but you will hate it. James is the world's most haphazard traveller, and you are the world's most organised. You will fall out twenty times a day."

In the end they travelled separately from the Godneys, because Nathan found it impossible to pin them down to a specific time or even day. He could not conceive of simply packing up and departing without the necessary planning beforehand. He waited, therefore, until word was received that they had left London, then he wrote his letters to alert the necessary coaching inns to their requirements. With an interceding Sunday, it was therefore three more days before they departed, plenty of time for Meg to fill the luggage coach with hat boxes and interestingly shaped packages.

They arrived at Daveney Hall to grey skies and drizzling rain, and Nathan had the amusement of watching Julia attempt to greet Meg with civility. He also noted the excitement amongst some of the servants to see Nell again. The butler and housekeeper were impassive, but the junior footmen smiled at her and bowed respectfully low, and a little cluster of housemaids hovered in a corner of the entrance hall, smiling and curtsying enthusiastically. There was also one other person there whom Nathan was curious to meet — Nell's younger brother Mr Jack Godney, who turned out to be a fine young man, tall, good-looking and sensibly dressed without fashionable excess. He hugged his sister and professed himself delighted to meet the others, with manners so easy and sincere as to make a striking contrast with his older brother and sister-in-law.

Having encountered no delays, they arrived in plenty of time to walk down to the parsonage and conclude their business with Mr Lumley that very afternoon, but Nathan had arranged to call on him the next day and so the next day it was to be. Sir James and his good lady showed no interest in proceedings, but Mr Jack Godney declared his intention of accompanying them.

"You will be whisking Nell back to Yorkshire at any moment, and there she will stay," he said, "so I must make the most of her short visit here. Besides, Mrs Lumley's cook has a very light hand with a gingerbread cake."

"I cannot say if I will be living at Percharden House or not," Nell said, with a small frown. "We have not yet found absolute proof that Jude and Felix were the same person."

"But it is certain, is it not?" Jack Godney said. "Surely there is no doubt remaining?"

"Not in my mind," Nathan said. "There is no knowing, however, whether the evidence we have managed to accrue is sufficient to convince the Master of the Rolls. I should have been happier to uncover a letter in Felix's own hand to prove it."

"Oh, something may yet turn up," Godney said, in his breezy way.

Nathan wished he could be so sanguine. He had been so sure that Felix would leave some sign of his change of name to avoid leaving the succession in disorder, but they had now exhausted all possibilities.

The entire Lumley family had gathered to receive them in proper state. Mr Lumley, his sister and his two sisters-in-law met them at the door and greeted them with affection, in the case of Nell and her brother, and great affability, in regard to Nathan and Meg. Mr Lumley was younger than Nathan had expected, having formed an image of a stooped and white-haired old man. This man was tall and upright and no more than forty or so, and his sisters were not much older than he was.

The whole party proceeded into the small front parlour, another chair was found for Jack, who had not been expected, and the marriage register was laid out on the embroidered cloth covering the small table. Nathan inspected the register, took a fair copy of the entry and tea was sent for, while Mr Lumley returned the register to its locked box in the church vestry.

When he returned, they drank the tea and sampled the cake, which was not the hoped for gingerbread cake, but a very acceptable marmalade version. Jack had three helpings and would possibly have had three more had not Nell suggested gently to Miss Lumley that it be removed forthwith.

Only then did Nathan produce his letter. "Mr Lumley, this was found amongst Captain Caldicott's effects after his death. It is addressed to you, or your successor, so I hereby discharge my duty in delivering it into your hands."

"Ah! Thank you, Mr Harbottle. I have been expecting this."

"You were expecting it?" Nathan said, astonished.

"Oh yes. In fact, when Miss Nell... I mean Mrs Caldicott came here in March, I felt certain that her purpose was to bring this to me. But perhaps you had not yet found it, my dear. He said he would hide it away, so that it would only be discovered after his death."

Nathan's head spun. "He? You mean... Captain Caldicott?"

"Or, as he once was, Felix Harbottle."

The silence in the room was so profound, Nathan was sure he could hear the mice behind the wainscoting.

"You know that? But can you *prove* it?" he said hoarsely, scarcely daring to believe it.

"Indeed I can, and, unless I miss my mark, this letter will authorise me to do so."

Nathan exhaled slowly, and then, to his own astonishment, he began to laugh. "The devious old fox! Such a merry dance Felix has led us, but the answer was here all the time."

30: A Voice From The Past

Mr Lumley sent his sisters out of the room before opening the letter, for it was a private matter. When he had read it, he showed it to Nathan.

'My dear Sir, If you are reading this, then it seems most likely that I have gone to meet my Maker, there to account for my immortal soul, and so I must needs also settle my earthly accounts. Please be so good as to forward the items left in your care to Sir William Harbottle of Percharden House, Sagborough, West Riding, or to the present head of the family, or the family lawyers, with my grateful thanks for your assistance, and your silence these many years. Your humble servant, Jude Caldicott, previously known as Felix Charles Harbottle."

The inner writing was in Felix's strong, flowing hand, which Nathan recognised from the letters to Aunt Amelie. The direction on the outside was in Jude Caldicott's cramped hand. Silently Nathan passed the letter to Nell and Meg.

"This is the proof," Nell said. "Thank goodness! Now we have all we need to secure Louis' inheritance."

"There is more that will be useful to you in that regard," Mr Lumley said. "Let me fetch the items that Captain Caldicott left in my care. I keep them locked away for safety."

When he returned, he carried a dusty wooden box. For a moment he looked uncertain. "I believe Sir William Harbottle is himself dead, in which case I am bidden to hand this to the head of the family or the lawyers."

"That is a problem," Nathan said. "Louis, I believe, must now be regarded as the head of the family, but as a minor perhaps it should go to his mother?"

"Or his guardian," Mr Lumley said with obvious reluctance.

Silence fell. No one wished to involve Sir James in the matter.

Eventually Nathan said, "I am Louis' nearest male relative on the Harbottle side of his family, if that would weigh with you. I am also the executor of Sir William's estate and have power of attorney to manage the business aspects of it."

"Ah," Mr Lumley said, brightening. "An attorney-in-fact… that would be perfectly acceptable, I believe. There, sir." He placed the box in Nathan's hands. "You should be aware, however, that what you will find therein may distress you all, and especially Mrs Caldicott."

"If you mean that my husband lied to me, Mr Lumley, I am very well aware of it. I do not imagine that any further revelations could cause me any greater distress."

He regarded her over the top of his spectacles. "I believe, my dear, you must be prepared for a very great shock, for what your husband revealed to me is very dreadful."

Nell paled, but lifted her chin a little. "I wish to know everything of my husband's past life," she said calmly.

"So be it," Mr Lumley said. "Let me tell you of my part in all this before you open the box and examine its contents. Captain Caldicott came to see me two days before his marriage. He told me his true name and of his family in Yorkshire, which you are already aware of, so I need not elaborate on that. He told me also of his first marriage, to Eliza Smith. It was a mistake, made in a misplaced sense of honour, and bitterly regretted. This too you know of, I surmise, and that his wife died tragically young in an accident, a fall from a balcony. What you may not know is that her fall was no accident — she was pushed off that balcony, and the person responsible was—"

"No!" Nell said. "No, I cannot—"

She stopped, and Nathan watched her face as she realised the truth — that her husband had been a violent man. It was all too plausible that he had injured his first wife, just as he had injured her. She shivered.

"He did not mean to do it," Mr Lumley said quietly. "It was an accident, but they were quarrelling, he pushed her and she fell."

Nell was mute, and Meg too was reduced to shocked silence, hands to face. Nathan felt compelled to share what he knew of the matter. He had hoped to shield Nell from this knowledge, but now it was out in the open.

"It is true, Nell," he said, in his gentlest tones, taking her hand in his. "I found it out in London from Lord Toller. He was there that night and saw it happen. He spoke up for Felix at the coroner's inquest, and loaned him the money to pay off various officials to ensure no one enquired too deeply into the matter. I am so very sorry."

"I am glad I knew nothing of this when Jude was alive," she said in a low voice. "It would have made my situation all the more pitiable. My husband beat me, Mr Lumley. Perhaps one day he would have killed me, too."

"Oh, my dear! If I had known!" Mr Lumley's face was suffused with distress. "He swore to me it was only that once, that it was merely the heat of the moment, he had not meant to push her... oh, how dreadful for you! How appalling! And I knew something of it. Had I suspected his tendency to violence was ingrained, I could have stopped the wedding. Oh, my dear Mrs Caldicott, I do not know what to say!"

She gave a wry half smile. "There is nothing to be said. He is dead, and here I still am, and at least I have my son. The past is gone for ever, and my husband can never hurt me again. I look to the future now."

So brave! Nathan squeezed her hand, and she gave him a stronger smile.

"Will you not see what is inside the box now?" she said.

He had almost forgotten the box, sitting unregarded on the table beside him. He opened it now, and spread the contents on the table. Two letters, one in Felix's distinctive hand, the other not known to him.

"My notes on all that was said," Mr Lumley said. "It seemed good to me to take a record, in case anything should happen to me. I also suggested that Captain Caldicott write down everything that he had told me. I shall, of course, be happy to recount any part of this to the authorities, should it ever be necessary."

Nathan drew out a ring with the Harbottle crest. "Ah, there it is. We wondered what had become of it."

Apart from that, there were his navy medals, papers relating to his navy career and his first marriage, the legal document recording his change of name, a small book of poems with the initials *'AB'* on the flyleaf and a shrivelled conker.

"I imagine that came from the chestnut tree on the south lawn at Percharden," Nathan said sadly. "Poor Felix. It is as if he left his past here in this box."

"Read the letter," Meg said. "I should like to know what he says. Read it out loud."

The first part of the letter was about his home and family, and then his disastrous marriage, but then he came to the fatal evening when Eliza had fallen to her death.

'Now I must relate the worst that any man can tell of himself, for I come to the moment when Eliza's life ended, and mine came within a hair's breadth of ending also. There were many wild, drunken parties at that time, and that evening's revelry was no wilder or more drunken than any other. Eliza was being difficult again. I say that not to blame her for my actions, but to explain, merely, how we came to quarrel. It was not two weeks since I had found her in Pulbright's bed, and I would not have minded quite so much if he had been an admiral, but it was beneath my dignity to be cuckolded by a lieutenant. We had got past that, or so I thought, but strong liquor brought out the worst in her, and the rum punch that night was very strong and she had had plenty of it. I had to extract her from the over-familiar attentions of a commodore, a captain and a ship's surgeon, and very degrading it was. So we quarrelled, as we had quarrelled a hundred times before.'

Nathan paused, shocked by this glimpse into Felix's married life. Poor Felix, shackled to such a woman! No wonder he had grown violent, exposed to such debauched behaviour in his own wife. His throat tight, he read on.

'We were pulled apart by friends, and I retreated to the card room to drink, although I was well disguised already. I mooched about there for a while, ranting to any who would listen, but my good friend Pascall persuaded me to go home, which I did. However, I must have gone back there, for I found Eliza...'

Nathan looked, up puzzled. "What a strange way to put it — that he *must have* gone back there."

"Read on," Meg said eagerly. "Let us hear it all."

'I found Eliza on the balcony and we quarrelled again, more violently than before. In my anger, I lashed out at her, pushing her backwards and she fell. Pascall helped me creep away and I went home, as I should have done before. God knows, I wish I had! But I do not remember any of this. I know it only because Pascall told me of it later. I remember the first quarrel, the card room, then leaving. I remember returning to our lodgings and preparing for bed. The next thing I knew, I was shaken awake by my man with the news that Eliza had fallen to her death. I heard this as if for the first time, for I had no remembrance at all of what I had done.'

Again Nathan paused, frowning, but Meg clucked at him, so he carried on.

'There was an inquest and the coroner asked me many questions, naturally, most of which I could not answer. It was not until Pascall came forward, good fellow that he is, and told them that he had seen me leave before ever Eliza went onto the balcony that the questions ceased. He then expended his own funds to a considerable amount to Admiralty officials — seven thousand pounds, no less, and where he got such a sum I cannot imagine, for he was ever short of the readies, but he said he could do not less for a good friend. I know not what he did but the effort was successful, for Eliza's death was deemed an accident and I was a free man, who should by rights have been executed. Pascall is indeed my truest

friend, and I owe him everything, even my life. I am determined to repay my debt to him, whatever it takes.'

Nathan was aware of a ripple of disquiet at this point. This was not quite the story that Toller had told, for he had claimed that Felix had done the bribing and Toller's only role had been to loan him the money. And where had he got hold of so much money? He recalled what Harry had said of him, that he never had a feather to fly with, and at the time he knew Felix, Toller had not yet inherited the viscountcy and would have been managing on whatever allowance his father gave him. No, there was something amiss with the story. But Meg was gesturing impatiently, so he read on.

'After this, I tried to pick up the threads of my life in the navy but I had not the heart for it. Father again rejected my attempts to heal the breach between us, and my requests to leave the navy were likewise rejected, I know not why. One of Pascall's cousins was in a position to facilitate this, but despite his efforts my appeals were refused. For four years I drifted along, trying to avoid Pascall, for his attentions were wearisome. He tried more than once to draw me into some devious scheme of his, and was displeased when I refused. I will repay the money I owe him as well as the interest he has asked for, and will always be grateful for his help, but just because he lied for me once does not place me under any obligation to lie for him in return. Then Father died, and at long last my request to leave the navy was approved. Pascall's cousin had moved on and the new man managed the business successfully. I then approached my brother, the new baronet, but he rejected my olive branch in such terms as to preclude my ever being accepted back into the family. So be it, but if the Harbottles wished for no further connection with me, I determined to satisfy their wish. I decided to shed my past altogether, and become Judas Caldicott. It would not only give me a fresh start, but also enable me to prevent Pascall from importuning

me further. Thus I left London, bought my first ship, the Rosy Dawn, *and settled in Southampton, where I have been accepted into society. Thus it was that I met my beloved Nell, soon to be my wife, who will give me the happy home life for which I have long yearned. She must never know of my dreadful past, for her affection for me, so innocent and sweetly given, could not be sustained if she knew the truth. However, I am the son of a baronet, and if Nell gives me sons of my own, there is always the possibility, however remote, of inheritance through my line. To that end, therefore, I have confessed all to the patient and understanding Mr George Lumley, who has undertaken to convey to my family after my death whatever items I leave with him. This is a true account of the circumstances of my life, so help me God. Felix Harbottle, also known as Jude Caldicott.'*

Nathan laid the letter down on the table. Meg looked sorrowful, and Mr Lumley was polishing his spectacles gently.

However, Nell was frowning.

"No," she said. "This is wrong. Jude never forgot. I have seen him drunk many times, but no matter how much rum or ale was in him, he always remembered everything he said and did. I cannot believe that he simply did not remember going back to the party or killing Eliza. Nor could he have pushed her off the balcony and then tamely gone home, got into bed and gone to sleep. It is inconceivable."

"That is true!" Meg cried. "And all he knew of it came from Pascall."

Nathan told them how Toller's story had differed from Felix's version. "There is but one explanation," he said. "Toller — Pascall, as he then was — allowed Felix to believe himself responsible. Perhaps Eliza fell accidentally, or perhaps Toller himself pushed her, who can say? Then Toller bribed the Admiralty officials and—"

"No," Mr Lumley said. "That was the part of Captain Caldicott's story that I always found hardest to accept — that senior officers in His Majesty's Royal Navy would accept bribes? Never!"

"A good point," Nathan said. "So Toller merely told Felix that he had bribed people, and then allowed him to fund his expensive manner of living for more than twenty years. And I do not think there is a single thing that we can do about such injustice."

"Oh, come now," Meg said, merriment bubbling into her voice. "Surely you can be more imaginative than that, brother. Toller lives by society's rules, does he not? Being good *ton* is all important to him, from what Harry tells me. Well then, let us use our wiles to undermine his position. Harry knows people now, influential people like Lord Carrbridge, who need only drop a word in an ear here and there quietly at the clubs, you know how it goes, and Toller would be ostracised."

"Would Harry do it?" Nathan said.

Meg laughed. "He will do it for me. Toller is finished."

31: The Folly

Nathan and Nell walked back from the parsonage side by side in silence. A gate beside the church led into the grounds of Daveney Hall, where a good path meandered the half mile to the house in a peaceful fashion, each turn bringing into view a fine tree or a statue beside a pool or a stand of shrubs, their limbs bent with blossoms. Meg raced along ahead of them with Jack, occasionally darting back to point out some interesting tree or vista, before dashing off again, her face full of merriment.

"She is happy," Nell said. "Everything is settled with Harry, then?"

Nathan smiled, relieved that she was not overset by the day's revelations. "So it would seem. That evening at the Marford House ball appears to have done the trick."

"Not the ball," she said with a smile. "The carriage ride home."

"Five minutes in a carriage?"

"Two people overflowing with love alone in a closed carriage?" she said. "Five minutes is more than enough time for a man to succumb to ardour and kiss his lady."

"Hmm... I imagine it was the other way round," Nathan said. "Harry promised not to breach the rules of propriety, but Meg would not feel herself so bound. She would have been the one doing the kissing, and no man in love could resist. Lord, what is she doing now?"

"Bouncing," Nell said, laughing. "She has so much energy."

"True, but it is not very ladylike to be so animated. She feels it herself — that she is too forward, too ready to speak the first thing that enters her head. She envies you your serenity."

"She should not," Nell said with some heat. "I was once lively, as she is now, and only developed my serenity, as you call it, as a defensive shield against the world. It is not a natural state for me."

"I have seen your natural state, in York," Nathan said, smiling broadly at the memory. "At Percharden House, too, sometimes. Your natural state is delightful."

She coloured slightly, but walked on composedly, pulling her shawl about her a little more tightly.

"Are you cold?" he said, but she shook her head with a smile.

They came to a branching of paths, and here she stopped. To the right it was only a short distance to the house, but to the left was a tunnel of roses, their myriad blooms filling the air with perfume.

"May I show you one of my favourite spots in the garden?" she said. "Meg has Jack to bear her company, and will not miss us for a few minutes, I am sure."

"I should be honoured," he said, as his treacherous heart surged in happiness. So precious, these moments alone with her. He treasured every one, small rays of warm sunshine in his otherwise dreary life, to be stored up to sustain him during the long, dark hours without her. And perhaps there would be years of darkness to be endured. Perhaps she would never be able to love him as he loved her. How would he bear it? With as much fortitude as he could muster. He would enjoy her company when he could and endure the aching loneliness when he could not, and hope always for better days.

They made their way beneath the arching roses, then skirted a rock garden with a pretty little pool and climbed a small hill between banks of sweet-smelling white flowers. A twist of the path revealed a ruined tower, its tumbled walls artfully arranged to make a sheltered seat with a fine view over the gardens and house. She sat on the stone bench, casting aside her shawl, gloves and bonnet, and turning her face up to the sun. When she looked round, she smiled up at him in a way that made his insides flip-flop in the most alarming manner.

"I see why you like this place," Nathan said, casting his gloves off likewise and sitting beside her, close enough to be aware of the soft rise and fall of her chest as she breathed, yet not quite near enough to feel her warmth. How he longed to sit closer, to wrap his arms around her, to bury his face in her soft hair and smother her lovely face with kisses. It hurt so much to be unable to touch her.

"This is where Jude first kissed me," she said. "Here we first declared our love to each other, and settled our future together."

That was an unexpectedly intimate revelation. Yet her voice was calm, almost as if she were talking about some trivial domestic matter. Perhaps she wished to talk about her husband, and this was an opening.

"You are remarkably composed, after all that has been learnt today," he said tentatively.

"Nothing about Jude can surprise me any longer," she said flatly. "I was living with a stranger all those years. If only he had confided in me, if only he had *trusted* me, we could have faced up to his past together. As it was, he shouldered that burden all alone for so many years, and it drove us apart. He shut me out of his life and I cannot forgive him for that. The other thing... the violence... all of it happened because he would not trust me with his darkest thoughts and fears. He kept everything trapped inside him until it exploded, and I was the one who drew his rage out of him."

"Surely you would not excuse his behaviour?" Nathan said, shocked.

"Oh *no!* Never! It was utterly indefensible. But I can *understand* it — the frustration, the boiling anger that drove him. We had both been used to a better life, and he must have felt that everything he touched was doomed to failure. Knowing now of his first marriage, imagine how desperate he must have been to find himself in difficulties again."

"Do you hate him?" Her openness thrilled him to his core.

"Not hate, never that. I feared him, but in the absolute belief that somewhere inside was still the man I loved. That was not true," she added sadly. "The man I loved — the man I *thought* I loved — never existed. He wrapped himself around with lies, so many lies, and that secrecy ate away at our happiness like a canker. I was little more than a child when we married, and I think he tried to keep me in innocence, while I wanted... something more. The closeness that comes from a perfect understanding and acceptance of each other. It could never happen, though, unless he shared his past with me. There can be no true intimacy without honesty, do you not agree?"

"I do. There are those who say that a man's world is different from that of a woman's, and she does not need to know all his concerns. Such men use that argument to justify any number of vices, but it is better, I feel, to have no vices that need to be concealed. I am of your mind, therefore, in believing that honesty is the best foundation for any relationship, whether business or friendship or marriage."

"Good," she said, glancing up at him with a little smile playing on her lips, "for I am about to test your honesty to its limits, which I do for my own satisfaction, careless of the injury it may cause you. I am being my natural self today, you see, and that means a certain recklessness of the consequences. I am risking our friendship, but only a little, for you are too generous not to forgive my boldness."

He was too much surprised to answer, but her sweet smile robbed her words of any concern he might have felt.

She went on, "I shall ask you a question and I wish you to answer me with absolute honesty, whatever the truth may be."

"Very well," he managed to say, although the blood was thundering in his veins. Whatever could she ask him that was so serious that she must approach the matter with such solemnity?

"Nathan, do you love me?"

Whatever he had expected, that was not it. For an instant, he felt as if he had plunged head-first down a well, and was struggling to breathe. He gasped, staring at her in stupefaction. Another breath, and then his wits began to recover, for surely it was the easiest question in the world to answer!

"Yes," he whispered. "Yes, I do."

"Ah. There it is! I was not mistaken, then." She was remarkably composed, considering the subject under discussion. She gazed into his face without any dissembling, and only a heightened colour about her face revealed some agitation within. "There is a certain look in a man's eye, sometimes — a look that is more than admiration. When he is swayed by strong emotion, when his deepest feelings rise to the surface and threaten to overwhelm him, then his voice changes and there is a light in his eyes that cannot be disguised. I thought I saw it in you once or twice. When you asked me to marry you for Louis' sake, and again as we sat beside the River Itchen in

Southampton, and then again after the Marford House ball, when you talked of being desperately in love… But then at other times you are quite different, very cool, very controlled. You speak of friendship and being practical about marriage and that love is not enough, so you will appreciate why I might be confused."

"Yes," he managed, although his voice was a mere croak.

"But there it was a moment ago, that light in your eyes, and it was not my imagination that saw it before. It is vain of me, and shallow and selfish and every other condemnation you can heap on my head, but I needed to know… that it was *not* my imagination. That I have your love, wherever that may lead to. But of course that brings us inexorably to another question, and again I must ask you to be entirely honest with me, for kindness and dissembling will not help. You understand that, I am sure, for you are my friend, and because I am *your* friend, let us agree that nothing we say here is binding. We may talk together with perfect openness, yet our words impose no obligations on either of us. Do you agree?"

"I do," he said at once, for he knew now where this was leading.

"Nathan, do you hope, one day, to marry me?"

Again, his answer needed no thought. "I do, but only when — *if* — it should be your wholehearted and unconditional choice. Not before. Nell, I once offered you everything that is mine in order to keep your brother away from Louis. I see now that it was wrong of me to press you in that abrupt way, when we were both ruled by the heat of the moment. For your own peace of mind, you must be free to marry when you wish and whom you wish, or not to marry at all if that is your choice."

"Ah… Thank you."

He watched her face, so beautiful, so serene, and was so overwhelmed with love for her that he could barely breathe. He could not imagine having such a conversation with any other woman. Her candour humbled and yet exhilarated him, for surely he could match it. Did he dare?

"Nell, do you love me?" he blurted.

She laughed suddenly, and her smile warmed his heart. "I deserve that, do I not? What is sauce for the goose, after all, is sauce for the gander. But I cannot give you an answer."

"Now that is not fair!" he cried, although he answered her smile with one of his own. "I have been honest with you, will you not be honest with me in return?"

"But I *am* being honest. I cannot answer you because I do not know."

Instantly he was deflated.

"No, no! Do not be discouraged!" she cried. "Consider my situation. It is not six months yet since Jude's death, and even though it was a relief in many ways, it is also a great loss to me. Whatever my marriage became in the end, for several years it was a joyful one, and for those years Jude was everything I had ever wished for in a husband. I cannot yet give up mourning him as he was then, and the long, happy marriage I looked forward to. Perhaps I never will, I do not know, but so I believed for a long time, such that I could not conceive of marrying again. There is so much fear deep inside me of making a mistake, of binding myself to the wrong man again."

She paused, and he held his breath, mesmerised by these revelations, waiting for her to find the courage to continue.

With a sigh, she went on, "But I have at last begun to notice that, even though Jude is dead, I am still alive. There is warmth and beauty and comfort in the world, and there are good people who show me nothing but kindness. And there is you, Nathan. My friend. My very good friend, who treats me, not as a feeble woman but as a sensible creature, helping when I need help and standing to one side when I do not. My very *dear* friend, who does not dissemble but answers my most impertinent questions with absolute honesty. And so, very gradually, I have come to realise that to marry again might not be so terrifying. To marry a kind man, an honest man, a dear friend — that would not be so bad, would it? I can see all the advantages to it, for myself and for Louis too. But..."

"Ah," he said, releasing the breath he had been holding.

"No. You must not look so... despairing," she said, and one hand reached up to his face as if she would stroke his cheek before falling back at the last minute. "It is your own fault that I am dithering so. You talked with such passion of being desperately in love... that one may love again just as intensely as the first time, and it is *not* so with me. Not yet, and I do not know... I cannot tell if it will grow, if I will come to love you just as desperately as I once loved Jude, or if I have expended all my youthful passion and there is nothing left but this cold shell of a woman who is glad to be free. I am very fond of you, Nathan, my dearest and very best friend, but I do not know if I will ever be able to offer you anything more than friendship."

The relief was palpable, now that he understood her mind. "Nell... dearest Nell..." He reached for her hand, and as he took it, a little tremor passed through him at the touch of her fingers. She looked up at him trustfully, her lips slightly parted, waiting for him to get his disordered thoughts into some semblance of coherence. He had supposed that he would make some non-committal little speech — that he understood, that it did not matter a bit and that he wanted only to make her happy. That no doubt was what she expected of him, and what he expected of himself. But it was a day for recklessness, and so the words that emerged were nothing like that.

"There is one way to find out," he blurted. "Let me kiss you and then you will know whether the fires of passion can be ignited again."

She moved sharply away from him, her mouth round with astonishment. He half expected indignant remonstrations, or worse. Perhaps she might even storm away from him. But she did not. Her hand quivered in his and then she gave a little laugh.

"I should like that, if it will not bind us irrevocably."

"Just a kiss," he murmured, as the blood raced in his veins. As if there could be such a thing as *just a kiss*, not with Nell, the woman he loved with every fibre of his being. As if his life would ever be the same again. But the world's strongest team of oxen could not drag him away from her now.

"Just a kiss," she said, smiling.

He shifted along the bench to sit closer to her, and gently slid one arm around her slender waist. She leaned into his embrace, gazing up at him with a smile of pleased anticipation on her face, and not a trace of fear. Slowly, oh so slowly, he leaned nearer and she moved too, inching towards him. Her eyes closed. Their lips touched, so softly he could not even be sure it had happened. He drew back slightly.

Her eyes flew open. "No, a *proper* kiss," she said.

With laughter bubbling up inside him, he pulled her more tightly into his arms. And then he kissed her.

Warmth and joy exploded within him. His other hand rose to cup her head, feeling the silky softness of her hair. One of her hands crept round his back while the other buried itself somewhere beneath his cravat, clasping his shirt. Her lips were velvety and yielding beneath his, and warm, so warm, setting him on fire. He was burning up, fire running in his veins, kissing her hungrily as the suppressed need of many months rose up to swallow him. She gave a little whimper and returned his kiss with fervour every bit the equal of his own. It was a long, long time before, with infinite reluctance, they drew apart.

"Ohhhh..." she said. Then she laughed, shaking in his arms. "That was... I have not the words." Another laugh. "But it was most definitely a *proper* kiss."

"Does it answer your question?"

She tilted her head to gaze up at him. "I... I am not sure. I am not sure of anything at this precise moment."

He laughed, and shifted his arm a little more closely around her waist. "Not to worry," he said. "Take your time. Take all the time in the world. Mourn your husband and your marriage, grieve for what was and what might have been, recover your natural self that so delights me. And if ever you feel that you would like to marry a dear friend, I shall be here waiting for you."

"Nathan... dear Nathan, it might be a very long time. It might even be... never."

"Then so be it. I shall wait for you for as long as my love endures – all the years of my life and beyond." And then mischief overtook him, for he added, "However, if you should wish to test out the fires of passion again while we wait — just a kiss, nothing binding — I shall be more than happy to oblige."

"Just a kiss?"

"Just a *proper* kiss," he said firmly.

She chuckled and laid her head on his shoulder.

Epilogue

JULY, ONE YEAR LATER

"Are you busy, dearest?" Nell said to her husband. He was hard at work at the big desk in the Percharden House study, making lists. Nathan was always making lists.

"Never too busy to see you, my love. Is the mail here yet? Shall we have some tea?" he said eagerly.

Nell smiled. It was part of their morning ritual. Somewhere in the middle of the day, whenever the footman had been down to the Sagborough post office to collect the mail, they would sit together and read their letters and drink tea, and enjoy a precious few minutes alone without the many other demands on their time.

"Craven is just bringing the letters, and the tea is ordered."

They moved to the small table by the window, just as Craven entered ahead of the little procession carrying the tea things. He himself bore the large silver salver laden with the day's post.

"So many!" Nell said, watching as Nathan deftly scooped up a large pile and placed them in front of her. Then a smaller pile for himself. "Replies to the invitations, I expect. Acceptances, let us hope."

"Bound to be," Nathan said. "Who in Sagborough would refuse to attend the first ball at Percharden House for a generation? Ah, this one is from the musicians. Good, that is all settled. You shall have music to dance to, Mrs Harbottle."

As Craven and the footmen withdrew, Nell poured the tea, while Nathan swiftly opened his mail. That, too, was part of their ritual. He read his letters quickly, for they were generally dull business matters, while hers were usually personal and all the better for being savoured."

"Ah, the attorney tells me the couple he has found to take care of the Davygate house are now in place. He has had all the locks changed and will bring the keys to you tomorrow, if convenient. Is it convenient?"

Nell looked up from the teapot, suddenly anxious. "Are you sure you want to do this? It is your family home, after all."

"It was what we agreed, and it is part of your marriage settlement, dearest. The house is yours, to do with as you please. Sell it, if you choose, and buy something more to your taste, but I want you to have a house of your own, where you will be safe."

Hesitantly, she said, "But you are not like Jude. You would never hurt me, would you?"

"*Never*," he said fiercely. "But if ever you feel that I might, or are afraid for any reason, you will have somewhere to escape. Darling Nell, I shall never forget my despair when I first met you, having to leave you in that house awaiting Jude's return, knowing that you had nowhere to go, no one to turn to, nowhere safe. I felt so *helpless*, and I cannot conceive how desperate your feelings must have been, to be trapped in that way. I want you to have a place to go, that is yours alone. It was my understanding that you wanted this. Was it not the reason you agreed to marry me? That was my cunning plan, after all, to make it impossible for you to refuse me."

She laughed, but said, "It was the offer of the house which convinced me that I would be safe with you, not the house itself. It seems a waste when I might never use it. It might stay empty for years."

"Good," he said at once. "I devoutly hope it may be so, and I shall do all in my power to make it so. But it is there for you and Louis if ever you should need it. Where is Louis, by the way? My ears have not been assaulted today by his enthusiastic attempts to coax a tune out of the schoolroom pianoforte. He has not your talent, my love."

That made her laugh. "No, Henny is a far better performer than he is. Perhaps I should suggest he gives it up. His talents lie in other directions, I think. The two Macs have taken him to Killingford Pond to collect more damselflies."

"That is becoming quite an obsession," he said. "Still, it is considerably better than grasshoppers. My ears are still ringing from Mrs Wells' screams. Grasshoppers and kitchens do not mingle, I fear."

"He has been told to ensure the lid is tightly affixed this time. That letter is from Meg — I would know her hand anywhere."

"It is. They have arrived at Highley Manor, only three days later than expected. Seemingly, little Edward screamed for the entire journey, but she is happy to report that neither she nor Harry murdered the child, despite the provocation, and he is perfectly contented now that he has the Squire and Mrs Smethurst to dote upon him. Grandparents are a wonderful invention. I suppose that perpetual screaming is something we shall also have to learn to endure, in a few months' time."

"Not a bit of it, for this child will be perfectly contented, just like his mama. Nathan, I am so glad that Harry and Meg resolved their differences. That brief carriage ride together after the Marford House ball secured all their present happiness."

He lowered the letter. "It was the ball itself which changed everything."

"Seeing Meg accepted into the highest society, you mean? Or seeing her admired by all those noblemen?"

"Neither of those. Harry told me that he had never before understood that the members of the *beau monde* were so shallow. There are good people, of course, like Lord and Lady Carrbridge, and bad, like Toller, but most are just ordinary men and women entirely devoted to a life of pleasure and excess. It offended his Yorkshire soul, he told me. Harry realised that evening that he was destroying his own happiness, and Meg's too, for nothing but vanity and ostentatious display. Meg will never be accepted by certain sections of society, and Harry may well lose his seat in the Commons at the next election, but he is still his father's heir and that will content him, since he has Meg by his side."

"Ah."

She looked so thoughtful that he said, "You disapprove? Do you think he should have put his career above his love for Meg?"

"Not at all," she said, "but if he loses his seat it will be a great loss to the country. Parliament needs men like Harry, who represent ordinary men — the mill owners and manufacturers and yeomen farmers and squires who have no titles or great power, but are vital to the strength of this country."

"Let us hope, then, that the voters of his constituency agree. Will you not read your own mail? That one is from your brother, I think."

She broke the seal and unfolded the sheet. "He and Julia are not coming to the ball... oh, wait, now he says that they are. *'Since Jack is determined to go, we feel obliged to accompany him, lest he fall into bad company.'* There now, that is what he thinks of us, that we surround ourselves with bad company."

"Or that we are ourselves bad company," Nathan said laughing. "He thinks us a dreadfully rackety crowd, I am sure."

"Lord Toller has been seen in Italy, seemingly, so that is where he hid away after society ostracised him. Oh, Julia is increasing again. Goodness, that was quick after Mary."

Nathan chuckled. "James still wants a son and heir, to displace the ungovernable Jack. Who is that one from?"

"Lady Craston. An acceptance for the ball. And Lord and Lady Gilbert will be coming, too. There, all our local nobles. We shall have an excellent attendance. Oh, this one is from Maria... oh! Oh, goodness! Well!"

"Now I am concerned," he said. "Is all well?"

"Oh yes..." she said absently, busily scanning the lines. "Well I never! Maria has an admirer."

"Oh, excellent. Anyone we know?"

"It is Mr Sherrard's younger brother, Mr Timothy Sherrard, who is almost as wealthy as he is. He came to one of Maria's card evenings and was so taken with the supper that he went directly to the kitchen to congratulate the cook. Maria says, *'He saw me there, covered in flour and grease, my hair in disorder and my face aflame from the ovens, and declared himself on the spot. Can you imagine it, dear Nell? And me with the cheesecakes and ice cream still to go up! But he wishes very much to buy the house, and settle the Lloyds elsewhere, and continue the business just as it is, only with his patronage to draw in the very best society. You will be hearing from his solicitor very soon with a proposal for the house.'* Well! If he will marry Maria and save her from a life of perpetual industry, I shall be very glad of it, although it seems that he wishes her to continue cooking, whatever happens. Or perhaps he will engage another cook to work under her supervision."

"Shall you sell the house, if he makes a sensible offer?" Nathan said.

"Oh yes! I should be very glad to see an end, once and for all, to that part of my life. Jude and I were very happy there for a few years, but latterly..."

He laid down the letter in his hand, and said gently. "Come here, wife, and sit on my knee for a while. We shall have morning callers arriving very soon and then we shall be caged in the saloon with Aunt Amelie, who will purse her lips and look disparaging whenever Henny speaks or is mentioned, and will gush excitedly over her dear, deceased son Felix." He sighed. "I love her dearly, but her views and mine do not coincide, and I have to force myself sometimes not to express my objections. But whenever I am tempted, I look at my lovely wife with her serene countenance, and bite my tongue."

Obediently she rose and he lifted her onto his lap, and kissed her long and lingeringly.

"I am glad you do not argue with her," she said after a while, resting her head on his shoulder. "We have inflicted upon her all your York household, except Meg, and it is a great trial to her, even though this is Louis' house now, and his wishes must prevail. He is very happy to have Henny here. He has been desperately short of friends of similar age."

"But he will be ready to go to school, when the time comes," Nathan said.

"You do not mind if he goes to Winchester?" she said, suddenly anxious. "I thought you might want to send him to your old school."

"In Edinburgh? No, he will do well enough at Winchester. It is an excellent school, and his Uncle James will keep an eye on him."

"But our own child will go to Edinburgh? If it is a boy?"

"Do you know, I see no reason why he should not follow his half-brother to Winchester. If you would like that."

"I should like it very much," she said happily. "But it might be a girl."

"Then she will tease the two Macs unmercifully, learn to dance and to play and to draw, and grow up to be almost as beautiful as her mama," he said complacently.

"That sounds delightful," she said, her throat absurdly tight. Even after four months of marriage, her husband could still reduce her to trembling tears of joy.

"I want you to have everything you dream of," he whispered, "for it is no more than you deserve, my dearest love. You have lived in darkness for too long. Now is your time to dance in the sunshine, and sparkle like the priceless jewel that you are."

"You are very good to me," she said, her voice a mere thread. "I love you so much, darling husband."

"As I love you, sweet Nell. I bless the day you threw caution to the four winds and dared to speak openly of love."

"Sometimes, one has to be reckless," she said. "There is a time to be good and obedient, but there is a time, too, to reach for the clouds, even if there is a risk of plummeting to earth. It was utterly selfish of me, but I needed to *know*. All the certainties of my life had been swept away, and I was not even sure of myself any longer. Who was the true Nell — the silent, fearful Nell of Southampton, or the confident society Nell of long ago, or the so-composed but barely alive widow, or some other Nell entirely? I needed to find my place in the world, and the first step on that path was to find out *your* place in that world. Did you want to set me free to make my own way unaided, or did you want to pull me along behind you, whether I would or no? I learnt that day that what you wanted was to walk beside me, giving me words of encouragement and helping me up whenever I fell. You were — *are* — the best friend I could ever have imagined."

"Oh Nell!" His voice was thick, and he squeezed her tight. "I once thought that I would happily take you however I could, even if it was only to protect Louis. In my arrogance, I was sure I could teach you to love me... that all you needed was a gentle, loving husband to be happy. It took me a long time to realise that you could not so easily set the past behind you. Do you remember when we first went up to London, and there was a dispute at one of the inns?" She nodded, remembering it all too well. "How easily the memories rose up to overwhelm you! You needed time to set the bad memories behind you... to find the true Nell, as you put it."

"There was another reason to delay, too," she said thoughtfully. "I rushed into marriage with Jude too impetuously. If only we had waited—"

"Hush," he said softly, pressing one finger against her lips. "We can all play the game of *'if only'*, but it is a game with no winners, only losers. We cannot change the past, and nor should we, for it has made us who we are. Let us have no regrets about what cannot be changed."

"True, and there is one thing about which I have not the slightest regret."

"And what is that?" he said, but he was smiling at her, surely guessing her next words.

"Marrying you. You make me so happy, my dear friend."

He laughed. "That is my life's purpose, as you must know. It is the only way I know how to repay you. I thought my heart would never be whole again, but you healed me, my dear Nell."

"As you healed me."

"No, it seems to me that you healed yourself. That day when you asked me to lay all my hopes and wishes before you, with nothing hidden or withheld, that was the moment when you seized your life back from your husband's grip. All I did was to watch and admire your courage."

"And to kiss me," she murmured.

She felt rather than heard his laughter. "That too."

"And you promised to wait," she said, in a whisper. "You waited for me, until I was ready. Kiss me, husband, and hold me tight."

"Always," he said.

THE END

The next book in the series is *The Lacemaker.* You can read a sneak preview of chapter 1 after the acknowledgements. For more information or to buy, go to my website at http://marykingswood.co.uk/.

Thanks for reading!

If you have enjoyed reading this book, please consider writing a short review on Amazon. You can find out the latest news and sign up for the mailing list at my website at http://marykingswood.co.uk/.

Family trees: Hi-res version available at my website at http://marykingswood.co.uk/.

A note on historical accuracy: I have endeavoured to stay true to the spirit of Regency times, and have avoided taking too many liberties or imposing modern sensibilities on my characters. The book is not one of historical record, but I've tried to make it reasonably accurate. However, I'm not perfect! If you spot a historical error, I'd very much appreciate knowing about it so that I can correct it and learn from it. Thank you!

Isn't that what's-his-name? Regular readers of my books will know that occasionally characters from previous books pop up again. There are a few in this book. Sagborough residents Sir William and Lady Harbottle were seen briefly in *The Seamstress*, as was Barbara Drabble, whose lovely daughter Celia became a great success after Fanny dressed her. The Marquess and Marchioness of Carrbridge first appeared in *Connie*, and Daniel Merton, Lord Carrbridge's very clever secretary, was first seen in *Amy* as Sir Osborne Hardy's friend.

Lawyer Mr Willerton-Forbes and his flamboyant sidekick Captain Edgerton have been helping my characters solve murders and other puzzles ever since *Lord Augustus.*

About the Silver Linings Mysteries series*:* John Milton coined the phrase *'silver lining'* in *Comus: A Mask Presented at Ludlow Castle*, 1634

> *Was I deceived, or did a sable cloud*
>
> *Turn forth her silver lining on the night?*
>
> *I did not err; there does a sable cloud*
>
> *Turn forth her silver lining on the night,*
>
> *And casts a gleam over this tufted grove.*

Ever since then, the term *'silver lining'* has become synonymous with the unexpected benefits arising from disaster. The sinking of the *Brig Minerva* results in many deaths, but for others, the future is suddenly brighter. But it's not always easy to leave the past behind...

Book 0: The Clerk: the sinking of the *Minerva* offers a young man a new life *(a novella, free to mailing list subscribers).*

Book 1: The Widow: the wife of the *Minerva's* captain is free from his cruelty, but can she learn to trust again?

Book 2: The Lacemaker: three sisters inherit a country cottage, but the locals are surprisingly interested in them.

Book 3: The Apothecary: a long-forgotten suitor returns, now a rich man, but is he all he seems?

Book 4: The Painter: two children are left to the care of a reclusive man.

Book 5: The Orphan: a wilful heiress is determined to choose a notorious rake as her guardian.

Book 6: The Duke: the heir to the dukedom is reluctant to step into his dead brother's shoes and accept his arranged marriage.

Any questions about the series? You can email me at mary@marykingswood.co.uk- I'd love to hear from you!

About the author

I write traditional Regency romances under the pen name Mary Kingswood, and epic fantasy as Pauline M Ross. I live in the beautiful Highlands of Scotland with my husband. I like chocolate, whisky, my Kindle, massed pipe bands, long leisurely lunches, chocolate, going places in my campervan, eating pizza in Italy, summer nights that never get dark, wood fires in winter, chocolate, the view from the study window looking out over the Moray Firth and the Black Isle to the mountains beyond. And chocolate. I dislike driving on motorways, cooking, shopping, hospitals.

Acknowledgements

Thanks go to:

All those fine people in Albany, Australia who restored the *Brig Amity*, and gave me the germ of an idea.

Shayne Rutherford of Darkmoon Graphics for the cover design.

My beta readers: Mary Burnett, Barbara Daniels Dena, Amy DeWitt, Melanie Savage

Last, but definitely not least, my first reader: Amy Ross.

Sneak preview of The Lacemaker Chapter 1: A Letter (March)

MARCH

Caroline laid the strip of lace flat on the counter, smoothing it carefully. Mr Turner, the linen draper, placed a neat pile of shilling coins beside it, while his sister looked on suspiciously. She was always suspicious, that one, suspecting Caroline of some subterfuge, even when the price was clear to see before her. Mr Turner, however, was old-fashioned. He still paid the traditional way, with the number of shillings that could cover the lace.

With delicate fingers, Caroline began to place the coins on the strip of lace, placing them as tightly as she could. Eventually, when not a scrap of lace remained uncovered, she stood back.

"That one is over the edge," Miss Turner said in her sour way, pointing to one of the shilling coins.

"It is just the angle from which you are looking," Caroline said easily. "The light is not the best just here."

"I can fetch a lamp," Miss Turner said, the fire of battle in her eyes.

"No need, Elspeth," Mr Turner said. "Let us not argue over a shilling. You know Miss Milburn's work is worth it. I never have any trouble selling her pieces, and this is a very pretty one."

Almost five guineas for three weeks' work — not a great deal, but much needed. Quickly, before he could change his mind, Caroline scooped up the coins and tucked them into her purse, hiding it away in a pocket. There was a great deal to be said for the old-fashioned fuller skirts, which had room for the concealment of pockets. She strongly disliked the new fashion for a reticule held in the hand. With a nod of the head and a quick bob to the Turners, she hurried out of the shop.

The rest of her day's business was more pleasurable. Winchester had shops in abundance, and her steps took her to the grocer for tea, cheese and spices, the apothecary for Lin's herbs, the silk merchant for more thread for her lace and — an indulgence — the milliner for a new bonnet for Poppy. Gradually her basket filled with neatly-wrapped packages. Only when she heard the clock strike the half hour again did she hasten back to the White Hart to catch the return stage to Romsey. She had no time to buy food at the inn, but she had had the foresight to buy a pie from a stall in the market, and that sustained her for the journey home.

Caroline was squeezed into the middle of a seat designed for two, but that didn't matter. She had seen the passing scenery many times before, and besides, she was busy designing her next piece of work in her head. She could already see the cushion laid out in her mind's eye, the placement of the first pins, the strip gradually growing under her nimble fingers. Mama might lie in the Abbey graveyard, but her skills were still alive in her daughters.

With a great racket as the guard blew his horn, the stage coach turned in to the crowded yard of the White Horse Inn. Caroline never rushed to alight, waiting for the dust to settle and the initial confusion to dissipate. When she descended, she picked her way past the carts and wagons, skirted the groups of people greeting arrivals or bidding farewell and made her way through the arch to the Market Place. From there it was only a short walk to the house she shared with her sisters, three other families and a linen draper's shop. The shop had once been her father's and the whole house theirs, but when he had died and everything had to be sold, they had squashed into just four rooms, and since Mama's death, it was only two, and the use of an attic room for the looms. Still, it could be worse, she supposed. They had a roof over their heads, and enough money for their modest wants, and today they had fresh cheese and a new bonnet for Poppy.

Lin was bent over the worktable, absorbed in her task, one fair curl falling unregarded from her coiled hair. "Gracious, are you back already?" she exclaimed, as Caroline set her basket down on the table. "Did you catch an earlier stage?"

"The coach was, if anything, a little late," Caroline said. "It wants but an hour until dinner. Have you finished the scarf already? I thought it needed two more days of work."

"Oh... oh, well, I *meant* to, but I had this wonderful idea. Peg dolls." She held up the work on which she was engaged, showing a clothes peg dressed in rather a fetching gown and bonnet. "We can sell them, you see, dearest," she went on eagerly. "It's another way to make money. You're always asking us to think up new ideas, and so I have. Don't you think it's sweet?"

"It is, yes. Very pretty. How much would you be able to sell it for — a penny? Tuppence? And how long has it taken you to make it?"

"Oh, not long… an hour or two… once I had got the idea." Sheepishly, she held up several failed attempts. "But… you mean we cannot make a profit by them? Oh… I am very sorry, Caro. It seemed like such a good idea."

"So it is, or would be if we didn't have Mrs Hasbroke waiting for that scarf."

"I am very sorry," Lin said again, hanging her head. "I am a great trial to you, I know. Shall I go and help Susie now?"

"No, I'll give her a hand. You can get an hour's work done on that scarf, while the light is so good."

Lin nodded and rushed away to the loom in the attic, leaving Caroline shaking her head ruefully. Lin was a hard worker, and enthusiastic, but too easily distracted. And yet it was so disheartening to watch her youth draining away in the hours spent up in the attic, bent over her loom. Sweltering in the summer and freezing in the winter, and exhausting all year round. Lin was too pretty to be wasted in that way. Some rich young man should sweep her up and dress her in silk and diamonds, and allow her to spend her days creating peg dolls or painting portraits or whatever her project of the moment was. She was nineteen already, and should be dancing at night, not huddled over a single candle with a needle.

Caroline hung her cloak and bonnet on a peg and took her basket through to the back room, where Susie was stirring a pot on the range.

"Had a good day, Miss Milburn?" Susie said, with her wide smile. She had been their nursery maid in the prosperous days, and still addressed the sisters with the formality their mother had insisted upon, even though she was now as much friend as servant.

"Good enough," Caroline said, as she always did.

"Winchester busy, was it?"

"As always. I bought some of that tasty cheese you like to melt onto toast. Our usual tea was far too dear, so I had to get something cheaper. Mm, something smells good."

"Made a seed cake."

Caroline tied on her apron, and settled at the table to pare vegetables. "These carrots are so old they almost bend in two. Was there nothing better in the market?"

"Not within the price you set, Miss Milburn, no. They'd keep better if we still had the use of the cellar. Gen'leman called to see you today."

Caroline laughed. "I don't know any gentlemen, Susie, not any more. I never knew many, and now there are none."

"Well, he looked like a gen'leman, right enough. Said he had somethin' to your 'vantage."

"Oh, selling some kind of patent medicine, was he? Only a guinea a bottle, and cures gout, freckles, the bloody flux and leprosy."

Susie chuckled, a low rumble that made her ample flesh wobble. "Nothin' like that. Attorney, he was. Card's over there, by the clock."

"An attorney?"

That was different. Caroline abandoned the carrots, and reached to the high shelf where the clock stood. Beside it was a neat rectangle of card. *'Mr L Stratton,'* she read. *'Stratton, Walsh, Stratton and Stratton, Attorneys At Law'.*

"I know Mr Stratton," she said thoughtfully. "A portly old gentleman, with a fine white wig and a fondness for snuff."

"This one were a thin, *young* gen'leman," Susie said. "Fine lookin' man, for a lawyer." She sniffed disparagingly. "Left a letter for you. Now where did it go to? Miss Poppy had it in her hand, I reckon."

"Then it has been cast aside somewhere, or thrust into a pocket," Caroline said. She sighed. "Ah well, it will turn up, I dare say. Where *is* Poppy, though? Is she in the loft?"

Susie looked sheepish. "Don't know, Miss Milburn, and that's a fact. Haven't seen her for hours, but then you know what she's like."

Caroline did know. "Well, I'd better go and find her. If she's not in the house, I'll send Lin down to do the vegetables."

"I can do them no bother," Susie said. "Mutton's stewing and everything else is ready. Off you go."

It was three flights of stairs up to the loft where their looms were. On each floor, she asked for Poppy, but was met with shakes of the head. In the attic, Lin was hard at work but there was no sign of Poppy.

"Mrs Bright has a new baby," she said.

"Ah. I'll try there."

Back down the stairs again, and out past the main kitchen to the yard, threading her way through Lin's pots of herbs and the lines of washing strung between posts. When Papa was alive, the laundry had gone out to the washerwoman and the yard was a pleasant, flower-filled place to sit, but with four families now sharing the house, there were always sheets and chemises hanging.

At the back of the house was a narrow alley, foul with discarded refuse, scavenging dogs and trickles of malodourous liquid. Crossing carefully, Caroline pushed open a gate and entered another yard. And there was Poppy, without her cloak and still wearing her working apron, the baby in her arms, crooning gently. She looked up at Caroline with a beatific smile on her face, tendrils of soft brown hair curling around her face. She looked angelic in such a pose, an enchanting Madonna. Almost sixteen, with sweetness of countenance and an innocence of such purity that Caroline feared for her future. Lin was a beauty too, but she had a deal of sense and knew how to keep out of trouble. Poppy had no such instincts.

"Isn't he sweet, Caro? So good — he's been asleep all afternoon. He is to be Baptised John — that's a fine name, isn't it?"

"A good, Biblical name," Caroline said, softly. "I'm afraid you'll have to give him back to his nurse now, dear. It's almost time for dinner, and Susie needs some help."

"Of course. Sally!" she called, and the maid's face appeared from an upper window. "I have to go now."

The maid nodded, and emerged into the yard a few moments later. Gently, Poppy laid the sleeping baby in her arms, then skipped away and out through the gate.

"Don't be cross with her, Miss Milburn," the maid said. "She loves babes so, and she's ever so good with them. Besides, I got the whole nursery cleaned, from top to bottom, so she's been a big help."

"I'd like her to be a big help to her own family sometimes," Caroline said. Then, since that sounded ill-humoured, she added, "I could never be cross with her, Sally."

And it was true, she reflected, as she followed Poppy back across the alley. No one could ever be cross with her, for whenever such a thing were attempted, she would gaze at the scolder with huge, reproachful eyes, and instantly all annoyance dissipated. Lin was remorseful and downcast when any neglect of duty was pointed out, but Poppy was simply incredulous that anyone could admonish her. How could it possibly be wrong to do whatever her heart told her was needful?

It was not until the three sisters sat down to their dinner that the letter from Mr Stratton finally emerged from its hiding place in Poppy's pocket. *'To the Miss Milburns'* it said, and so Poppy, with her own form of logic, had decided that it could not be read until they were all three together. Caroline could not remember the last time they had had a letter to open. A few condolence letters, after Mama's death, and how expensive that had been. One had come all the way from Scotland and had cost a shocking one and tenpence. But this one was a pleasure to open, for it had been delivered by hand, and therefore had cost them nothing.

"Read it, Caro," Lin said. "It must be important, seeing as he's an attorney."

'To Miss Milburn, Miss Elinor Milburn and Miss Penelope Milburn. It gives me great pleasure to inform you that I have some tidings to impart to you of the most interesting kind, which will be greatly to your advantage. Please call on me at the offices of Stratton, Walsh, Stratton and Stratton at any time convenient to yourselves. I am readily available between the hours of eight and two, but may be obtained at other hours by appointment. Yours in anticipation of an early meeting, Lester Stratton.'

Caroline laughed out loud. "Now I imagine him sitting behind an empty desk waiting for us to appear and give him something to do. I have never heard of an attorney who was readily available before. Papa always had to make an appointment to see the elder Mr Stratton. It will be some scheme or other — some investment he wishes us to participate in. He's misinformed if he thinks we have money to spare for such nonsense."

"But it could be something wonderfully exciting!" Poppy said, her eyes aglow. "A prince wishes to marry one of us, or... or... a long-lost relation wishes to claim us. A duke, perhaps, and we should go to live in his castle and eat peaches every day."

"Then you would be very ill, eating so many peaches," Caroline said.

"But you will go to see this Mr Stratton?" Lin said anxiously. "So little ever happens to us that, even if it's a mistake, it will be amusing, won't it?"

"Oh, yes, and the letter is addressed to all of us, so we may all go and meet this young Mr Stratton, and hear his tidings of a most interesting kind. In fact, let us attend him promptly at eight, so that we may have the rest of the day to do our work. I have a new piece to begin and I should like to make a good start tomorrow."

The following morning, therefore, as soon as the Abbey clock had struck eight, they donned their cloaks, bonnets and gloves and walked the short distance to the premises of Stratton, Walsh, Stratton and Stratton. The door was locked and the shutters were closed.

"Typical," Caroline muttered, but even as they loitered uncertainly, debating whether to go home again or to wait, the clerk arrived with a rush.

"Good day, good day, good day, ladies! Miss Milburn..." He bowed perfunctorily to Caroline. "Miss *Elinor* Milburn." Another, much lower, bow. "Miss... um... um... Do come inside, ladies. You will be wishful to see the younger Mr Stratton, I perceive."

He unlocked the door and they meekly followed him inside. Caroline could not help smiling. Every clerk and apprentice in Romsey knew Lin's name and face, and accorded her that special courtesy reserved for a beautiful woman. Caroline was known to most of them only as Lin's older sister, and Poppy was of no account at all. If only Lin could attract the notice of a gentleman, someone of independent means who could afford to marry her and perhaps support her two less pretty sisters. One day, perhaps, but the months and years were passing by, with no sign of such a person.

Not two minutes later, the elder Mr Stratton arrived, accompanied by a younger man. Caroline had to agree with Susie's description of him as *'a fine looking man'*. He was slender and not above average height, but he had a charmingly pleasant countenance, which was currently wreathed in smiles, as if his day afforded him no greater delight than to meet three uninteresting spinsters with neither money nor prospects. He dressed well, like a gentleman, and... yes, he had noticed Lin. They always noticed Lin.

"Well now, how delightful to see you all again, and under such happy circumstances," the elder Mr Stratton said. Happy circumstances? For the first time, Caroline felt a flicker of interest. "Miss Milburn, may I present to you my nephew, another Mr Stratton you see, who has just joined us from Portsmouth now that my father is unhappily not able to undertake as much of the business as was his wont. Nephew, this is Miss Milburn, and Miss Elinor Milburn, and Miss Penelope Milburn."

"Delighted! Delighted!" he cried, executing his bow with a flourish. "So happy to make your acquaintance, especially with such wonderful news to impart. Such an exciting day for you all, and for me also, for you are my very first clients. Do come into my office. Mind the rug! There is a worn patch just there, so do take the greatest care. My uncle will be just next door if you have any questions which I am unable to answer, but he is entrusting your case entirely to me. This way, ladies."

All the time, the wide smile on his face never wavered, and Caroline decided that his enthusiasm was genuine. Whether he was always thus, or it was related to the information he had to convey to them, or whether it was merely the effect that Lin had on him was uncertain. Probably the latter, she decided, for he could scarcely take his eyes off her.

The clerk followed them into the office, and fussed about arranging chairs on one side of the desk. When they were seated, the clerk withdrew and Mr Stratton took his own seat. The desk was entirely empty, and although the shelves lining the room were laden with serious-looking tomes, there was not a thing out of place, not a document or a pen holder or an opened book to be seen anywhere. Mr Stratton was indeed very new to Romsey if he had not yet had time to clutter his office with the detritus of his occupation.

"Now then, ladies, to business," he said, the smile widening even further. "There is good news, but, as is so often the case, there is some rather sad news for me to impart first." The smile faded, replaced by a solemn expression, and his voice dropped to a low, sympathetic tone. "I am very sorry to have to inform you that your grandfather has died."

There was a long silence in the room, as the sisters exchanged glances.

"This is indeed sad," Caroline said, "but it is hardly news, Mr Stratton. Both our grandfathers died some years ago. Grandfather Milburn departed the world some ten years ago, and Grandfather Carter before Mama was even born."

"Ah," he said, and for the first time he looked uncomfortable. "Is that what you were told? I regret to inform you that you have been misled. Your maternal grandfather was *not* called Carter and he did *not* die until last month."

"That cannot be so," Caroline said. "His name was George Carter, and he was a soldier in the 37th Regiment of Foot. He was killed in action in India."

Mr Stratton gently shook his head. "His name was Abraham Wishaw. He was a hop merchant, primarily, although he dabbled in other commodities. He died just a few weeks ago when the ship bringing him from Ireland foundered."

And in that moment, every truth in Caroline's life crashed in pieces to the floor.

END OF SAMPLE CHAPTER of *The Lacemaker*

For more information or to buy, go to my website at http://marykingswood.co.uk/.

Printed in Great Britain
by Amazon

65299009R00229